PRAISE FOR
THE
LIGHTHOUSE
TRILOGY

In *The Lighthouse Trilogy*:

The Lighthouse Land

The Lighthouse War

The Lighthouse Keepers

THE LIGHTHOUSE WAR

THE LIGHTHOUSE TRILOGY

• BOOK II •

ADRIAN McKINTY

AMULET BOOKS

New York

The Library of Congress has cataloged the hardcover edition as follows:
McKinty, Adrian.
The lighthouse war / Adrian McKinty.
p. cm. — (Lighthouse trilogy ; bk. 2)
Summary: When Jamie and Ramsay answer a summons to return to Altair, accompanied by Ramsay's half brother Brian, they learn that the Witch Queen wants to capture the Salmon from them and use it to transport her people from that dying planet to Earth—and that Jamie's beloved Wishaway has agreed to marry someone else.
ISBN-13: 978-0-8109-9354-9 (hardcover w/jacket)
ISBN-10: 0-8109-9354-6 (hardcover w/jacket)
[1. Space and time—Fiction. 2. War—Fiction. 3. Magic—Fiction.
4. Ireland—Fiction. 5. Science fiction.] I. Title.
PZ7.M4786915Lik 2006
[Fic]—dc22
2006100361
Paperback ISBN 978-0-8109-7265-0

Originally published in hardcover by Amulet Books in 2007

Text copyright © 2007 Adrian McKinty
Map illustration copyright © 2007 Bret Bertholf

Book design by Chad W. Beckerman

Printed and bound in U.S.A.
10 9 8 7 6 5 4 3 2 1

HNA ▌▌▌▌▌
harry n. abrams, inc.
a subsidiary of La Martinière Groupe
115 West 18th Street
New York, NY 10011
www.hnabooks.com

FOR MY MOTHER, JANE MCKINTY, AND IN MEMORY OF MY FATHER, ALFRED MCKINTY. *GO RAIBH MAITH AGAIBH.*

CONTENTS

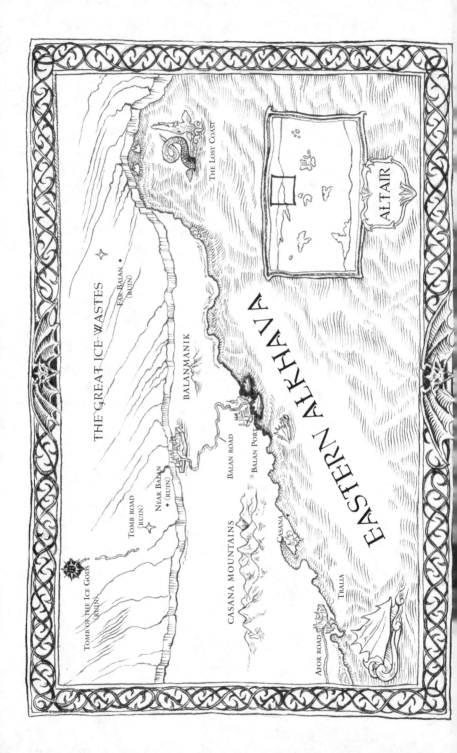

Anythin' for a quiet life, as the man said w[h]en he took the sit[ua]tion at the lighthouse.
—Charles Dickens, *The Pickwick Papers* (1837)

Chapter I
THE QUEEN

THE CITY WAS DOOMED. Everyone knew it. If it hadn't been for the Stop Laws, the peasants and the workers would have evacuated years ago.

Winds howled over the battlements, moisture froze in the air. Snow and ice blew off the top of the ice sheet, and the awful groaning noise was the sound of the glacier as it rumbled inexorably on.

The sky had a gray, malevolent cast, but no sensible person ever looked anywhere near the sky. The blinding whiteness of the ice-filled wind restricted the field of view to the few steps of skidding pavement in front of your feet.

The city smelled of emptiness and fear.

The climate had been like this for years, for centuries. It snowed nearly every day, and except for a few weeks in high summer, it was seldom above freezing. Plants could not grow, and all the food had to be brought in from Balan Port on the icy sea twenty miles to the south. The glacier moved slowly, only a few feet a year, but it wasn't its speed that was the problem, it was its implacability. Its stubbornness. Nothing could stop it: not the massive brick walls they had built, not the ditches, not even the enormous fires previous generations had constructed at the glacier's face in the hope of cracking or melting the great monster.

None of it had helped. The fires had burned and the glacier marched on. The walls were breeched and still it came.

It moved like some ravenous beast, hungrier every season, swallowing forest and farms and then isolated houses and now whole streets, schools, and meeting-houses.

Gag Macak, the local people called it. The insatiable one.

The Twenty-seventh Queen of Balanmanik surveyed the apocalyptic landscape from the high window of her fortress. She rubbed her hands over the logs burning in her grate. Few, very few of the citizens were permitted a fire, and no one was allowed to burn wood. Resources were far too precious for that.

She smiled.

The old Queen, of course, was above the law. The old Queen made the laws, was the law.

Through the thick glass window she watched a *draya* suddenly stumble to its knees, stone dead, skewered by a stalactite blown off the glacier's south face. Its owner whipped it a few times and then got off his box to examine the animal. Without a *draya*, his source of living was gone. Probably he wouldn't survive the winter.

The Queen turned away.

Such scenes were depressing. An injection of the pedestrian into the concerns of the wider world.

There was nothing she could have done for that peasant, but there was something she could do for her people. Yes. She sat in the leather chair nearest the fire and clicked her long nails on the marble mantel.

She waited.

He was late.

I cannot abide a lack of punctuality, she said to herself.

She stood and walked to the large north window. Here the view was worse. Here one stared right at the glacier, big and malevolent, as unwelcoming and inescapable as death itself.

A third of the old town of Balan and all of Manik on the other side of the frozen river were now part of the ever-expanding wasteland. A pity, a real shame, because that had been the prettiest par—

A knock at the door.

"Enter," she said in base Alkhavan.

Her maidservant Anda came in with pursed lips.

"What is it?" the Queen asked.

"It is the Lord Protector, my lady. He seeks an audience with the Witch Queen," Anda said.

The Queen disliked and discouraged the use of the title *Witch* Queen. Other queens enjoyed the title, feeling that it engendered an atmosphere of fear, but she knew that only fools believed in magic or the supernatural. It was also an attack on her gender. There were few female rulers on the planet of Altair; women seldom got the chance to wield power, and it was insulting that one of the rare female sovereigns was known as Witch.

The Queen knew it was a losing battle, the epithet would stick no matter what she said, but the Lord Protector's use of it irritated her.

"What does that fool want this time?" she asked.

"It is about the capital, my lady."

The Queen nodded.

It was always about the capital. The Lord Protector wished to move the capital of Alkhava two hundred miles southwest to the relatively ice-free and pleasant city of Afor.

"What did you tell him, Anda?" the Queen asked.

"I told him you were engaged, that tomorrow morning would be a better time," Anda replied.

The Queen smiled. It wasn't every afternoon that you could ignore an audience with the Lord Protector, but today was special.

"Make sure he is escorted out of the palace and have his spies amused until the hours of dusk. I want no interference in our work," she ordered.

"The agent in the library will not be easy to divert," Anda said.

The Queen looked at the girl. She was sharp and bright for a peasant. She would go far. She had very fair skin, and her brown hair was tied in a plait behind her head, north country fashion.

It was a contrast to the Queen's own withered features and bright blond wig that she used to cover her bald head.

"Then have him killed," the Queen said.

Anda did not bat an eyelash. "He is a cautious man, he sups his own food and is a swordsman, I believe," Anda said.

"Have him taken to see the Machine. He will be giddy with excitement. His guard will be down. When he has seen it, arrange for an accident off the adjoining battlement. Whether it looks like murder or not is hardly relevant at this stage, I think, Anda."

"No, my lady."

"Go now."

The servant scurried out, and the Queen returned to her chair.

She waited some more.

Finally, almost an hour past the appointed hour, Sarpa of the Science Guild was announced. He was a wild-haired, fussy little man, typical of his breed but atypical in his brilliance.

For hundreds of years the Balan science guilds—and before that the metalworking guilds—had been poring over the Machine. Of all the masters who examined the device, only Sarpa had had the wit to understand its operation or had the ability to reactivate its power source. His genius forgave a lot.

"You are late, Master Sarpa," the Queen said.

Sarpa knew better than to make excuses. He merely bowed and then after a moment's hesitation he added: "We are ready, my Queen."

"Come then," she said.

They exited her quarters.

Master Sarpa offered the old Queen his arm, but she ignored him. Although she was well into her nineties, she was not yet infirm, and certainly not foolish enough to be seen needing assistance walking about her own palace.

The position of Witch Queen was elected, not hereditary. Any one of a half dozen contenders for the throne would jump at the chance to eliminate an old and ailing woman. Terror was what kept them in line. Nothing else.

They can wait their turn, she thought to herself testily.

She was not long for this world in any case. A year perhaps, probably less.

Sarpa led the Queen along the dark, freezing corridors of the palace, now lit only every few paces by torches.

They took the back staircase that led to the audience chamber and the theater.

It was dark, cold, slippery, and more than once it occurred to the Queen that perhaps Sarpa had not in fact discovered the secret of the Machine and was merely bringing her here to assassinate her. Perhaps the Lord Protector had paid in gold to be rid of her.

She had an anxious few moments, but they reached the bottom of the stairs without incident.

"This way, my Queen," Sarpa said with reverence.

The Witch Queen smiled at her own fears. It was right to be paranoid, but the intelligent ruler didn't waste energy worrying about their trustworthy subjects.

"Lead on, Master Sarpa," she said.

Sarpa opened a side door into the old theater. Once performances had taken place here. Plays, operas, music. At one time this city had been a bastion of the arts, even rivaling Aldan in its embrace of higher culture.

The Queen sighed.

Those days were long gone.

But none of it mattered.

Mighty Aldan too would fall in time. What the Lord Protector singularly failed to see was that it wasn't just this city that was doomed. It was the whole planet. Moving the capital to Afor would only delay the execution.

Sarpa pushed open the door to reveal a well-lit room

and a dozen men buzzing around the Machine like expectant fathers.

The Machine itself was a long silver box connected to what resembled the half shell of a giant sea lizard's egg. The whole thing was as large as a cottage. It had been found in Tarak Land in the year 20, not far from what the ignorant called the Tomb of the Ice Gods. At first, the peasants venerated it too as a god, but then they turned it over to the rulers of Niassa, a kingdom long since obliterated by the ice.

No one in the Witch Queen's employ thought it was a god anymore.

They knew better.

It, like the Salmon of Knowledge that the Ui Neills used to jump between worlds, had been left by the Vancha—the Old Ones.

Aside from the famous tomb, few Vancha artifacts had turned up over the years. Nothing as big as this, nothing as complex as this. The Vancha had left writings on the Machine itself, but no one had ever understood them.

None that is, until now.

Only one man had been able to discover the Machine's meaning, its purpose. Only one in all these years. This man, who in his excitement had taken the Queen's arm anyway, was leading her toward the massive object.

She smiled gently and removed his four fingers from her elbow.

Master Sarpa, the son of a carpenter, practically the grandson of a slave. Yet his competence in this field was unquestioned. The Witch Queen prided herself on her ability to spot talent. Anda, Protector Rasman, several others; but Sarpa was the cream of the crop.

Seeing the way he excelled in the arithmetical tests, she had taken him out of trade school at the age of thirteen and sent him first to the Black Monks and then to the Science Guild.

There he had come into his metier.

With meteoric progress he'd passed through the ranks of apprentice, journeyman, and guilder to become master of the order at the age of twenty-five.

The Witch Queen had been patient.

She had waited until he had donned the purple robe before revealing the secret of the Machine. She personally had taken him to the vaults of the palace and shown him the alien artifact.

He had begun work the very next day, and amazingly, in a comparatively short ten years, he had discovered its power and its function.

"I have solved it, I know what it does, and I know how to make it work," Sarpa had written her in the last month. A brief note in an inelegant hand, but never had she received a communication of such import. She had summoned him immediately, and he had explained.

At first the Queen had been disappointed.

The Machine, alas, could produce no instant magic. It would not push back the glacier. It would not save their city.

Perhaps that was one of the many reasons she didn't want the Lord Protector to know about it. Such a man had shortsighted ambitions. He couldn't see the big picture, he couldn't play the long game.

No, the Machine would not bring help within the lifetime of the old Queen, nor of any of her immediate successors.

But, if she was right, it would bring help.

The theater was cold, and the Witch Queen shivered involuntarily.

Sarpa had thought of everything and immediately an apprentice appeared with a coat made from *moxy* fur.

It was cold because Sarpa had removed the theater's roof, exposing it to the darkening sky. Snow was drifting down onto the thick eggshell part of the object. She took the coat and said "thank you" to the apprentice, who was too frightened to mumble any kind of a reply. The Witch Queen draped the fur about her shoulders.

It was then that the other members of the Science Guild noticed her entrance. They immediately stopped working and made their bows.

"Get back to work," Sarpa barked and then added, "if Your Highness pleases."

The Witch Queen nodded her approval.

Sarpa began explaining what would happen that night.

"We have lined the Machine up where we want it to be. Kammiaquai will connect the power source, the uh fire, if you will. Once the dials light, the Machine will be ready to speak. The power source is a *battery*, a kind of storehouse of energy, which will be good for one long signal, the current having—"

The Witch Queen shook her head; she had never understood any of the technical details of the device. Merely, that it would serve her needs.

"Enough, Master Sarpa, spare me," she commanded.

"Yes, Your Highness," he replied.

They waited until full night came.

The Witch Queen declined a chair. "Which one is the Ui Neill world?" she asked, looking at the cold stars for the first time in years.

"After trawling the Vancha's star charts, we believe Earth to be near the yellow star in the constellation Snake," Sarpa said. "The one just above the Eye."

"I am getting cold. Are we ready, Master Sarpa?" the Witch Queen asked.

"We are ready," he said.

"Carry on then."

Sarpa gave the order to power up the device.

Apprentice Kammiaquai attached the light rods to the battery source. The Machine came alive with a low hum.

Some in the room clapped, others cheered, most did nothing but look at Master Sarpa and the Queen, who had remained stony faced.

"Quickly now," Sarpa said, and then a dozen apprentices manhandled the Machine into its final position.

"It is done. We are ready to send our words to the stars," Master Sarpa said proudly.

The Witch Queen reached into a hidden pocket in her thick woven gown.

"Send this message," the old Queen said, and handed Sarpa a note.

Sarpa attempted to read it. "What does it purport to say, my lady?" Sarpa asked, baffled by the meaningless words.

"It is in the script of another world," the Witch Queen condescended to explain.

"I do not understand it," Sarpa protested.

"You do not need to understand. You need merely to obey," she ordered, summoning up her full authority.

"It will need to be converted to our number system and then into binary, a language of—" he said, trying again.

"Very well. Do what is necessary. Send and resend this message until the 'battery' is done."

"But, Your Majesty, this is our chance to talk across the stars, to tell them of our world and culture, perhaps some of our poetry, our—"

"Send this message and repeat it all night. I will not command thee again, Master Sarpa," the Queen said in a voice so quiet and deadly the very snow seemed to stand still in the air above her head.

Sarpa's blood chilled in his veins, and he immediately set to work.

He coded the words and then tapped in the Queen's message in a simple binary language of ones and zeros.

The Witch Queen called for an enclosed litter to take her up to her chambers.

She could relax now.

The message had been sent.

Whether it would be received or not was another question. But the Ui Neills came from a world of wonders, and it might be that they would have a similar Machine on their planet.

The Witch Queen lay down upon her bed.

She had accomplished her mission.

She had thrown a lifeline out into the void of space, and perhaps, just perhaps, that line would reel in its catch.

She slept for a while.

The dawn was lost in a blizzard out of the east, but as Sarpa predicted there was enough energy in the alien device to allow it to transmit for all of the night and well into the next morning.

Finally around noon, the Machine's power source gave out.

After that the Witch Queen's health began a steady decline.

The days shortened, the long winter came, and before the spring, the Witch Queen died in her sleep, fortunate not to have been poisoned.

She was interred in a stone sarcophagus in the traditional burial ground outside the old palace garden. In a week drifts had buried the tomb, and in a year or two no one even remembered where it had been.

Her successor dealt with the intrigues and problems of her own reign. The peoples of Courland rebelled and were crushed. The Lord Protector had no heir and there was a crisis over the succession. The ice walls broke and the barrier collapsed and the glacier marched ever closer to the city of Balanmanik.

The successor ruled a long time, and then she too died.

Her replacement was assassinated in a palace coup, and the new Queen had the folly to lead an expedition north to find the lost passage to the Soura Sea. She was never heard of again. In a plundering raid in Perovan another Queen found a horribly mangled copy of the Salmon of Knowledge. It had excited everyone, but the

Black Monks had never been able to get it to work and the Queen who had brought false hope was murdered.

Such were the events of history. Trivial things, when all around them the most pressing concern of all was the gradual shrinking of their sun, the cooling of their world.

Years passed, decades, and a new Queen took the throne.

This one was patient. This one believed in the future.

Even when her brother became the Deputy Lord Protector and launched his invasion of Aldan, even when one of the Ui Neills, a boy called Jamie, returned to defend the land, she knew the time was not yet ripe.

The message was crossing the stars. The light-years of space. It would arrive when it was supposed to arrive.

The authorities would learn. The boy would come again. He would fall into the trap. The real Salmon would be theirs. And she and all her people would have salvation. To Earth they would go and somehow make it their own . . .

The Thirty-second Witch Queen stood on her balcony on the edge of the frozen city.

Only her palace and a few outlying houses remained. The terrible glacier was a mere mile away. In a decade or less everything that had been Balanmanik would be wiped from existence. It did not matter. It was approaching midsummer and a cool frigid sun shone in the southern sky. She looked up at what the uneducated called the Black Tower, which was really a dark gray. And why was black seen as the color of evil, when it was the horrible white glacier that imperiled them?

Ninety-six Altairian years, three months, and twelve days had gone by since the Twenty-seventh Queen had sent the message to the stars and set in motion this chain of events.

Precisely the amount of time Master Sarpa predicted long ago.

The guards were ready, her servants were ready, the Science Guild was ready. The Black Monks were ready too.

If it was going to happen it would happen soon.

"We will kill him and take the Salmon and we will escape this terrible fate," she said, staring at Gag Macak—the hungry ice.

Her handmaiden Tara smiled and did not reply. The Witch Queen often spoke to herself, Tara noted. Tara, a rough-faced, strong peasant girl, was the descendant of Anda, handmaiden to the famous Twenty-seventh Queen. And although the city had fallen on hard times, her clan and family had done well for itself.

"We will kill the Ui Neill and we will all be free," the Witch Queen muttered angrily.

She stood on the balcony, and on this bright early

summer day, instead of snow dropping from the sky, for once she felt an icy rain fall gently onto her face.

A sign of hope.

The Witch Queen smiled.

Things might be going their way at last.

In Belfast it was raining too. A light rain admittedly, but more than enough to damp the spirits of the festival crowd.

Most of the spectators had gone home, and even passersby, shopping on Royal Avenue, were no longer stopping to stare. Jamie was sensing the bad karma coming from the roadies who wanted them to finish their set.

The other three members of the Ayatollahs of Funk were deep in the music. Ramsay still playing despite the water bouncing off his drums; Brian and Mike completely out of step on bass and lead guitar, practically fighting each other to gain control of the song.

All four were on a stage set up in front of Belfast City Hall for the regional heat of *Ireland's Most Talented Youngsters*, a Dublin TV show. The Ayatollahs were the very last act, and halfway through their first song, the judges (the DJs from the quasi-legal but popular Pirate Radio 252 ship parked out in the Irish Sea) had decided that they'd seen enough and had retired to a local pub. Jamie knew they weren't going to win, and later that night the judges announced that they were sending a seven-year-old tap-dancing magician as the representative from Belfast.

Ramsay banged the drums, ending the agony of Mike's guitar solo.

Jamie grabbed the microphone stand.

"This is our final song today, it's called 'A *Yasi* Is a Type of Six-Legged Rhinonceros," Jamie said, and when the drums kicked in, three beats late per usual, he began to sing a simple G A D, three-chord rhythm-and-blues progression played at Undertones/Ramones/Pistols speed for the first bar and then twice that for the rest of the song.

"I left my girl on another world / On a far-off distant star / I left my girl on another world / Can't pick her up in my car / I left my girl on another world with a boy I don't really trust / He says that he likes my girl too, but you can substitute like for lust."

Ramsay kicked in with the chorus.

"A *yasi* is a rhino, a *draya* is a horse, a *seecha* is a squirmy cat that doesn't meow of course."

There were two more verses and choruses, and when the wall of noise ceased assaulting the half dozen citizens who had remained to see them, Jamie held the microphone high and bowed.

"You've been great, truly great," he said, then put the mike on its stand and exited the stage.

Ramsay stared at him as he walked past the drum kit.

"There are still two songs left on the set sheet," Ramsay said.

"We're done," Jamie muttered.

There was a smattering of applause, and the crowd, such as it was, drifted away.

"Freebird!" some wag called out, but there weren't going to be any more songs this day. A grip turned the power off before anyone got electrocuted, and the roadies began tearing the set to pieces.

Backstage Ramsay was feeling philosophical about their less-than-stellar performance.

"In retrospect a song about Kurt Gödel's Incompleteness Theorem wasn't maybe the wisest choice to begin our set," he mused.

"No, it wasn't," Brian said. "What were you thinking, Jamie? We shouldn't have allowed him."

"I was thinking," Jamie said defensively, "that it was our best melody and judges are a sucker for a good melody."

"The judges were bored to tears," Brian insisted.

"The judges hated us anyway. I tried to send that Pirate Ship radio station a tape of our stuff and they sent it back unopened," Jamie said.

Ramsay seemed as if he was about to cry and Brian reached over and put his hand on his shoulder. Ramsay looked at the hand as if it were a tarantula, but much to Jamie's surprise he didn't shake it off.

Brian shouldn't really have been in the band at all, and he was hardly one of Ireland's most talented "youngsters." He was Ramsay's half-brother, from his dad's first marriage. Ramsay had only met him three times in his whole life before he had come to live with them two months ago.

He was thirty now, which was sixteen years older than Ramsay, though he looked considerably younger. He was an angular, skinny character with a mop of blondish red hair that seldom met shampoo and never conditioner.

Brian, as Ramsay's father sometimes darkly hinted, was the "clever one" of the family. After the divorce, he had lived with his mother in Scotland, where he had excelled in school, gone to Oxford, graduated with a double first in physics and mathematics, and then gotten a scholarship to MIT.

But there the trajectory had been less than stellar. Always a big fish in a small pond, Brian had found himself among people in Cambridge, Massachusetts, who were not only as smart as he was but sometimes smarter.

Six years he had been working on his PhD thesis on superconductivity in nonmetallic polymers. But with progress going nowhere and his scholarship money running out, his advisors had ordered him to change his topic. Brian had refused, quarreled, and finally quit the school. His mother was traveling the world, so Brian, reluctantly, had gone to Ireland to live with his father and his sometimes annoying, always precocious half-brother.

"And whoever heard of a drummer singing anyway?" Mike fumed.

"Mickey Dolenz from the Monkees, Phil Collins in Genesis, Dave Grohl in Nirvana and Foo Fighters—what you lack, Michael, old boy, is a musical education," Ramsay said good-naturedly.

Mike had frizzy brown hair and pale skin overburdened with freckles. He was a hot-tempered character, a year younger than them, but Jamie and Ramsay liked him immensely. Still staring daggers, he stormed off to get his coat.

"You know what's going to happen now?" Ramsay said.

"What?"

"I'll bet you ten quid he's going to quit the band again," Ramsay said.

"No, no, that's a given. You have to give me odds." Jamie laughed, for Mike had left the band at least four times since they had started playing together at Christmas.

"I'll bet ten quid on it, give you odds of two to one. If

he stays in, you get twenty; if he quits, I get ten. It's a good deal," Ramsay said with his big trademark smile.

"I'm not taking that bet, I know his ways. Not a chance, pal," Jamie replied.

In the year and a bit Jamie had been in Ireland he had lost some of his American colloquialisms but none of his New York accent. And the final definitive "pal" made both Brian and Ramsay grin at each other.

"He was playing too fast anyway," Brian said to Ramsay. "It was your job to slow him down."

"What do you mean?" Ramsay asked.

"You and me should stick together, not just from family loyalty but because we're the rhythm section, you on the drums, me on the bass," Brian continued. "We're the natural enemies of lead singer and lead guitar."

Ramsay was about to defend Mike's prima donna tendencies, but the dude himself came back with his coat buttoned to the top and wearing a rain hat.

"I suppose it's the train," Mike said.

Both boys looked at him expectantly.

"And?" Ramsay asked.

"And nothing," Mike replied, irritably. His mouth closed and formed into a thin line of annoyance. He was finished with his end of the conversation.

He picked up his guitar case.

"That's it?" Jamie asked.

"That's it," Mike said suspiciously.

"Wow, I should have taken your money, Ramsay," Jamie said.

"You certainly should," Ramsay replied.

Mike cocked his head in puzzlement like a particularly stupid collie dog.

"We thought you were going to quit the band after tonight's debacle," Jamie explained.

"Nah, now that my dad's got religion he's thrown out the TV, so it's either the band or Scrabble with the folks on Saturday nights," Mike said.

"The very reason Led Zeppelin stayed together," Jamie said ironically.

Half an hour later they were on the train, the bad feelings gone and they could even joke about the audience.

Brian had seen a hack from the *Belfast Telegraph* in the crowd and they debated the possibility of a write-up. Ramsay and Brian thought a review would be a good thing, Jamie and Mike came down against it. This was enough to keep them distracted through the short train ride out of central Belfast.

Brian and Mike got off the train at Carrickfergus. Mike to go home, Brian to go to the pub. Jamie and Ramsay stayed on, since they were taking it all the way to Ballycarry, another fifteen minutes up the line.

"It was the rain that defeated us," Ramsay mused, gazing out the window as the train pulled out.

Jamie put down his copy of Bob's Dylan's *Chronicles* and looked skeptical.

"It was that Kurt Gödel song," Jamie disagreed. "It was too esoteric. You know what people like: 'She loves you, yeah, yeah, yeah,' that's what they want."

"I don't think it's esoteric at all, if you even know what that word means," Ramsay said with fake haughtiness.

"How does it go again?" Jamie asked, his sarcasm spread so thin Ramsay didn't notice.

"Kurt Gödel, you did quite well revealing the problems of mathematics / Even Einstein said you were swell despite being an asthmatic / If you—" Ramsay sang in a warbling baritone before Jamie cut him off.

"OK, that's enough. Do me a favor, never sing that again. Never even think it again. It is a nice melody but I thought you'd worked the kinks out of the lyrics. And Mike had a good point. While you were singing I was standing there like Davy Jones from the Monkees, looking like an idiot with a tambourine."

"You got your time in the spotlight, mate," Ramsay muttered.

"Yeah."

"You think if I worked on the lyrics some more it would help?" Ramsay asked.

Jamie didn't reply. He was peering through the window at the darkening sky. There was still a little light in the north and west. At this time of year it didn't get fully dark until eleven. He mugged at his reflection in the glass. His curly hair looked greasy and awful from the rain. Normally it swished to one side in a way that he thought made him look interesting. Now it was like half a drowned cat hanging there. Even the blue-green of his eyes were washed out, and his complexion was not at its most attractive.

"Thought the band might help us get girls," Jamie said almost to himself.

"We don't need help," Ramsay replied.

Jamie scoffed. "What? Are you kidding? You're a big, tall goofball who plays Warcraft all the time, and I'm a one-armed gimp who deserted his girlfriend on an alien planet, who can't play rugby, and who sucks at school."

"*Au contraire,* mate. You're a wormhole-traveling, hereditary laird who saved a whole planet from destruction who might be good at soccer if you gave it a try, and I'm a big, tall goofball who happens to be one of the top ten Warcraft players in the world. The girls should love us."

"Whitehead, all change Whitehead," the conductor cried before Jamie could reply.

"Do we get out here?" Ramsay asked.

"My mom said Ballycarry. One more stop," Jamie said.

"Your mum's a trouper to meet us off the train like this," Ramsay said.

"She is."

"We'll tell her we did great at the show," Ramsay said.

"No, we'll tell her like it was," Jamie said in an imperative tone Ramsay knew better than to contradict.

Jamie didn't want to tell Anna O'Neill any more lies than were strictly necessary. After their two-week disappearance to the planet Altair they had already built an entire cathedral of falsehoods.

In the hospital, when Jamie explained to his mother what he and Ramsay had been doing for the missing fortnight, at first he had attempted to tell her the truth.

They had found an alien artifact called the Salmon of Knowledge that allowed them to jump through a wormhole in space to a planet named Altair. There, they had defeated an Alkhavan invasion fleet using the Cortez/H. G. Wells trick of giving them the chicken pox. After that Jamie had decided to stay and be with a girl he'd met there called Wishaway, but he'd heard his mother screaming that she was in trouble through the wormhole, so he changed his mind. He had to get back. Then the leader of the Alkhavan invasion, Protector Ksar, had tried to grab the Salmon before they wrestled him off and shoved him into the black-ness of folded space-time. They came back through the wormhole and saved Anna from drowning in her overturned car.

As a story it was hard to believe, and even in her morphine-addled state Jamie's mother didn't buy it for a moment.

No one, in fact, believed it.

Not Jamie's mother, not the police, not Ramsay's parents.

If they'd told a tale about satanic child abuse, they could have invented any old rubbish and had twenty people in jail by now, but aliens, other worlds . . . it was too hacky. Too *Alice in Wonderland*, too *Peter Pan*.

In the end Jamie and Ramsay had had to confess that they'd cut school to hitchhike round Ireland.

That story *was* believed. Especially when they threw in a couple of subplots about Gypsies, pot smoking, and a six-pack of beer.

Both were severely disciplined, Ramsay losing his pocket money and Jamie getting grounded for six months.

But Jamie's mother couldn't punish him too severely because after not speaking at all for nearly a year, from the shock of losing an arm to cancer, the backpacking trip round Ireland had brought him out of his shell. He spoke, talked, and now even sang in front of an audience.

In any case the boys' bad behavior was well behind them now. Neither had attempted anything like it since.

It was pitch-black as the train pulled in to Ballycarry halt, and the rain was very heavy. Anna flashed the Volvo's lights to show where she was parked. Jamie opened the carriage door, and both boys ran across the platform and jumped into the car.

"Well, how did it go?" Anna asked when they had their seat belts on.

"I don't want to talk about it," Jamie grumbled in a little bit of a huff.

"I thought it went well," Ramsay said cheerfully.

"You played all your songs?"

Ramsay shook his head in the darkness. "Nah, we only did three, two that Jamie sang, one that I did, we were a big hit," Ramsay said while Jamie marveled at his ice-cold ability to fabricate.

Anna backed out of the parking spot and drove the car toward Islandmagee.

"And everyone played together well?" she asked.

"Mike and Brian tried to go off on tangents but I kept them in line," Ramsay said.

Anna knew better than to ask whether they had won the competition.

"I once saw Lou Reed play," she said in an attempt to show that she was hip.

"We should be like him, Jamie, all cool onstage and everything," Ramsay mused.

"Yeah, that's what we're missing in our act, junkie chic and twelve-minute cello solos," Jamie said.

Two minutes later Anna left Ramsay off at his cottage. Jamie said good night and told him that he'd see him in school. "Good night, Jamie. Night, Mrs. O'Neill," Ramsay said. Anna preferred to be known as "Ms." but in Ireland "Mrs." got applied to any woman over the age of thirty, like *Madame* in France. She had given up on the "Ms." a long time ago.

"Good night, Ramsay," she said, smiling at the big Irish boy.

She negotiated her way through the village of Portmuck and drove the Volvo onto the causeway that linked Muck Island to the mainland.

Ever since her accident, she was very careful about the causeway. Now she never drove when there was any water on it at all and even then always at five miles per hour over the thickest part of the strand.

Jamie stared out the window at the old lighthouse from which he and Ramsay had jumped to Altair. There was something melancholy about the place now. Jamie had left Wishaway on the other world, and there was no way he would ever see her again. The lighthouse had a sad, depressing air about it.

He knew Ramsay felt the same way, and now they rarely went to the lighthouse at all.

Rain was lashing the granite stone walls. It was lonely and bleak, but it did have one secret left. And someday, to prove to the world that they weren't making the whole thing up, they were going to show someone the Salmon of Knowledge, the alien device that was able to create wormholes from the planet Earth to the planet Altair . . . Someday, but they both agreed that the time wasn't yet ripe for that. Scientists would take the Salmon away from them, to a museum or a lab, someplace they would study it, dissect it, ruin it. Jamie and Ramsay would certainly never get their paws on it again.

"OK, we're home," Anna said.

Jamie got out of the car and went inside the Lighthouse House.

It smelled of food. Not Irish food. Real food. Edible food.

Anna had made hamburgers, New York style, with a big fat piece of meat, fried onions, and thin melted cheese.

"Thanks, Mom," Jamie said, grabbing the burgers and sitting down at the kitchen table.

Anna put a cup of decaf coffee in the microwave. She sat opposite him and pushed a loose hair out of his eyes.

The coffee *dinged,* and she added sugar and thick Irish cream.

"It wasn't that bad was it?" she asked.

"Look, I don't want to talk about it," Jamie said, wolfing a burger.

"You played though. You got on?"

"Yes. We got on. We were the last act. That's it. Now please, could we not discuss it?"

"It didn't go so wonderfully, did it?" his mother asked, looking at Jamie with concern.

"Mom, it went fine. Ramsay was practically telling the truth. Three songs, I sang two, the judges left during the first one and the crowd not long after the rain began. But Mike didn't quit the band, so we can't consider it a complete disaster."

"Well, you did three songs in front of a crowd, that's not a bad start," his mother said optimistically.

At least no one heckled me for having one arm, Jamie thought but didn't say.

Anna sipped her tea.

Jamie finished his burgers in under two minutes.

"That hit the spot. Thanks, Mom," he said.

"It was my pleasure. You don't have to do chores, you can slip on up to bed if you're tired."

"I think I'll do that. I'm crashing now," Jamie said.

He stood and stretched. His long right arm pointing

out horizontally, his stumpy left arm only making it as far as a twitch in the elbow.

"Oh, I forget to tell you, there's a big story on the Internet. It's right up your alley," Anna added.

"What is it?"

"Something about aliens or something. It was on the BBC as well, but I didn't catch it, there was a David Beckham exposé on the other channel."

"What about aliens?" Jamie asked.

"Oh, there's a rumor we've had a message from the aliens, I really don't know what they—"

But that was all Jamie needed to hear. He took off his coat, ran to his computer, and turned it on.

Chapter 11
THE MESSAGE

O F COURSE somebody somewhere on the Internet was always saying that we'd be contacted by aliens. Crazy people mostly. From frequent Googling, Jamie knew that if you typed in "Alien Contact" or "Aliens Among Us," you'd get about a million hits.

But this time the report was slightly more credible. For a start it was coming from the Associated Press, a normally quite sober news organization. And apparently the AP had gotten the leak from someone at the Jet Propulsion Laboratory in Pasadena, California—an extremely respected part of Caltech that was staffed by some of the cleverest people on the planet.

The background to the AP story was that JPL's *Cassini* probe in orbit around the planet Saturn had picked up a radio signal coming from outside the solar system. Not knowing what else to do with the signal and assuming it was from its controllers back in California, *Cassini* copied the message to its memory banks and then relayed it back to Earth for confirmation. At first the JPL technicians had thought *Cassini* was malfunctioning, but then the truth began to dawn.

Cassini had picked up an extraterrestrial signal emanating from a star in the constellation Pegasus.

JPL told NASA, and the head of NASA called the White House. The White House instituted a long-standing procedure, and the president signed a temporary executive order expressly telling everyone involved that they were not to talk to the press until he had given the go-ahead.

When the AP tried to probe further, they were told that NASA was using the Very Large Array radio telescope in Arizona to investigate a potential spatial anomaly, and moreover, JPL, NASA, and the White House were now all officially denying that they had received a message from aliens.

It was fishy and the AP knew it, but for the moment their inquiries were put on hold.

No one was satisfied, but the final fly in the ointment came from SETI, who were the real bridesmaids at the party. The Search for Extra-Terrestrial Intelligence hadn't heard any signal and couldn't quite believe that after all these years of patient listening, they could have been pipped at the post by anyone else; so SETI muddied the waters by saying that it was more than likely the whole thing was a mistake.

Even so, the president and his advisors knew that they weren't likely to keep this quiet for long, so without a lot of fuss, the secretary of state was flown back from vacation in Utah, the defense secretary returned from the Middle East, the head of NASA jetted up from Houston, and a meeting of the war cabinet was called to discuss the issue.

There were two main questions.

Was it a message from aliens?

And if it was, what did it say?

A lot of people got to working on it. Even some of the very same experts who'd been on TV dismissing it were discreetly contacted by men with tailored suits and earpieces and given first-class tickets to Washington, D.C.

The NASA chief wanted some answers before he had to stand in front of the president.

Unfortunately he wasn't going to get them.

He wasn't going to get them because the two foremost experts on alien life on Earth, the two people who really could have cracked the communication and told the president who it was from and what it said, were not contacted and were certainly not working on deciphering the message. Ramsay, initially excited enough to phone Jamie, had weighed the evidence and dismissed the whole thing as a typical Internet story, and Jamie, convinced by his friend's skepticism, had gone to bed.

"The whole thing smells like a hoax," the vice president said as Samuel Hutchenson, the new head of

NASA, walked into the Oval Office. Hutchenson nodded nervously. And he was right to be nervous. It wasn't every day someone from NASA got invited to a meeting of the war cabinet.

The president of the United States did not look up at first. He was having trouble with his pens. Twice he had tried to sign the executive order, twice the pen had not worked.

"What's the matter with these things? Can't anyone get me a pen that works around here?" he asked.

"Mr. President, Director Hutchenson of NASA," a tall aide whispered.

The president stood and offered his hand.

"Good to see you, Sam," he said cheerfully. "Sit down."

Sam Hutchenson sat in the only remaining chair.

He cleared his throat.

Arranged in a semicircle around him were the four most powerful people in the world. The president of the United States, the vice president, the secretary of state, and the secretary of defense.

The presidential aide and a photographer left the room.

"What's all this nonsense we're hearing about aliens," the secretary of defense snapped before Hutchenson's posterior had even begun to warm the seat.

"It's a very complicated situation," Sam Hutchenson began uncertainly.

There was a long and awkward pause. The vice president grinned like a lionness who had just spotted a baby zebra separated from the herd. "Sounds like something the Russians or the Chinese would pull to trick us, eh?" the vice president muttered

"Well, Sam, why don't you begin at the beginning," the president said helpfully.

"The beginning. Uhm. Of course. Well, it turns out that JPL, that's the Jet Propulsion Laboratory—a private body, not part of our agency—has picked up what they think is a message from an, uhm, intelligence in space."

The president narrowed his eyes. "A nonhuman intelligence?" he asked.

"Yes, so they say, sir," Hutchenson said warily.

"And what does this message say?" the vice president asked.

"It's a long string of ones and zeroes. Ninety-eight digits long—some of that is the message being repeated. The broadcast, if that's what it is, may have been going for weeks, possibly longer, but JPL's probe only caught the last couple of hours before it stopped."

"Where was it coming from?" the president asked.

"The constellation Pegasus. We can't be sure where exactly, but that's the general vicinity. We're trying to track it down," the NASA director replied.

"Are we certain this is the work of an intelligence?" the secretary of state asked.

"No, ma'am, not by any means. It may be the radio waves from a dying pulsar, it may be associated with a gamma ray burst, it could be ejecta from a spinning black hole. The truth is, we don't know exactly what it is. It was picked up by the JPL's *Cassini* probe around Saturn. *Cassini* thought initially it was a message from Earth and when it realized it wasn't, it sent the message back to Pasadena for confirmation. JPL jumped the gun a little bit, but they followed the protocols. They called us and we called you. Everyone wants to get an OK from the White House before the information gets released to the media."

The president leaned back in his chair. "Do you have a copy of this so-called message?" he asked.

"Yes sir, of course," Director Hutchenson said. He took an envelope from his inside jacket pocket, opened it, and handed a piece of paper to the president.

The president looked at it and passed it around the semicircle.

It was a piece of paper with this printed in the middle:

```
11111111 11 1111 1101 101 10101
   1001 1110 101 1001 1100 1100
11111111 11 1111 1101 101 10101
   1001 1110 101 1001 1100 1100
```

The president took the note again and handed it back to Sam Hutchenson.

"If it is aliens, what do you think they're trying to tell us?" he asked.

The NASA director sat forward in his chair. He was on safer ground here and was beginning to relax a little. "It's in binary, sir, the simplest way of transmitting a message across space by radio telescope. If you convert it to base ten we think it means this," he said, handing the president a second piece of paper on which the number 2553151352191459121225531513521 914591212 had been written.

"And what does that mean?" the president asked.

The NASA director grinned awkwardly. "Uhm, we don't know."

"Could it be an alphabet code?" asked the secretary of state, a former specialist in security matters.

"Well, if the aliens, if they are aliens, somehow know Earth alphabets, which is unlikely, it doesn't produce words we can understand. We've had the FBI's Cray parallel computers run it through every known language on Earth, but it's nonsense," the NASA director said with some complacency.

"The computers couldn't find any code or message at all?" the president asked.

"No sir, nothing. If it *is* a message, we don't know

what it means. It might be music, it might be poetry, it might, on the other hand, be a scientific phenomenon unconnected to an intelligence."

"Like what?"

"Like I say, sir, we don't know, two stars colliding, the dying radio burst of a quasar, something like that."

There was another long pause.

The vice president took the two pieces of paper, examined them intently, and passed them around.

No one could make heads or tails of any of it.

"How far away are these aliens? Could they be coming here anytime soon?" the vice president asked.

Sam Hutchenson laughed nervously.

"Oh no, not by any means. The source of the message is about a hundred light-years from Earth."

"And to a layman that means what?"

"Oh, well, we estimate that the fastest a ship could ever travel and still remain within the boundaries of the laws of physics is about ten percent of light speed. So it would take them a thousand years to get here," Sam said.

The president stroked his chin and smiled.

At first he'd been concerned, but this was beginning to look like less and less of a problem. Certainly not in the same league as the Iraq business or the coming elections.

"What's your hunch, Sam? Is it something we should be worried about?"

"I'm skeptical, sir. In the 1970s SETI—that's the Search for Extra-Terrestrial Intelligence—claimed to have had an alien contact, the so-called Wow signal. It turned out to be nothing. In the Clinton administration, NASA got egg all over its face from that Mars rock they said contained life, but that also turned out to probably not be life at all. I think we may be looking at a similar phenomenon," the NASA head said with growing confidence.

"You don't think it is aliens?" the secretary of state asked with a curious smile.

Sam had really not come to any conclusion, but he could sense the mood in the room: They wanted to disbelieve it. He, however, was not going to be badgered.

He shook his head. "I don't know. I just don't think we have enough information to say definitively one way or the other."

The president nodded.

"So what do we do?" he asked.

"The story's already leaking. JPL only showed it to us first as a courtesy. And your executive order will only keep them quiet for a while. They want to release the message to the world. They *will* release it sooner or later. They don't really run a tight ship over there. Bunch of hippies actually, very smart, but you know . . ." His voice trailed off as the president stood and walked to the window.

He looked out at the brown grass and the scrubby rosebushes. Someone wasn't doing a very good job with the gardening.

Was this really the answer to the question of whether humanity was alone in the universe? It was certainly too big to keep a secret. The NASA director was right about that. Secrets didn't last very long in this country.

Indeed, on his inauguration day, no one came to brief him about the Bermuda Triangle or the Kennedy assassination or Area 51. He learned, with a little bit of disappointment, that there were no big classified plots hidden away. Oswald shot Kennedy, Area 51 was an ordinary aircraft base, the Bermuda Triangle was statistically one of the safest waterways in the world. There were no secrets and no conspiracies because Americans didn't do a good job of keeping secrets. Once free of the Puritan restraint, his countrymen had become blabbermouths. Everything that could leak would leak.

"Mr. President?" the vice president prompted at last.

He turned to face them. "OK, I've decided what we're going to do," the president said to the expectant quartet.

"What?" the vice president asked.

"We're going to have a press conference. Let's tell the world before the hippies do. Sam, you'll run it."

"Me, sir?" the director said, grabbing onto his tie like it was a lifejacket.

"You. You'll tell them we're not sure what it is. It might be a message from an extraterrestrial intelligence, it might just be a freak of nature. But we'll put it out there. Every time we've tried to hush things up, it's bit us on the ass," the president said, and gave the secretary of defense a pointed look.

"What if the Chinese crack the message first?" the vice president objected.

"We let everyone know. We'll put it out there. So what? Maybe the Chinese will crack it, maybe the French, hell, maybe two boys in a basement in Milwaukee will figure it out."

Milwaukee, Wisconsin. A lovely spring evening. Birdsong. Apple blossom. Kids bicycling under the trees. Women pushing strollers in Congress Park. Pies cooling on window ledges. Teenagers playing street hockey in cul-de-sacs. A breeze off the lake rattling the air conditioners on the rooftop of the Harley-Davidson plant.

A beautiful and arresting scene.

Spielbergian. *Happy Days*ian.

Something is going to happen.

Definitely.

But not here . . .

Muck Island, Northern Ireland.

The dark sea, storm clouds, smoke from Ballylumford power station blowing over the rainy islet nestled off the Islandmagee peninsula.

The phone ringing in the Lighthouse House.

"What the fuuu . . ."

Jamie looked at the clock.

It was three in the morning.

"Somebody better be dead, or giving birth," he said.

He let it ring and eventually it stopped. He waited. But they didn't call back. Wrong number, Jamie concluded, but now he was awake. Groaning, he got out of bed, put on his slippers, walked downstairs.

He flipped on his computer.

A new message from Ramsay. He opened it. Nothing about the aliens. Instead a novella Ramsay was working on called *A Screaming Comes Across the Sky*. He read a bit of it. It was about aliens who come to Earth looking for the meaning of life, but no one on Earth knows the meaning either and the aliens get very pissed off— Ramsay wanted to know if they could turn it into a rock opera.

He checked his other account and read an e-mail from Thaddeus, his octogenarian friend back in New York. Thaddeus had just been offered a lot of money for his apartment in Harlem, and he was thinking about taking the cash and moving. "I love progress, but I hate change," Thaddeus had written, explaining that it was a quote from Mark Twain, and then, feeling that kids today knew nothing, he spent the rest of the e-mail explaining who Mark Twain was.

Jamie sighed and shut off the computer. He sat for a moment at the kitchen table. For the hundredth time since the alien message story had broken he thought about Wishaway, who for a moment on Altair had been his girlfriend—his only girlfriend.

The phone started ringing again.

He grabbed it.

"What?" he said.

"I was wrong. It *is* aliens. Check out the Internet."

"I knew it was you that called. Do you know what time it is, Ramsay?"

"Did you vibe what I said? 'I was wrong.' Those are words you're not likely to hear again from me in this lifetime. NASA held a press conference. They released the message. They're saying it could be a natural phenomenon. It's not. I've read it. It's dynamite. I think I'm on to something. I'll talk to you tomorrow," Ramsay said hurriedly.

"Say all that again slowly."

"I gotta go," Ramsay said, and hung up.

"Wait," Jamie said, but his friend was gone.

Groggily he set down the phone.

"Kid's totally crazy," Jamie muttered to himself.

He stood there for a moment and then walked to the living room window and looked out to sea. In the channel the lights were bobbing on the Pirate Radio 252 ship which was broadcasting pop and rock from beyond the three-mile limit. They wouldn't care if there were aliens or not, just as long as it didn't interfere with Britney Spears's or Jessica Simpson's ability to pump out horrible music.

Jamie stared at the lighthouses across the lough in Scotland. He yawned and inwardly swore at Ramsay, for he knew that, tired as he was, there was no way he was ever going to get back to sleep this night.

Chapter III
THE PROPOSAL

STILLNESS. QUIET. A waveless silence. Nothing moving save the almost imperceptible motions of the heavens. Stars, planets, the two moons—one crescent, one full.

She shivered but it wasn't cold.

It was high summer, there was a warm breeze from the south, and the day, when it came, was going to be hot. Regardless, she wrapped a shawl about her shoulders and shuffled from the window seat and onto the balcony itself.

She walked to the rail and looked out.

In this new house, they were right on the water, and in the daylight the ocean was a gentle blue or blue-green, inviting and lovely; but at night it was a black solitude that seemed to stretch forever.

It spooked her and she turned round so she was facing the city.

A crimson haze in the west. A stranger would have thought it was the dawn but it wasn't—not yet. It was vapor transpiring from the fresh plantation of *axney* saplings. A grove of these trees, whose lustrous oil was highly prized, had been felled by the Alkhavans for mere timber. The new trees were doing very well, but it would take fifty years of careful growth and shepherding to fill the void of that foul deed.

All those foul deeds.

Invasion, fire, pillage, murder.

However, the twelve-month anniversary had come and gone and those terrible days were fading into history. For well over a year now the city had slept the sleep of contentment. It slept still. The quiet shops, houses, markets, minarets, towers. No movement, no noise. Just her and the night together.

She started at the sound of bells but it was only the return of the *dragga* fleet. A dozen little boats lighting their way into the harbor with yellow lamps and a few men calling to one another with more than the usual joy. A good catch.

The fleet threw ropes and moored, and then for a while the silence returned. She took a knot out of her hair and considered returning to bed.

But the thought of the boats had stirred her.

Shoeless, she walked out onto the terrace to the sculpture garden. Her father, being rich, had commissioned a piece to commemorate his elevation to the position of Council president, a term he would hold for the next year.

Wishaway examined the new replica sculpture of a ship

glinting in the moonlight. It was quarter-scale, lifelike, carved from a single piece of Perovan crystal. The masts, the rigging, all cut with a precision and fragility that took the breath away. It was beautiful, yes, but there was something melancholy about it too. The artist had carved the ship without a crew. Among the more conservative peoples of the Middle Sea, it was not considered seemly to draw or make copies of individuals. Some people bucked tradition, but her father was a bit of an old reactionary too.

She yawned as the *rantas* began calling on the harbor wall. Dawn was definitely coming.

She hadn't slept at all. She'd been up all night. How could she not be? This was going to be the day. This was going to be the morning in fact. Her heart began pounding in her breast, and she had to force herself to calm down.

She walked deep into the gardens, bent low, and drank some of the water from a ceremonial fountain. It tasted bad. But then everything had tasted bad for days. Nerves. She returned to the terrace. Her bare feet touching the cool stones with what the dancing instructor would have said was the grace and elegance of those highborn. She smiled. Of course she was *not* highborn. Her father, yes, a councilor, a scholar, but her mother was a peasant from the mountains, of no name, no stature, with nothing to offer but her beauty, her intelligence, and her love.

Wishaway's hand went to the place around her neck where the pendant had been that contained her mother's picture. But the hand stopped itself. The pendant wasn't there anymore. Jamie had it, on Earth, which, as she understood it, was millions of miles away from here. Millions of unconquerable, uncrossable miles . . .

She breathed deeply and closed her eyes and nostrils. In a human, the gesture would signify a kind of deep sigh. In an Altairian it just looked sad. Very sad.

She opened the patio doors and went into the library. Books were rare, and few on Aldan other than her father had copies of almost all that had ever been made. About two thousand titles in total. It was one of the best collections in the city outside of the university library—though in truth, several of the rarer volumes had been borrowed from the university and not quite yet returned.

They were written in all the languages of the world, some printed, some handwritten the old way before the Ui Neills came; but of all the volumes in this room, the one she went to most was the *Book of Stories*.

When the Ui Neills had arrived all those centuries ago they had brought precious few books with them. A paltry number of religious texts or histories or poems. These of course had been copied and studied and disseminated—for the Ui Neills were famous, godlike, and they had done wondrous things. They had saved the city from invasion, they had brought new technologies and founded the hospital, the university, several schools.

They had thrived.

And then they had died.

They had had no offspring, and when the last great Ui Neill, Morgan of the Red Hand, was on his deathbed, a Black Monk—a scribe—came by ship from Balanmanik. When asked what his business was in Aldan, the monk said that he merely wished Morgan to speak, to tell everything he knew so that it could be recorded for posterity. Despite the hostility of the Aldanese people to the presence of one associated with the Witch Queen, Morgan was flattered and charmed by the idea. For this was a man who could talk. He had been educated in the old Irish way, where the bardish traditions died hard. Even in his eightieth year he knew thousands of lines of poetry, history and Brehon Law by heart. For several months Morgan filled the scribe's sheets with tales.

And then he grew too ill to speak. The Black Monks offered the services of their physicians, but the Aldanese would have none of it, and soon thereafter Morgan went to be with his fathers. With Morgan safely dead, the Aldanese Council imprisoned the monk and seized his book. The Alkhavans protested, and after a long wait—years—the monk was released. Meanwhile, the Aldanese had copied Morgan's book and had it printed. It was a huge success. As a girl, Wishaway had read Morgan's famous *Book of Stories* many times until all those Earth-born kings and knaves, heroes and heretics, fighters and fools had become jumbled up together. Cortez had met with Alexander by the shores of Lake Texcoco. Wicked Macbeth had fought Hector, tamer of horses, on the field of Bannockburn. Cuchulainn of Ulster gave aid to Caesar in his war against the Turks.

Her father had three copies of the *Book of Stories* in his library—one of which came with engravings. That was her favorite. She took down the well-thumbed volume, opened it at random, and read a little of the tale of Arthur, King of Britons, who had died but would come again.

On Earth such things were possible.

She knew that because she had been there herself—had been there for one magical hour and experienced a little of its marvels.

They could do almost anything on that world. And when Jamie had returned home to save his mother, she felt in her heart that he would return. But then the hours had become days and the days weeks, and the weeks months, and now it was a year and more.

She had to face the truth.

Jamie was no longer able to make that journey. His device, the Salmon of Knowledge, was broken beyond repair.

"He comes not," she whispered in English and closed the book. And not in this world, in this life, would she see him again. Seamus of the Black, Guardian of the Way, Heir of Morgan, Smiter of Alkhava. Jamie, lovely Jamie, the boy from Earth.

She found that she was crying. "No, I will not do this, I will not give in to tears," she whispered.

But she did. She let herself sob for a few minutes and then walked onto the balcony to catch her breath. The false dawn was past. The sun, rich and yellow, was rising from the western sea.

It wouldn't be long now.

In Oralands it was traditional to come with the dawn. You propose at dawn, you marry at midnight. She knew it. She knew their customs. He would arrive in his best clothes, bearing a gift for the house and a necklace for her.

Traditionalist that he was, he had already asked her father and of course her father had given his blessing.

It was a good match.

He had never boasted of it, but she knew that he was of the royal house in Oralands. A princeling. More than that, a prince.

His grandfather was the king, and he himself was fifth or sixth in line to the throne. He was also handsome, charming, intelligent, kind, and most important of all—he loved her.

He had loved her when they had been students together. He had loved her when they had been prisoners on the iceship. He had loved her when they had battled and defeated the Alkhavans.

He shared her passions too. English, music, science, history.

He was the perfect husband.

Except.

And in the stories there was always an "except."

"Except, I don't love him," she said to the sea.

And what was more, she would never love him.

She loved someone else.

After all this time. For what was a year? It might as well be a hundred. It wouldn't matter. Now and forever.

"I like him, I like Lorca very much, but I don't love him," she whispered.

The sea did not reply. The sea never replied. It kept its own counsel. And as the sun ascended, it slowly, quietly, turned from a twilight indigo into a soft aquamarine.

She was not too young to be married. She was fifteen years old, almost sixteen. Fourteen Altairian years was the minimum for wedlock, and at her age she no longer needed the consent of her father. Not that that would ever have been a problem. He was a prince of Oralands who had distinguished himself so highly in the now storied Final Battle Against the Iceships. He had been made an honorary citizen, been given a rank of captain in the army, and even—in a somewhat scandalous breach of protocol—been awarded his degree without the necessity of taking his examinations.

He was everything a dutiful daughter could have wanted in a future husband. A tall, dark, handsome prince with a good nature and a kind heart. Of course her father had consented. It was supposed to be a secret. But how could you keep such a thing secret? Her father knew, the servants knew, the vendor of blossom in the central square knew . . .

She walked back to her bedroom and stared at herself in the looking glass.

Her eyes were puffy, her hair a disaster, and she looked pale and exhausted.

Would he want to marry this wretch? she thought.

At the very least she would have to go through the motions. She opened the dresser, took out her mother's comb, and removed the knots from her hair. She washed her face, applied *grama* bark to her eyes, and found an emerald dress that was subdued but nonetheless, flattering.

She went back to the sculpture garden.

And not a moment too soon.

There he was, walking down the lane.

She ran to the gate and opened it.

"Lorca," she said, affecting surprise.

He was wearing a military jacket and blue trousers. His long untamed locks had been unnaturally smoothed onto his scalp. He was carrying a box. "Wishaway," he said, somewhat taken aback by her appearance.

"Yes?"

"I, uhm, I had intended to wait in the garden until I heard the house stir," he said in formal Aldanese.

"Well, I'm awake," she said cheerfully, again pretending complete innocence.

His cheeks reddened. "Uhh—"

"Come in, I assume you want to see my father?"

Lorca shook his head. "No, no. That is, yes, but I wish to see you first."

"Me?"

"Yes, I want to talk to you."

"Hmm, you look serious. We should go to the terrace."

She led him to the balcony and tried to keep herself from shaking. She sat by the wall with the sea behind her. Lorca sat opposite on the stone bench.

"Wishaway—" he began, but she interrupted.

"What's in the box?"

"I beg your pardon?" he said, thrown again.

"What's in the box?"

"A gift for your father, well for the house, really."

"What is it?"

"A globe of the world, made by craftsmen in Oralands. And for you I also bring a necklace, a token of my—"

"A globe, he'll like that," Wishaway said. "Who made it?"

"I had it commissioned by the finest craftsmen in Oralands," Lorca said a little stiffly.

"My father will appreciate it. It will be a distraction. He is under much pressure. There was a theft of several barrels of the 'gunpowder' from the university; the army and Councilor Quiller are threatening to take away his entire research supply. He's very upset."

"Such important things should, perhaps, be taken out of the hands of civilians," Lorca said, losing his battle with tact.

"Oh, you think so?" Wishaway said, trying rather obviously to begin an argument.

Lorca was getting exasperated. "Wishaway, I need to speak to you. It concerns something important."

Her throat went dry and she grabbed the rail to steady herself. "Speak then."

Lorca did not hesitate. "I know of your affection for the Lord Ui Neill. I know that you and Seamus, Jamie, uhm . . ." he began uncertainly.

"Jamie, yes, what of him?"

"When the Ui Neills deserted us to go back to—"

"They didn't desert us, Lorca. They saved us," Wishaway said, her eyes looking at her bare feet. She had forgotten to put shoes on. How embarrassing.

Lorca coughed and realized he had gotten off on the wrong foot.

"The thing is, Wishaway, Jamie isn't coming back. He can't come back. We're all grateful for what he did, but his part in our story is over. You see that, don't you?"

It was the crucial question, and Wishaway knew that she had to give a truthful answer. She took a deep breath and slowly let the air exhale.

"I do see that," she said in a tiny voice.

He smiled. A charming smile. Behind him the sun was well above the horizon and the sky had taken on a pinkish tone. The day couldn't have been more perfect. Many girls, she knew, dreamed of a moment like this.

"Wishaway," Lorca said hesitantly.

"Yes?"

"There's . . . uhm, there's something on my mind, something I've been meaning to talk to you about. It's about us."

Wishaway again pretended ignorance, not to make it more difficult for him, but just to delay the inevitable moment.

"Yes?" she whispered.

Some lowered their head in supplication, others bowed, but Lorca copied the tradition of the Earthmen and got down on bended knee.

He took out the necklace and began to speak.

She didn't hear a word. She thought about Jamie. She was never going to see him again. By now he had probably forgotten her. He was undoubtedly "dating" some girl on Earth. He would have many admirers. Wishaway had no doubt that he was a hero on Earth too. A traveler between worlds. A great champion. But he was gone, and Lorca was here, now, and she might never get a chance like this again.

Lorca finished his speech. She hesitated and then, in the old way, she lifted his face to hers. His long eyelashes blinked expectantly, almost girlishly. He really was very beautiful.

She smiled. "Yes," she said in a shy voice, and then louder: "Yes, Lorca, of course I'll marry you."

* * *

It was a Saturday and there was no school, so Anna O'Neill was surprised to see Ramsay appear at the front door of the Lighthouse House. Especially at eight in the morning when she was hoping for a little quiet time. She put down her mug of coffee and raised the latch.

"Hello, stranger," she said.

Ramsay nodded, took off his wet coat, slung it on a

hook, and sat down at the kitchen table. "Is, uh, is Jamie up?" he asked, a bit of nervous tension creeping into his voice.

"Still asleep, I think," Mrs. O'Neill replied.

"Have you got any coffee, breakfast?" Ramsay asked.

"Come in, make yourself at home," Anna said, more amused than irritated by Ramsay's easy way with her house.

"Shall I go wake him?" Ramsay said.

"Sit there, I'll get you some coffee. Do you take cream and sugar?"

"I don't know. I'm not really old enough to drink coffee, but I was working all night, so I'd really like some please."

From experience Anna knew better than to ask Ramsay what he'd been working on. Chances were, he'd tell her and it would be something incomprehensible or illegal or both.

"Lots of cream, lots of sugar, and don't tell your parents I'm corrupting you with the demon bean."

Five minutes later she handed him a creamy coffee and a slice of cherry pie.

"Thanks very much," Ramsay said.

She sat opposite him. "So, Ramsay, this is your terrain, what do you think of all this alien message stuff?"

Ramsay's eyes narrowed. "Uhm, not much actually."

"Really?"

"Yeah, it's natural causes. Personally I think it's Hawking radiation from a black hole . . . I don't think it's a message at all," he said a little haltingly, and took a monster bite of the pie.

Anna eyed him suspiciously, but before she could probe him further Jamie appeared.

"I thought I heard voices," he said.

Ramsay put down the pie and coffee. "Uh, Jamie, we have to talk. Mike called me last night, he's thinking of quitting the band, wants to form his own group, the Red Branch Warriors. Dumb name. Something to do with Cuchulainn. Anyway, we can't lose Mike," Ramsay said fast, put his arm round Jamie's shoulders, marched him back to his bedroom, and closed the door.

"What is all this?" Jamie asked, pushing Ramsay off of him. "Let Mike quit if he wants I don't—"

"Forget Mike. This isn't about Mike. That was just to throw your mother off the scent. Get dressed. Don't you ever return your calls? Voice-mailed your cell twice this morning. We'll go to the lighthouse for some privacy. Come on, hurry up."

Five minutes later they were in their "den" at the top of the old lighthouse. Although they didn't use it much, by now they'd made the place very comfortable. They'd thrown in some rugs and chairs, and they even had a gas stove to provide a little warmth. Jamie's portable tablet PC was beeping.

"Hey, I think I have an e-mail. Maybe it's Thaddeus," Jamie said excitedly.

Jamie looked at the computer; however, it was only spam. He started to delete it, but before he could Ramsay turned the machine off.

"Hey, that was rude," Jamie said.

"Forget it. It can wait. This is serious," Ramsay said. "Sit at the table and pay attention."

"You can't boss me around. I—"

"Sit at the table and pay attention. I don't want to have to explain everything twice."

Jamie sat down, feeling oppressed by his own generous nature. Ramsay could be overbearing at times, and it was the saintly figure who could let it slide. Thinking of his own beatification someday, he nodded and said nothing. Ramsay took out a sheet of paper on which he'd written a series of numbers. "Look at this," Ramsay said.

"Were you playing battleships?"

Ramsay snatched the paper back. "Gimme that. OK, so I assume you ignored my midnight call, but you must have watched the news or logged on. NASA showed us the radio signal they got from space."

"Midnight. If only. Three in the morning, buddy. And yeah I saw it, no one's really sure what it is."

"That's what *you* made of it?" Ramsay asked.

"What's there to make? It was just little beeps with spaces between the beeps. What of it?"

Ramsay rubbed his hands. "Beeps with spaces between the beeps. Good grief. It's binary. You know? Computer language. The simplest language there is."

"If you say so."

"OK, so I've written it out in binary and it looks like this: The spaces are where NASA says there was a gap longer than the space that might represent a zero, OK?"

Among the many calculations on the page Ramsay pointed to where he had written:

$$1111111 \quad 11 \quad 1111 \quad 1101$$
$$101 \quad 10101 \quad 1001 \quad 1110$$
$$101 \quad 1001 \quad 1100 \quad 1100$$

Jamie looked at the paper and nodded.

It was completely meaningless to him.

"Great," he said.

"Now there's any number of ways to interpret the beeps and spaces, but let's assume that this is the correct one. Small spaces represent zeros, dots are ones, and the big spaces are gaps between letters or bits of information," Ramsay said.

"Assume away," Jamie said.

"Now there's no way aliens could know our counting system, but if they could, in base ten that list of binary digits comes out as 255, 3, 15, 13, 5, 21, 9, 14, 5, 9, 12, 12, or if you ignore the gaps, 25531513521914591212 with the same number repeated once."

Jamie was getting peevish now.

"And what does that mean? It looks like a pretty random number to me," Jamie said. "I mean couldn't it be a radio burst from a star or something? I heard the Hayden Planetarium guy on TV, and he discounted the whole thing."

Ramsay leaned back in the chair and licked his lips.

"Yes, it could be a load of rubbish and NASA obviously doesn't think it's a message from aliens or they wouldn't be so free to give it out as information. And true, if you convert those numbers into an alphabet-substitution code with, let's say, 1=A, 2=B, and so on, you are bollixed from the start. I mean what letter does 255 represent?"

"Unless the alien alphabet has 255 letters, in which case we'll never get it."

"No, we wouldn't."

Ramsay stood and walked to the window.

A silence descended on the room as silences often do with a boy who spent a year not talking and another who was occasionally lost in his own thoughts.

"You ever look at the rocks on the causeway, Jamie?" Ramsay asked finally.

"Sometimes," Jamie replied noncomittally.

"They're all cracked and wrinkled like W. H. Auden's forehead. Or since you probably don't know who he is, let's say the surface of Europa," Ramsay said a little dreamily.

Jamie got up from his seat and went over to his friend.

"What are you talking about? What's got into you?"

"The cracks in the causeway. They look man-made but they're a completely random fissure in the granite and the bedrock."

"And don't insult me. Of course I've heard of W. H. Auden. Have you heard of Francis Scott Key?"

"Yes."

"Dorothy Whitbornth?"

"You just made her up," Ramsay said.

"Did not."

"Did too."

"Did . . . What's this got to do with the message?" Jamie asked.

"If I were sending a message across the stars, the first thing I'd want to do is make sure the people getting it know it's not a random radio signal from a star or a black hole. I wouldn't want them to think it's like cracks in the granite, I'd want them to know it's something I made."

"How?"

"What I'd do is give them the list of the prime numbers or something as a marker. Right? I'd go, 2, 3, 5, 7, 11, 13. That list doesn't occur in nature. And then when we've established that, I'd go straight in and say what I wanted to say. But the aliens didn't do that here, did they?"

"Uhm, I guess not."

"They just sent out an utterly meaningless list of numbers."

"If it is aliens," Jamie insisted.

A smile began to creep around the edges of Ramsay's mouth.

"There's something you're not telling me," Jamie said.

"Did you know that dolphins only sleep with half their brain at a time?" Ramsay said mysteriously.

"Why's that then?"

"Because otherwise they would drown."

"You're being more annoying than usual today," Jamie muttered.

Ramsay's big eyes were wide with pleasure.

"You see, you have to think like the other species, not like the humans. Do you follow?"

Jamie examined his friend's face. "You've cracked, it haven't you? Haven't you? It is a message and you've worked it out. Tell me."

"Patience," Ramsay said. "Now, come over here."

"How did you solve it when bloody NASA couldn't?" Jamie asked.

"I have had the advantage of going to the place from which the message was sent, and knowing that there they count in base eight, not base ten," Ramsay said with satisfaction.

"Altair? It came from Altair, it came from Altair? How is that possible? You said they didn't have the technology to send any message—"

"OK, so I was wrong about that too," Ramsay interrupted. "Plain wrong. It's a completely backward civilization, haven't even got the internal combustion engine, but somehow they did it, don't ask me how, but they did."

"What does the message say?" Jamie asked desperately.

Ramsay ignored him and took out a pencil.

"Let's look at that list of ones and zeroes again. 11111111 11 1111 1101 101 10101 1001 1110 101 1001 1100 1100," Ramsay said and took a deep breath.

"OK."

"Now, I think the first eight ones are a marker telling us to count in base eight. They're not part of the real message at all. That's why NASA won't crack it. You have to ignore the first eight digits," Ramsay said with a wicked grin.

"Brilliant," Jamie muttered, and slapped his friend on the back.

"So ignoring the first eight ones and converting the rest of the message to base eight gives us 3, 17, 15, 5, 25, 11, 16, 5, 11, 14, 14."

"Great, now what?"

"Now, what NASA doesn't realize and no one on Earth could possibly know is that the aliens *know* we use English here on our planet. So all you have to do is substitute that list of numbers into our own alphabet using the plain text code 1 for *A*, 2 for *B* and so on."

"OK, and you've done that I'm sure."

"Yes, I have," Ramsay said grimly.

"The suspense is killing me, for God's sake tell me."

"OK, remember we're counting in base eight. OK, so, 3, the third letter of the alphabet in base eight that's *C*. The seventeenth letter is *O*. The fifteenth letter is *M*. Fifth letter is *E*. Then 25, that's *U*. Then 11, that's *I*. Then 16, that's *N*. Five is *E* again. 11 is another *I*. Then two 14s, that's two *L*s. The message is . . ."

"Yes?"

"Come Ui Neill."

"What?"

"Come Ui Neill."

Jamie was too stupefied to speak. He stared at his friend and saw that this was no joke. *Come Ui Neill.* Ramsay filled the silence with Jamie's unspoken thought.

"The message sent to the whole planet was actually

addressed to you, Jamie. It came from a hundred light-years away in Pegasus. That means it was sent a hundred years ago."

"What, how, who?" Jamie gasped.

"I assume they didn't know it was going to be you, unless they can see into the future, which is impossible—at least in my understanding of the laws of physics. But they wanted the current Lord Ui Neill, whoever he was going to be, to use the Salmon and come to Altair. Whoever sent the message a hundred years ago is in the middle of a long-term problem, and they need our help."

"But it's broken. We couldn't go even if we wanted to," Jamie said, Ramsay's statement just beginning to sink in.

"That's right, we couldn't go even if we wanted to," Ramsay repeated. "Because the Salmon has run out of juice."

Jamie thought of that mysterious artifact resting on a pillar in the secret room above their heads. He had stolen several peeks at it since his return from Altair, but he had gone up there less and less over the months. The memory of his experience on that world was wrapped up with his loss of Wishaway, and it was just too painful.

"But they need us, Ramsay," Jamie said after a long pause.

"They do," Ramsay agreed.

"So what do we do?"

"Somehow we've got to fix the Salmon, recharge its freaky alien batteries, lie to our parents, and jump back to Altair," Ramsay said, drumming his fingers on the table.

"And have you thought about a way we could possibly do that?"

Ramsay did not reply but he gave a slight, almost imperceptible nod of the head.

A seagull began crying outside the window. And when it stopped, since the tide was out, there was now no sound at all, not even the sea.

"Let's go get the thing," Jamie said to break the tension.

They pulled the table over, Jamie stood on it, and they removed the false bricks in the ceiling they had placed over the entrance to the upper room of the lighthouse.

"Flashlight," Jamie said.

Ramsay handed it to him. Jamie turned it on, climbed into the upper room, and walked over to the Salmon. Of course it was untarnished by the damp and erosion. Gleaming there, fishlike, strange, this machine that made wormholes in space-time and broke humans into molecules and sent those molecules across the eternities of space to other worlds.

Jamie lifted it up and looked at it with wonder.

"Well?" Jamie said.

"Well what?"

"Answer the question. Have you thought of a way we could possibly fix it?"

Ramsay took the device from Jamie's hand and examined it. There was one thing he had considered months ago. Considered and dismissed as too risky.

He shook his head. "There is an idea I've been toying with. But it's going to be a gamble, Jamie. It's going to be all or nothing."

"What do you mean?"

"Well, it'll either fix the Salmon or it will completely destroy it."

"Then I'm all in," Jamie said. "We'll go for it. We have to. We've no other choice. They've summoned us, and by hook or by crook we're going to come."

The Thirty-second Witch Queen put on her furs and walked through the underground passage from her palace to the Black Tower of Balanmanik.

She was greeted by a representative of the Black Monks, a young novice of soft complexion, taken no doubt on a slave raid to the southlands when he was still a child.

"This way, my lady," he said.

She ignored his impertinence. In her day one waited to speak until one was spoken to by a superior. The Twenty-seventh Witch Queen might have had him whipped. The Twentieth would have had him killed on the spot.

She sighed. Such was the decline of the world. "Lead on," she barked.

The monk bowed, and she followed him up the spiral staircase to the top of the Black Tower. The windows had long since been bricked up against the howling gale, but the large circular room at the top was well lit with torches.

In the center of the floor lay a gold circle and within the circle, a gold triangle and within that an oval object broken into several pieces.

Half a dozen people awaited her approach.

Monks, priestesses, and one hooded supplicant who lurked in the corner away from the others. The wretch was burned down one side of his body and could only walk with the aid of a stick. He was in some considerable pain and required the application of a healing balm morning and night.

As usual he was wearing the accoutrements of a senior monk, a full cassock and a hood pulled up to conceal his badly scarred face.

He was a pathetic sight, and she kept him near, not from fraternal obligation, but from respect for his genuine abilities.

He limped in her direction.

Although he didn't feel it at the moment, he knew that

he was lucky. Lucky to be alive. Lucky that the monks had long preserved this room in the Black Tower of Balanmanik, keeping it pristine and protected from the elements. This room where once beings from a distant star had leaped between worlds.

Lucky that the monks had scrambled into action once they had known that an Ui Neill was here on Altair using that great talisman—the Salmon of Knowledge—using it and here over a year ahead of schedule.

Lucky that they had been trying to catch the jumper and divert him on his path from Altair to Earth. *Lucky.* The fiery heat of the wormhole would have killed him and torn him to pieces but for the actions of these monks.

Yes, he was very fortunate that they had pulled him from the wormhole and saved his miserable life. Of course he knew that he had not been their object. His rescue was only happenstance. They didn't really care about the jumper, be it him or the Lord Ui Neill, or one of the Old Ones for that matter.

What they wanted was the Salmon. What she wanted was the Salmon.

And if he knew his sibling, she would have it.

"Darling sister," Ksar hissed through a face that was only now beginning to recover its full mobility after months of healing ointments.

"Brother," she replied without affection.

"The monks believe that by now the Earth people will have received the message sent a century ago by your predecessor," Ksar said in the high Alkhavan dialect of the Witch Queen's court.

He drooled as he spoke. It was quite disgusting. The Witch Queen turned away.

"So they tell me," she said.

"Of course you can't know if the message will be passed on to the boy Ui Neill."

"You are naive, brother. When the message arrives on Earth, as a man of some personage, no doubt the Lord Ui Neill will be informed immediately."

"Ahh, no doubt," Ksar said with a gurgle that may have been an attempt at laughter.

"And when he comes, with the other two towers destroyed, we will divert him here with the remains of our Salmon," the Witch Queen said with some complacency.

Ksar looked at the monks holding the horribly mangled second Salmon.

This second Salmon of Knowledge, which had enough power to save his life, to pull him from the vortex, did not have enough to enable one to make a jump.

"Yes, you will *attempt* to drag him here, with the remains of the other device," Ksar corrected.

The Witch Queen noticed the conditional tone in his voice.

"That certainly is the idea," she agreed.

"And if you succeed?" Ksar asked.

"And then, dear brother, we will have a working Salmon and escape to Earth."

Ksar laughed. "You think the Lord Protector will permit such a thing? It is you that are naive, sister. He will take the Salmon for himself. His spies are everywhere, even here."

The Queen hesitated. "You know this?"

"I know him, dear sister," Ksar slurred.

The Witch Queen *knew* her brother would not have mentioned this if he had not already been concocting a solution.

"What do you have in mind?" she asked.

"Give me gold—give me gold to recruit my men. With gold I can achieve much. I will take care of the Lord Protector so that he will not interfere with our plans."

"You think yourself able to go against the Lord Protector?"

Ksar rose to his full height and stretched out his burned arms and shoulders. It was a gesture he had been working on for days.

"I am certainly match enough to go against that fool," he said, fighting hard to keep a steady timbre in his voice.

The Queen said nothing for a long time. She knew her brother was intelligent, she knew he was efficient, but was he wily enough to go against the Lord Protector and his Palace Guard? Could Ksar carry something like that off in his present condition? The old Ksar could have. But could this burned, deformed creature in front of her be half as capable?

"How many men will you need?"

Ksar shrugged. "Not more than a dozen."

The Witch Queen's lips thinned.

"Thou art dreaming, brother. How will you storm the palace in Afor with so few soldiers?"

"I have my ways," Ksar said.

She regarded him for some time.

"It must not come back to me if you fail," she said.

"I will arrange poison vials for myself and my companions," Ksar said quickly.

"No, I will see to that, that is my area of expertise."

She looked into his cold blue-black eyes. The will was certainly there. And if it went wrong, she could always denounce him, urge the Lord Protector to execute him at once. It would be a victory either way.

"I will trust you, brother," she said at last.

Ksar smiled and winced as drool fell from his mouth to the cold floor.

"Yes, you will take care of the Lord Protector and I will procure the Salmon," the Witch Queen said.

"And the Lord Ui Neill?" Ksar asked with a hint of

deference. For he was positionless, rankless, powerless, and she was still the Witch Queen.

"I have no interest in the Lord Ui Neill. I want only the device that will enable us to escape this world," she said.

"It will be my pleasure to dispose of him, to avenge myself on him. If the Queen permits it," Ksar added hastily.

She sniffed.

"Oh by all means, he is of no use to us. Kill him, kill his accomplices—you may have your diversions, brother. It is the Salmon we seek."

Ksar nodded. Kill him and his accomplices. He would do it, slowly and lovingly, inflicting great pain in recompense for the great pain done to him. (Jamie had robbed him of victory in Aldan and rived his body.) He bowed and walked away from the others. He sat down painfully on a cold stone seat in an alcove near the stair. He caught his breath. *Read the message, heed the message. And then come, Ui Neill,* he said to himself and repeated it like a mantra. *Read the message, heed the message, and come, Ui Neill.*

Chapter IV
THE COUP

ACCORDING TO RAMSAY (who had never traveled) the County Antrim coast (where he had lived all his life) was one of Europe's loveliest vistas. Pressed, Ramsay could get quite prolix, explaining that, carved by glaciers and softened by the warm, moist air of the Gulf Stream it was a paradise of winding roads, isolated harbors, bird sanctuaries, wild cliffs, and secret beaches.

But every Eden has a serpent, and Ramsay was quick to point out that the beauty of the coast was spoiled by the monstrous, brutalist power station at Kilroot lying just outside the twelfth-century town of Carrickfergus. Constructed as a series of gigantic, concrete rectangles, the plant was so big it could be seen across the Irish Sea in Scotland, as could its two enormous chimneys stretching skyward and belching black smoke over Belfast Lough and much of Eastern Ulster.

It was one of Ramsay's least favorite places in the whole of Ireland and he hated to be here. Wild horses couldn't drag him here. He wouldn't come here for all the tea in China. He wouldn't come here for Lindsay Lohan on toast.

Nonetheless he was here.

At least now it was night and the worst excesses of the 1970s utilitarian architecture were concealed by the darkness.

Still they had to be careful.

Powerful spotlights illuminated the perimeter fence, and there were arc lamps every fifty feet on the chimneys so that on a clear night, when there wasn't mist, rain, fog, or low clouds, airplanes wouldn't crash into them. Unfortunately, Irish days without some form of precipitation are as rare as Irish snakes. And this wasn't one of them. Ramsay and Jamie were soaked through as they lurked on the slip road between the fence and the cold waters of the lough.

"Do you think he's going to come?" Jamie asked, looking at his watch.

"He'll come. I can tell he was intrigued."

"I should have brought an umbrella."

"He'll be along in a minute," Ramsay said.

"A hat at the very least. You think he'll keep his mouth shut?"

"I think so. One, he's my brother, two he's a bassist. Bassists don't want any trouble. They just want to keep the rhythm. They like order," Ramsay said.

"Uhm, this is a crime we're contemplating here," Jamie observed.

Ramsay nodded—a pointless gesture in the dark.

"Listen, I know you hate me to bring up Dungeons and Dragons—" Ramsay began.

"So don't," Jamie pleaded.

"But bassists are mostly Lawful Evil. They commit evil but keep within the limits," Ramsay said.

Jamie said nothing because he didn't want to encourage him.

Ramsay let the rainwater fall on his tongue for a while. "What time is it?" he asked.

"I don't know," Jamie admitted.

"You're wearing your watch."

"You have to press a button on the watch to get the light to work and you need two hands for that," Jamie said.

"I'll do it," Ramsay said and leaned over to grab his friend by the wrist. Jamie shook him off.

"Leave my watch alone. Wear your own watch."

"I don't hold with watches anymore. Watches are for squares. I like to follow my own sense of time," Ramsay said with a sniff.

Jamie guffawed sarcastically. "Seriously, Ramsay, who writes your dialogue? You should fire him."

Ramsay knew it was a fair point and slipped into silence.

Jamie coughed.

"If this were a movie, one of us would pull out a pack of cigarettes and have a smoke now to fill the silence," Ramsay observed after a while.

"Nothing wrong with a good silence," Jamie said.

"Tried smoking myself once. For scientific reasons. I tell ya, the nausea, carcinogens, cancer-producing oxidants, and the diminishing of my lung capacity did not outweigh the mild narcotic effect," Ramsay said.

Jamie ignored him. Ramsay's nerves were obviously getting the better of him. He wanted to draw Jamie into a conversation, possibly a dispute, but Jamie wasn't going to take the bait. If they were going to do this thing tonight one of them had to keep a level head, and that person was clearly not going to be his tall Irish friend.

"If you're not interested in what I'm saying, just tell me to shut up," Ramsay said a little huffily.

"Shut up," Jamie muttered.

"Right then, I will shut up. Shut up I will. Not another word. I'll learn ya. You'll be the sorry boy when I do," Ramsay intoned.

"If you do do," Jamie said.

"Do, do, that's funny," Ramsay muttered, walking from under the tree and putting his hand out. It was still raining but perhaps a little less intensely.

"Tail of the cold front," Ramsay said knowledgeably.

"Hmmm," Jamie said.

Ramsay wiped the rain from his face and beckoned Jamie over.

"So this is the famous Kilroot Power Station. Big mistake if you ask me. Oil burner originally, coal now, conceived when oil was cheap. You know they had to demolish Jonathan Swift's house to build it? Swift, the writer."

"So?" Jamie said, completely uninterested.

Ramsay tried a different conversational gambit. "That bitter taste in your mouth, that's adrenaline. But don't be nervous, I have everything under control. You see—"

Before he could continue what was obviously going to be a lengthy spiel, Jamie interrupted. "Look, I don't have a bitter taste in my mouth. I don't care about Swift. Just be quiet until your stupid brother comes, if he comes."

They waited for another five minutes. Finally Jamie relented and let Ramsay look at his watch. It was 9:15. Brian was quite late.

"Hurry up, Brian," Jamie said under his breath.

"Aye, where is that Spawn of Satan?" Ramsay wondered out loud. "I'm telling you, if he's chickened out, I'll kill him."

The Spawn of Satan had not chickened out.

In fact at that moment he was less than five minutes away.

He was furiously driving his employer's pickup truck from Islandmagee to Kilroot. Brian worked for the United Fisheries, delivering boxes of fresh and frozen fish to various fish and chip shops throughout East Antrim. Bit of a comedown for a PhD candidate at MIT, but since he had no local references and was suspiciously overqualified for everything else in Northern Ireland, this was the best he could get.

Normally he wouldn't risk his job going off the route, but his annoying little brother had left him the following note: "Urgent. Bring your truck and come to the slip road to at Kilroot Power Station at 9 o'clock sharp. Ramsay."

This better be important, he said to himself as he got the van up to fifty miles per hour.

It was 9:20 and Jamie and Ramsay were beginning to think about abandoning the whole plan, when they smelled a strong whiff of fish and then saw a pair of headlights appear at the end of the power station slip road.

"Told ya," Ramsay said in triumph.

Jamie said nothing. The boys walked out from under the tree.

Brian stopped the vehicle and got out of the truck.

He looked ticked off. "What's this all about, Ramsay?" he asked furiously.

"You stink," Ramsay said.

He did too, but this was not the place to mention that, Jamie reflected. "We need your help, Brian," he said.

"Aye, come on, Odor Wan Kenobi, you're our only hope."

"Did you just say 'Odor Wan Kenobi'?" Brian asked.

"Yeah," Ramsay muttered.

"Even for a pun that's really lame," Brian said.

"Just help us, Han Smello," Ramsay exclaimed.

"OK, I'm leaving. Idiots, the pair of you. Angry at myself more than you. This is what you get when you hang out with wee children. Oh, and by the way, I'm out of your stupid band too."

"No, don't go. We need you, Brian," Jamie begged.

"We do. I'm sorry," Ramsay said.

Brian hesitated for a minute. He wiped the rain off his forehead.

"OK. I know I'm going to regret asking this, but why?" he asked finally.

Ramsay took a deep breath and launched right in.

"We're going to break into the power station, go to one of the high-voltage relays, syphon off some power, scale the fence, and get out of here. There is a possibility that the relay will explode, so we'll need a getaway driver, and there's no one else we can really trust or who knows how to drive, so you're it."

Brian rocked back on his heels and said nothing. Ramsay kept his foot on the metaphorical gas: "You're not heavy, you're my brother, we need ya mate, there's security everywhere. We're dead ducks if we can't get out of here incredibly fast."

The wind changed direction and the smell of fish became overpowering for a moment. Brian sighed, found his keys, and got back into the cab. He closed the door. "I'm surprised to see you here, Jamie, I thought you had more sense. You're going to be the Laird of Muck someday, you should learn to be responsible," Brian said.

He turned the starter, and the engine kicked into life.

Jamie looked grim. Ramsay gave him a questioning glance. Jamie nodded.

"Will we tell him?" Ramsay asked.

Jamie shrugged. It was fine by him. It wasn't that big a secret. He'd already told his mother everything, although obviously she'd been way too overmedicated to take in such a fantastic tale.

Ramsay reached into the truck window and turned off the ignition.

"Don't do that," Brian cried, and tried to slap Ramsay on the top of the head, but his nimble kid brother easily ducked the clumsy blow.

"Don't ever touch my wheels, man," Brian growled, his face wrinkling up in irritation.

"OK, OK. Just listen to me, big brother. I've something to tell you and it's going to blow your mind," Ramsay said.

"Let me guess, you finally got that signed photograph of Gwen Stefani you've been after," Brian snapped.

"No, no, no," Ramsay said indignantly. He paused. "Well, yes, actually, I did get that photo on eBay, but that's not what I was going to say."

"It's a forgery," Brian muttered.

"Is not, but anyway, that's not what I was going to tell you."

"Well, tell me then. I'm sure it's something equally amazing."

"It is actually. See, for your information, mate, Jamie and I went to another planet last year," Ramsay intoned defiantly.

Jamie could see the look of profound skepticism in Brian's eyes.

"We did, we really did, we went down a wormhole, to a planet called Altair, to a country called Aldan," Jamie said.

"Sure it wasn't a rabbit hole?" Brian wondered.

"No, a wormhole. There was a big battle and we sort of, uhm, well we sort of saved them, actually, from an invasion. The Alkhavans had these great big iceships and we gave them chicken pox and I invented Greek Fire, except we called it Ramsay Fire, and anyway we're big heroes over there," Ramsay said.

Brian looked at the boys for a long time. He ran his hands through his hair.

"You vouch for this story, Jamie?" he asked.

"It's all true. We went to Altair and met a girl called Wishaway and saved the world from the Alkhavans."

Brian shook his head very slowly.

He turned the key in the starter again, opened the truck door, picked up the two boys by the scruff of the neck, and threw them in the cab. He closed the door, locked it, and climbed in the driver's side. When they were both belted in he articulated an idea that he'd suspected for some time.

"Drugs," he muttered sadly. "Come on, the pair of you, I'm taking you home and we're going to have a serious talk."

He drove down the lane and the power station transformers sat snug in their cages, unaware of the fate that they had just escaped.

The clouds were gone. The moons were out. The flat disk of the Milky Way formed a line across the still, clear night, like an enormous spine. The stars, yellow, red, and gold, basked in the enormous quiet of the vacuum of space. Here on Altair, light-years from Earth, the Milky Way galaxy looked substantially the same as it did on Earth. As it would on Earth if General Ksar ever got his chance to see it. A grimace slipped across his face. In the language of Alkhava even thinking in the conditional tense was considered to be a sign of weakness. He *would* get his chance to see it.

Ice on his gloves.

Ice on the leathery wings of the huge, pit-reared *ranta*.

He tightened his grip on the reins and pulled downward. The *ranta*'s black lizard head snarled at him and the water vapor in its breath froze in the air.

His legs ached and his arms were sore. He had taken his pain medication—the boiled essence of the *gurya* plant, but that did nothing to keep out the cold. He looked across at the five other great lizardlike beasts gliding next to him in the air. Except for sea monsters, nothing, he thought with satisfaction, on the planet Aldan got bigger than these creatures. And the largest ones of all were in Ksar's personal stable. A secret breeding program begun by his grandfather, and then continued by his father, had finally born fruit three years ago with the birth of six enormous stallions from a single clutch.

He had seen to their care personally before setting off on the ill-fated invasion of Aldan. An invasion that the Lord Protector had insisted upon but that Ksar thought was extremely foolhardy. A waste of time, a waste of resources, and a waste of talent.

Why attack and destroy a prosperous country like Aldan?

It was thinking from the old days.

No. If they were going to attack, they shouldn't have gone looking for plunder, they should have gone to colonize the country. They should have been looking to settle there permanently, not merely to see what loot they could bring back to Alkhava.

Of course his objections had been ignored and overruled in council.

Later he had tried to speak to the Lord Protector privately, but that too was a pointless discussion.

The Lord Protector was no visionary. A coarse, brutal man who barely saw into the next week, never mind the next year or the next decade.

Well, his days of making decisions for the Alkhavan people are numbered, Ksar thought.

The ice was hurting his throat.

He moved his tongue to stop the saliva from freezing in his mouth. Fortunately the wind was blowing from the south, otherwise flying would have been next to impossible, and the whole plan would have to have been abandoned. Years ago summer would have brought nothing but south winds, but now gales from the north were increasingly common. The whole planet was changing, and they were increasingly under the sway of the thousand-mile glacier that stretched from the pole deep into their beloved homeland.

This breeze however *was* coming from the southern

ocean, moist and comparatively warm. Though up here at a thousand feet above the city the *rantas* were at the limit of their tolerance.

"Karaka, sstatha, ah," he soothed, and patted the big beast on its scaly neck. The *ranta* looked back at him and blew more frosty air from its nostrils.

It was a stout animal but it couldn't last much longer at this height. It wouldn't need to. They were close now. Another few minutes and they would surely see the—

Ah, and there it was. The city of Afor stretched out in all its ugly glory around the wide bay. Fifty thousand souls lived within those walls. Rich, poor, male, female, old, young, free, slave. Some in the large houses next to the coast, but most in the densely clustered tenements that lacked windows, plumbing, and often even a chimney stack, so that they were always smoky, dirty, and unpleasant.

Of course it was night, and none of this was clearly visible. No one from the lower orders could really afford to waste timber or *ghana* oil on mere illumination.

Still, there was enough light to show them the way. Bonfires burned within the granite castle, and lights eked from the windows of the larger homes.

"Dara cool?" Ksar's faithful lieutenant Krama shouted from the beast next to him.

Ksar nodded, raised his arm, and gave the signal to begin their descent.

"Dara, dara," he shouted to the others. Down. Down.

He tugged the reins, dug in his spurs, and the *ranta* banked, dropping lower, beneath the clouds. They would have to time this exactly. *Rantas* were gliders, not flyers. They wouldn't get another stab at this. If they overshot or were spotted, they were in trouble. He lost another hundred feet, and suddenly the castle loomed close and massive out of the darkness. Tall, thick, unbreachable walls, a guardhouse, a keep, even a full squadron of *draya* cavalry in the grounds—always on call in case of attack.

He urged the *ranta* on and it sailed over the southern abutment. He pulled hard on the reins, it flapped its massive wings once and then glided over their final destination—the flat roof of the citadel.

Here they definitely could be seen by any of the rooftop guards. Time was of the essence. Every second was precious. They had to land.

He tugged hard on the *ranta's* bridle and slapped it across the nose.

"Dara," he hissed.

He took the loaded crossbow from his shoulder. The *ranta* folded its wings and put out its claws for landing. And the guard on the rooftop didn't see the arrow that killed him. One moment he was staring out into the impenetrable darkness of the western sea, the next he was clutching at his chest, bleeding to death.

Down, down, down, Ksar urged with a final tug on the reins.

The *ranta* landed, scraping its talons on the smooth granite roof, sending up sparks for a second before skidding to a halt.

Four more of the beasts came down beside it.

Four? They had lost someone. He waited a moment, but the final *ranta* didn't appear. Its wings had frozen or its pilot had fallen off.

Could they do this with five men? *Well,* thought Ksar, *we have no choice.* A frontal assault on the castle complex was impossible. If you managed somehow to get over the outer walls the guards would get you, and if they didn't there was an entire brigade of elite soldiers garrisoned on the lower floors of the keep who would.

The direct approach was suicide.

They also did not have enough time for the more traditional Alkhavan methods of regime change: bribing a cup bearer to poison the Lord Protector's wine or arranging for a tragic hunting "accident."

No. If Ksar wanted power immediately it had to be a lightning-quick coup d'état.

And naturally he understood that this was going to be his one and only chance. He was fortunate to be alive after his encounter with the Ui Neill, and that fortune would either hold steady or turn to cinders in his mouth.

By the time the sun came up today, he knew he would either be the ruler of the Alkhavan dominions or he would be dead.

Krama approached him. "Sir, it seems that we have lost Voorta," Krama muttered in that lower-caste Alkhavan drawl of his.

"So I see," Ksar replied.

Krama offered no observations on what had happened to their confederate, and he certainly didn't ask if the plan was to be abandoned. He knew better than that.

Ksar began untying his heavy overcoat.

"Do you wish me to go ahead and secure the residence?" Krama asked.

Ksar smiled. Krama had remained loyal through all his travails. If this worked, he would see to it that he got promoted to a general of the armies.

The deputy was waiting for a reply.

"No. We are so few we must remain together. We will have but one opportunity. If he is in his bedchamber, we will kill him. If he is elsewhere in the residence or on one of the lower floors with his personal guard, then our chances are slim . . . The direct attempt is our only play. Tie up the beasts."

Krama nodded and tethered the *rantas* together.

Ksar faced the other soldiers. Friends he had known since his first campaign against the Perovans. The only men he could trust. They were few, but better a few good soldiers than an army of cowards.

He drew his curved blade out of its leather scabbard and threw off his thick skin jerkin. He stretched to show that he had regained much of his old strength and form. They had no idea he was in so much pain, but he would keep this weakness from them.

His tiny troop was staring at him with expectation in their eyes. Another man might have made a speech here, exhorting his fellows to give their best efforts.

"Come," Ksar said simply. He turned and kicked the dying guard into the guttering.

The citadel roof was flat, with a trapdoor that led down to a guardhouse below. Ksar, weakened though he was, knew that it was his prerogative to lead them through this initial danger.

He opened the trapdoor and steeled himself for the fight to come.

Gingerly at first and then with increasing confidence he went down the steps two at a time until he arrived in a large room lit with torches, glittering with armor, and filled with men.

Every single one of them sound asleep.

Ksar hesitated and tightened the grip on his sword.

A fire was kicking in a grate and the room smelled of sawdust and spilled liquor. Was it a bluff, had the

Lord Protector been forewarned and these men were waiting to attack?

A noise. Ksar turned. Krama.

"Sir?" his deputy whispered, looking at the scene.

"Drunk to a man," Ksar said.

"Their platoon must have been paid today," Krama said. "We couldn't have timed this better."

"Yes."

"Then the ice gods view our objective with favor," Krama said seriously.

"Apparently," Ksar agreed.

"What do we do? Should we—?" Krama began.

Ksar silenced him with a look. He sheathed his sword and took out the poison vial the Witch Queen had given him to take his own life.

"We will kill them while they sleep," Ksar hissed to his men.

There was a moment of silence. He knew they would balk at the task. Even for an Alkhavan warrior it was an ugly thing to do. It was dishonorable and might bring disfavor from the spirits of their ancestors.

Ksar understood that the way to break the spell was to act immediately.

He found the nearest sleeping man. A fat sergeant, with pale skin and yellow hair, probably a freed slave. Ksar put his hand on the sergeant's cheeks, forced open his mouth, and poured in a drop of the Witch Queen's deadly poison.

In a moment the guard went rigid, thrashed his legs once, and died.

Krama and the others stood at the bottom of the stairs, breathless, watching Ksar set about a second man. Now Krama knew the onus was on him to act. His actions would convince the others. Ksar, perhaps, was half mad, but Krama was a hardheaded soldier.

He removed his poison vial and knelt beside another one of the sleeping guards. He dropped the potion into the man's mouth, who also expired noiselessly.

The rest of the men filed into the room.

But this time their luck did not hold.

A sleeping guard was disturbed by the sound of a scabbard scraping on the floor. He opened his eyes and grabbed his axe. "Alarm!" he cried.

Half a dozen of the others woke from their drunken stupor.

"Have at them," Ksar said. Ksar's men drew their weapons and attacked.

The intoxicated guards fought with a grim determination, and in the confusion a lamp was broken. The room was plunged into darkness. But in two minutes it was all over. Nine Alkhavan soldiers lay dead, and only one of Ksar's men had been killed.

"Are you hurt, sir?" Krama asked.

Ksar shook his head.

"The butcher's bill?" Ksar asked.

"Bania, sir," Krama. "A good man from Alakak."

Ksar nodded. Only one, but one of five was a serious loss.

"Well done, lads," Ksar said. "One more obstacle and we're there. There should be half a dozen guards outside the residence chamber itself. We'll have to cross the inner courtyard and then traverse the old King's Corridor without the general alarm being raised."

"But surely the guards will see us in the King's Corridor?" Krama asked hesitantly. He had been there before and knew it was a long wide passageway with no place for concealment.

"If we can get close, our crossbows will take care of them," Ksar said. "Now, follow me."

They walked through the diorama of corpses and opened the hall door.

They crossed a small storage room and then an empty dining chamber. They entered a cellar that looked as if it hadn't been used in years. It was warm in here, and the men, unused to a heated building, began to sweat.

"This way," Ksar said, and took them through a large circular opening into an exterior space.

The smell of the night came in. The sound of bubbling water.

They had entered an inner courtyard filled with exotic plant life from the central islands of the Alkhavan sea.

Up here in the northern latitudes such a garden required a lot of care and attention, and Ksar knew that a dozen attendants were employed maintaining this tiny, extravagant plot of greenery.

He snorted. The Lord Protector was fond of such comforts.

A decorative fountain burbled in the center of the court and next to it a long-haired man in a robe was apparently sleeping on a bench. Ksar recognized him as Balza, the Lord Protector's chamberlain. Krama looked at his leader and in a questioning gesture ran his finger across his throat. Ksar shook his head.

Balza was no threat and at some point he might even be useful.

The night was wearing on, and Ksar noticed that he had developed a limp in his left leg. He ignored the extraordinary pain in his calf and forced himself to walk normally.

I must not show weakness, he told himself.

He led the party across the courtyard to an archway above a golden door.

"No one say or do anything without my lead," Ksar told his men.

In single file they slipped through the golden door and

into the famous King's Corridor, a long elaborate passageway filled with treasures from a thousand years of plunder and conquests—paintings, statues, goblets, sculptures. The usual gaudy rubbish that impressed feeble minds.

The guards at the end of the passageway did not look up from a game of chance they were playing with sticks and a ball. Nine or ten burly men in the blue uniforms of the Protector's Legion. More than Ksar was expecting, and this time none were drunk and all were wide awake.

Ksar checked the bolt in his crossbow and let the weapon fall to his side. The corridor was dimly lit and the guards might not see the bow until he was close enough to shoot.

"Fan formation, let everyone spread out so that you are able to take a clean shot," he whispered.

It was about a hundred paces to the residence chamber entrance. If he got half that distance without an alarm being sounded, he knew he'd be in with a chance.

He marched brazenly toward the guards. Almost immediately one of them looked up and shouted a warning: "Who goes there?"

"A message for the Lord Protector from the Witch Queen, there has been an attack on Balanmanik," Ksar said confidently.

The other guards stopped playing with their sticks and ball and stared at the strangers.

An attack? A message? Such a thing was entirely plausible, even at this late hour. Ksar saw that their suspicions were not immediately raised. And in any case they had to be wondering how someone could have gotten this deep into the castle complex with a fraudulent story.

Ksar walked confidently on. Seventy-five paces to go.

"By whose authority do you disturb the Lord Protector?" an older guard asked. An officer.

Sixty-five paces.

"By the authority of the Witch Queen," Ksar said.

The officer sniffed and drew his sword.

Fifty-five paces.

"Her purview runs not in the keep of Afor," the officer said.

"True," Ksar said. "However, this is a matter of great importance to the state."

Fifty paces.

Ksar tightened his grip on the crossbow.

"Halt. Come no farther," the officer said. A whiskered man, Ksar noted, with the scarred face of a veteran. Promoted from the ranks. Experienced.

Forty-five paces.

"I said come no farther," the officer barked.

Lightning quick, Ksar lifted his crossbow, shot it from the hip, and struck the officer in the chest. Krama and the others fired their bows, killing two more of the guards instantly.

The rest were momentarily frozen.

A moment that was the tipping point between life and death.

Ksar dropped the crossbow, drew his sword, and ran as best as he could at the survivors. He crossed the remaining gap between them in a clutch of seconds. One man tried to block him with an outstretched arm. Ksar raised his sword, hammered it down, and sliced the man's arm off at the shoulder. He pushed him to one side as another big black-haired guard hit him with a wooden club. The blow caught him in the ribs and staggered him for a moment, but a timely crossbow bolt from behind struck the club-wielding guard in the head.

A palace guard threw a hand axe that killed one of Ksar's men instantly. Krama killed the axe thrower with a sword swipe to his head, and then skewered another guard in the neck—arterial blood sprayed from the wound for a moment and the man was dead.

Ksar left the sword jammed in the man's throat and pulled out his twin daggers.

A melee of two, perhaps three seconds.

"I'm hit!" someone yelled, though whether it was friend or foe was impossible to tell.

Krama killed a man with his short sword, and from behind Ksar another crossbow bolt struck a palace guard in the mouth.

Ksar ran another opponent through the stomach with a dagger thrust, and immediately after that there was a cry for quarter.

In half a minute it was all over.

"Krama. Report," Ksar asked, wiping the blood from his eyes.

"Draga is dead, I am slightly wounded," Krama said.

Only two guards were left. Surrounded and outnumbered three to two, they both fell to the ground in prostrating gestures of surrender.

"Please don't, please don't," they begged.

"Cowards," Ksar said, and ordered his men to execute both of them immediately. When that was done, he wiped the blood from his sword and caught his breath.

"Who did you say was dead?"

"Draga," Krama replied. "Now we are three."

Ksar nodded. "Three or thirty, it matters not. The night is in our favor," Ksar said.

He opened the double silver-handled doors leading to the Lord Protector's residence.

He knew there would be one or two final guards inside. Perhaps some servants.

He stepped into the room. A wall of heat from a *wood*

fire reached him. More decadence, more shortsighted ignorance.

There was someone sitting in the window seat.

He didn't wait for the man's challenge. He limped fast across the floor, and by the time the nervous guard had opened his mouth to scream, Ksar's sword was entering his rib cage, driving through nerve, fiber, and muscle into his rapidly beating heart.

Another guard, who was sleeping on a rolled-up mattress, got groggily to his feet.

Ksar withdrew the blade, ignored the waking guard, and stormed into the Lord Protector's bedchamber.

The room was as he remembered. Exotic tapestries hanging from the walls. Furs on the floor. A massive bed covered with expensive fabrics from Oralands. Above, a crystal device from Aldan that held dozens of candles illuminated the entire room with a yellowy brilliance.

By now the Lord Protector had heard the commotion and was standing by the bed with some kind of ceremonial axe he had obviously just pulled off a wall.

He was a squat, red-haired man in a flowing crimson robe. His beard was not kempt, and his blue eyes showed the fear that coursed through him.

The Lord Protector knew it was a coup attempt, but he was momentarily stunned to see a trusted lieutenant standing before him. Worse, a trusted lieutenant he had assumed had died a year before. "What is the meaning of this intrusion, Ksar?" the Lord Protector demanded when he had recovered from his shock.

Ksar turned to see that his men had killed the final guard and entered the bedchamber.

"The room is secure," Krama said, and handed Ksar back his crossbow

Ignoring the Lord Protector and with great sangfroid, Ksar reloaded the weapon.

"I say again, Ksar, what is the meaning of this intrusion?" the Lord Protector bellowed, summoning up some of the power and dignity that had elevated him to this post in the first place.

Ksar smiled. "The meaning, Dorpa, is that I am taking over this miserable place."

The Lord Protector took a step back, holding on to his axe like it was the last spar of a sinking boat. "What did you say?"

"We need your army, Dorpa. We must control all three of the towers on Aldan that were built by the Old Ones. The Witch Queen owns the Tower of Balanmanik, but we must seize the one on the Sacred Isle, and we must destroy the one in Aldan itself."

The Lord Protector laughed. "You are mad, Ksar. Twice we have been thwarted in our attempt to take that city. The army has not yet recovered."

"We do not need to take the city. We need only destroy the tower. I have already set the wheels in motion. It is called planning, Dorpa. A thing you would know nothing about."

Behind the Lord Protector someone whimpered under the bedclothes.

"See who that is, Krama. I'll give you three to one it is not the Lord Protector's lady wife," Ksar ordered.

Krama approached the bed, delved underneath it, and dragged out a young blond-haired girl in a white nightgown.

"Dorpa, stop them," the girl whimpered.

"Leave her, Ksar, she is irrelevant to you," the Lord Protector said.

"I have nothing to do with this," the girl agreed desperately.

"Silence her, Krama," Ksar ordered, and without further ado Krama smacked her on the head, hard, with the butt of his dagger. She fell sickeningly to the floor, bleeding from a cracked skull.

The Lord Protector screamed and would have immediately launched a foolish attack were it not for the three battle crossbows pointed at his chest.

There was a terrible sound of gurgling on the floor as the girl's blood spilled into the expensive rug. Would she live or die? It mattered little to Ksar. He would have Krama see to her after Dorpa was taken care of.

The Lord Protector seemed to wilt a little now.

He eased his grip on the axe. "Why, Ksar?" he asked after another long pause.

"It is a simple matter of necessity. We have summoned the Ui Neill, and he will come. We must have him. We must have the device which he controls."

Dorpa looked baffled. It was a mad, incomprehensible scheme from a quixotic, disturbed man. Ksar had always been an odd one. He and his satanic sister. Their father, Vartigern, had been a bad one too. It would have been better to have assassinated them all years ago.

"What are you going to do with me?" Dorpa muttered, defeat replacing panic in his bleary eyes.

"You're going to die, Dorpa. But worry not, it will be quick. You are one of the lucky ones that got to live. Pity those who never experience life at all. Pity the lost future generations of Alkhava when the planet of Altair becomes a frozen world of ice."

The Lord Protector nodded at this bizarre remark, as if he were humbly accepting his fate. Which he wasn't at all. You didn't get to be Lord Protector unless you had something up your sleeve (sometimes literally).

The Lord Protector was doing what Lord

Protectors did best. Plotting to stay alive. And now he thought he saw his way out of this.

Ksar was the key. It was Ksar who held this little bunch together.

He didn't have to kill all three men. He only had to kill one. Slay Ksar, and the others would fold like paper toys.

"The court will not approve you, Ksar, you'll be shunned, just as your father was shunned," the Lord Protector said, and slid a thin blade out of his robe and held it in his hand.

"No, they will follow me. They respect my skills as a warrior. They know I was against your foolish Aldanese adventure. They know I do my best for my country—not for my own comfort or gain," Ksar replied.

"No one will follow you. You are disfigured, you do not have the favor of the gods. Your men will be cursed if you assume the Lord Protector's throne," Dorpa said and looked pointedly at Krama.

Dorpa took a step nearer and prepared a lunge. A slash at Ksar's throat or a stab right into his heart. "And you are foolish, Ksar. Another Aldan expedition will destroy this country. You will be leading these men to their deaths," the Lord Protector said, almost in a whisper now.

He leaned delicately on his right foot. He clutched the knife, got ready to drop the axe. This was the moment.

"And you have not considered the new Aldanese defenses," the Lord Protector suggested, inching closer.

"You, Dorpa, have not considered anything in your whole life," Ksar said, annoyed at the Lord Protector's accusations.

Dorpa dropped his axe and lunged at his former deputy.

The knife glistened in the candlelight.

Ksar's eyes widened.

"Stand fast!" Dorpa yelled to Ksar's accomplices.

But it was too late. Pain. Terrible pain. There was a crossbow bolt in his throat. Another thumped into his head. There was a third in his chest.

There was . . .

Nothing.

"It is done," Krama said.

"Yes," a voice said from the door behind them. And now that the contest was over, Chamberlain Balza ran into the chamber from the anteroom. He was still wearing his long night robe. In his right hand he was holding a small oil lantern, in his left a curved dagger.

He stopped in front of Ksar. The lantern wavered and the dagger fell from his grip.

"General Ksar? But I thought you were . . . ?"

"You have improperly addressed me, Balza, a crime punishable by a year on the ice cliffs."

Cautiously Balza peered at the Lord Protector's corpse. The scene of bloody murder disgusted him. He put his hand over his mouth and stepped backward.

"Lord Protector, I—I salute thee," Balza said wisely.

"Yes, very good. You are right. I am the new Lord Protector, Balza. Now if you wish to retain your head, bring me something cool to drink."

"I-I-I . . . Yes, Lord Protector Ksar," Balza muttered and shuffled backward from the room.

Ksar turned to Krama. "Bring me the captain of the guard," Ksar said.

Krama nodded and led his last man away. When the room was empty, Ksar steadied himself, somehow walked to the window shutters, opened them, and took in the air. The heady air of victory. Yes. After all these years he had attained the post his father had failed to gain. He had become the Lord Protector of Alkhava. And with that title came the power to wage war, the power to make peace, the power to do whatever he pleased. His head felt light. He walked out of the bloody chamber onto the large balcony overlooking the city and the sea. Night was ending. The stars were disappearing like lamps being extinguished by the morning watch.

The town was coming alive.

Carts on the cobblestones.

The smell of bread turning in the turf fires.

Furnaces from the iron foundries sending sparks through chimneys.

Balza appeared with a tankard of icy water mixed with raw spirit. As was the etiquette of these troubled times, Balza sipped it first to show that it was not poisoned.

Ksar took the drink and dismissed the chamberlain with a nod.

When he was alone he gripped the balcony with both hands as a wave of tiredness rippled through him.

His ribs ached. His feet hurt. He was exhausted.

He drained the tankard and set it on the balcony rail. He sat on the ground. He knew that he was on the verge of keeling over, but he fought the collapse, failed for a moment, and then mastered himself again.

He stood.

Down in the city he began to hear the cries of produce sellers, the singing of milk boys, the calls of the wild *rantas* ascending the thermals above the cliffs.

Foamy crests on the magenta ocean.

A green dawn.

And then, out of the endless waters of the Western Sea, the sun began to rise.

Chapter V
THE PROMETHEANS

ANOTHER CITY. Midnight. The sound of bells. Startled, she looked toward the plaza and thought she could just make out the torch-lit procession leaving from the central square.

She felt sick with nerves.

He was coming.

And here she was with the same emotions, in the same place, waiting again.

Except that that was dawn and this was midnight. This time it was much more serious. On this occasion there really was no way out.

Her heart began to beat fast.

She peered through her father's octoscope.

The procession had reached the university and was coming across the central square. She couldn't yet make out individuals, but by Oralands custom she knew that the leading lantern was being held aloft by Lorca.

She put down the octoscope and tried to breathe normally.

Nothing is inevitable, she said to herself.

She slipped out of her shoes, walked to the edge of the balcony, and gazed into the black nothingness of the sea.

Her toes lifted slightly.

How easy it would be to tumble over the rail and into the harbor.

A brief fall through the night air. A crash.

She had never learned to swim, and the sea was so cold it would paralyze her movements anyway. Drowning would be instantaneous.

Would she be afraid?

Would she regret it the moment she did it?

Surf broke against the seawall. A song drifted up from the town. Deep beneath the waves phosphorescent creatures flashed in the dark water.

How easy it would be . . .

A shadow fell across her mind and she stepped back from the edge. No, she would not do *that*. Nothing so dramatic or so foolish. The time for despair was a year ago, when the city was ravaged and the people enslaved. Now Aldan was rebuilt, her father's fortunes restored, and she herself on the verge of a new life.

The bobbing lights moved closer.

She could discern a dozen individuals carrying lanterns. Definitely a wedding procession.

The wedding procession.

She shivered. Nervous. No, more than nervous. Afraid.

"Wishaway," her father called from inside the house.

She didn't reply.

There was a long, significant silence while he waited for her response.

The song. The distant bells. The waves breaking over the ghosts of a thousand shipwrecks.

"Wishaway, it is nearly the hour," her father said with more urgency.

She stared into the black ocean and tried to catch her reflection. Once before she'd been able to do this, but not tonight. Tonight it was cloudy, and the moons and most of the stars were hiding themselves from view.

"It is nearly the hour," her father said in his most bellicose of tones.

In a fit of pique she dropped the expensive octoscope into the water. It vanished without even a splash. "Nearly the hour," she muttered to herself. Before the Ui Neills had come there had been no clocks on Aldan, no clocks, no watches, in fact no reliable or universally accepted system of dividing up the day. But the Ui Neills had brought two pocket watches, which had been examined and copied and scaled up into clocks. Such was the reverence for the great Ui Neills that their system of hours and minutes had been implemented, even though it had been calculated that the Altairian day was longer by at least seven hundred seconds; which of course meant that all the city clocks had to be reset every fifth cycle.

It was preposterous really.

Still, now everyone knew the time. Everyone knew the very minute of their appointment with fate.

Hers was midnight.

The ceremony was to begin at midnight.

Marriage was not an Earth-brought custom, but on Altair pair-bonding was only one of many forms of family arrangement. Polygamy, polyandry, single parenthood, communal parenthood were all common, especially in the southern islands. But marriage's popularity had also grown with the coming of Ui Neills.

They brought blessings as well as curses, she reflected ruefully.

In Oralands the proposal took place at dawn and the wedding at midnight of the same day. Lorca had indeed proposed to her at sunup, but he had not been so presumptuous as to assume her acceptance.

The wedding had taken weeks to prepare. His father had had to come from Oralands, guests had been invited from all over Aldan, and musicians and entertainers had been brought in from as far away as Kafrikilla.

Sometimes, mercifully, it had seemed like the preparations would take forever.

But nothing takes forever.

Not even the slow heat death of the universe will take forever.

And the weeks had become days, which had become hours, which had become seconds.

Well, at least I'm ready, she told herself.

And indeed she was. Bathed. Perfumed. Preened. Dressed in gold lace slippers and a gown of spun Athea silk, embroidered with wild *hurty* plant.

Her hair had been plaited and arranged with flowers. Nothing had been done to her face. It didn't need to be. She was nearly sixteen summers old; she had never looked lovelier.

Her father appeared behind her on the balcony.

"Lorca's party is coming from the town," he whispered softly in the dialect of her mother's people.

She turned, and he was momentarily taken aback by the sad beauty in her eyes.

"His uh, the uhm, the old prince is coming up the—"

"I know. I saw," Wishaway said.

"Well . . . Are you ready?"

"Of course," Wishaway snapped, then regretted it instantly when she saw him visibly wince at her sharpness.

"I am sorry, I did not mean to speak so. Perhaps, I have fears," Wishaway said, lapsing into English for a formal apology.

Her father smiled and took her hand. "You know, there is nothing to be afraid of. The ceremony is simplicity itself. Lorca asks for my consent, I grant it. He asks for your consent, you say yes, then you are wed. It will take mere moments," Callaway explained.

"Yes," Wishaway concurred.

"Your mother would be so proud," Callaway whispered, squeezing her palm.

Would she? Wishaway wondered doubtfully, and then for some reason she started to cry.

Callaway knew better than to say anything or put his arm around his willful daughter. In these circumstances it was best to leave her alone.

Besides he had a feast to prepare.

"I shall see you anon," he said, and stepped back inside the house, where there was a different scene completely.

Servants and cooks scurrying everywhere.

Because the city was still in recovery from the Alkhavan invasion, the wedding was purposefully small, but even so, the bare minimum of his fellow citizens he could invite (and not cause offense) was three score; and he had been warned that the prince's party contained nearly that number.

Cooks had been working for days. The food, honey wine, and oat beer had been brought in from half a dozen kingdoms. The servants and entertainers numbered at least forty now, and with regret he saw that the whole thing was probably going to cost him almost his entire accumulated savings.

"Better your daughter marry a carpenter than a prince of Oralands," he had secretly confided to his friend the city treasurer, both men of course realizing that Callaway couldn't have been happier and wouldn't have wanted it any other way.

Still, it wouldn't be easy for him after this.

Undoubtedly she would follow her husband to that happy and prosperous isle of Oralands, and he would be left alone.

A small pink-faced man in a black smock ran up to him in the middle of his reverie.

"Master Callaway, one of your incompetent staff has poured sour milk instead of cream into the soup. It is a disaster. It cannot be saved. There will be no soup. Without soup there can be no meal. You have ruined me, Master Callaway. My reputation will be in tatters. You have made me a laughingstock . . ."

Callaway forced a smile onto his face.

"Come, come, Master Greenaway, there are a dozen other courses, which I'm sure will be delicious and more than compensate for your spoiled soup," he said in a soothing voice and led the chef back into the kitchen.

They passed Wishaway, who was retreating to the library for a few final moments of meditation.

"Do you wish me to send your lady's maid?" Callaway asked his daughter.

"Send no one. I wish to be alone with my thoughts," Wishaway said a little sternly.

She entered the library and sat down. Her heart was beating fast, the blood thumping in her ears. On Earth they would call what Wishaway was experiencing a panic attack, perhaps even an incipient nervous breakdown.

She breathed deeply and drank a little water from a pitcher near the book repair stand. *I must calm down. He cannot see me like this*, she told herself.

Her eyes were watering and her face, she knew, was glowing red.

She took another gasp of air, then grabbed the family copy of Morgan's *Book of Stories*, flipped open the volume randomly and read:

> Some call the lost kingdom that existed between Ireland and Scotland the Land of the Lost, and still others, the Land of the Drowned. Many are the tales of this harsh place, which, like the Atlantis of Plato, has since sunk beneath the gray waters of the Irish Ocean. Here, in the Chronicle of the Fintoola, bard Nacallum tells his story. "In the Land of the Lost there were two souls walking. They were together on the back of

the mountain and in the vast expanse of the wilderness. They had not spoken, and each had met up
with the other along the road. Neither had seen the
other's face, even by the red light of the campfire—
sheathed as they were by their hoods and cloaks
against the dust and the knife edge of the biting
wind. Each had kept to his own provisions and
supply of water. A few short words had passed
between them, for in the hard country it was better
to save one's breath than waste it with the spinning
of tales or stories. So they walked, neither man
leading nor following, each keeping his own counsel about the way.

They journeyed the long day, over streams and
marshland and rock, traveling until they were too
worn to continue, and then they stopped. At dusk
they built a fire from timber and gorse and the
bones of animals.

The night came and in the moments before sleep
each wondered if his companion would perhaps kill
him in the darkness. Augment his own meager supplies with those of his fellow traveler. Each felt the
dread of being awakened with violence and with the
promise of steel slipping beneath his furs and into
the folds of his cold skin. Even so, there was nothing that could be done, and the fear was overcome,
and finally they slept. On the third day there was a

storm. A black togetherness of thunder and hail that had come from the Antrim Hills in the west. They walked through it and pitched camp, sleeping under the overhang of a whetting stone. In the morning it was calm, and as the sun came up over the great plains both men lay dead on their backs.

In the night the men's shadows had been wakened by the forks of lightning. The shadows had quarreled and fought and slain each other.

And as all know, no man can wake without a shadow to guide him through the world.

The dead men lay and the frost covered them up, and in the spring there were two earth mounds where the men had been."

Such is the harsh way of the Land of the Lost. We can expect no happiness or reward in this life. All comes to us in the future time in the Kingdom of the Saved.

She closed the book and almost laughed.

Well, that was cheerful, she told herself.

She put the volume back on the library shelf with an ironic thud.

She had been hoping to read one of the stories of Finn MacCool and the giant, or the wooden horse and Troy, or Theseus in the labyrinth. But the gloomy little tale had served its purpose. She stood and wiped away her tears.

There were worse things in the world than marrying a handsome prince.

She walked out into the main hall.

"Just in time," her father whispered.

"Why?"

"The royal party is here," he said unctuously, and bowed as Prince Lanar, Lady Lanar, their son Prince Lorca, and their retinue appeared on the pathway of his humble dwelling.

I will do it, Wishaway told herself and forced herself to curtsy low to her father's guests.

The clock at the university struck one.

An hour had gone by in a moment.

It was almost over.

The Rector spoke in a dream.

In Aldanese: *"Ashara, by tala, fasss."*

In the high dialect of Oralands: *"Hurt ma, cor di."*

In English: "And now my children. Thou art wed."

Lorca grinned happily, brought her face to his with a gentle hand, and kissed her.

It was the only time she had ever kissed him.

It was only the second time in her life she had ever kissed a boy. The first, being of course—

"I love you, Wishaway," he said.

It was as if he were speaking to her under water.

She looked at the gleaming faces about her. Lorca's father, a gray-haired, corpulent man in a singlet of plain black cloth braided with gold. One of Lorca's brothers, a flighty, skinny boy a year or two older than his sibling. Lorca's mother, a youngish brown-haired woman with a condescending but not unkind smile on her face. Her own father, elegant in a white shirt and his best blue pantaloons, his hair cut, his beard trimmed.

The rector muttered something else and the room erupted into cheers.

Fubble, gabble, Lorca seemed to say.

"Sorry? What?" Wishaway asked.

"Our yacht leaves in the afternoon, I have arranged everything," Lorca repeated.

"Tomorrow? We leave tomorrow?" she asked.

"Later today really. You will get your Council's approval at the morning session, we will sail to Oralands to present ourselves before my grandfather, the king."

Wishaway felt ill. She put her hand on his broad shoulder. He steadied her.

Tomorrow. Later today.

Of course, from now on they would be inseparable. From now on they would be sharing the same bed.

Her head was swimming. It was hard to breathe.

Someone passed her a glass of wine. She drank it, pulled herself together, and smiled through half a dozen toasts.

At the earliest opportunity, she slipped away to the balcony. The plain-faced Alkhavan refugee girl who had been acting as ladies' maid for the last few days inquired if she was feeling ill.

"No. I am quite well," she replied. "I am merely taking some of the night air."

She had just managed to calm herself when Lorca appeared and put his arms about her. The maid excused herself and went inside.

Wishaway wiped the tears from her cheeks. Fortunately he seemed oblivious to her distress.

"We will be so happy in Oralands. You will have a dozen servants to cater to all your needs. You will sail with me, we will go to the theater, the opera, to our lodge in the mountains," Lorca said softly.

"I have no need of servants," Wishaway said.

"Oh, but you shall have them. They will look after you."

"I can look after myself."

"Of course. But they will be there to aid you. You will enjoy yourself in Oralands. You will be comfortable, happy. You will have many companions so that you will not be lonely," Lorca said, trying perhaps to convince himself as much as her.

"Books have been my companions, these long years," Wishaway said. A thing that was obvious to all. Wishaway had always been an odd girl. No giggling bosom friends helped her prepare for the *big day*, no close companions helped her cope now.

Lorca turned her to look at him.

He was not lacking perspicacity, and he could see the hint of melancholy in her expression.

He embraced her gently and then kissed her cheek. Perhaps attempting in that gesture to show her that he would be patient with her and that his love would be enough for both of them.

"Books. You shall have books by the hundred. My grandfather, the king, has a library of three thousand volumes. We have an original of *The Book of Stories*, with art by Morgan Ui Neill himself," Lorca said, knowing that this would please her.

He grinned, and some of his happiness spilled over into her.

She turned up the corners of her mouth and forced a smile.

"Lorca, I know that you—" Wishaway began but was interrupted by a large distant bang that came rolling unexpectantly across the city.

"What was that?" she asked.

She looked at him. Perhaps his father, the prince, had arranged for a fireworks display. Fireworks were no longer a military secret. Not since Ramsay, Jamie's friend, had brought them to Aldan so spectacularly last year.

"I do not know," Lorca said candidly.

There was another muffled bang, and people along the

shore began pouring out of their houses. Half a dozen guests joined them on the balcony.

"What is happening, Wishaway?" her father asked.

"I can see something on Steward Hill," Wishaway said, noticing a commotion in the center of town but unable to tell exactly what was taking place, as it was a good mile from where they were.

More people crammed onto the balcony, voices murmuring. Concern floated among the crowd.

Another smothered bang and smoke.

The bells calling out the watch were sounded.

Something was definitely wrong.

And then it came.

A much larger explosion and an aftershock that shook several people to the floor. The blast had a muffled, peculiar sound and obviously occurred somewhere near the White Tower.

"It is an attack," Callaway said, aghast.

Wishaway remembered the missing barrels of "gunpowder" from the university. The missing barrels that had so infuriated General Feeaway and Councilor Quiller, and that had generated a scandal that almost cost her father his job.

"I see no evidence of destruction. They have failed to ignite their infernal devices," Prince Lanar said confidently.

Only a small tail of smoke was drifting from the plaza

near the White Tower. There were murmurs of agreement from the people on the balcony.

But Wishaway shook her head.

Smoke from beneath the ground could only mean one thing. She knew what had happened, and she knew what was going to happen next.

"Agents from Alkhava have gotten into the sewers beneath the tower. We must stop them," she began.

Her father nodded and grabbed her arm. He too understood the implications instantly.

"Alert the city watch," he called out desperately across the balcony. "Tell them that Callaway of the High Council—" But his remaining words were lost beneath the sound of half a dozen barrels filled with high-explosive gunpowder detonating in the main city sewer, which ran under the square in front of the White Tower of Aldan.

The structure was by far the most ancient in the city, perhaps in the entire island. It was built by an unknown people centuries before the Aldanese ever came here. It was old and in a state of some disrepair, but it had withstood millennia of storms and tempests, and its foundations went deep into the bedrock.

What the foundations could not withstand however were six barrels of black powder going off in a natural fissure in the rock. The explosion thundered from wall to harbor, shattering glass sculptures and blowing out windows.

In an instant the whole city was awake. People ran into the streets, alarm bells sounded, *hanyans* barked, *seechas* cried, *rantas* screamed on the harbor walls.

"What is happening?" Prince Lanar asked.

"Look," someone called, and even through the dust and the murk of the wee hours, the watchers on the balcony like those all over the city could clearly see the White Tower of Aldan totter horribly on its foundations.

"It's coming down," someone said, mouthing the obvious.

And sure enough, the tower swayed for a moment, then a huge crack ran up the outside of the structure. It leaned abruptly to the left and fell with an awful rumble into the central city plaza and the surrounding streets.

There was a huge, terrible crash, and then a frightening shroud of dust and debris poured down upon the city from Steward Hill. It rained soot and pulverized stones for five minutes, and after that there was nothing but a long, vacant, dreadful silence.

Even the animal life knew that something bad had happened.

"*Gurrsa fea Mek,*" Prince Lanar muttered, which Wishaway knew was an invocation to the sun god.

She felt faint, and her maid brought her a drink.

Because it was the middle of the night and because the tower itself was not used anymore (as it had been in the past) as a prison or a lighthouse, it was unlikely that anyone would have died.

But few at the wedding party could be consoled by that.

As the last of the detritus from the White Tower was propelled skyward into the blackness of the Altairian night, everyone in the city was thinking the same thing.

The great symbol of the city of Aldan was destroyed in what could only be described as a sneak attack; and whether it was the Perovans or the Alkhavans or someone else entirely, one thing and one thing alone was clear, the Aldanese people were again at war.

According to the theory of relativity, you can't say that two events in the universe are happening at the same time. Each event is dependent on an observer, and since the observers are in motion and motion slows down the action of time, nothing in the universe happens simultaneously.

But if you could say that two events in the universe were occurring at the same instant (what Einstein contemptuously called "spooky action at a distance"), then the very moment the White Tower of Aldan crumbled into the plaza beneath it, on Earth, a hundred light-years away, a van on a dangerous part of the Carrickfergus–Whitehead road known as the Bla Hole stopped moving forward and suddenly screeched and skidded to a halt.

It was not a good place to park a vehicle. It was a blind corner on a precipitous cliff face that fell sheer to the Irish Sea three hundred feet below, and over the decades it had been the site of many accidents and one or two death plunges.

Why the van stopped there can be explained by again defying Einstein and rolling back time a few minutes.

During the entire, brief car ride from Kilroot Power Station to Islandmagee, Brian's pesky—possibly crazy—little brother had been patiently reiterating everything that had happened to him and his friend Jamie over the past year. How they had discovered the secret room in the lighthouse on Muck Island, how they'd used the Salmon of Knowledge to make the wormhole to go to Altair, how they'd helped fight the enemies of Aldan and won the city back from these enemies using biological warfare and Earth technology.

Brian had heard the ridiculous story once before from his father when he'd come to Ireland from MIT. Both of them had had a good laugh at Ramsay's flights of fancy.

"Yeah, Ramsay, you're full of crap, but you always were. No one believes you. You, a hero that saves the day? Of course that makes sense—"

"But it's—"

"I'm still amazed at you though, Jamie, backing him

up on this," Brian said in disgust. "You're normally pretty levelheaded."

Jamie smiled and said softly, "But it is the truth, Brian. We went to another planet and we met the aliens and we talked to them. We used the Salmon to create a wormhole in space-time to travel there."

"Oh aye, and what did these aliens look like?"

"They looked a bit like us. Two arms, two legs, small almost nonexistent noses, pointed ears, weird blue eyes; they were a bit like the faeries or leprachau—"

Brian snorted and then faked a laugh. "See, that's where I have you boys. Aliens would look nothing like us. they'd be like big squids or . . . or . . . huge bundles of mud or energy beings or whatever. There's no way they'd be bipedal and have two arms and legs. That's just an Earth bias. All that *Star Wars* and *Star Trek* silliness, aliens looking like humans. Ridiculous."

"Listen mate, first of all *Star Wars* is a metaphor for events that took place in another galaxy a long time ago, the actors are representing alien forms, they don't actually have to look like them; and second, I agree with you, *Star Trek* is ridiculous in that every time they go to a new planet most of the aliens look like us. But, crazy as it is, it's still a fact. They do look like us. Either there's a shared history between our worlds, or it's because of convergent evolution."

"Convergent evolution," Brian mocked.

"You know, the way the eye evolved separately six or seven times in different species," Ramsay explained.

"OK, so I'll let you have that one, but seriously you expect me to believe that you two boys went to another planet and you didn't tell the BBC or CNN? Kept it a big secret. That's likely."

Jamie couldn't take much more of this. "Show him the Salmon," Jamie suggested. "Show it to him."

"Yeah, show me this device that allows you to jaunt off to flipping Narnia whenever you feel like it," Brian said with deep sarcasm.

Ramsay took the Salmon of Knowledge out of his backpack and passed it to his skeptical older brother. Brian stared at the object for a moment.

And that was when the brakes got hit.

The van skidded to a halt in the middle of the Bla Hole bend.

If a fast car came from the blind corners to the north or south, either the van or the car or both of them were going to end up a hundred yards below in the sea.

But Brian McDonald couldn't care less.

He took the Salmon of Knowledge, held it up to the light, and gazed at it openmouthed. To the untrained eye it meant very little, but Brian knew immediately he wasn't being hoaxed and that the boys could not have made this small, glinting fish with what looked like machinery inside. This was beyond their power, this was not a practical joke. He knew it because the Salmon was constructed from a superconducting polymer that he had never seen before, not at MIT, not at Motorola, nowhere. A fantastically advanced material, cool to the touch, light, yet he could tell that it had taken a lot of energy and engineering to fuse it together. It was much colder than the air around it, and if you dinged it, it vibrated at a very low frequency. This material was something far advanced of anything they could do anywhere in this world.

"Where did you get this?" he asked, flabbergasted.

"I told you, the lighthouse on Jamie's island."

"I-I don't think this c-comes from Earth," Brian stuttered.

"It doesn't."

"Wha?"

"Aliens made it. Listen, it's all true. We went to another world. We gotta go back there. The message NASA got wasn't a quasar or a binary star going nuts. It was a message for us," Ramsay said

"That 'message' was sent a hundred years ago," Brian muttered, turning the little fish over in his hands.

Ramsay put his hand on his big brother's shoulder. Jamie wound down the window to let in some air.

"It was sent for the present Lord Ui Neill. Jamie. The person who lives on Muck Island. They sent it in

English, Brian, in base eight. I figured it out. I'll show you my workings," Ramsay said and took out the piece of paper with the deciphered message from Altair.

Brian read that note, looked at the NASA announcement, did his own calculations, and sure enough the message from the star system a hundred light-years from Earth said: "Come Ui Neill."

There was an engine in the distance. Jamie stuck his head out the window.

"Think there's a car coming," Jamie said.

"This thing makes wormholes in space-time?" Brian said. His face white, pale, covered with sweat.

"It does when it has power. I got to fill it with DC current, or at least try to," Ramsay said.

Brian nodded.

He understood.

He believed. Sort of.

It was against all logic, all sense. If there was intelligent life out there in the universe, wouldn't they be here already? Wouldn't they have been here for centuries? Perhaps they had been. But then again, why be so coy?

"I still say that there's no way aliens could be bipedal," he said quietly.

"Car coming," Jamie said, listening to the increasingly loud drone of a vehicle approaching from Whitehead.

"If you want my help, I want to go," Brian insisted.

"Don't know about that," Ramsay said.

"Car!" Jamie screamed as the headlight beams showed up on the road in front of them.

All three of them yelled at once as the car, a big Volvo SUV doing sixty miles an hour, appeared on the bend fifty feet in front of them. It honked its horn desperately, and Brian put the van into gear, started it, stalled it, put it into neutral, started it, and drove into the left lane just a split second before the SUV would have plowed into them.

"OK. Are you going to help us or not?" Ramsay asked, completely ignoring their brush with death. Brian said nothing, but his eyes were glazed over. Not surprising for someone whose worldview had been completely changed in the last five minutes.

"Come on, Brian," Jamie said. "We've got to go. We've got to get back to the power station."

Brian sighed. "I know I'm going to be sorry I did this . . ."

Ten minutes later they parked the fish van in the wooded access road next to the power station. Ramsay took a tool kit, a length of chain, and a pair of binoculars from his backpack.

He put the binocs round his neck and scanned the power station for security guards.

"All clear," he said. "Looks like we just missed a patrol.

Gives us a while."

As if he'd done this a million times before, he attached one end of the chain to the tow bar of the van and hooked the other to the top of the fence.

"Now, Brian, go," Ramsay said.

Brian drove the vehicle forward, and after only a moment's jangly hesitation, the barbwire roll tumbled off the top of the fence.

"Stop," Ramsay commanded. The van shuddered to a halt.

"What now?" Jamie asked.

"Now we go. Fast. We got about forty minutes before the next patrol comes round. Come on."

With the roll of barbwire pulled down, it looked a fairly easy task to get over the fence. Ramsay quickly climbed the mesh and, dodging the arc lights, ran across the open concrete of Kilroot Power Station to the nearest high-voltage transformer station. Jamie only had one arm, so he climbed the fence with much more difficulty. In the end, and with some loss of dignity, Brian had to heave him over.

They walked together to the small enclosed structure Ramsay had made a beeline for.

Naturally Jamie had never been inside a power plant before, and he was surprised at how empty it seemed. The generating building itself was massive (at least fifteen stories tall) and the chimneys were much bigger than that. Huge turbines hummed ominously in the middle distance, but, even so, out here near the perimeter fence they were relatively isolated from the noise, the spotlights, and hopefully the security guards.

And to help things along, it was full dark now, and at last the rain had to turned to drizzle.

When they got to a sign saying TRANSFORMER SUB-STATION #23, Ramsay had already climbed a small protective wall surrounding it and was fiddling with the high-voltage cables within.

The power plant was dotted with dozens of these sub-stations—large relay boxes packed with high tensile lines and wires. It was an extremely dangerous place to be, hence the protective walls, the posted warnings that said things like DO NOT ENTER and EXTREME DANGER and the many diagrams of men being electrocuted, in case you didn't speak English.

"Probably going to kill himself. I'll get the blame, of course. Only adult here. Press will have a field day, never get a university job after this," Jamie heard Brian muttering to himself.

"Be careful, Ramsay," Jamie said.

But his friend hardly paid him any mind. He was busy doing things with his pocket solder and his tool kit.

Sparks were flying from the cables.

It didn't look at all healthy.

"Are you sure you know what you're—" Jamie began.

"It's done. Give me the Salmon. Throw it over. Quickly," Ramsay said in a stage whisper.

"That's it? Are you sure? Is it safe?" Jamie asked.

"Throw it. Come on," Ramsay barked.

"What's going to happen to the Salmon?" Jamie asked.

"Well, it'll get recharged or utterly destroyed," Ramsay said candidly. "The calculations go both ways."

Yup, it was either going to be a complete success or a total failure. But that was the way Jamie liked it. He threw the Salmon over the fence.

"What exactly are you doing in there, Ramsay?" Brian hissed.

"I'm reversing the polarity on the transformer. The cables will conduct through the nearest available object, which is going to be the Salmon," Ramsay explained.

"When the transformer suddenly reverses polarity, isn't that likely to cause some sort of electrical short?" Brian asked.

"Very likely," Ramsay agreed.

"And won't that short cause a bang that will bring every single security guard running over here immediately?" Brian suggested.

"Do you ever listen? That's why we need a getaway driver."

Brian nodded to himself. "Yeah, I'll definitely not get

into a university after this, might even get jail time, or the loony bin when I tell them I did it so I could meet aliens," Brian said with almost cheerful resignation.

Ramsay finished what he was doing, packed up his tools, and climbed out of the transformer cage. He stood next to his brother and his friend with a satisfied grin splayed over his face.

"So is that it?" Jamie asked. "What do we do now? Wait?"

Ramsay shook his head.

"Nah. I have to pull that red lever on the outside of transformer box. I'll cut the connection, the power will trigger the safety, fall back on itself and the polarity will reverse . . . in theory," he said.

The red lever was some kind of emergency shutoff. There was a sign above it that said DO NOT TOUCH in very large letters, and beneath the sign there was a picture of a man spread-eagled with a lightning flash above him.

"You see that sign, right?" Jamie wondered.

"Well, they wouldn't have the lever there in the first place if they didn't want anyone to pull it," Ramsay said.

"Brian, what do you think?" Jamie asked.

Brian's doubts were beginning to surface again.

"You know, maybe this isn't the best idea," he said cautiously.

"It's not the best idea, but it's the only one we've got,"

Ramsay said, and walked to the transformer substation. He put his hand on the lever.

For a second he hesitated.

It was only a second, but in that time Brian managed to shake himself from the daze he'd been in for the last forty-five minutes. He was a theoretical physicist, but even theorists don't forget the fundamentals of cause and effect. He did a quick calculation in his head. If Ramsay disabled this transformer, then the effects would not merely be localized. Surely it would lead to a chain reaction in all the other transformers which would suddenly be faced with a huge power surge that would inevitably cause an overload. There would not be one small self-contained short or explosion; it was more likely that every transformer in the entire power station would blow up, causing an immediate emergency grid shutdown and then a power outage in the whole of—

"No. Ramsay. Wait. Don't do it," Brian said, but by then of course it was too late. Ramsay pulled the lever.

Feeling parental, Brian rugby-tackled his brother to the ground, pulled Jamie down, and shielded them with his body just as the transformer burst into a huge ball of fire.

All three of them were thrown off their feet at least six or seven yards backward into the security fence. Jamie's jacket caught fire and he had to roll on the ground for a moment to put himself out. The others were singed, bruised, but unhurt.

The Salmon of Knowledge, their only link to the planet Altair, was blasted a good hundred feet in the air before tumbling to the ground somewhere in front of them.

There were red and blue sparks flying everywhere, igniting anything that would burn within a radius of fifty feet. Curves of electricity were streaming off into the atmosphere like fork lightning, and tiny pieces of burning metal were raining down on them like snow from hell.

But that wasn't the worst of it.

As Brian had guessed, naturally as the first transformer exploded, a surge went through all the other transformers in the power station complex. There followed a rapid series of brilliant, deafening bangs as every substation in the plant blew up.

A minute of sparks, fire, and popping cables was followed by total and instantaneous darkness.

Power went out in the town of Carrickfergus, and then as the overload worked its way through the system, gigantic circuit breakers shut down the grid in Greenisland, Belfast, and even the northern suburbs of Dublin and western Scotland.

All three of them stood transfixed as complete blackness reigned supreme in Belfast Lough for the first time since the Bronze Age.

Their hair was standing on end and their clothes stank of burnt rubber.

There was a sustained, uncomfortable silence punctuated finally by the sound of a police siren.

"Look, with all the light pollution gone, the stars have never been more visible," Ramsay said dreamily.

"Aye, you can see all of Orion," Brian replied in a similar stupor.

"Snap out of it, you two. Let's get out of here," Jamie said.

He hunted on the ground for the Salmon, found it, picked it up, and put it in his backpack. He pushed the two brothers in front of him, and then, with some difficulty, they all reclimbed the perimeter fence, ran to the van, and got inside. Brian drove down the access road and turned left for the Tongue Loanen, the long but safer way back to Whitehead. They drove high into the Antrim Hills into a dead black world of silent farms and sheep pens, the villages of Beltoy and Ballycarry seemingly thrown back in time hundreds of years. There were no lights anywhere, except in the far distance—the hospital generators in South Belfast and the twinkling lighthouses up and down the coasts of Ireland and Scotland.

"What's that smell?" Ramsay asked after a time.

"Ionized electrons," his brother explained. "When we were caught in the explosion the electrons attempted to earth themselves in—"

"The fishy smell," Ramsay asked.

"Fish," Brian said.

Ramsay looked at the boxes of fish at his feet. "Oh yeah."

"Atlantic salmon," Brian muttered.

"Typical fraud. Says PRODUCT OF PERU on it," Ramsay said.

"So what?"

"Well, it can hardly be *Atlantic* salmon if it's from Peru."

"Atlantic salmon doesn't have to be from the Atlantic, it's a type of fish and—"

"The Salmon. Oh my goodness, I totally forgot," Jamie interrupted them.

"Totally forgot what?" Ramsay said.

"Did it work? Did it actually work?" Jamie replied and began rummaging in his backpack.

He took out the alien device and examined it.

"Look," he said excitedly. "That tiny little bead in its eye. There's light behind it now. It's fixed. You did it, Ramsay! You're a genius. You did it."

Ramsay grabbed the Salmon from his friend's hand and checked it.

"Cool to the touch, not even singed, and it's been recharged."

"It's a superconductor, of course it's been recharged," Brian said, as if he'd known it all along.

"Uh-oh, put the Salmon away," Jamie said suddenly. "There's a police car up ahead."

Sure enough just outside Ballycarry on the road to Whitehead there was a police roadblock.

"Get your seat belts on and say nothing," Brian ordered.

The policeman was pointing a flashlight at them. Brian slowed the van and stopped. He turned to Ramsay. "Don't say a word," he muttered.

The policeman was a tubby, gray-haired man in his late fifties. The serious type. "Wind down the window," the cop said.

Ramsay put up two fingers, waved them at the cop, and said in a low tone: "These aren't the droids you're looking for."

Jamie nudged his friend violently in the ribs.

"For the last time, Jedi mind control doesn't work in the real world," Jamie hissed.

Ramsay continued waving his fingers, his face scrunched up in concentration.

"Shut up, you two," Brian said, wound the window down, and smiled.

"Is there a problem, officer?" Brian asked innocently.

"Been some kind of an incident at Kilroot Power Station. Checking all the vehicles heading away from there. Looking for suspicious characters," the policeman said.

"Well, nothing to do with us, we're just delivering fish. That's my job. Delivering fish. Yup. Fish deliverer.

Humble fish delivery boy, that's me—" Brian said and would have continued on in this way for hours had not Jamie pinched his leg.

"Why the binoculars?" the policeman asked, looking at Ramsay. Ramsay clutched at his throat. He still had the stupid things round his neck.

"Uhm, the binoculars. Well, we're part of the Islandmagee Astronomy Club. The power outage is a perfect time to examine the heavens," Ramsay said, wildly improvising.

"Islandmagee Astronomy Club, eh?" the policeman said skeptically. "What are you carrying in the back of the van?"

"Atlantic salmon," Brian said.

"From Peru," Ramsay clarified.

The policeman nodded and thought for a while. "Astronomy Club. Yeah. Good night for the stars now the rain clouds have moved on."

"That's right, officer," Jamie said.

"Aye, we live in a beautiful world. The sun, the moon, the planets. How many planets, boys?" he asked with an attempt at cunning.

"What?"

"Question. You're the Astronomy Club. How many planets?"

"Eight, officer," Ramsay said.

"Eight? You mean nine, sonny," the policeman said.

"Used to be nine, but they downgraded Pluto," Ramsay said.

"Is that a fact? Eight planets? *Eight* planets? You're saying what I learned in school is wrong?" the policeman said with a little hostility in his voice.

"It was all over the news," Ramsay muttered.

"Oh, but it's not confirmed. There's still nine planets in most of the textbooks. Isn't that right, Ramsay?" Jamie added.

"Uhm, could be," Ramsay said.

But the copper was ticked off now. "See your driver's license please," he said to Brian. Brian gave it over. The policeman examined it carefully and handed it back.

"What's the one with the rings, smart guy?" the policeman asked Ramsay.

"Saturn, officer."

"And the one with the canals?"

"Mars, officer, but they aren't really canals. You see, it was a mistake in the translation of an Italian astronomer's notebooks and Percival Lowell thought that—" Ramsay said until Jamie pinched him very hard.

"Mars," Jamie said.

"You're from America?" the policeman muttered, shining his flashlight onto Jamie's face.

"Yes, I moved here last year," Jamie said meekly.

"Aye. America. Some place. Daughter went out there. New Mexico. And when she came back at Christmas you would have thought she was Indian the way she was carrying on with the beads and all. Beads and crystals and crap like that," the policeman said bitterly.

"She was caught up in the New Age movement?" Jamie suggested.

"Very. The wife was embarrassed in front of the neighbors the way she was moping about. Chanting and everything."

"I can see how that would create a disturbance," Jamie said sympathetically.

The policeman nodded solemnly and turned off the flashlight.

"Well, can't stand here chatting all night. Be on your way, boys. Don't be surprised if your electricity is out at home. Like I say, some kind of incident at the power station. I'm sure the techies'll take care of it. OK, go on, no pun intended but I've bigger fish to fry than a salmon delivery van and the Islandmagee Astronomy Club."

"Thank you," Brian said, nodding. He put the van in gear, and with a huge collective sigh of relief, they drove off into the night.

Chapter VI
THE JUMP

O N 125TH STREET, in Harlem, Thaddeus Harper was sitting at a computer terminal in the George Bruce branch of the New York Public Library, occasionally looking at the screen in front of him, but mostly gazing out of the window at the Hudson River and the Jersey shore beyond. It was a task rendered extremely difficult by forty years of unwashed grime on the glass and by the impatient staring of two teenage boys who wanted to use the PC. Thaddeus had just finished an e-mail to Jamie, but he was in no hurry to send it. It seemed bland and not very interesting.

He reread it:

> To: jamieoneill47@yahoo.com
> From: thaddeusharper@hotmail.com
> Dear Jamie, I know I haven't e-mailed for a while now and I'm sorry. I've been very busy lately with other things. Well, one other thing. As I mentioned before, real estate in Manhattan has gone totally crazy and I've been offered a lot of money for my apartment in Harlem. The whole neighborhood is

being gentrified, which means that they're kicking out all the old-timers and moving in a bunch of yuppies. Is that the word people use these days? Anyway, I have decided to take the offer and move to a retirement home in New Mexico. Do you think I'm doing the right thing? Please drop me a line and let me know your opinion and also let me know how things are going in Ireland. Take care. Best, Thaddeus.

The two unkempt, smelly teenage boys waiting for Thaddeus to send his e-mail were getting increasingly restless. They were desperate to get online so that they could download pirated movies, play a little Warcraft, and then upload a sophisticated computer virus that would, they hoped, bring Western civilization to a grinding halt and show the adult universe that they were badasses who weren't to be messed with.

Fortunately for Western civilization, Thaddeus Harper wasn't easily intimidated by the ironic sighing of teenagers and took such a long time at the computer that the kids gave up their plans for world destruction and went home.

When Thaddeus finally did send the e-mail, he knew Jamie would take a while to get back to him.

But when Jamie didn't reply for a long, long time,

Thaddeus called Jamie's mom. When Anna didn't reply either, or answer repeated phone messages, Thaddeus reluctantly called the police. When the police went to the Lighthouse House and failed to find anyone there they launched an investigation. When the investigation turned up no leads whatsoever, the Royal Navy, the Royal National Lifeboat Institution, and all inshore vessels were alerted to the possibility that a tragedy might have occurred on the Muck Island causeway and people should be on the lookout for remains floating in the water.

And, a few days later, maybe it was this that saved Jamie's life.

Maybe.

* * *

The waves were high, the wind strong. Every dip of the large warship into the raging sea brought white water pouring over the gunwales that drained like a flood tide through the scuppers.

Speed is relative. The boat probably wasn't going more than sixteen or seventeen knots (not quite eighteen miles an hour), and yet with the sea raging, the spars creaking, the ropes and sails at their breaking points, it seemed incredibly fast to those on board.

"Prepare to broach," someone yelled as the ship leaned horribly over.

"More men on the lee rail," the admiral commanded, and immediately several crew ran from the windward to the lee side of the vessel to prevent a capsize. Gradually, the ship returned to a comparatively safe thirty degrees from the vertical.

Admiral Farar put a piece of *jama* leaf in his cheek and frowned.

Another huge wave struck, and the barefoot sailors jumped as a gush of freezing ocean raged over the wooden deck.

The thin, old, gray-bearded admiral shook his head.

"Steer well clear of the ice," he ordered the helmsman, who was having enough trouble just keeping the wheel steady, never mind worrying about the many small floating icebergs.

"Yes, sir," the helmsman said.

They were going as fast as the admiral had ever seen one of his vessels move, and he was becoming increasingly concerned for the sails and the integrity of his hull.

"Ease off on the main sheet," he ordered the ship's captain.

"All the way, sir? Reef the whole thing?" the captain asked hopefully.

"No," Farar said, for he knew he couldn't risk taking in an entire sail without first getting permission from the young prince.

Still, all the big black spinnakers were very taut, and it didn't help that they got a good ducking every time a swell broke over the windward side.

"Storm force," the captain told the admiral, looking at the wind ties on the main. "Yes," Farar agreed, for the heavy ties were standing out almost to vertical.

"Squall," someone warned, and almost immediately, from dead north, there was a huge polar gust, so cold that it made even the hardiest of souls gasp in pain. The thick wooden mast creaked sickeningly, and the boat rolled for a moment before righting itself.

"Can't take much more of this," the captain said, and looked significantly at the two young people at the scoop.

The admiral nodded, popped another leaf in his cheek, and scratched his beard.

"I will tell them then," he said finally.

"You must," the captain agreed.

The admiral took off his hat and warily approached the two figures on the observation scoop near the lee rail. The young prince and his foreign bride, the Aldanese woman—a girl really.

"Please excuse me, sir," he asked deferentially.

"Admiral, yes, good to see you. It must feel strange to be in command of only one ship and not the whole fleet," Prince Lorca said.

Lorca was dressed in leather trousers and wearing a

woven, *loka* sweater that obviously had some waterproofing capacity, since he was comparatively dry. The girl however was still in her wedding dress and, but for a boat cloak, was more or less soaked through. Why she hadn't changed was beyond the admiral, but then, the Aldanese were noted for their eccentricity; some said they cultivated it.

"Sir, uhm, I was thinking that for the safety of the ship and, of course, your good selves that, uhm, well, perhaps we should reduce sail," Farar suggested.

Lorca looked at his new bride to see if she had understood.

She had but she shook her head.

"We must get to the Sacred Isle before the Alkhavans do," she said simply. *"Arala toof a car,"* she added in a clumsy approximation of the Oralands tongue.

Lorca nodded. "If Wishaway says we must press on, then press on we must," he told the admiral. "It can't be more than a few leagues now anyway."

Farar nodded. "Yes, sir," he mumbled.

It was an Oralands ship and an Oralands crew and in that country there wasn't just respect for the royal household, it was almost a kind of reverence. Lorca was only fifth in line to the throne and, as a younger son, with two older brothers, he was unlikely ever to become monarch. Even so, he was still the representative of the king, who was the absolute and unchallenged ruler of the state. If Lorca had ordered them to set fire to the vessel or sail it over the edge of the world, the admiral would have obeyed.

Farar bowed obsequiously.

Normally Wishaway would have been disgusted by this kind of subservience, but here it served her purpose. Prince Lanar's ship was the fastest one available in Aldan harbor. And she knew they had to get to the Sacred Isle as quickly as possible.

All in all it had been a dizzying twenty-four hours.

After the explosion, a competent, exhaustive search by the city watch had discovered the Alkhavan saboteurs hiding in a warehouse near the harbor, obviously waiting to slip out with the trawling fleet at dawn. As the guard approached, two committed suicide by taking poison, but two others were captured alive.

Under what Watch Commander Savlona called "intensive questioning with moments of considerable duress," the saboteurs explained that they had been sent to Aldan to carry out their mission by the new Lord Protector Ksar.

The new *Lord Protector Ksar*. That was a phrase to strike panic into stout Aldanese hearts. Ksar, the leader of the bloody invasion of their fair city, whom most assumed was dead, was now, apparently, the leader of the most powerful country in the northern sea.

With further questioning it became apparent that the saboteurs' goal was not to destroy the entire city of Aldan with their infernal devices, but merely to disable or destroy the White Tower itself.

And in that goal they had been most successful.

As soon as Wishaway heard this news, she grabbed her sea boots, put on a boat cloak, and asked Lorca for a fast ship. Ksar might be clever, he might have animal cunning, but he was never subtle. It was obvious to her what his next move was going to be. Why had he destroyed the White Tower? To sow panic? To destroy Aldanese morale? As an act of revenge?

No.

He was a practical man with a good, logical reason for everything.

The White Tower was one of three locations on Altair where Jamie could use the Salmon machine to swim his way from Earth to Altair. With the White Tower gone, that left only the Black Tower in Balanmanik, which was in Alkhavan territory, and the tower on the Sacred Isle, where the Ui Neills had first come to Altair. Why would Ksar destroy the White Tower? Because the Lord Ui Neill was coming, and Ksar knew he was coming and wanted to bring him to Balanmanik.

Seventeen hours of hard sailing to the Sacred Isle had

passed since the wedding feast had become a council of war.

No one had slept, the watches had been doubled up. Lorca had taken none of his retinue but had insisted that Wishaway, as befitted her rank, be surrounded by servants.

It had been a long, strenuous night but the Oralands warship *Proud Star* was now close to the Sacred Isle itself.

"I think I recognize these waters," Wishaway said. "The lookout must sight the tower soon."

Lorca put his arms about her and smiled happily to himself.

Could this girl really tell one patch of sea from another?

Of course she could, she was Wishaway, daughter of Callaway, one of the brightest students at the university, a savior of her city, a guide to the Ui Neills.

"I'm sure he will," he whispered in her ear, and grinned again.

When he brought her home, there would be resistance to a foreigner at the court in Carolla, but her brains, beauty, and wit would win over the men at least and perhaps the jealous ladies would come around too, eventually.

"We must arm ourselves," Wishaway said.

"Do you expect trouble on the Sacred Isle?" he asked, holding her tighter.

"I expect there to be minions of the new Lord Protector," Wishaway replied, still not entirely sure how she felt about being in Lorca's strong embrace.

"Do you . . ." *expect to see Jamie?* Lorca almost asked but fortunately stopped himself in time.

"Do you . . . like my father's yacht?" he wondered instead.

"All but the name. The Aldanese do not give names to their ships; it is a superstition," she replied haughtily.

Lorca smiled.

"Full of pride on the *Proud Star*," he said, but in the Oralands language it was a pun within a pun that Wishaway didn't get.

"Land ho!" someone called from the masthead.

"An iceberg?" the admiral shouted.

"No, sir, land a few points off the starboard beam. An island," the sailor replied.

Lorca handed Wishaway an octoscope.

Wishaway gasped.

It was the Sacred Isle, but apparently they were too late.

A small Alkhavan war schooner, perhaps the only such vessel that tree-deprived country actually possessed, had anchored on the far side of the island. At least two dozen warriors had landed with ropes, scaffolding, and a pulley, and they were now attempting to pull down the tower on the western side of the island.

"We have not arrived in time. If the Lord Ui Neill attempts to come, he will not succeed," Wishaway said, trying to keep back a flood of tears.

"Nonsense. We will stop these thugs in an instant," Lorca said and immediately summoned Admiral Farar.

The admiral bowed. "Sir?"

"We must land. Prepare your men for an assault," Lorca said.

The admiral shook his head. "There can be no landing for several hours, Prince Lorca. We are at low tide, I dare not risk the ship in these waters. However when the tide is high we may safely anchor close and—"

"Forget the safety. We need to move now. Ram the ship up onto the beach next to those Alkhavan soldiers," Lorca ordered.

The admiral blanched. "Impossible. The *Proud Star* will be holed and the Alkhavan vessel will surely escape, but if we blockade them, wait just a few hours until—"

"I am in charge here, Admiral. Do as I say and you will be a peer by nightfall. Disobey and I will see to it that you are sent before the mast," Lorca said harshly.

Both men were talking fast, and Wishaway could barely follow their conversation, but she was impressed by the command in Lorca's voice and the bearing that suddenly seemed to drape itself over his shoulders. This was someone who, from birth, had been schooled in taking responsibility for himself and others. She noticed other things too. Spray and salt had matted his hair, and he looked tanned and rough. Older. The previous year had changed him. This was a boy no more, this was a man.

The admiral bowed and barked the order to the horrified sailors: "Prepare to run aground. Captain, beach the ship next to the soldiers, when we stop I want everyone over the side immediately."

There was a groan of disbelief from the crew.

"Silence on deck there! Prepare to beach, arm yourselves for combat," Admiral Farar barked.

Lorca grimaced and bit his lip. Some of these men were going to die because of his decision.

Wishaway could see the troubled look in his eyes. She leaned over and kissed him tenderly on the cheek, filled with admiration for her young prince. It was, she realized, not yet love, but perhaps that would come with time.

After a moment's hesitation, the helmsman turned the ship into the wind and headed it straight for the old lighthouse on the shore; this was where the Alkhavans seemed most concentrated and the beach at least was on a low gradient.

It was a place Wishaway knew well, a place where she had lived alone for several weeks before that amazing day when she had met Ramsay and Jamie—the Lords Ui Neill come back after four centuries.

The *Proud Star* cruised right past the small, fast Alkhavan ship. The incredulous Alkhavan crew managed to launch a few arrow shots and crossbow bolts, which hit nothing. They sailed fast toward the shore and in a minute were almost on the gravelly beach.

"Sir, we are a rope length from the bottom!" a young sailor cried, holding up a depth line.

"Seize a stay, a bulkhead, anything solid. Steady now!" the admiral cried.

Wishaway held tight to Lorca and he grabbed the stern rail. The keel struck an obstacle and then there was a tremendous, ugly grinding noise as the *Proud Star*'s hull scraped over the larger rocks on the beach.

"Touched bottom, sir," the sailor with the sounding line called out, rather obviously.

The grinding noise grew louder, the ship shuddered, and then a large portion of the hull seem to buckle. The vessel stopped and then lurched forward, sending a dozen sailors flying to the deck.

Seawater began pouring in through a hull breach, but such was its initial momentum that still the ship managed to scrape forward up the shore.

Wishaway held Lorca still tighter as the *Proud Star* suddenly leaned over to port and continued up the beach, almost sideways, thrashing and bucking like a *dragga* in a net. A mast shattered, sending splinters down onto the crew gathered on the deck. There were screams and terrible wounds, and one man was killed instantly.

"The knees give," the first mate yelled and there was a tremendous crashing from below decks.

For Wishaway all the voices and noise seemed to come at once:

"I'm hurt!"

"My eyes!"

"Tora is overboard!"

"The keel is gone!"

"I need the surgeon!"

"She's breaking apart!" the first mate yelled, but then, suddenly the grinding noise lessened, the *Proud Star*, slowed, shuddered again, and finally stopped.

Lorca stood upright and surveyed the damage.

The vessel was intact, most of the crew unhurt.

"Grab your weapons and follow me!" he yelled, and leaped over the side onto the sand. He ran straight toward a group of amazed Alkhavan warriors. The sailors and Wishaway did not hesitate to follow, and in a second the fight was on.

* * *

For a thirty-year-old, barely employed student like Brian, Sunday-night entertainment in Islandmagee was usually: take the bus to Belfast, drink several pints of beer, attempt to meet girls in the pub, fail, get a curry somewhere, attempt to meet girls at the curry house, fail, get the bus back to Islandmagee, attempt to meet girls on the bus, fail again, accidentally fall asleep, get out of the bus at Carrickfergus by mistake, chase after it, yell fruitlessly for it to stop, and then walk the remaining seven miles to Portmuck, just as the heavens open in what seems to be an eerie echo of the biblical deluge that drowned the earth itself.

But not this Sunday.

Now he was standing in the round tower on Muck Island, holding the rebooted Salmon of Knowledge, and apparently, like the *Apollo* astronauts, about to journey into space. Over Ramsay's and Jamie's objections, he was going to go first. This was his price for the help at the power station and for having to put up with Ramsay's terrible song- and short-story writing over the last few months.

There was no time like the present. Jamie's mother was at the cinema in Belfast, the tide to Muck Island was low, Brian was well rested and well fed. Everything was perfect for a quick jaunt to Altair and back again.

"Are you ready?" Jamie asked.

Brian nodded nervously, but before he could answer his cell phone rang.

"Hi . . . Oh hi, it's you . . . Fine, nothing special . . . Yeah, I might see it. Probably won't. 'Course the golden age was *Bananas* to *Annie Hall* and really, with the odd exception, no classics since about '86 . . ."

He looked at the boys, who were standing there with varying levels of patience. Jamie: pretty relaxed. Ramsay: furious.

Brian nodded and put his hand over the receiver.

"Friend from MIT," he whispered.

"Get off the phone," Ramsay said.

"OK," Brian said, chagrined. He removed his hand from the mouthpiece. "OK, OK, listen, Ganesh, it's great to hear from you and everything, but I think, well, I've got to go . . . Yeah I'm heading out the door. Little trip, might be interesting . . . I don't know, if I can't get my act together I'll be back in the fall term. No, fall of this year. Thanks. Bye."

Brian clicked his phone shut. Ramsay smiled at him and shook his head.

"What?" Brian asked.

"What? I'll tell you *what*. Fall term my foot. You still don't really believe us, do you? I'm telling you, mate, after this experience you won't *want* to go back to MIT."

Brian stared at the two boys. Being honest with himself, he wasn't that sure that he believed everything they had told him. Or *anything* they'd told him; but he was in too deep to have fundamental doubts now. What other choice did he have? He'd already broken several laws and caused a four-hour power outage over Ireland, western Scotland, and parts of northern England. If this was an elaborate practical joke, then he didn't know how he'd react. His anger with Ramsay would certainly take a long time to dissipate.

He stared at the timer on his digital watch.

"OK. What am I supposed to do now?" he asked them.

"Step back a bit . . . Good. Now push the button, near the eye," Jamie said. "And hold on tight . . . if you drop that thing we're all in the soup."

"OK, push this button near the—" he began and then disappeared.

Jamie laughed with delight.

Ramsay, grinning, turned to his friend. "Well, well, I suppose it works," he said.

"Yeah, I guess it does," Jamie replied.

"Good to have a guinea pig," Ramsay reflected.

"Yeah . . . How long do you think he'll be?"

"Oh, I don't know, maybe have a quick shoofty round the island, breathe the air, grab some fossils. An hour or two maybe. Course he's a bit more of an existentialist than either of us," Ramsay said.

"Exist— What?"

"Lives in his mind. Solipsistic. Overthinks things. Might take him a long time to recover from this fundamental paradigm shift in his worldview."

Jamie shook his head, sighed. "OK, you win. I think I prefer your Dungeons and Dragons speak," Jamie said.

"Knew it. They all come round to Dungeons and Dragons eventually," Ramsay muttered, almost to himself.

"Yeah, anyway, scintillating as always, Ramsay. Back to important stuff. I've a question for you," Jamie said.

"I'm all ears," Ramsay said with mock interest.

"OK, the last jump we made was from the White Tower in Aldan City. Isn't there a chance he could end up there instead of Wishaway's island? The Sacred Isle. You know, the Salmon could sort of home-back to the last place it went from?"

Ramsay nodded. "Didn't think about that. It's possible. Yeah. Not quite sure how the Salmon chooses which of the three towers to go to. Just sort of assumed it always went to the same place. Well, if he goes back to the city, then we're screwed. He'll find that place totally fascinating, we might not see him for days or even wee—"

Brian appeared in front of them, exhausted, sweating, and apparently bleeding from a cut on his finger. He seemed distressed, but when he saw the boys he smiled from ear to ear, ran over, and hugged them.

He held up the Salmon and said something incoherent.

"Are you OK?" Jamie asked.

"Holy crap," Brian managed after a moment.

"What did you see?" Jamie persisted.

Brian sat down on the stone floor of the old lighthouse and caught his breath. After a minute he stood, grabbed a bottle of water, and drank. He stopped the timer on his watch.

"Ever notice the more functions a watch has, the lower the IQ of its owner," Ramsay muttered impatiently.

Brian ignored him and sat down again.

"Come on, the suspense is killing us," Jamie said.

Brian nodded. "OK, OK, first let me just say this. Yes, it's the most important scientific or archaeological discovery in the history of mankind. Probably the most significant event in human history since we discovered fire. If you tell the authorities about this, without a doubt, you and Ramsay are going to be the subject of high school essays, PhD theses, and books for the next thousand years. You are going to be famous. Second, let me add that the journey itself was an incredible, awesome experience, it was just amazing to cross the galaxy through a wormhole and then bear witness to an independently evolved alien culture. Totally mind-blowing and impressive."

Ramsay was looking at his older brother with a curious half grin on his face.

"And yet . . ." Ramsay said.

"And yet?" Brian asked.

"And yet . . . Come on, I sense a 'but' in there somewhere," Ramsay said, cocking his head to one side questioningly, rather like a puzzled dog.

"You sense a 'but,' well . . ." Brian began and then stopped.

"What?" Jamie and Ramsay said together.

"Well there is a 'but' in there. You see, as amazing as the journey was and it was amazing—the aliens, the lost artifact, the whole thing, wonderful . . . I'm not complaining about that."

"What are you complaining about?"

"Well, I might be wrong, but didn't you say there would be beautiful girls and music and they all thought you guys were heroes and stuff?"

"We did. We are," Ramsay said.

"Funny way to treat a hero. I jump through the wormhole, catch my breath for about two seconds, and there's a big commotion, and some crazy chick starts yelling at me. Then there's a bunch of shouting and all these other guys come right at me."

"What are you talking about. Where were you? On the island?" Ramsay asked.

"Island? Don't think so. A very dank, nasty place in fact, surrounded by dudes in hoods chanting some diabolical language. Literally for a quarter of a second I thought that the jump had killed me and I'd ended up in hell, and then for another quarter of a second I thought, no, you can't go to hell for stealing pencils at MIT. That's not very fair."

"But then?"

"Well, then some woman notices me and screams something and comes all the way over, getting in my face, and she's pretty hot I guess. Catherine Zeta-Jones crossed with the Evil Queen from *Snow White*, you know? And then there's the yelling and it looks like she wants the Salmon or something and I panic, drop the thing, pick it up, cut my finger, flip the button, and come back here."

Ramsay and Jamie were completely perplexed. Ramsay was the first to shake himself out of a daze. "None of that happened did it? You're making it up. Did you pass out or something? Did you have a bit to drink before you jumped?"

"Straight up. It's all true. Amazing but true."

"Good-looking woman? Who might that be?" Ramsay wondered out loud.

"Hmmm, don't know . . . Maybe Callaway got married again. Could be his new wife? Were you on an island or in the city?" Jamie asked.

"I told you I don't know. It was very dark," Brian said.

"It must be night there," Ramsay said. "That won't tell us anything . . . There's only one way to really find out."

Jamie nodded. "I'll go," he said and took the Salmon from Brian's still trembling hand.

"Why you?" Ramsay asked.

"Because it's my lighthouse and I am the Lord of Muck," Jamie said, and felt foolish as soon as the words had left his mouth.

Ramsay laughed. "I'll go first. I'm bigger and tougher than you. Sounds like there could be the hint of trouble on the other side."

"I'm going. You won't handle things diplomatically. You'll blunder in," Jamie said.

"I'm going. I'm older than you. I'm fourteen and a half. You're fourteen."

"Going where?" Jamie's mother asked, standing at the top of the stairs.

Everyone froze. Foolishly Jamie tried to hide the Salmon behind his back.

"And what's that you're hiding? And who are you?" she asked Jamie and Brian in turn.

Brian was momentarily stunned. He hadn't seen Anna O'Neill up close before. Only from a distance driving over the causeway onto Muck Island. He'd been expecting a much older woman, not this flame-haired, attractive, thirty-five-year-old who looked seriously annoyed.

"I'm, I'm, I . . ." he explained.

"My brother Brian. Half-brother actually. You know, from the band?" Ramsay said apologetically.

"Oh yes, from the village. I think I've seen you. You deliver the fish, don't you?" she said, sniffing the air.

"Yes," Brian said self-consciously.

Anna marched toward them. "And what is this?" she asked, pulling the Salmon from behind Jamie's back.

"Uhhh, that's the Salmon of Knowledge," Jamie said truthfully.

"How long have you been standing at the top of the stairs there? Thought you were supposed to be at the cinema," Ramsay asked cautiously.

"I'm asking the questions. The movie was sold out. But I'll tell you one thing, Ramsay McDonald, I've been here long enough to make me very curious about what you two, you *three*, get up to up here. What is this thing? What's it for? Where did you get it?" Anna asked, her eyes wide and almost a little afraid—as if the answer to that question was going to bring a whole host of other problems into her life.

"I told you, Mom," Jamie said quietly.

Anna looked at him strangely.

"I told you. I went to another world and my arm came back and I learned how to speak," Jamie said, almost in a whisper now.

Anna looked at the beautiful, golden fish in her hand. The light of memory came into her eyes.

She nodded absently.

"I told you, Mom. I told you everything in the hospital,

but you were on morphine at the time and afterward I knew you didn't believe me, but it's all true," Jamie said, without even an attempt to invent a cover story.

Ramsay groaned.

"You did tell me that story. You went to another world and you saved people and your voice came back. You told me that in the recovery ward," she said.

"I did, Mom," Jamie replied.

"But, but I thought it was just your own way of explaining how your voice came back. That's what the child psychologist said, anyway."

"It's true, last year—" Ramsay began, but Anna cut him off.

"Last year when the pair of you supposedly ran away, you used this thing to travel to another dimension?" Anna said, incredulously.

Brian cleared his throat. "Another planet, Mrs. O'Neill, another planet, same dimension. The Salmon creates a wormhole, a fold in space-time that allows one to—"

"Quiet, fishmonger," Anna ordered. "I'll see for myself if you're all lying. How does it work?"

Jamie stepped in front of her.

"No, you can't go. We don't really know where it's going to take us right now. It might not be Wishaway's island after all."

"Wishaway's that girl you met? In your story, you met a girl," Anna said.

Jamie nodded.

"OK, I'll ask one more time. How does this work? Is it going to take off? Am I going to fly?" she asked, determined now to meet this *girl*, this alien thing, who might be trying to corrupt her son.

Brian grabbed hold of the Salmon. "No. Mrs. O'Neill, you clearly don't understand the physics of warp travel. I think I should go with you," he said, trying to sound smooth, for he was quite captivated by the extraordinary emerald of her eyes.

"If he's going, I'm going," Jamie said, shoving his hand onto the Salmon, like it was the game One Potato, Two Potato.

Ramsay sighed and stared at the three of them holding on to the alien device for grim death. "Stop. Just stop, all of you. Calm down. Come on, things have come to a pretty pass when *I'm* the voice of reason around here," he said. "No one is going anywhere."

"The switch near the eye is the 'on' button it seems," Brian said, ignoring his brother.

Anna started fumbling for the button.

"Don't press the button. we need food, water, rucksacks. Last time we brought supplies. We can't go halfcocked in jeans, fleeces, and T-shirts. This isn't a trip down to the chip shop, this is interstellar travel," Ramsay said.

"I want to see what this is all about. If you're all into drugs or something, I want to know," Anna said, looking at Brian accusingly.

"That's what I thought, but they're not," Brian said.

Anna found the button, hit it, and started to disappear. Brian and Jamie held on tight and began to vanish.

"Wait for me," Ramsay said, jumping toward them and grabbing on to the Salmon, just as the wormhole sucked them all off Earth completely.

His arm was back. His arm! On Altair the Salmon reconfigured his molecules to give him two arms.

Jamie opened his eyes.

A black room. A dozen men in hoods were coming toward them.

"Bloody hell, he wasn't joking," Ramsay said.

"Is it always like this?" Brian asked.

"Whuuuu," Anna said.

"Look! On the ground, there's a broken Salmon. They must have used that to bring us here," Ramsay said.

"Where is here? Is this the White Tower?" Jamie asked.

"Whuuuu," Anna said.

"Kaara, vass, tama!" the Witch Queen yelled.

One of the monks grabbed the Salmon. Brian punched the monk in the face. Another jumped him and pulled Brian to the ground. Another one grabbed Anna and began wrestling with her.

Jamie felt someone hit him on the top of the head.

"Push the button," Ramsay cried.

Jamie fumbled for the Salmon of Knowledge.

Falling.

Projections of color.

Grays, greens, browns, black. Black for a half a minute. A burnt sky.

The smell of acid.

Jamie blinked.

He felt like he was swimming in a dark pool. His body being tugged in several directions at once. Crystal shapes. Static.

This hurts, he thought.

Then all sensation of movement abruptly stopped.

He couldn't see the others.

"Mom?" he asked.

Another form became visible. Ramsay?

His arm was gone again. Here so briefly and gone again. The matrix for Jamie on Earth was one-armed and the teleportation device had returned him to the way he was. They were back in the old lighthouse on Muck Island.

"What now?" Ramsay said.

"Can't leave them there. Gotta go get them," Jamie replied.

"Jump again? God knows where we'll end up."

Jamie shook his head. "Really, do we have a choice?"

Ramsay grabbed the Salmon and Jamie pressed the button.

Falling.

The arm coming back.

But of course . . . Whatever power had disrupted the last jump was no longer operating.

Sunlight streaming in through a window.

They were definitely on Altair, but the air smelled of the strange, alien sea, and it was cold.

"Where?" Jamie asked, looking at his restored left arm again in amazement and happiness, which quickly changed to worry when he looked around for his mother.

"Sacred Isle, I think," Ramsay said.

"What's that noise?" Jamie asked.

From outside they could hear yelling and the banging of metal against metal.

"What happened? Do you think Mom and Brian got back to Earth somehow?" Jamie asked.

"I don't know," Ramsay said.

The noise of fighting grew louder outside and then without warning, the lighthouse began to shake violently.

"What's going on outside?" Ramsay asked.

Jamie stuck his head out of the window, and the first thing he saw was Lorca leading a charge of Oralands sailors against a horde of Alkhavan troops who were standing beside what looked to be an enormous crane.

"Lorca," Jamie said. But then he noticed . . . her.

There she was. Running, determined, a few paces behind Lorca, wearing an elaborate and impractical dress and carrying a heavy wooden staff.

Wishaway with a huge beefy man beside her that Lorca had ordered to look after her.

"Her bodyguard," Jamie guessed correctly.

The Alkhavans were slightly outnumbered by the attackers, but even so—

"We gotta help," Jamie concluded.

Just then the lighthouse gave another tremendous shudder. Tiles and bricks fell from the roof, and a hole appeared in the flagstones on the floor.

"What's going on?" Ramsay said, but Jamie was already sprinting toward the spiral staircase.

"Come on," Jamie said.

Mortar was spilling out of the walls, the steps cracking under his feet.

He reached the bottom of the stairs where he saw that Alkhavan engineers had erected a system of pulleys and attached ropes around the base of the round tower.

Stones, rubble, and the dust from a dozen millennia were falling from the lighthouse roof over the two warring groups.

"Can't see a thing," Ramsay said.

"Forget the plan! Back to the ship!" someone shouted from the beach. The command was in Alkhavan but Jamie recognized the voice immediately.

"Ksar!" Jamie said, horrified.

And sure enough, when the dust cleared, he saw the black-clad general running in a loping hyena gait to a rowboat waiting for him in the surf.

"It is Ksar," Jamie muttered as an Alkhavan warrior loomed out of the dust and tried to smash his brains out with a heavy wooden club.

"Ksar, right, I'm on him," Ramsay called, and the big-legged Irishman set off in pursuit. Jamie rolled out of the way of the clumsy blow, picked up a dead man's sword, and parried the club as it came down again.

Jamie thrust the sword into the Alkhavan's leg and stepped aside as the big warrior tumbled to the ground. There was no need for a death blow. Instead Jamie ran to a little hillock and surveyed the action.

Lorca had killed two Alkhavans outright in a surprisingly deft display of swordplay, and Wishaway was holding her own against a smallish Alkhavan engineer who was trying to get past her and back to his departing ship.

"Cala fak, cala far!" a huge, blond-bearded Alkhavan shouted, and clearly this meant something like "Every man for himself," for the warriors not engaged in a life-and-death struggle all immediately disengaged from combat and began running for the surf.

"After them!" Lorca shouted as he stabbed a third Alkhavan with his short sword.

Jamie's attacker dropped his club, turned, and began limping for the beach.

Ksar leaped into his boat and did not wait for his men to join him. He gave the command to row. Some of the Oralands sailors tried to fire arrows at him but no one was close enough to be accurate, and within seconds he was out of range.

"Come back, you dog," Ramsay shouted, running into the surf and pushing a couple of pleading Alkhavan marines out of his way.

Ksar stood up in the boat.

His face was red, disfigured, but his bright eyes flashed even from fifty yards away. He drank something that seemed to revive him.

"Ahhh, Lord Ramsay, we meet again!" Ksar shouted over the surf.

"Come back and fight me," Ramsay called.

"No doubt that time will come," Ksar replied, and sat down again. Ramsay watched in frustration as Ksar reached his ship and climbed aboard. It immediately weighed anchor and set sail for the north.

Seeing their master desert them robbed the other Alkhavans of their will to fight. The dozen or so who yet lived dropped their weapons and bowed their heads in the traditional Alkhavan manner of supplication.

It was over.

Jamie waved to Wishaway.

"Wishaway!" he called out, "Wishaway, it's me!"

Wishaway noticed him, but then for some inexplicable reason she pretended not to see. She turned her head.

"Wishaway!" Jamie yelled again.

He ran to her. "Wishaway," he said when he was at her side.

"Lord Ui Neill," she replied.

"I've missed you," Jamie said and was about to put his arms around her, but she stopped him with a look. She took a step back and then placed her hands in front of her, making the apparently universal "halt" sign.

"What?" Jamie asked confused.

"Do not embrace me, Lord Ui Neill," she said formally.

Jamie was taken aback. "Are you joking?" he said and tried to hug her again.

"I do not jest with thee, Lord Ui Neill," she said softly.

Jamie noticed the sad distance in her eyes. As if she were looking at him from the bottom of a deep well.

He couldn't fathom it. "I don't understand," he said.

"I am wed, Lord Ui Neill. And as per the custom of Lorca's people it is not now my intention to touch another man save my husband or my father."

Jamie laughed. He still thought that she was somehow kidding him. (Or at least he hoped so.)

"You're married? Pull the other one. You're fifteen . . . And yeah I know, your year is longer, your day is longer. Still, you're barely sixteen in human years, and that's a bit too young even for a Southern state—"

"I am wed," she said again, firmly.

Jamie's face contorted, his expression went from amused to confused to disappointed.

"How? Who?" he managed, his voice barely above a croak.

Wishaway turned her back on him and walked away.

Of course she was crying now.

She walked to the water and stood there as the freezing tide sluiced over and ruined her expensive shoes.

And for what seemed like an age she watched the waves coming in over the stony beach.

How many times had she come to this beach during her exile from Aldan, waiting, hoping that the great Ui Neill would return and deliver her city.

And in the shape of a boy he *had* come and he had saved them.

And now she had betrayed his trust.

She sobbed.

Her shoulders shook from crying, and she hoped that from a distance it would seem that she was merely cold.

Jamie stared after her in amazement, and seeing his wife in apparent distress, Lorca wiped the blood off his sword and ran to her.

"Wishaway, my darling, the enemies are dispatched, and the Lords Ui Neill are safe," he said cheerfully in English, pretending not to notice the tears.

Wishaway threw her arms about his neck. "Oh, Lorca. Thank you, you have . . . you have done a man's job," she said haltingly in his language.

They kissed and held each other.

Jamie watched the scene from farther up the beach. It hurt him. But after a minute or two he felt he understood. *Yes, of course,* he said to himself. *She didn't think I was ever coming back. She had to move on. Lorca proposed. He's young, rich, a prince. How could she refuse?*

He let the couple talk for a few moments before feeling strong enough to approach them.

"Thank you, Lorca, for all your best efforts," Jamie said, and offered his hand. Lorca shook it happily.

"You are welcome, Lord Ui Neill. I am glad to return some of the debt which I owe thee, for saving me on the iceship."

"That was nothing. Our fault really. Anyway, thank you, oh and, and uhm, many, er, c-congratulations on your wedding. Wishaway just told me, and I know that you two will be very happy together."

Lorca squeezed Jamie's hand a little tighter than before. He looked Jamie in the eye. "And I have your blessing, Lord Ui Neill?" Lorca asked after a long pause.

"Well . . . for what it's worth . . . yes," Jamie said.

Wishaway smiled and took the hair from her face.

She closed her eyes to conceal the quiet sadness no longer hidden under her hair. But Lorca laughed and slapped Jamie on the back, genuinely affected by the Earth boy's words. "Thou art a true friend, Lord Ui Neill, a true friend," Lorca said.

Jamie nodded.

Ramsay jogged over to the group. "Looks like Ksar got away again. More escapes than Houdini, that guy," Ramsay said, and from the blank expressions realized of course that he alone of the four of them knew who Houdini was.

"Well, we better get back to the White Tower in Aldan. If they're not on Earth, that's where the others will be. They are going to be freaked until we get there. About a day's sail in that big boat?" Jamie said with false bonhomie.

Wishaway looked distressed, and Jamie knew instantly that something was wrong.

"What is it?" he asked.

"Why dost thou speak of the White Tower, Lord Ui Neill?" Lorca asked with concern.

"Well," Jamie began cautiously, "Ramsay and I jumped here from Earth with my mom and Ramsay's big brother. We really couldn't stop them from coming, though believe me we tried. Anyway, we ended up here, and we don't know where they went. But we think it must be Aldan."

Wishaway put her hand to her mouth.

"What is it?" Jamie asked.

"The White Tower of Aldan has been destroyed by Ksar's men," Lorca said.

Jamie felt a cold chill run down his back. "But if they're not there, where are they?" he asked.

"Jamie, they're not in Aldan. That's not where we went. Remember, there's a third tower, isn't there?" Ramsay said.

"A third tower?" Jamie asked.

Lorca and Wishaway both nodded.

"In the realm of the Witch Queen in Balanmanik," Lorca said.

"Where is . . . ?" Jamie asked, but he knew the answer.

"Alkhava," Ramsay said simply.

"Al-Alkhava?" Jamie stuttered.

"They're Ksar's prisoners now," Ramsay croaked.

Jamie's head was spinning. He was finding it hard to breathe. The veins in his forehead throbbed. He hyperventilated. He almost fell. Ramsay steadied him. "My mom? What? Ksar's prisoners. My . . . What are we going to do, Ramsay? What are we going to do?" Jamie asked.

Ramsay did not reply.

"What are we going to do, Ramsay? You're the brains, think of something . . . Come on. What are you going to do?" he shouted, on the verge of panic.

"I don't know, Jamie," Ramsay said. "I'm sorry. I just don't know."

Chapter VII
THE COUNCIL

NOT IN THE LAST THOUSAND YEARS had there been such a summer snowfall in the city of Afor. In Balanmanik several hundred miles to the north this was now an increasingly frequent phenomenon, but here on the southern tip of the continent, where the moderating currents of the trade winds kept the climate temperate, it was almost unheralded.

Ksar looked through the windows of the old King's Chamber. Wet hail glistened on the roof of the great stone Temple to the Ice God.

"Appropriate," he murmured.

He watched a wooden ship turn for the headland and tack south. It had only just landed two hours before, carrying him from the Sacred Isle, now it departed with two generals, several of his trained *rantas*, and the greater part of the city treasury. On assuming full control of the city, he had found to his surprise that Lord Protector Dorpa had acquired or inherited several dozen chests of gold. Perhaps to any other leader this ready cash would have been used to buy luxuries or military supplies. But not for Lord Protector Ksar. The departing ship was taking the majority of that gold to Aldan.

He did not fear the Aldanese, but several barrels of gold would be enough to keep them off his back for a considerable amount of time.

His sister entered without knocking. An impertinence which from anyone else could have meant a premature ejection from this world.

"Snowing," she said. "One could even call it a blizzard. It is the shape of things to come."

"Yes," he replied.

He turned to look at her. She was dressed in a purple gown with gold brocade. Ksar was surprised to see her in anything but black. Her hair was tied back and plaited, her cheeks had taken on some color. She must have been exercising her *draya*.

"Thou hast seen a glass? Thou art in rude health, sister," he said, beginning the conversation as he always did, in English, to thwart spies and eavesdroppers. Or at least the poorer educated of the spies and eavesdroppers.

"Hardly," she replied. "I have merely been outside."

She pointed out the window. Ksar followed her gaze.

"It is the beginning of the end. Master Sarpa and the Twenty-seventh Queen predicted this over a century ago," she said in Alkhavan. And soon they would all feel it. The peoples of Aldan, Kafrikilla, Oralands, it would come to them all in time.

"Thou art troubled by the snow?" he asked.

"The Old Ones, it seems, have abandoned us to the ice gods," the Witch Queen said with sarcasm, hinting perhaps that she did not believe in either of those two entities.

The Lord Protector did not reply. Despite his recent successes it would not be wise to mock the unknown forces that ran the universe. Their father had been a blasphemer, and his career had ended ignominiously in shipwreck, drunkenness, and disaster.

She sat on a divan and regarded the snow for a time. "Our plan was partially successful," she said at last.

"Or mostly a failure, depending upon your point of view," Ksar replied with a smile.

The Witch Queen's lips narrowed. Eight fingers folded themselves carefully onto her lap.

The order of Black Monks and Sisters had long ago taught her patience.

"It is true that we do not yet have the working Salmon," she said simply.

"No," Ksar replied.

"But the message we sent a century ago has born fruit and brought to our world the latest incarnation of the Ui Neill. If that indeed was Lord Seamus that you saw on the beach of the Sacred Isle."

Ksar knew that she was attempting to bait him, to mock him for not getting the Salmon when he had the chance. He refused to let himself be angered.

"Oh he's back, I saw both of them. Lords Jamie and Ramsay," Ksar said.

She knew there was more.

"Yes?" she said.

Ksar stood and grinned at her. A deeply disturbing gesture from such a man, brother or no. "And I believe, dear sister, that despite your spoken doubts, you have already confirmed this by an independent means," Ksar said.

The Witch Queen showed no emotion.

Obviously someone had talked. Now was not the moment to be coy. She was found out. She had to come clean.

"I was going to tell you, Lord Protector. That is why I came to see you," she added in a voice dripping with conciliation and honey.

"Tell me what, sweet sister?"

"At the same time you beheld the Lords Ui Neill on the Sacred Isle, apparently two others came with them from Earth," the Witch Queen said.

"You amaze me," Ksar said, highly amused to see her so discomfited.

"Yes, Lord Protector. We intercepted two of the Ui Neill's companions in the Vancha Tower in Balanmanik."

"Did you indeed? And who are they?" Ksar asked eagerly.

Now it was her turn to smile. Obviously this was information his spies had not yet passed on.

"I believe you will be quite pleased, Lord Protector," she said, unable to resist drawing the moment out a little more.

"Yes?"

"A woman, Anna Ui Neill, *Lady* Anna Ui Neill presumably . . . for she is the Lord Ui Neill's mother," the Queen said with satisfaction.

"By the gods themselves!" Ksar cried, smacking his fist on the table. "And the other?"

"Lord Ramsay's kin. A brother, Brian of the McDonalds."

Ksar did something he hadn't done in twenty-five years. He leaned over and kissed his sister on the cheek. For a moment she almost thought there were tears in his eyes.

"Then all is not lost," Ksar said. "We *will* have the Salmon."

Ksar stormed out of the room and called for Krama, his trusted lieutenant.

"Sir?" Krama replied, and seeing the Queen, he bowed low.

"Krama, we must call back the ship for Aldan, I have a message to send to the Lord Ui Neill."

The Alkhavan messengers arrived in that country's only wooden ship. It would have been quite a blow to their navy to seize or burn the vessel, but because they had come under a flag of truce they could not in all conscience be detained or arrested. They knew exactly where they were going and walked unmolested through the town until they came to the new ambassador's residence overlooking the cliffs and the sea.

They conferred with the new Ambassador Balza for several hours, during which time many chests were seen to be delivered to the Ambassador's house. Several of the chests seemed to contain something that was alive.

After the conference, Ambassador Balza directed the messengers to the home of Council President Callaway.

It was a market day, and at first Callaway's servants assumed the strangers had come to sell their wares, but when the nature of their errand was ascertained, the guard was called and the house alerted.

It was, after all, not every day that two Alkhavan generals showed up on your doorstep.

Despite their rank, the generals were somewhat surprised to see a prince of Oralands approach them at the gate. He would not permit them to enter the grounds, but he did accept the message neatly folded in a leather tube. He rewarded the Alkhavans with gold, which, in breach of all protocol and the dignity befitting their status, they accepted.

The tube was addressed to "Seamus of the Black, Prince of Ulster, Laird of Mugh, Defender of Shore" and the message inside was sealed in red wax, with the imprint of the Lord Protector of Alkhava.

Lorca walked to the rear of the house. He had a fairly good idea what the note contained. Jamie was sitting with Ramsay in the sculpture garden, pretending to eat bread and a kind of runny cheese, but actually far too worried to consume either.

"I heard the guards get called out. What was all the fuss about?" Jamie asked. "Are there visitors?"

"I think this will contain the answers to many of your concerns," Lorca said solemnly.

Jamie took the letter and tore open the wax seal.

The note was written in English and said simply:

A trade, Lord Vi Neill. Thy mother and the Lord Brian for the Salmon of Knowledge. On receipt of this note ye shall have one Earth week to present thyself before the gates of the city of Balanmanik. It is mayhap unnecessary to tell thee, Lord Vi Neill, that a delay, or a failure to produce the Salmon, will prove costly for thee and thine. In expectation of an equitable exchange, I am, Sir, your servant, Ksar, of the Ninth House of Alkhav, General of the Armies, Lord Protector of the Alkhavan Peoples.

That night, Callaway convened a special meeting of the Council of Aldan in the rebuilt Council Chamber overlooking the harbor and the sea. It was a secret session, with only the twelve councilors, the Alkhavan ambassador, Jamie, Ramsay, Wishaway, and Prince Lorca present.

The general public would be informed later, but for now this was a matter of war and peace.

Jamie considered the Council Chamber a rather unimpressive room: a bare floor, stone tables, wooden chairs, and a pitifully empty gallery. With its sea smell and vacant interior it reminded him of an old warehouse on the New Jersey waterfront. This was not the Aldan Council's fault, though. The old chamber, which had been destroyed during the Alkhavan invasion, had had intricate sculptures and decorative glass windows and beautiful antique, wooden furniture. They were having to make do with this unadorned room until money could be raised for a new building.

Still the councilors themselves looked impressive. A dozen men and women sitting in a semicircle wearing flowing multicolored robes, flecked with blue stars. Callaway, sitting in the center of the half circle, was dressed in a thick purple gown with delicate gold braid on the sleeves.

Callaway began the proceedings in High Aldanese,

with the occasional burst of English. Wishaway translated for the Earth boys when necessary.

Callaway thanked the councilors for answering his summons and then showed them the note Jamie had received from the Lord Protector.

With great dignity he read its contents to the assembly.

The Council discussed the communication briefly and audibly and then called upon Ambassador Balza for his explanation. The children moved to the very front of the visitors' gallery so they wouldn't miss a word.

Ambassador Balza bowed to the assembly.

He was offered a seat but declined.

He was an inflated, elongated fellow who looked like he had spent most of his life outside the Spartan conditions of the frozen north.

"What do you know about Balza?" Ramsay asked.

Wishaway whispered that he was supposed to be quite clever, with a knack for oratory and languages. He had been chamberlain to and a close friend of Lord Protector Dorpa, and apparently the local wine merchants could testify that he had a taste for the finer things in life. His blond hair was certainly curled artificially and his pale skin had been painted darker.

Callaway began his speech: "Ambassador Balza, I thank thee for coming tonight on such short notice. But the urgency of this case will not brook delay until the morrow. You have heard the contents of the note which I have read to the Council?"

The ambassador nodded.

"I must ask you one question before we continue these proceedings. Is this note that the Lord Ui Neill received today a genuine communication from Lord Protector Ksar?"

The ambassador smiled. "It is," he said.

"It that case, such a threatening letter, coupled with the attacks on our city by the Alkhavan nation, means that, unless undertakings are given by you this night repudiating such attacks, and recommending the immediate release of Lord Ui Neill's family, then a state of war shall necessarily exist between the people of Aldan and those of Alkhava and her dominions."

Wishaway whispered her translation and Ramsay nudged Jamie in the ribs.

"Now we're talking," Ramsay said.

Jamie and Lorca also nodded with approval and there were shouts of "Well done," and "I agree" from several of the councilors.

Most of the councilors, however, said nothing, and Councilor Quiller, a tiny man with a squat, kindly face, shook his head and said rather loudly: "That is still for us to decide, Callaway. Let the ambassador give his response."

The Alkhavan bowed. "Do you wish me to say something?" he asked in a honey-voiced English.

"If you please," Callaway said.

He cleared his throat and smiled unctuously. "People of Aldan," he began, this time not in English, but in polished Aldanese. "I am ordered to convey to you the immense regret the Lord Protector Ksar feels when he recalls the unpleasantness of the past. As many of you are no doubt aware, he was forced to carry out the orders of the depraved Lord Protector Dorpa, whose wish it was to attack your fair and beautiful city. Lord Protector Ksar regrets that in the time he spent here he could not have gotten to know you all better—"

"He killed people in cold blood!" Jamie yelled upon hearing the translation.

"Silence," Callaway ordered and gave Jamie a withering look. "Proceed, Ambassador."

"Yes, Councilors, the Lord Protector Ksar expresses deep sorrow over those tragic events. I cannot emphasize enough that he was only following orders—attempting to carry out his duty, as any of your generals would no doubt also have done," Balza said.

"General Ksar's duty no doubt included the killing of several of our Council colleagues and the attempted enslavement of the others," Callaway could not help but say.

This time Ramsay restrained himself, but there were

murmurs of encouragement from the other members of the council and a melodramatic shake of the head from Councilor Quiller.

Balza smiled. "The attack on your city, the murders, the wanton destruction, was the perverted wish of Lord Protector Dorpa. General Ksar's efficacy and soldierly abilities are well known, and he regrets that he had to demonstrate them to a people for whom he has always had the greatest admiration and respect."

"Funny way of showing it," Ramsay muttered loudly.

Ambassador Balza looked at Ramsay in the visitors' gallery but hardly missed a beat.

"Fortunately, it is my pleasant duty to inform you and all the Aldanese people that Savi Dorpa and his criminal associates have now been completely removed from power."

"Is that so?" Callaway asked, pretending to sound slightly surprised, although Aldanese intelligence agents had independently confirmed this fact days ago. Indeed when Balza himself had shown up as the new ambassador, it didn't take a genius to realize that change was sweeping through the Alkhavan hierarchy.

"Yes, Councilor Callaway. Lord Protector Ksar has now assumed full control of Alkhava while Dorpa and his degenerate gang and have been dealt with by summary execution."

There were nods of approval from the Council. The ambassador continued.

"On going through Dorpa's papers, we learned that a rogue unit of Dorpa's guard sought to destroy the White Tower of Aldan. An attempt was made to warn you, but alas that warning did not arrive here in time. Those rogue units have all now been captured, tried, and either executed or sent to work on the ice cliffs for the rest of their lives. We are glad that there was no loss of life in the incident at the White Tower, and we are pleased to announce that Lord Protector Ksar has opened the Alkhavan treasury and in recompense—and in the hope of better relations between our two lands offers—offers you a thousand gold ingots for reconstruction of the White Tower or for whatever purpose the Council of Aldan sees fit."

There were gasps of shock and amazement from all around the room. A thousand gold ingots was more than ten years of tax income for the Aldanese Council. Alkhava was not a rich country, and this had to represent almost all the gold in their coffers. It was an extraordinary gesture and could only be seen as a serious attempt to let bygones be bygones in the expectation of a better future.

The ambassador smiled beatifically.

"Can you say the amount again?" Callaway asked, letting the surprise show on his face.

"A thousand gold ingots, Council President, which we hope will be proof of our continued goodwill."

"He's trying to buy you off—he destroyed the tower in the first place!" Jamie yelled, really starting to get furious now. His mother's life was at stake here.

The ambassador did not need Callaway's help this time. He responded to Jamie directly.

"Of course, any claims that Lord Protector Ksar had anything to do with these incidents are laughable and untrue. He had nothing to do with the attack on the White Tower or the invasion of your Sacred Isle—"

"I saw him myself!" Ramsay yelled.

"That's enough," Callaway said angrily.

Balza shook his head. "He has a right to his opinion, however misguided," Balza said, and turned to address Ramsay. "I am sorry to say that thou art mistaken, Lord Ramsay. Lord Protector Ksar was tracking down Dorpa's associates in the city of Balanmanik at the time when supposedly ye did spy him on the Sacred Isle. There are dozens of people who will vouch for this."

"I'll bet," Ramsay said.

Balza turned to the councilors wearily, as if it were a great burden to have to deal with the outbursts of a petulant child.

"Please believe me, Councilors, Lord Protector Ksar wants only peace between our lands and hopes that a new era of cooperation and trade is upon us. We all sincerely desire and trust that good relations will flourish and long remain between our two nations."

There were murmurs of approval from the Council.

When Wishaway finished translating for the two boys, Jamie could not contain himself.

"You've taken my mother and Ramsay's brother!" Jamie yelled.

The ambassador nodded and bowed. "Ah, yes. Lord Ui Neill, it is my understanding that two of thy people have become guests of the Alkhavan Protectorate and are currently being entertained in the Vancha Tower in Balanmanik. The people claim to be respectively, thy mother, the Lady Ui Neill, and Lord Ramsay's brother, Lord McDonald. Alas, we have not yet confirmed this. They may be spies or agents of a foreign power. If, however, these folk are who they purport to be, then of course we will endeavor to reunite thy families. If thou art willing to travel to Balanmanik thou willst be able to confirm their identity in person. Of course I can assure thee of safe conduct until thee and thine are brought together once again," the ambassador said.

"You think I'm going to fall for that?" Jamie said angrily. "You just want the Salmon, it says so in black and white."

The ambassador frowned.

"Lord Ui Neill, I know nothing of this Salmon of

which ye speak. I have been told that there is some dispute about the ownership of this thing. However, it is a small matter."

"You do know all about it. This is all about the Salmon," Jamie said.

Quiller stood up. "President Callaway, surely it is time to clear the gallery of these children," he said angrily.

"These *children*, lest we forget, saved our city," Callaway said.

Many of the councilors nodded and shook their heads at Quiller. These weren't urchins from off the street. These were Ui Neills from Earth and a prince of Oralands.

Quiller cleared his throat. "They must either leave or restrain themselves," he said.

Ambassador Balza shook his head. "Nay, that will not be necessary. Let the children stay. I can assure you, Councilors, I know nothing and care less about this Salmon. But I do know that Alkhava wants peace. We demand nothing from you as a people, but we do desire your goodwill and your understanding."

"If you don't give me back my family, I'll burn Balanmanik to the ground!" Jamie yelled.

The ambassador smiled. "That might prove difficult in a city comprised primarily of ice and stone," he said with studied coolness.

There was laughter in the chamber—almost all of the Council, unable to resist chuckling at the remark.

"You want a third beating in a year? The people of Aldan won't stand for this. You are asking for war, and war you will get," Lorca said in English.

There was a mild uproar for a moment before Councilor Quiller stood and addressed the throng in high Aldanese.

"Quiet, please. Please . . . thank you. Now, as vice president of this body, I think I speak for everyone here in saying how grateful we are to thee, Lord Ui Neill, for thy efforts in favoring our city with thy presence and, in the last year, thy aid . . ."

There were nods of approval. Many of the councilors were still in awe of Jamie, the latest incarnation of the great Earth clan who had come to Aldan from Ireland in the past and done much to found their city centuries ago.

"However, what is past is past," Quiller continued. "The ambassador's words and our own investigations have led us to believe that Lord Protector Ksar knew nothing of the assault on the White Tower and that he has indeed deposed that felonious criminal Shiva Dorpa, the madman who ordered the invasion of our city and, apparently, this new and most outrageous attack . . . In light of these changes of government in Alkhava I think it is incumbent upon us to accept the Lord Protector's offer of amity and peace. It would not do to jeopardize relations between our two countries with hasty accusations or, heaven forbid, a declaration of war . . . No, we must study further these incidents and await confirmation of the political developments in Alkhava. Now is not the time for foolish haste. Now is the time to give peace and understanding an opportunity to flourish."

Quiller sat down. There was near unanimous applause from those in the Council Chamber. Everyone clapped save Callaway and the four teenagers.

"It is the gold, not the peace, that blinds them," Callaway whispered to himself.

"I too agree that this is not the time for hasty action . . ." another councilor began.

Jamie had heard enough.

He stormed out of the gallery and into the cool night. He sucked the air into his lungs and fought back a panic attack. He felt helpless and afraid. His mother was being held by that monster, Ksar. A man who was capable of anything. What was he going to do? What could he do?

There was a plaza outside the new Council Chamber with a half-built fountain in the shape of some kind of sea creature.

He sat down on the edge of the structure. Ramsay and Wishaway appeared in the doorway. "Come back inside, we haven't lost this yet," Ramsay said.

Jamie smiled at him. "Yes, we have. Tell him, Wishaway," Jamie said.

Inside, the debate was heating up, but they heard Callaway being shouted down by his fellows. Wishaway walked over and sat next to Jamie, while Ramsay darted back inside to hear what was going on.

"Our people have short memories," she said sadly.

Jamie felt Wishaway's hand next to his on the stone surround.

He wanted to hold it, but he could not, and its almost magnetic draw was making his body shake. He stood and moved cautiously away from her.

He looked out to sea.

A boat putting out from the harbor.

Mist across the moons.

Yellow lamplight all over the city.

He waited for her to say something, but she didn't.

Finally Ramsay came out of the chamber and walked across to his friends.

"What's happening now?" Wishaway asked.

"Callaway's making the case, but it's obvious that they're not going to do anything," Ramsay muttered.

Wishaway nodded. "I thought not," she said.

A few moments later Lorca appeared outside.

"Any further developments?" Ramsay asked.

Lorca ignored him and went straight to Jamie. "Lord

Ui Neill," Lorca said formally. "Thou seest that they shall do nothing for thee."

Jamie nodded. "It looks like it."

Gently Lorca put his arm about his bride and attempted to draw her away from Jamie and a little closer to him.

"They are ingrates," Lorca muttered, genuinely angry.

"I don't need their help. I can sort out my own problems. I'll go to Alkhava," Jamie said.

"We'll go," Ramsay concurred.

Wishaway shook her head. "If you go alone to Balanmanik, you will be killed or imprisoned," she said.

"But what choice do we have?" Jamie said.

Lorca's eyes glittered in the moonlight. He seemed nervous, excited.

"There is another way," he said.

"What?" Wishaway asked, suddenly seeming to realize for the first time that he was there at all.

"Leave here, Lord Ui Neill. Come with me to Oralands. I will send messengers to ready the Red Star fleet. We will meet them in midocean. I will talk to my grandfather, the king. I will explain the situation. He will give me command of the prince's squadron and we will go to Balanmanik in my ships, land at night, attack the city, free your mother and thy brother, and sail for home," Lorca said and turned to Wishaway eagerly, as if seeking her approval for the idea.

"What about the ambassador? The note?" Wishaway said.

"We will not even respond to the note. We will leave now. Tonight. Before port spies can follow us. With fair winds we can be off Oralands in two days, and in Balanmanik two days after that. The Lord Protector will never be expecting an invasion. Alkhava invades other lands, not the reverse," Lorca said happily.

Jamie looked at Ramsay. "You think we could do that?" he asked.

"I don't know," Ramsay muttered.

Lorca grinned. "Tell them, Wishaway. Tell them that we can do this." He wanted her to speak, he wanted her to tell them that he wasn't merely a student at the university, he was a prince of Oralands, privy to the councils of the king. And although he was not a legendary Ui Neill like them, Jamie should understand that Wishaway was marrying a leader, a statesman, a future high-ranking official in the Oralands government.

"Will the king give you a fleet?" she asked.

"Of course. I have proved myself in the battle for Aldan and again on the Sacred Isle."

"What would we do? How would this work?" Ramsay asked, warming to the idea.

"We will storm Alkhava before they are expecting us," Lorca said. "For years Oralands spies have been telling us that Balanmanik is a dying city. The latest intelligence that I have seen states that there are no more than a thousand souls left in the whole town, and most of those are slaves or monks or servants of the Witch Queen."

"There's still the Alkhavan Army in Afor," Jamie said.

Which you, in your foolishness, spared last year, Lorca thought, but said: "It will take them a week to muster and march from Afor to the Black Tower. If they come at all. There is no love lost between the two cities, perhaps the Lord Protector would wish to see his sister fail. Maybe he is playing a more subtle game than we can imagine."

The others nodded, and Lorca knew he was impressing them with this stuff. Perhaps his grandfather would give him the fleet, perhaps not, but either way it was better for them all to be among friends in Oralands, where Lorca was a respected member of the royal house, not just an honored guest in a foreign country.

"Could we do this?" Wishaway asked softly.

"Of course, Wishaway. The Witch Queen's position is precarious at the best of times. This year alone our spies say that there have been two assassination attempts on her life. Faced with an Oralands army at the gates, I am convinced someone will see the wisdom of deposing her and freeing the Lord Ui Neill's family."

"And if they don't?" Jamie persisted.

"We will storm the city, seize the Queen, demand the

return of Anna and Brian," Ramsay said, getting into the spirit of the thing.

Lorca laughed and slapped Ramsay on the back, and Jamie too looked at Lorca with a deep feeling of gratitude. Lorca had married his girl, but he was still a good friend.

"Yeah, Jamie," Ramsay continued. "He's right. We'll do it. We'll sail there and we'll find your family and we'll take that godforsaken city completely by surprise and we'll use the Salmon and leap from the Black Tower and go home."

Jamie nodded. It was a horrible plan fraught with uncertainty and the potential for disaster, but they didn't have any other choice.

"Let's do it," he said.

Balanmanik was a city of few surprises. A city of the inevitable. A city of cold certainties. If you were clever you contrived a way to leave. If you were dull-witted you remained there until your premature death.

If you committed a crime in such a place you were simply executed. There was no prison, no jail, no place to hold suspects prior to trial. Justice, if it could be called that, was meted out quickly.

Where then to hold two enemy aliens, people from Earth, who had come to Balanmanik seemingly by accident?

Lacking options, the Witch Queen put them on the highest floor of the Vancha Tower. It was not an unpleasant place (it had formerly been the sleeping quarters of the Queen's steward and his wife), but it was extremely secure.

A large circular room with two hard wooden beds, a wooden dresser, a few odd-looking stone statues that resembled gargoyles. Nothing else.

The walls were a curious amber color, a thick, almost transparent type of granite, cold to the touch and covered with a greasy layer of damp. There was a mossy substance on the floor for insulation and underneath that the same thick, hard stone. There wasn't much light, but there were two small oval windows that overlooked the frost-caked city, the plain beyond, and to the north the huge outer face of the Gag Macak glacier.

Brian woke.

Anna was holding his hand.

He tried to sit up.

She pushed him down again.

"Don't," she said. "They hit you pretty hard."

Brian said nothing for a moment.

Who had hit him pretty hard?

He'd been six foot tall at the age of eleven. No one had hit him since primary school. And where was he? And who was speaking? What was going on?

His mind couldn't make sense of it.

Fear flooded through him for a second, but he calmed himself almost immediately. He was an Oxford graduate, a scientist, a scholar at MIT. He would use his empirical abilities to pose the pertinent questions and figure this one out.

"Whaaa?" he asked.

"Lie down," Anna said. "You've had a nasty bump. Take it easy."

He lay back on the thin blanket over the hard bed and decided to try that question again.

"Where . . . ?" he began.

"Altair. One of the Queen's guards hit you on the back of the skull. You've been unconscious for a couple of days. I thought it might be serious for a while, but your breathing stabilized yesterday."

"My head hurts."

"I'll bet. He clubbed you with a mace. For a while there I was worried that you were slipping into a coma."

"Altair . . ." It was starting to come back. "Jamie's planet?"

"Apparently."

"Where are they? The boys?"

"We've been separated. From what I've been led to believe, Jamie and Ramsay have gone to a city called Aldan. The Queen is attempting to reunite us."

"The Queen?"

"An unpleasant woman. We're her, er, guests."

Brian stared at the circular prison cell.

"Guests?"

"That's what she said."

Brian shook his head. *Guests* wasn't close to the word that he would have used in a place like this. Still, different worlds, different standards of hospitality. He looked at the heavy wooden door.

"Do they keep us locked in?"

"The Queen says it's for our own protection."

"Where is the Queen?"

"She's gone to Afor, wherever that is."

Brian sat up. A ringing noise in his ears. "Can you help me get up? I want to get up, get the blood into my feet," he said.

"OK, but take it easy."

Anna put her arm round him, and Brian swung his legs off the bed. He stood, and once he was steady, he walked to the damp, oozing walls. He touched them with the palm of his hand and sniffed. The smell was quite revolting.

His head felt light. Clearly enough effort for the moment. He hobbled back to the bed and sat on it.

"So this is another planet? I don't think much of it," he said.

Anna nodded and smiled. "Yeah, it's a bit grim, isn't it?" she said.

"No unicorns, harp music, nothing like that."

"No," Anna agreed. "Nothing like that. Have some water. It's fresh. There's a sort of spongy bread too, I think it might be a fruit of some kind."

Brian drank water and ate the fruity bread, which was actually quite good.

"So, what happened exactly?" he asked. "Everything's still a bit hazy."

"Well, we grabbed the fish thing. Ended up here. A bunch of men in robes went for us, you struggled, and one of them hit you. Jamie and Ramsay got out. The monk characters have been in to check on us a couple of times."

Brian nodded. "And what about this Queen?"

"She came in to see me before she left town. She was courteous but pretty thorough about asking questions. Unfortunately, I told her everything before I quite realized who and what she was."

"What is she?" Brian asked.

"It looks like Jamie and your brother were telling the truth about everything. I suspect that these guys are the ones that Jamie and Ramsay were fighting last year. The Queen is the enemy."

"So you think Jamie's story was all true? Coming here and fighting the Alkhavans and freeing that city, whatever it was called."

"Don't you?"

"Well, I guess. I don't know. We are on another planet. Are they definitely not human?"

"No. They're not."

Brian took a sip of water.

"Well there is one silver lining," Anna said excitedly. "If it is all true, that means he's got his arm back. Jamie said that when he went to Altair, he always got his arm back."

Ramsay nodded.

"Weird," he muttered, and took another sip of water. "You said the Queen was trying to unite us all together?"

"That is what she said. I hope it won't take long. I left the gas on in the Lighthouse House," Anna said with a wink.

"Maybe I'll try walking again," Brian said.

He got to his feet and went to the windows. He looked out over the bleak city and the bleaker surroundings.

"It's like they've taken Dracula's castle and dumped it at the North Pole, and then let everything fall apart for a couple of hundred years," Brian complained, but really he was quite impressed with the view and the fact that he was alive and observing another world.

"How do you go to the bathroom?" Brian asked.

"There's a latrine in the corner. It's just a gutter in the floor that leads to a hole in the wall."

"A hole in the wall?"

"Don't get excited. I already checked. It's shot through with iron bars so you can't escape through it, and even if you could, it looks like there's a three-hundred-foot drop to the courtyard below."

"Where is it?"

"Oh, I put a blanket over it to keep the breeze out."

"Ah I see it, uhm, listen, Anna, I sort of need to—"

"Just go. I'm raising a teenage boy, I've experienced much worse."

Brian relieved himself, zipped up his trousers, and hobbled back to the edge of his bed.

They talked in low tones for a bit until a monk came to bring them more food and water. Brian's hopes were initially raised when the door opened, but he quickly saw that there was no possibility of making a break for it. Bruce Lee couldn't get past the dozen guards waiting outside the chamber armed with axes, stone clubs, and staffs.

That night the chamber got very cold, and Brian shivered under the thin blankets, hardly sleeping at all. Anna seemed to do much better, but perhaps, he thought, she was just more stoical.

Morning brought the sun, a smidgen more warmth, and a knock at the door.

"Keep her talking," Anna whispered.

"What? Who is it?" Brian asked.

"It's the Queen," Anna said.

"How do you know it's her?" Brian replied.

"No one else would have the courtesy to knock. Keep her talking. Make her like you. I don't think she digs me much."

The knocking grew louder. "Come in, it's open," Brian said.

The Witch Queen entered with two burly men carrying crossbows. She was wearing a kind of red sari under a dense fur coat.

Brian saw that she was a strikingly handsome woman in what—on Earth—would be her early forties.

"Ye art awake," she said.

Brian nodded. "That's right, Sherlock, I can see that nothing escapes you," he said.

Anna gave him a black look. "How was Afor, Your Majesty?" she asked sweetly, not wanting the conversation to descend into unpleasantness.

"I do not care for that city, Lady Anna. This, for better or for worse, is my home," the Witch Queen said candidly.

"Sit down," Brian said, getting off his bed and moving next to Anna on hers.

"I thank thee, I shall sit, I am quite tired."

With great economy of movement the Witch Queen crossed the chamber and sat delicately on the edge of Brian's bed.

"Ye art well? We were concerned," the Queen said, looking at him with piercing gray-blue eyes.

"Yes, I'm feeling much better," Brian replied.

She nodded and said nothing.

There was a long silence during which one of the Queen's guards yawned and moved his crossbow from his left to his right hand and everyone else remained motionless.

"So, uh, what can we do for you?" Brian asked to break the spell.

"We seek to harness the magic of the Salmon of Knowledge, so that we may travel to your world," the Queen said.

Brian and Anna were surprised and taken aback at her frankness. Both had assumed that there would be more of a game before she got down to business.

Anna was the first to recover. "Salmon of what? I really don't—"

The Witch Queen raised her hand. "Try not my patience," she said quietly. "We seek thy magic."

Brian shook his head. "Uhm, don't take this the wrong way, but really, uh, there's no such thing as magic," he said.

The Witch Queen smiled. "I have seen it with my own eyes. Twice now. When ye first came and when ye and Lady Anna came together. My own brother has felt some of its power. Do not lie to me, Lord McDonald."

"I'm not lying. That wasn't magic. That was just the application of the laws of physics. A quantum mechanical distortion of space-time."

"Call it what ye will, I have seen it," the Witch Queen said, staring at him intently. Something told her that Brian knew quite a lot about this subject. Interesting. She muttered a sentence in Alkhavan to one of the guards, and a man outside the door replied and ran off down the corridor.

"Thank you for the bread, it's excellent," Anna said.

The Witch Queen nodded, and then after a beat or two she sighed.

"Long day?" Brian asked.

And yes, she was tired. A full day it had taken her to return from Afor. By boat to Balan Port, and then by grueling, *draya*-drawn covered wagon to the city itself.

She wilted a little on the bed.

So, she's as frail as the rest of us, Anna thought.

"Your Majesty, I know that you are very busy, but may I ask you a question?" Anna said in a meek voice.

"Ask."

"Uhm, well, when do we get to be reunited with our families? You said you'd do it. And I'm sure you will, and I really want to see Jamie, soon," said Anna.

"A message has been sent to Aldan. I am assured by

the Lord Protector that the Lords Ui Neill will come here to Balanmanik before the week is out," she said.

"You could let us go to him, Your Majesty," Anna said.

The Witch Queen smiled. "Not while you are our guests here," she said.

Anna was going to get indignant, but she knew that that would be a mistake. Why shatter the pretense of host and hostess? It might be inviting a whole heap of trouble on their heads if the Queen took off her mask and was completely unrestrained by the bounds of fake civility.

"Your English is very good, Your Majesty," she said instead.

The Queen snorted.

"We speak English in the new fashion coming from Aldan. We are a backward country. Our clothes are modeled after the artists in Oralands, our music and poetry are from Aldan, our wooden ships are made in Kafrikilla."

"Oh, I see," Anna said.

"No, you do not see. It was not always thus. Once we were a beacon for this world. Now we are a dying country."

Brian looked at her. "Dying? How so?" he asked.

"Each year the ice wall comes closer to our city. Already it has destroyed our northern towns, the Tomb Road, most of Balanmanik itself."

"How long has this being going on?" Brian asked.

"Centuries," the Witch Queen said. "Last year our former leader, the Lord Protector Dorpa, attempted to secure for us wood and slaves and plunder south in the City of Aldan, but the expedition ended in disaster when the Ui Neills came," the Witch Queen said with disdain.

Brian nodded. "But you didn't agree with that policy, did you?"

"I did not. Even if we moved to Aldan it would do us no good," she said, admiring Brian's perspicacity.

"Because you know that this climate change is going to affect everybody sooner or later. Your country, Aldan, all the countries on this planet. And that's why you want the Salmon, isn't it? So you can escape to Earth," Brian said.

The Witch Queen nodded.

She was beginning to enjoy this conversation. Perhaps this was what it was like for the legendary Twenty-seventh Queen in her talks with Sarpa.

Brian glanced at Anna. She raised her eyebrows in encouragement. They were getting good information out of this little chat. Anna had seen immediately that the Witch Queen was sympathetic toward the good-looking Irishman.

"The Lord Brian is a great scientist on our world," Anna said.

The Witch Queen regarded her icily. Anna winked at Brian, prompting him to speak again.

"Where did you hear about the Salmon in the first place?" Brian asked quickly.

The Witch Queen hesitated but then, after a moment's internal debate, decided to tell him. "The Vancha, the Old Ones left . . . certain . . . artifacts," was all she was willing to say.

She would not tell them about the Machine, which had summoned the Ui Neill, or the secret that lay beyond the glacier at the Tomb of the Ice Gods.

"And what do you know about the Old Ones, exactly, if you don't mind me asking?"

"The legends are many and diverse. They do not agree."

"Legends never do," Anna said.

"What's the gist?" Brian asked.

It seemed the Witch Queen didn't understand the word.

"What are the most credible stories, Your Majesty?" Anna asked.

The Queen looked embarrassed, as if what she was going to say was too fantastic even for travelers between the stars.

"They were beings of many limbs and no hands. Many eyes and no mouth. They neither ate food nor slept," she said at last.

"Sounds a bit like an octopus with insomnia," Anna suggested cheerfully.

"What else?" Brian asked.

"Some stories say that the reason they have not visited us in thousands of years is that they have abandoned their bodies completely. They travel from world to world by thought alone."

Brian nodded. "I guess that's possible. Certainly explains why they haven't used their wormhole technology for millennia. But it doesn't explain why they've abandoned you. If they could just think themselves to Earth or Altair, they could be here in a second."

"What dost thou say?" the Queen asked.

"Well, I don't know, but I think its more likely that these Old Ones, the Vancha, went extinct centuries ago. If you look at the history of Earth, ninety-five percent of the species that ever existed have gone extinct. Probably the same story throughout the galaxy."

"Thou dost not believe that they will ever come back to us?" the Queen asked, sounding a little shocked.

Brian shook his head. "No. I really don't. Sorry."

The Witch Queen pursed her lips. "Ye art a liar! It was said that the Ui Neill would not return. And yet they art here. Thou art here," she shouted.

"I'm only venturing an opinion," Brian said.

Before the Witch Queen could explode there was a knock at the cell door.

"*Aaka,*" the Queen said angrily.

A monk opened the door and presented the Witch

Queen with a small felt bag. She dismissed him with a wave and gave the bag to Brian.

He opened it and poured the contents onto his hand.

He knew immediately what it was.

A Salmon of Knowledge, but horribly twisted, burned, and weathered by the elements.

The Witch Queen watched his face.

"Ye knowest what this is?" she said.

Anna coughed. Brian shook his head warily.

The Witch Queen smiled. "Do not test me. Thou knowest."

"I'm not testing you. I really don't know. If you tell me what you know about it, maybe I could help you."

"Ah, Lord Brian, I can tell that ye art wise. But perhaps thy knowledge does not extend to our world," the Queen said with moderate cunning.

"Well, I wouldn't go that far," Brian said, his ego hurt. "Where did you get this thing?" he asked.

"This Salmon of Knowledge has been in the possession of the Black Monks for decades. It is the same as the famous one of the Ui Neills, save that their machine worked and ours is broken."

"Hmmm," Brian said.

"Can this one be mended?" the Witch Queen asked greedily.

"Not a chance," Brian said far too fast.

Anna shook her head. *Don't give her anything so definitive,* she thought.

The Witch Queen pursed her lips. "Thou liest."

"No, I don't. This thing is kaput," Brian said sadly. "Kaput for quite some time, by the looks of it."

"Pray over it, use thy magic, thy power. If ye mend it, we shall have no need of thy Salmon. Thee and thy friends may go as they please. I give thee my word. I shall bind my brother to his. Pray on it, use thy wiles."

"Yeah, maybe we *can* fix it," Anna said and looked at Brian significantly.

Unfortunately he didn't pick up on the hint. "Praying? Nah, that's what I was saying earlier. See, it's not just a difference in names. Magic versus science. There is no magic. Good job too. You want to live in a world where voodoo curses really work? That's the problem with Harry Potter. A whole generation of kids out there who want to be magicians not engineers. No, no, no, this device works by science not by magic. You need the science of the Old Ones to fix it. It's beyond me."

The Queen looked at him for a moment and then violently snatched the remains of the Salmon out of Brian's hands.

"If ye cannot help us, then I will have thee—" She stopped herself just in time.

Outside the wind howled, and the snow began again.

"Look," Brian began with a conciliatory smile, "Earth's not so great either. It's messed up. Pollution's increasing, the ozone hole's growing. And those are only the minor problems. You know, go to Earth, wait a billion years, and our sun is going to die too. It's the natural life cycle of a star. And don't say you'll go to a new planet with a new sun. All the suns are going to die eventually. Eventually all the stars in the universe are going to go out. It's called the Second Law of Thermodynamics. There will be nothing to record the fact that humans, whales, Martians, ever existed. No Shakespeare, no Mozart, no nothing. Don't you see? You know why I couldn't finish my PhD? Because I didn't see any point. From nothing to nothing with nothing in between. Do you understand? Whatever temple we build, whatever we write or discover, it's going to be for nothing. Forget about going to Earth. Just accept that everywhere's doomed. Best thing for ya."

Anna and the Queen were staring at him. Anna knew he'd said far too much.

The Queen stood. Anna stood too out of respect.

"We will continue this conversation another time. Thy accommodations are satisfactory?"

"Excellent, thank you, Your Majesty. But we could do with some air. A walk outside perhaps?" Anna asked.

The Queen nodded. "Perhaps . . . Until the morrow then," she said.

The guards opened the door, and the Queen and her crossbow men walked out.

When she was gone, Anna and Brian let out a sigh of relief.

Anna almost collapsed onto the bed.

"I can feel your look. Stop looking at me," Brian said. "You think I should have egged her on more."

"I didn't say anything," Anna muttered.

"No, you don't have to. I screwed up. I know it."

Anna nodded but said nothing.

Brian didn't yet realize what the stakes were. He didn't understand what type of person the Witch Queen was. She did. She had met the type before in her law firm back in New York. The Queen was like a tort attorney sniffing around a road accident. She was like an assistant district attorney on a double homicide. She was like a judge about to bang her gavel.

Brian was only five years younger than Anna was, but he'd never been much out of the ivory tower. He still didn't understand the seriousness of the situation facing them. It was obvious what the Witch Queen wanted. She wanted to escape from her dead world. She wanted the Salmon of Knowledge. That and that alone was the only thing that mattered to her. Brian and Anna were completely expendable. And if they didn't please her somehow, then they were going to die.

Chapter VIII
THE FLEET

THE ORALANDS FLEET stank like the perfume floor of Macy's on the day after Valentine's. The smell a heady mix of spice boats, trawlers, unwashed sailors and civilians.

To avoid Alkhavan, spies the refitted *Proud Star* had departed in the middle of the night without full provisions or even a complete crew. Lorca's brother and mother had missed the tide, and his father, Prince Lanar, had only just gotten on board by the skin of his teeth.

Shorthanded, it had taken them a little longer than it should have, but now, thankfully, they were here at last.

Here was a rendezvous spot in midocean, a day's sail from the Oralands city of Carolla.

It was dusk, and night was falling fast, but Jamie could see that the massive Red Star fleet was made up of sailboats, rafts, and trading junks filled with merchandise from all over the southern seas. Hundreds of vessels, including several huge slab-sided barges that were the king's floating palaces.

The ships were packed with people. Altairians of all colors, countries, creeds. There was also, Jamie noted, a heavy military presence. White-clad members of the Royal Guard mixed with green-shirted Oralands soldiers and marines.

The *Proud Star* had put in at a kind of floating harbor, and already a great fuss was being made at the arrival of Prince Lorca. Trumpets were blowing, drums beating, and a few assembled dignitaries had begun to cheer. With a feeling of jealousy and disgust, Jamie watched Wishaway and Lorca disembark. He knew these were cheap emotions, but he couldn't help himself.

Prince Lanar, Lorca's father, had arranged the whole thing. He wanted a big display because he knew that the plan was a good one. If all went well, Lorca would sail to Alkhava, battle the Witch Queen, take Balanmanik, save the life of one of the immortal Ui Neills, and then return to Oralands in triumph, to formalize his marriage to the only daughter of the Council president of Aldan. It would be spectacular. And the implication for the people would be obvious. If Prince Lanar's last and least prom-ising son could do these amazing things, what could the prince himself do when he became king . . .

Jamie, however, was oblivious to the politics and was quite irritated by the sight of men in elaborate costumes bowing to Wishaway and the young prince.

"Lord Ui Neill, your *fourga* is ready!" Admiral Farar shouted to Jamie from the poop deck.

"OK, I'm coming!" Jamie replied.

Jamie and Ramsay disembarked from the ship and sat down in the *fourga*, which turned out to be an ornate, gilded longboat pulled by men chained to the oars.

"Whew, it's hot here isn't it?" Ramsay said, settling down next to his friend.

Oralands was on Altair's equator, and it was the warmest place Jamie had been to on the planet, but it wasn't exactly hot, nor even humid. For everyone but an Irishman it could be described as comfortable.

Certainly not a patch on New York City in July.

"We should have brought a camera," Jamie said to Ramsay. "Next time we come here, please, let's bring a camera. We're like those poor saps who see UFOs and Bigfoot and no one believes them."

"Video camera would be better."

Yeah they'd need a video to get everything. The fleet wasn't so much a collection of ships as an entire floating city. Thousands of individuals were crammed into narrow rafts, boats, canoes: selling food, jewelry, clothes. Everywhere they could hear the tinkling of odd musical instruments, the crying of hawkers, loud haggling at stalls, the pleading of beggars, the wailing of religious preachers, and the yelling of soldiers and marines.

One thing even a video camera couldn't capture were the smells. The uneasy perfume of roasting meat, rotting fruit, cooking *ranta*, the guano of thousands of small animals for sale in small cages, and a vile stench from the sea, which of course was one big open sewer.

They were rowed closer to a huge rectangular, floating barge or palace. It was domed and ornate and covered with jewels that glittered like stars. Even in the dusk Jamie could tell that it bore a striking resemblance to the Taj Mahal. Had one of the Ui Neills brought a picture of that Indian mausoleum to Altair? It seemed unlikely. Perhaps it was just another example of the convergent evolution Ramsay sometimes spoke about.

They made their way among dinghies, rafts, and rowboats. The sounds of musical instruments and revelry drifting across the water grew louder.

They were met by an elaborately costumed servant, greeted in a foreign tongue, and led inside. There was a small antechamber filled with soldiers, and at the end of it double doors that led into a huge central ballroom. The two boys walked in. Crystal oil lamps provided a glittering illumination of a large Byzantine room filled with more than a hundred people. It was ornamented with precious stones, tapestries, and expensive-looking displays of carved wood, iron, and gold. (All were extremely rare commodities on Altair.) A short older man (apparently the king himself) was sitting at the head of the chamber at a long table with a few notables, while his other guests were seated at rather basic-looking benches perpendicular to the throne.

Incense was pouring from two enormous burners, and a gang of child musicians was playing assorted horns and flutes in a band pit at the far end of the hall.

Obviously this meal or banquet had been going on for several hours, because even with a kind of forced bonhomie most of the guests had a weary, intoxicated look—though not as weary as the slaves who were still bringing tray after tray of exotic food and drink.

The room was a heady and disorientating place, but it was the floor that disturbed Jamie the most. A tapestry hanging from the ceiling revealed in pictorial and gruesome detail the information that the white "porcelain" floor was made from the pounded skulls of the king's enemies. Obviously such a delicate material would need constant repair, but fortunately it appeared that enemies of the king could always be found.

"Did you see that tap—" Ramsay whispered.

"Yeah, I did."

Jamie spotted Lorca and Wishaway sitting next to Prince Lanar and the king.

He waved, but they didn't see him.

"This way," someone said in English, and he and

Ramsay were led to chairs at the far end of the king's table. Food and a purple drink were placed in front of them. Their near neighbors bowed briefly but then immediately turned their rapt gazes back to the king in the middle of the dais.

"They behead them and boil off the bones and—" Ramsay began.

"I saw it," Jamie interrupted.

"What do you think this food is?" Ramsay asked.

Jamie tried to hazard a guess, but the king shouted something, and the children playing the odd, discordant music suddenly increased the volume by a factor of three.

"The food?" Ramsay yelled.

It looked to be various kinds of small animals, cooked in viscous, brightly colored sauces. Jamie sampled a piece of a bony animal, but it tasted sour and unpleasant to his Earth palate.

"It's not great!" Ramsay yelled. "But the purple stuff is OK!"

Jamie sampled some of the drink, which was like lemonade mixed with wine. It was horrible, but the others seemed to like it or pretend to like it.

In fact the whole room had an air of pretense. Almost everyone was wearing costumes. Some had come dressed as animals, others in elaborate gowns, and (presumably in imitation of the Ui Neills) many were dressed in faux

Elizabethan clothes, with ruff collars, tight-fitting jackets, and pantaloons. All the women and men were heavily weighed down with jewelry and large chains.

The king was leaning across the table to question Lorca and Wishaway, and Jamie saw that he was a stout, red-bearded man in a white gilded shirt that was stained with food and drink. He was the only person in the whole of Altair that Jamie could have described as obese. His ruddy skin and thick nose might almost have allowed him to pass for human. He was clearly intoxicated, but Lorca and Prince Lanar were doing their best to patiently explain the situation to him.

After a few minutes Jamie began to feel uncomfortable. He was sweating, and his head ached. "Are you hot?" Ramsay asked, but it wasn't the heat. It was the whole gig. The purple drink, the music, the skull floor, the incense, the crowd of strange people, and the rocking motion of the floating palace—all of it conspiring to make him feel quite ill.

"I think I'm going to have to go back to the ship," Jamie muttered.

"Get some food in ya, try some of this," Ramsay said, tucking into his fourth portion of what looked like deep-fried guinea pig.

Before Jamie could reply the king suddenly stood. "And where is this new Ui Neill from Earth?" he boomed in English. The banqueting hall fell quiet. Lorca put his head in his hands. This was all supposed to be kept as secret as possible. Lorca's father, Prince Lanar, touched the king's arm and tried to make him sit down again. But he was not to be dissuaded.

"I said, where is this Ui Neill of which ye spake?" the king demanded.

"Get up and bow, Jamie," Ramsay whispered to his friend.

Reluctantly Jamie got to his feet. He was extremely nervous. The room was now so silent he could hear people rowing past outside.

"Thou? Thou art the Ui Neill?" the king asked, looking at him.

Jamie nodded, but his throat was so dry he couldn't say anything.

"The books tell us that the Ui Neill are giants. Giants. I have seen bigger things than thee in my privy pot!" the king yelled and burst into riotous laughter.

Of course everyone else began to laugh too.

"Eh, chamberlain? My privy pot!" the king yelled again, and thumped the table.

When the laughter at last subsided, the king recollected himself and made the smallest of bows in Jamie's direction.

"Thou art welcome to the waters of Oralands and to

the presence of King Laman the Twentieth, Lord Ui Neill. Thy needs are our needs and thy presence honors us. Thou art a friend to my son and grandson, and that is recommendation enough. Welcome," the king said. He sat down again and proceeded to drain almost an entire flagon of the purple wine.

Jamie refound his seat, his head spinning.

Food.

Music.

Dancing.

The banquet dragged on. The king, Lorca, Prince Lanar, and a thin, yellow-haired little man with a gold chain around his neck were now all in a heated discussion about something. Lorca was leaning back in his chair and looking very pleased.

"I got to get out of here, my brain's twirling like a merry-go-round," Jamie said.

Ramsay shook his head. "Protocol, mate. You have to stay until the king leaves. Eat more of that rat on a stick, it's quite good."

Just as Jamie was getting to his feet, the king banged the table, startling the crowd and musicians into another worried silence.

"No, my lord chamberlain, no chamberlain, one does not get to be king by being cautious," Laman the Twentieth barked in English, obviously for their benefit.

There was a scattered applause from the exhausted guests.

"No, you get to be king by being born ahead of your brother," Ramsay whispered.

Jamie kicked him under the table. He didn't want Ramsay to become part of that skull floor too.

"What sayest ye, Lord Ui Neill?" the king boomed, as if Jamie had somehow been part of their whole conversation.

Jamie stood. He knew he had to be careful not to say too much in case spies were listening. But he also had to flatter the king and do his best to promise that it would be in his interest to help him.

"Uhm, Your Majesty, I assume that you have been apprised of the events that have led us here tonight. We are honored to be at your table and to be in your august presence. And I would be forever grateful if you would help me reunite my family, er, thank you," Jamie said and sat down.

The king appeared to think for a moment, but Jamie could see that he had already made up his mind.

"You *will* have your squadron, my boy. Take care of her, I have but one other," the king said to Lorca in a lower voice, but still audible to everyone in the room.

He drank another glass of wine, pushed his chair back from the table, and after a time, appeared to be singing gently to himself.

Jamie noticed Wishaway excuse herself, bow to the royal personages, and slip out a side door.

Wait a minute, if she can split, I can split, he thought.

"Back in a tick," Jamie said to Ramsay. He did a clumsy bow and followed Wishaway outside.

She was standing at the rail that went around the barge, looking out across the pitch-black sea to the fleet beyond.

There were dozens of smaller boats on the water, and even though it was late, smoke burned from hundreds of cooking fires, sending a pungent aroma into the still night air. Jamie walked to Wishaway and stood next to her.

"Hi," he said. Wishaway nodded. They had hardly talked on the voyage from Aldan. They had barely exchanged more than a few sentences since she had told him that she was married to Lorca. But then what was there to say? Jamie hadn't shared his feelings of disappointment, betrayal, loss. He hadn't needed to. She knew, and he knew that she knew.

They heard melancholy chanting from one boat and saw a body being heaved over the side.

"It's very different here than in Aldan," Jamie said at last.

"Yes," Wishaway agreed. She put her hand on the safety rail. Jamie nudged his left hand a little closer to hers.

"Ramsay thinks it's hot. Do you find it hot?" Wishaway shook her head. "No, me neither," Jamie said.

Wishaway cleared her throat and stole a glance at him.

"Jamie, I'm glad you came out . . . I . . . I want to tell you something," she said.

"OK," Jamie said, looking at her.

"I married Lorca because I did not think that you would return," she said simply.

Her blue eyes were filled with sadness, visible even in the gathering dark.

"That's OK. Neither did I," Jamie said.

She bowed at this conciliation.

The silence became heavy.

"So there's no way out then. You're definitely married?" Jamie said at last.

"Yes . . . All but a few formalities in both of our home cities. Those were obviously postponed because of the Alkhavan attack."

"What? Say that again."

"The wedding ceremony is finished. All but the formalities."

Jamie's eyes sparkled with hope. "Are you kidding me? What formalities? So you're not really married quite yet? Is that why you slept in separate cabins on the *Proud Star*?"

Wishaway shook her head. "I am married. We await a formal confirmation, that is all."

"What does that mean exactly?"

"In Aldan all marriages must be confirmed in Council before a daughter of that city can marry a foreigner, and here in Oralands, before a royal prince may wed, the king's approval must be sought and given."

Jamie's heart almost leaped out of his chest.

"So technically speaking you're not actually, totally, married yet then are you?"

Wishaway smiled sadly. "You misunderstand. I *am* married, Lord Ui Neill. It is a mere legal procedure that the approvals be given. It has not yet been given in Aldan. However, Oralands law will be followed soon. Lorca tells me that his grandfather will sign the proclamation tonight giving a royal approval to our wedlock."

But Jamie's brain had seen the opportunity and he was running with it.

"Yeah, you keep saying you're married, but being nit-picky, you're not actually totally done yet are you? Even after tonight you won't be really, really wed until you get back to Aldan and present yourselves at the City Council and they give you the OK too. Right?"

"Well I suppose . . ."

"I knew it," Jamie said excitedly. "So there is a way out."

Wishaway was finding this less charming by the minute. "No," she said sternly. "There is no way out. I am married to Lorca. The last 'technical' detail, as you call it, will be accomplished when we get back to Aldan."

"Do you want to be married to Lorca?" Jamie asked.

"Of course. I love him," Wishaway said.

Jamie touched her on the shoulders and turned her to face him. "I don't think that's true," Jamie said.

Wishaway sighed impatiently. "It is true, Jamie. And it is done. I am wed. In the eyes of my father, in the eyes of the state, it is over."

But Jamie was not to be silenced quite yet. "You say you didn't have time after the tower fell in Aldan? But when we came back with us you had plenty of time to present yourself before the Council. It would have been the easiest thing in the world for you to have taken your father aside and asked him to have the wedding formally declared to the Council. Piece of cake. But you didn't—"

"Stop it, Jamie," Wishaway interrupted.

"No, I won't. You didn't get the marriage formalized because you couldn't. You couldn't because you didn't want it to be formalized. See, I think you don't love Lorca, I think—"

"Stop it. Stop it. Stop it!" Wishaway exclaimed, and almost slapped him across the face.

"Let me finish—" Jamie barked furiously.

"No!" Wishaway yelled. One of the guards patrolling

the deck looked at her briefly before moving on. "No. No. No," Wishaway continued in an exhausted whisper.

Jamie took a deep breath. He could see that she was tearing up. He knew he'd gone too far and he was sorry for it.

"Wishaway, look, I apologize, I only wanted to—"

"Stop it. It is finished, Lord Ui Neill. Never speak of this to me again. If you are unable to restrain yourself on this topic, then simply do not speak to me at all," Wishaway said, tears now running freely down her cheeks.

Jamie was shocked into silence. He thought she was going to storm off, but she didn't. She stood there, looking at the water, hardly noticing the junks, sampans, and rowboats ferrying people, cargo, and animals among the bigger boats.

"Dost thou understand, Lord Ui Neill?" Wishaway asked quietly.

Jamie nodded.

She nodded back and then, exhausted by the conversation, she sat down, took off her shoes, and put her feet in the water. Jamie watched her for a bit.

"How's the water on your toes?" Jamie wondered.

"It is cool," she said.

He sat next to her and removed his shoes too. They did nothing but look at the boats for a while, but then an enterprising child in a crude canoe paddled up to them—a girl about seven or eight years old. She smiled and put her hands out in a begging gesture. Jamie grinned, suspecting that it took a great deal of courage to ask for help from two strangers on a royal barge filled with guards and soldiers. He took off his watch, passed it to her. "Sell it," he said.

The girl didn't understand the words or what she'd been given but happily accepted the gift, bowed, and paddled off into the darkness. Wishaway turned and briefly looked at him. This time he really didn't need to say it: *You're marrying into all this? You want to live here, a privileged royal princess, while these people struggle daily to survive? That's not you, Wishaway. That's not the Wishaway I know.*

Their eyes met, and she quickly cast her gaze back to the water. "Lorca will change all this when he comes into his majority," she said.

"Will he?" Jamie asked.

"We have had many discussions. Aldan is a model for the other countries of Altair. It is these people's foolish superstitions that are holding them back," Wishaway said defensively.

"Foolish superstitions? Not the tyrannical power of a royal house?"

Wishaway shook her head and fought back another bout of the waterworks.

Jamie could tell that she was deeply hurt. "I'm sorry," he said.

He reached out for her hand. "Do not touch me," she snapped.

"Wishaway, come on I—" Jamie tried.

"Do not touch me, Lord Ui Neill," she insisted.

He felt Wishaway's pendant against his chest, and for a moment he thought about taking it off and giving it back to her. He shook his head. That would be shabby.

He heard footsteps and turned. Ramsay and Lorca.

"Hey, are you crying?" Ramsay said.

Jamie and Wishaway got to their feet. "It's all the cooking smoke out here, making my eyes water," Jamie said quickly.

"Well, forget that. We are sorted, me old mate. Lorca came through for us big-time, big-time," Ramsay said excitedly.

"Yeah?" he said, staring into his friend's grinning face.

"It is indeed done, Lord Jamie," Lorca said formally.

Jamie didn't look at him. He couldn't. Not yet. Not now.

"The fleet is ours. On the morrow we will go to Alkhava," Lorca said.

Jamie nodded. Behind Lorca the moonlight was making prisms of the blue-green water, shifting it down the spectrum in a deep maroon. "What?" Jamie said in a faraway voice.

"The fleet is ready, we will be provisioned and armored by morning, Lord Ui Neill. That is, if you still wish to go."

"Oh yeah, absolutely. Of course," Jamie said. "Let's go get them."

"We will sleep on the *Proud Star*," Lorca said, and offered Wishaway his arm.

"Good night," Wishaway said to Jamie and Ramsay.

"Night," Jamie managed.

He watched them walk along the deck. Ramsay grinned and slapped Jamie hard on the back. "Hey, it's all going be great. Big fight. Big fun," Ramsay said.

Jamie turned sharply and pushed the big Irishman violently away from him.

"Idiot," Jamie seethed.

"What's your problem, mate?" Ramsay said.

"My problem? Are you drunk? How can you be so glib? My mom and your brother are still hostages. Anything could be happening to them. This isn't a big joke, this is serious."

Jamie's eyes were blazing. Ramsay knew he wanted to have an argument. The tension had been building for days. But Ramsay didn't want to fight.

"Sorry," Ramsay said and stepped back to give him space.

Jamie sighed. He shook his head and sat down heavily

on the deck. He picked up Wishaway's soft felt slippers, which would have been big on a foot-crushed Ming emperor's daughter.

"What's that you've got?" Ramsay asked.

"Wishaway's shoes."

"She forget them?"

"Yeah."

Ramsay turned to call out to them, but a guard opened the door and they watched Lorca and Wishaway, prince and princess, reenter the overwhelming banqueting hall, the music still playing, Laman the Twentieth still bellowing, and Wishaway's bare feet treading delicately on the crushed and flattened skulls of the king's enemies.

❁　❁　❁

They were in the middle of a silly argument. Even at the worst of times Anna was a fairly easygoing person, as long you didn't do anything foolish like mess with her son or criticize her cooking.

But Brian was another story. He'd been a virtual recluse at MIT, and now that he had left that university and been revoked of his J1 visa, forcibly relocated to rainy Ulster, and removed from all human companionship save his misanthropic father and a couple of weirdo fourteen-year-old wannabe musicians, his social skills had not improved to any significant degree.

The argument was about films. Although he claimed

otherwise (especially in front of Ramsay), Brian was in fact a supernerd. Largely passionless about everything else in his life, he was fascinated by the movies, especially those involving technology or science. Anna liked films too, but she had many friends and a diversity of interests. Brian spent hours e-mailing the C++ and UNIX blogs about why *Star Wars: Revenge of the Sith* was inferior to *Star Trek II: The Wrath of Khan.* In Cambridge, he had once taken a date to an all-night marathon of the original five *Planet of the Apes* movies (long held to be the science fiction equivalent of the *Ring Cycle*). The date had walked out during either *Escape from the Planet of the Apes* or *Return to Planet of the Apes*—he couldn't quite remember. Even the stoic Charlton Heston would have been pressed to last that long.

This particular debate in the odd surroundings of a prison cell on the planet Altair was about the film *Sleepless in Seattle.*

"A mawkish, lifeless manipulation of the emotions, lacking grace, direction, story, or charm, and because it's a rip-off of a sentimental Cary Grant movie, its even inferior to the risible *You've Got Mail*, and that was a bad movie."

"I liked it. I thought it was funny and sweet. And it had a good ending. You have to be a pretty cold-blooded individual not to be a little moved by *Sleepless.*"

"Mindless drek for mindless dreks."

Anna bristled. "Can you name a film you like that doesn't have the word *Star* or *Space* in it?"

"*Blade Runner.*"

"You've proven my point."

Anna didn't know what was worse. Being imprisoned by sadistic bullies a hundred light-years from Earth or being imprisoned by sadistic bullies, a hundred light-years from Earth, with *him*.

There was a period of silence during which Anna reflected on life, her incarceration, and the brave prison memoirs she had read by Nelson Mandela and former Beirut hostage Brian Keenan. Brian McDonald reflected on the well-known uncanny ratio of even numbers and *Star Trek* films, wondering why the odd-numbered ones always sucked while two, four, six, and eight were great. The inverse was true for James Bonds—there the even-numbered actors in the role fared very badly.

Anna could take the quiet no longer, but they had already done movies, television, childhoods, and they had played I Spy and Twenty Questions.

"Books," Anna said at last.

"What books?"

"Favorite books."

"Well my favorite is the *Mac 2 Manual*. Oh that's a classic. Macs are so great. Don't you think? How can anyone love a PC?" Brian said.

"Good grief. Don't you read novels?"

"Novels?" Brian asked, as if the word confused him.

"*Pride and Prejudice, Jane Eyre*, you know?"

"What's the point? They take a long time and you don't learn anything from them, they're all made up."

"I don't even know how to begin to answer that. You don't read novels? OK, forget that topic. Travel? Tell me about Boston," Anna said, getting a little desperate now. For if they didn't talk about something the silence was going to become unbearable again.

Brian frowned. "Boston. Uh, well it's a nice enough place. MOFA is nice, and the North Shore I like. Better than the snooty Cape anyway. But Cambridge really depresses me. Every year there's a new crop of twenty-year-old geniuses, you know? I'm going to be thirty-one in August. I just feel past it when I'm there now."

Anna laughed. "You feel past it. Ha. I'm thirty-five and everyone in Ireland treats me like I'm sixty."

Brian was taken aback. "You're only thirty-five?"

"Well, you're a charmer. What are you saying? I look older?"

"No, you look fabulous. I just, uhm, well, you must have had Jamie when you were pretty young," Brian said.

Anna sighed. "Junior year of college. I was supposed to go to France with Mike, it was going to be this big thing, but then Jamie came along. You know how it is . . ."

Brian nodded with sympathy.

"Did you finish college?"

She shook her head sadly. "I never did . . . But don't get me wrong, I wouldn't trade Jamie for any number of degrees."

"I've got more degrees than a protractor; it doesn't mean a thing."

Anna nodded. "If it's not a touchy subject, how come you never finished your PhD? You said it was cosmic despair, but there must be something more to it than that," she asked.

Brian laughed. "I don't know. I got fed up with the whole business. And like I say, Cambridge isn't a good place to develop an inferiority complex, with so many brilliant Harvard and MIT grads milling about. I just didn't think I was getting anywhere, and every year there were new faces coming along younger than me, working harder than me, and better than me," Brian said in a monotone.

"What was your topic?"

His face brightened. "Electrical applications of superconductors. At room temperature of course," Brian said.

"Of course," Anna said, but she had no idea what he was talking about.

Before this détente could continue there was a knock at the door.

"The Queen," Brian and Anna said together.

"Call her 'Your Majesty' or 'Your Royal Highness.' Queens like that," Anna whispered.

"How do you know?" Brian asked.

"From novels," Anna said pointedly.

Brian grinned.

"And we really should stand until she chooses to sit down. Queens like that too. I was wondering why she was so ticked off yesterday. Think that was it, us not being respectful or something?" Anna said.

The Queen entered with her guards. She was wearing a somber brown cloak that was flaked with snow. She had obviously been outside.

"Pleasant trip to the battlements, Your Highness?" Anna asked.

The Queen looked at her with a jaundiced eye. Anna frowned at herself for showing off.

"Nice snow gown," Brian added.

"The peasants say that in Balanmanik even Death himself doesn't go out without his hat and coat," the Witch Queen intoned.

Anna broke into a smile. "Thou art humorous," Anna said.

"Yeah, have a seat, Your Maj, that was a good one," Brian said.

The Queen shook her head. "My visit today is brief," she said with mock sadness.

"OK," Brian replied.

"I have something to tell thee, but first I have a question," the Witch Queen said.

"Fire away, Queenie," Brian said.

"Who is this Harry Potter of which ye did speak in our last conversation?" she asked.

"What?"

"Ye didst spake of a Harry Potter well versed in magic. Does he accompany the Lords Ramsay and Ui Neill?"

"Uhh. No. He doesn't," Brian said. "Harry couldn't make it. He was doing *Equus* nude in the West End, probably in some Indie flick now about carnival freaks in the Deep South."

The Queen nodded, satisfied. "I trust that ye doth speak the truth," she insisted.

"Ye trust right we doth speaketh the trutheth," Brian replied.

"Good . . . Well then, all are accounted for. Ye shalt be pleased to know that Lord Ramsay and Lord Ui Neill, are, as we converse, on their way to Balanmanik."

"Are they safe?" Anna asked.

"They are well protected, but not perhaps as well concealed as they believe," the Queen said with a smirk.

Anna could feel the malice in the Queen's face and did not reply.

"Well, I've something to tell you: This cell is too much

for us. We're getting on each other's nerves. We want to take a walk outside. You said the other day that you would let us exercise outside. Even at Guantánamo they let them walk outside. It's in the bloody Geneva Convention," Brian said.

The Queen blanched. "Methinks ye doth overreach thyself, Lord Brian, considering thy position and my position," she said.

And now even Brian picked up on her foul mood. It annoyed him.

"Well, we're not going to be together long are we? Obviously the boys are coming to get us," he said.

"They come," she agreed. "Whether they get thee or not will be my prerogative."

"Of course. What's your big plan? Wee swap? Us for the Salmon, is that how it's going to go?" he said boldly.

The Witch Queen was bored with the interview. She signaled the guard to open the cell door.

"The Lord Ui Neill knows what I seek. He will bring it to me in person. If he is tardy then I will relish the opportunity to kill thee, Lord Brian, in such a dreadful way that it will concentrate his mind fully on the fate awaiting his mother . . . Good day."

The Queen got up and exited with her guards.

When the cell door closed Brian grinned. "Well, that went well," he said.

"Didn't it though," Anna agreed, forcing a half smile onto her deeply troubled face.

*   *   *

It was their second full day on the ocean, and Jamie was looking at the strange bird that had been following them all the way from Carolla.

Jamie had no clue what it was.

Rantas apparently never got so big or strayed so far from land. There were no other large lizards or flying creatures that Wishaway had told him about on Altair, so there was no other obvious solution: It had to be a bird. The problem of course was that there were no birds on Altair. Could some crazy seagull or albatross have slipped through the wormhole from Islandmagee to the Sacred Isle?

Unlikely, and this thing was all-black. Even weirder, from time to time it almost looked as if there might be a person riding on top of it.

He was just going to ask Ramsay if he could rustle up an octoscope when Lorca came toward him along the side rail of the *Proud Star*.

Jamie was in no mood for conversation. Not with anyone, certainly not with the person who had effectively stolen his girl. And actually it had disturbed him from the beginning that Lorca had wanted to help him so badly. What did he have to gain from all of this? He appeared the big man in front of Wishaway? He trumped his brothers in the succession stakes? He showed the Lord Ui Neill who the real royal was around here?

Jamie couldn't help but be a little cynical about the prince's motives. He watched the black bird dip beyond the horizon. He knew it would be back again in an hour or two.

Lorca coughed. Jamie pretended not to hear and looked out at the seven magnificent vessels of the king's Red Star fleet arranged in a line along the horizon. They resembled a cross between Armada-era cruisers and nineteenth-century clipper ships. Doubtless the rules and limits of naval engineering were similar on both Earth and Altair.

Lorca coughed again. Jamie turned and faced the young prince.

"Yes?" Jamie said with deep annoyance. "Your ship is huge. Isn't there anywhere else on this vessel you can stand except next to me?"

Lorca's face reddened. "I am sorry to disturb ye, Lord Ui Neill, but I wished to tell ye some things," he said simply.

"Tell away," Jamie said.

"Tomorrow when we land at Balan I will be in command of the fleet and the army. It is almost certain that there will be a battle."

"Yeah, I know."

"I wish to warn thee, Lord Ui Neill. My father and my grandfather, the king, they, they—"

"They what?" Jamie muttered, irritated by this foolishness.

"They fear thee, Lord Ui Neill, " Lorca said.

"Do they indeed?" Jamie said, mildly interested.

"They fear thy power to leap between worlds."

"I see," Jamie replied. "They want it? Thry want the Salmon for themselves?"

"I do not know," Lorca said.

"Then why are you telling me this?" he asked.

"In the heat of battle, if it comes to that, I wish thee to beware of any accident that may befall thee, *from our side*," Lorca said.

Jamie nodded slowly. "Ahh. I get it. For all you know some of the officers might have been given instructions to bump me off in the middle of the fight," Jamie said.

Lorca nodded. "I have no proof, but I have suspicions," he said.

"Well, thanks for the heads-up," Jamie said, and turned away. He looked deliberately out to sea, but he knew that Lorca, infuriatingly, was still standing there.

"Is there something else?" Jamie asked a little rudely.

"As I say, there may be a battle, Lord Ui Neill. Things may not go as planned . . ." Lorca began.

"Yes, I know."

"In the event that things go against us or I am killed, I wish you to have this," Lorca said, giving Jamie a rolled-up piece of vellum.

"What is it?"

"The Oralands intelligence network is among the best in the world. We have compiled a map of Balanmanik and the eastern portion of Alkhava. In the event of disaster, there are several ways to the coast. Our ships will cruise the bays between Casana and Tralia for one week following our landing. If thou art able to make it to the ships, please take care of Wishaway. Instruct the captain in my name to take you to Aldan, not to Oralands; without my influence thy position there would be perilous."

Jamie examined the map for a moment. He traced his finger along the line of the huge glacier that was swallowing up Alkhava. How terrible it must be to be confronted with that thing every day. That was one battle that the Alkhavans would never win.

Jamie rolled up the map and bowed in gratitude to Lorca.

"Thou hast understood?" Lorca asked.

"In the event of trouble, head south, get a ship to Aldan."

Lorca nodded with relief. Jamie looked into his honest, handsome face. His irritation was gone. Lorca was a decent-enough fellow. In fact he was more than that. "You're a good man, Lorca," Jamie said.

And indeed this *man*, who was to command an army in the morning, was still really a child himself. On his next birthday he would be seventeen in Altairian years. And although the year was longer here, on Earth Lorca wouldn't be allowed to vote, to drink, or even to enlist in the army. And Lorca had had a hard life too. You had to grow up fast in that court with that king. They were both survivors in a way.

Jamie offered Lorca his hand. "Yeah, you're a good man and I know you'll make Wishaway a good husband," he said sincerely.

"I appreciate that very much, Lord Ui Neill, uh . . . Jamie," Lorca said, able to lose some of his formality now. They shook hands for a full thirty seconds.

"I must attend to my duties," Lorca said, touched.

"Until tomorrow then," Jamie said.

Lorca nodded. "Until tomorrow."

Chapter IV
THE AMBUSH

ARAK KRAMA WALKED through the ice-filled courtyard with an odd sensation of elation and nervousness. He'd heard a rumor from his adjutant that this moment was going to be the culmination of all his wildest hopes and ambitions. Of course it might just be that—a rumor, and certainly only twice before in the history of Alkhava had someone without noble rank been appointed to the rank of Protector. He had been born a peasant and, even worse, the child of freed slaves. Orphaned at the age of three in a Kafrikilla raid and without a House of his own, he had been taken in by the Ksars and put in the servants quarters. He was the same age as Irian Ksar, and he'd been brought up less a servant and more a family friend. He had known the Witch Queen when she was merely Vartigern's wild, unruly daughter. He had known General Ksar when he was a child who dreamed of running away to sea to explore distant foreign lands.

Now, could it be that his years of service were going to be rewarded?

"Sir," the guards said and saluted him.

He nodded, saluted back, and began the wearisome ascent of the Black Tower of Balanmanik.

Seven hundred steps later he found Ksar waiting for him on the rooftop observation deck.

It was windy, snowing.

"Lord Protector," Krama said, trying to catch his breath after the exhausting ascent.

Ksar turned. He was holding a brass octoscope that he must have gotten from Aldan or Kafrikilla. Krama was surprised that there had been any monies left in the treasury to purchase the thing after Ksar had given most of the Alkhavan reserve to the Aldanese.

To Krama and most of the Alkhavan court this had been seen as something of a cowardly move, but neither Krama nor the Protectors had dared venture this opinion out loud. Although Ksar had made mistakes in the past, he had been supremely deft in the last few months, and the Lord Protector, Krama was sure, knew what he was doing.

"Ah, Krama. At last. Tell me what you have observed," Lord Protector Ksar said in a low Alkhavan dialect common among soldiers.

"We have been diligent, sir—" Krama began.

"I expect no less. Get on with it."

"Yes, sir. My men and I followed the *Proud Star* from Aldan to Oralands waters in a disguised Kafrikilla trading ship. We sent up the *rantas* in rotation and kept the Ui Neills under close watch."

"Your ship was not seen?"

"No. We were able to keep the vessel beyond the horizon. The mounted *rantas* may have been seen, but I do not think that anyone could have guessed what they were."

"What happened at the rendezvous?"

"They did not quite spend one night with the fleet. The prince's squadron left with the morning tide on a course for Balan Port."

"How many ships?"

"Seven."

"Which represents?"

"I am not sure, Lord Protector, but no more than three or four thousand men."

Ksar looked surprised. "So few?"

"They do not expect a difficult assault on the city. They have been informed that Balanmanik contains less than a thousand souls, and most of those are monks, nuns and peasants."

Ksar laughed. "But that is true, is it not, Krama?"

"Yes, sir."

"No one has attacked Balanmanik in five centuries. Why would you? It would be like invading a morgue. Isn't that what they say?"

"Not in front of the Witch Queen, sir," Krama said.

Ksar laughed again. "You have done well, Krama. Very well."

"Thank you, sir."

"You are expecting the assault today?"

"Yes, sir. They have already disembarked at Balan Port. We thought it wise to let that process proceed without harassment."

"Lest they become discouraged, eh?"

"Exactly, sir," Krama agreed.

Alkhava had warred with most of its neighbors over the years, but the Kafrikillans or Frantanese had always raided the eastern coastal towns like Balan Port or Casana. Few had ventured inland, none had marched an army across the ice fields to launch an assault on Balanmanik. But that was precisely what Ksar wanted, and it wouldn't do to put the Oralands marines off by burning their ships too soon.

"So they suspect nothing?" Ksar said.

"No, sir. They think our army is in Afor and Balanmanik is a ghost town teetering on the edge of collapse."

"Excellent. You have read the instructions from the Witch Queen?"

Krama was proud of his ability to read and he wondered for a moment if Ksar was making a slight about his humble background.

"Yes, sir. She wishes to hand Lord Brian and Lady Anna to the Lords Ui Neill before the battle . . ."

"Yes?" Ksar asked, seeing the hesitation in Krama's honest face.

"I am not quite sure why though, sir."

Ksar sighed. "Use your head, Krama. So that in the eyes of the world—specifically the king of Oralands—the fault will lie with the invaders, not us. We returned the hostages to the Ui Neills, and they did not give us what we sought. We were willing to trade the hostages for the Salmon, and after we kept our end of the bargain, they broke the agreement. Not us."

Krama nodded. "And will they not give this *Salmon* to the Witch Queen?"

"They will not, Krama. I assure you of that."

Krama nodded, but he still looked troubled.

"You do not like the plan?" Ksar asked.

"If Prince Lorca is killed, the king of Oralands will be very angry. The prince is his youngest grandson after all . . ."

Ksar thought for a moment. He wiped some snow off the battlements with the back of his hand and watched it fall seven hundred feet to the courtyard below.

"Yes, all right then, if you can spare the prince then do so, but do not allow it to interfere with your battle plans."

"And the prince's bride? Wishaway?"

"She needn't concern us. Kill her."

"And the others?"

"Kill them all," Ksar said. "Ui Neill controls the

Salmon. We must not permit him to use its power. Before this day ends he must no longer be drawing breath."

"Yes, sir."

Ksar brought the octoscope up to his eye again. He didn't quite know how to focus the device and all he could really see was a blurry mist in front of him, but he couldn't lose face in front of Krama and had to peer through the haze for a half minute before putting it down.

"You are dismissed, Krama," Ksar said.

Krama nodded, trying not to let his emotion show. He saluted and turned on his heel.

So the rumors were not true. All his years of service had been—

"One more thing. You are improperly dressed, you are setting a bad example for the men," Ksar said harshly.

"Sir, I have been on the back of those flying—"

"You dare contradict me, Krama? You have grown impertinent and familiar. Watch yourself or I will not hesitate to throw you off this tower," Ksar barked.

"No, sir. You are correct, sir."

"I am always correct, Krama, you are never required to reaffirm that," Ksar said.

"No, sir."

Ksar smiled. "Do you wish to know why you are improperly dressed, Krama?"

"Yes, sir."

"You are in the wrong uniform. Your uniform should

be that of a general in the Alkhavan Army. You are to assume the rank of Protector from this moment."

Despite his mental preparation, Krama almost burst into tears. "Thank you, sir, I am—"

Ksar raised his hand. "Enough. You have done well, Krama. But we need to finish the job. The Oralands Army must be annihilated, the Ui Neills killed, and the Salmon taken. Is that understood?"

"Yes, sir."

"Good. Now go and attire thyself for battle."

Krama bowed and walked off the observation platform. Never before had he felt so happy. Only in the great country of Alkhava could loyalty alone allow a man to rise so high. And he owed it all to Lord Protector Ksar and his family. He would give the Lord Protector and his sister what they wanted. If needs be, he'd kill a hundred men and cut a bloody swath through the invading Oralands host; he'd dispatch the bodyguards, grab the Salmon of Knowledge, and slay that Ui Neill boy with his own hand.

After running down the tower's steps and gasping for breath he made it back to the ice-filled courtyard. He drank a flagon of ale and walked to the city gates.

The sun was rising over the glacier top.

Soon the invaders would be coming.

Good.

Enjoy this sunrise, Seamus of the Black, Lord Ui Neill, he said to himself. *Enjoy this sunrise, for it is to be thy last.*

Balanmanik already looked like a defeated city. The effects of centuries of ice, snow, and wind could be seen everywhere.

The battlements were cracked and split in many places, support towers had fallen, and repairs if they had been done at all were rough and haphazard at best.

The northern villages were completely submerged under the great advancing glacier of Gag Macak, and weathering and frost erosion had so destroyed the north-facing walls of the inner city that they were down to a few feet high in places.

Refuse, dead animals, and people lined the Balanmanik road, and yellow coppery ice gave the granite curtain walls a glittering, sepulchral feel.

Only the Black Tower of Balanmanik looked to be in good condition, and perhaps that was because it had been built by the Old Ones and not by Altairians at all.

The boys, Wishaway, and Lorca were dressed in fur of the *moxy*, a small rodentlike animal from Perovan. It was an expensive and comfortable material that was surprisingly light and provided great protection against the chill polar air. Even so Jamie was glad that it was the Alkhavan summer.

The soldiers were wearing *draya*-hide coats, which were thicker and cheaper. They kept out the cold, but they also made movement much more labored.

Jamie for one hoped that the Oralands Army had been given instructions to discard their coats if it came to fighting.

They even had cavalry. One of the Red Star ships had brought several *drayas* from Carolla. Several more had been seized at Balan Port when the population had fled at the sight of the advancing fleet.

Lorca, Jamie, Wishaway, Ramsay, and Admiral Farar rode together at the head of the force to the Balanmanik gatehouse. Lorca would have preferred that Wishaway stay in the rearguard of the army, but until they were formally wed he could not *order* her to do so. Still prudence did dictate some things: "Wait here," Lorca said to Ramsay and Wishaway. "Jamie, the admiral, and I must go on ahead."

Jamie nodded to affirm this instruction.

Gently he tapped his heels into the flank of the six-legged, giant beast, which seemed to be a cross between a Komodo dragon and a Galápagos tortoise.

The army halted behind them, and the three men urged their animals up the final few meters to the huge Balanmanik city gates.

"Dost thou understand the plan, Lord Ui Neill?" Lorca asked as they got close.

Jamie nodded. "Say it," Lorca ordered.

"If I can get Brian and Mom outside, then I am to do

so. If I can't, honor dictates that I let the Queen get back inside before we attack," Jamie said.

Lorca looked satisfied. "Are you sure the Queen will come out at all?" Jamie asked.

"I am a representative of the king of Oralands. She will come," Lorca said.

They rode closer, almost to within hailing distance. They couldn't see anyone mounted on the battlements, but there were dozens of slits carved into the walls from which a concealed archer could let fly an arrow.

"Dost thee, uhm, thou note the, uhm, condition of the gate, sire?" Admiral Farar asked Lorca in poor English.

"Wow, yeah, the gates look rough," Jamie replied.

"What do you see, Admiral?" Lorca asked in the royal dialect of Oralands.

"They have been stripped of their iron and much of their wood. They may fall even at the first heave of the ram," Admiral Farar said confidently in his own tongue.

Lorca nodded. "Good. Have your men be prepared, Admiral. If she will not accede to our demands, then we will allow her and her retinue to return to the safety of the citadel and then we will attack immediately."

"Yes, sir . . . I had thought that we would attempt a breach over the north walls, but now that I've seen the gate, I believe that a frontal assault will prove rewarding," the admiral said with glee.

The admiral was a wily old dog, the veteran of many campaigns on land and sea. Lorca bowed to his experience.

"So be it, I will leave it in your hands, Farar. Only recall that the Queen's life as a royal personage is inviolate and that no action must be taken to jeopardize the lives of Lady Anna and Lord Brian."

"Of course, sir."

Jamie turned to Lorca. "What was all that yakking about?" Jamie asked.

"The admiral thinks a frontal assault will be the winning strategy . . . I concur." "OK. But remember we're going to do this peacefully if we can," Jamie said.

Lorca nodded with condescension. "Of course. Now it is up to thee, Lord Ui Neill. Go to the gate and announce thyself," Lorca said.

Jamie rode to well within bow shot. If they wanted to pick him off, now they certainly could. He looked about him. Light snow was falling from a gray sky. There was utter silence in the city and the plain.

He stood up in the leather *draya* saddle and cleared his throat.

"I have come, Queen. Show yourself!" Jamie yelled.

His voice echoed off the stone walls.

There was no answer.

"It is me. The Lord Ui Neill," Jamie said, trying to keep the embarrassment out of his voice.

He was about to yell again when chains began to rattle, there was an awful creaking noise, and the city gate opened.

A woman—the Queen—on foot was walking toward him, alone.

Jamie looked back at Lorca. "What do I do?" he mouthed.

"Dismount," Lorca whispered.

With some difficulty, Jamie climbed down off the *draya*.

He walked to meet her, and they stopped when they were a few feet apart. The Witch Queen examined him closely. Not in her wildest imaginings had she thought that he would be so young. This pipsqueak had freed Aldan, sunk the ice fleet, bested her brother?

It disgusted her.

"Lord Ui Neill," she said, and bowed.

"Queen of the Alkhav," Jamie replied, and also bowed.

"What do ye seek in Balanmanik to enter our domain so boldly with an army of pirates and marauders?" the Witch Queen asked.

"I want my mother and my friend," Jamie said.

"Thou wert to come here two days from now," the Witch Queen said.

"I come and go at times of my choosing, not at the dictates of kidnappers," Jamie replied.

"Thy mother and the Lord Brian have been our royal guests in Balanmanik. No one speaks of kidnap," the Witch Queen seethed.

She was smaller than him and quite alone, but even so Jamie couldn't help but be afraid of her. He summoned his courage for a reply.

"*I* speak of kidnap. Now let them go, or be prepared to see your city leveled by a superior force," Jamie said.

The Witch Queen considered him for a moment, but she could take this charade no longer.

"Thou hast brought the Salmon?" she asked greedily.

Jamie reached into his backpack and took out the alien teleportation device.

The Witch Queen gasped.

This thing, which her order had desired for four centuries, the thing that would save her and her people. So close, so close . . .

"Give it to me, and I will send out thy kin," the Witch Queen barked.

"Send out his family, now!" Lorca, fifty feet behind, couldn't resist yelling.

The Witch Queen looked back at Lorca, as if noticing him for the first time.

"This is not thy fight, prince of Oralands. We have no quarrel with thy country or thy lands."

Lorca kicked the *draya* forward a few yards.

He shook his head. "I choose to quarrel with thee, Witch Queen," he said.

There was a long half minute of silence during which all three of them seemed to communicate much. Ramsay had told Jamie once that quiet was also a form of conversation, and in a way that was perfectly true.

Finally the Witch Queen nodded, turned, and yelled something in Alkhavan.

The gate again opened and a column of black-clad soldiers marched out, leading Brian and Anna. The troops were all heavily armed with crossbows and spears.

"*Carava ak,*" the Witch Queen said and the troops formed a semicircle behind her, crossbows loaded and pointed at Jamie, Lorca, and the admiral.

"Mom! Are you OK?" Jamie cried.

She had to be restrained from running over to him. "I'm OK, Jamie," Anna replied, wiping away a tear.

"Thanks for coming to get us, Jamie," Brian said.

"No problem, buddy."

The Witch Queen looked at him. "I have brought Lord Brian and Lady Anna. Now give me the Salmon and thou willst be allowed to leave here with thy kin," the Witch Queen said.

"Thou art in an unfavorable position to give orders, Witch Queen!" Lorca yelled, nudging his *draya* still closer.

Indeed it looked bad for the ruler of Balanmanik.

Her forces of perhaps a few score of black-clad troops were facing several thousand Oralands soldiers and marines.

The Witch Queen smiled. "Perhaps thou art correct, Princeling," the Witch Queen said.

She turned to Brian and Anna, bowed. "I will remember our talks with affection. Go to thy kin," she said.

They didn't need to be told twice. They broke free from their guards and ran across the no-man's-land to Jamie. He hugged his mother.

"Your arm, Jamie, I don't believe it," Anna said, staring at him in wonderment.

"Mom, listen, we don't have much time. Go back to Ramsay, he's brought coats for both of you. Go back there now, there's going to be trouble. Take Brian with you," he whispered.

"And you'll be—"

"I'll be fine. Go."

Anna led Brian back to where Ramsay was waiting next to his *draya*.

The Witch Queen smiled at Jamie.

"A touching reunion. Now . . . I have given thee what ye desireth. Give me the Salmon of Knowledge."

Jamie shook his head. "We both know that's not going to happen," he said.

The Witch Queen spat onto the icy tundra at her feet.

"Then thou has broken our bargain and forfeited thy right to live. I so declare it in front of witnesses! Ye also, prince of Oralands, who hath dared violate our land this day. My judgment falls upon thee and thy entire army of assassins."

She turned and walked back to a platoon of soldiers, who tried to escort her back inside the city, but she waved them off with a dismissive hand. *You have to admire her panache*, Jamie thought.

The gates closed, and there was a deafening, empty silence.

"That was easy," Brian said.

Jamie was perturbed. "It's like what they say in the movies," Jamie replied. "'Too easy.'"

Admiral Farar looked at Lorca. "What now, sir?" he wondered.

Although he had foreseen the possibility that a show of force alone might be enough to convince the Witch Queen to give up the hostages, Lorca hadn't considered it a likely scenario. He was baffled for a moment.

"I do not know, Admiral. Back to the ships?"

Just then a horn blew from the Black Tower and a rain of arrows, stones, and other missiles came pouring from the city walls.

Jamie and the others moved out of bow range.

But then, from behind cunningly constructed snow

dykes, thousands of screaming fighters appeared from the west and south and ran as fast as they could to reach the Oralands flank and encircle the invading force.

"What's happening?" Ramsay asked.

"I don't know," Jamie said. "Lorca?"

Lorca stood tall in his saddle.

A trap.

A huge force of soldiers was surrounding them. The enemy had let them march to the gates of Balanmanik, and now with the city to the west and the Alkhavans to the south and east they were not only outflanked but also cut off from the Balan Road and all the routes to the coast.

"What's happening, Lorca?" Wishaway demanded.

"The Alkhavan Army is not at Afor," Lorca said in a stunned monotone.

"What? What are you talking about? What's happening?"

"We are ambushed, my lady," Lorca said.

"I don't understand," Wishaway said.

But then they all understood as the Alkhavan Army, composed of the toughest and most experienced raiders and warriors on the whole planet, let loose a terrifying battle cry and launched their attack.

The assault commenced with two hundred *draya*-mounted cavalrymen smashing into the Oralands left flank, scattering the surprised Oralands marines, killing dozens with their first charge.

"How many of them are there?" Wishaway yelled.

"By the look of it, the entire army and its reserve. Well over fifteen thousand men," Lorca whispered, awestruck.

He took his sword from its scabbard, examined it, saw his reflection in the blade, and there, somehow too, a glimpse of the inevitable future: a stunned young man, not yet seventeen, lying on an enemy funeral mound, his body cut to shreds, stripped naked of its princely finery. He looked at the dead eyes, the blue lips.

"But what's happening, Lorca? Who are those people? What's going on?" Ramsay yelled, still unclear as to the nature of the threat.

Lorca put down the sword and regarded him cooly. Was it his own vanity that had taken him to this place of death? A desire to prove himself in front of Wishaway and two lords from Earth?

"Lorca, do you know what's happening?" Ramsay asked desperately.

"I do," Lorca said calmly. "We have been outgeneraled, Lord Ramsay, and sad to say, before the day is out, we will all pay for it with our lives."

❖   ❖   ❖

Jamie dug his heels into the *draya*'s side. Whatever was going to happen, he wanted to be next to Wishaway and his mom. But before he could even get the beast moving, it thrashed out and tossed him off its back.

A heavy crack on the head.

Pain.

He was on the ground.

Uhhh.

A sky made of arrows.

A rain of death.

The air smeared over with smoke.

In the city a *ranta* was rising from the battlements. Straggled and hung down, it had a tarsal bone in its yellow beak and a soldier on its back. *So that's how they knew we were coming,* Jamie thought.

The creature soared over the remains of a hundred men, flattened now, and soon to be swallowed up by pyres or the Gag Macak.

Jamie wiped blood from his eyes.

He rolled to the side, and the sky waned, dieseled black ebbing into the tundra. Lorca, next to him, offering him his hand.

No, Lorca. Go. Take them away. Take them away, O Prince. Cross to her embrace, over the web of battle; flash your smile and your golden hair; journey over the stone and the water. Go. Swim her away with you. Sink not under the weight of your rubies.

Lorca speaking. His lips moving. His lips . . .

"Get up, Jamie. Get up."

A hand on his hand. Jamie found himself on his feet.

"Are you all right, Lord Ui Neill?"

"No . . . Yes. I'm a little dazed. I hurt my head. I think I'm—"

"Good, I will find Admiral Farar," Lorca said, all business.

"We must protect Wishaway," Jamie said.

"A battalion of our best has already been assigned. Now, I must find the admiral," Lorca said.

Jamie nodded, touched his scalp. Blood on his fingertips.

Lorca ran into the throng.

Jamie took a breath. *Get your wits together, kid,* he told himself.

Jamie saw a *draya* munching at a pack of snow. He grabbed some of the snow and smeared it on his face.

The cold shook him, and he climbed on the *draya*'s back, surveyed the field. Alkhavan cavalry was still pushing deep into the Oralands flank, but now the vanguard of the Alkhavan Army was charging too. Jamie watched it crash into the rear supply columns of the Oralands Army, butchering the largely unarmed sailors and quartermasters in a horrible slaughter.

"Sun god protect us!" an Oralands officer yelled beside him in English.

"Help us!" another officer echoed.

Outnumbered three or four to one, hemmed in by

the glacier and assaulted from the south, east, and west, they were being killed by the hundreds and the thousands and now Oralands discipline was breaking down completely.

The weakness of the Oralands troops was obvious. The marines were used to shore raids and quick attacks that depended upon surprise and overwhelming numbers to defeat an enemy, but they had no training or even concept of defense. And apparently no notion of what to do when faced with such a superior force.

Whole platoons were deserting their officers, and men began scattering by the score, desperately trying to get away from this scene of massacre.

Sensing a quick victory, the Alkhavans pressed from all sides. An armored column drove in from the center while mounted troops on the flank wiped out a detachment of Oralands scouts who had been sent there to examine the west walls of Balanmanik.

Jamie could see the pincer closing tighter and tighter. On *National Geographic* once he'd seen footage of the pilot whale cull in Tórshavn harbor. This was eerily similar.

"Help us!" came the cries from all around.

"*Tooav!*"

"*Sava khan!*"

Admiral Farar tried to form the forces closest to him into a defensive square.

"To me, to me!" he cried, but barely a dozen soldiers answered his call.

"Look to the women," Jamie heard Lorca cry from behind him.

And then, to make matters worse, clay pots filled with Greek Fire began bursting among the Oralands troops.

Screams.

Terror.

Men burning horribly, diving into the snow to put themselves out.

Who was doing it? Jamie looked back to the city to see gleeful Alkhavans hurling the Greek Fire at them from the backs of flying lizards.

"Jamie, they must have stolen the secret of the—" Ramsay yelled but was cut off as his *draya* reared on its hind legs, hit by an arrow, throwing him. Ramsay went down and had to roll fast to avoid being crushed by the massive beast.

"Ramsay!" Jamie cried. "Ramsay!"

Cheering went up from the Alkhavan side as the royal Pennant of Oralands, a blue river on a green field, was captured from its defenders.

"We are done," someone nearby said.

And indeed for the Alkhavan Army it was high times come at last after their horrendous defeats in Aldan the previous year.

The attackers came in wave after wave, the Oralands lines buckling and giving and breaking to pieces. On Lorca's orders, a platoon of men formed themselves around the young people in a protective semicircle, but Jamie knew they wouldn't be able to keep the Alkhavan hordes away forever.

And then, as if the butchery and chaos were not yet enough, from inside the city walls the gates opened, and a column of black-clad mounted cavalry galloped out on armored *drayas*.

Jamie recognized the man leading the new assault.

"Ksar!" Jamie yelled. "Lorca, it's Ksar!"

"We must rally!" Lorca yelled back.

Ksar's outriders flew into the attack, brandishing spears and axes, knocking aside friend and foe alike, trampling them under their heavy steeds.

Jamie saw an Alkhavan ram Wishaway's *draya* and watched her tumble from her mount.

"Wishaway!" he screamed, jumping off his animal and weaving his way to her through the mess.

She was lying on the ground, shaken but not hurt.

"*Challa, challa,* to me, to me," Jamie heard Admiral Farar call out.

But no one came.

And Admiral Farar knew now what he had to do.

He had been given explicit instructions from the king

himself. In the event of a disaster, he was to kill Jamie and take the thing in his backpack that all the great lords of Altair seemed to covet.

The battle was lost. The prince's son was lost. Perhaps he could at least carry out that part of the plan.

The boy was utterly preoccupied with the Aldanese harlot.

Admiral Farar lifted his spear and approached. A thrust in the neck would kill the Earthling. As a witness she would have to die too, but in all this confusion no one would be the wiser.

"What's happening?" Wishaway asked Jamie.

"You fell off the *draya*. It's OK, we've all fallen now."

Jamie helped her to his feet. Her eyes were wide with fear.

"What can we do?" she asked.

"We've got to get out of here," Jamie said.

"Do we lose the battle?" Wishaway wondered.

Jamie looked to see if she was concussed.

"Do we lose the battle? We've *lost* the battle," Jamie said. "It's over."

There was another almighty cheer from the Alkhavans.

Jamie turned to see Admiral Farar, only ten yards from him, speared through the back with a metal javelin. The admiral tried to yell something at Jamie, but then his face contorted in pain. He dropped to the ground as another javelin, expertly thrown by the new Protector Krama, killed him.

Jamie turned Wishaway to face him. "Have you seen my mom and Brian?"

"I cannot hear you," she shouted.

Krama waded through his enemies, removed his two spears from the admiral's back, stood triumphantly on the corpse, and took a loud cheering salute from his men.

"Have you . . . never mind, come on, this way," Jamie said, and they crawled back to the diminishing Oralands lines, front and rear now only a few yards apart in places.

The Lord Protector's cavalry tightened the vise and began throwing pots of Greek Fire and shooting burning arrows at the last of the Oralands soldiers. Now they were actually laughing and whooping with delight at the confusion of their enemies.

"My mom?" Jamie tried again.

Wishaway pointed to a large group of Oralands troops trying to form themselves into a defensive infantry square.

"I think they are over there," she said.

Jamie's mind was racing. What should they do? What could they do? There was only one choice. Flight not fight.

Jamie stared at Wishaway, her tiny, pale face contorted

with panic, her eyes alert, her hair matted with sweat and snow.

"It's going to be OK, Wisahaway, I promise. We're going to be OK. Do you understand?"

She nodded.

"Good. We're going to get everybody that's still alive and get out of here," Jamie said.

He stood up and surveyed the slaughterhouse.

"Mom! Brian! Ramsay!" Jamie called, looking for them in the boiling mass of people.

"Here," Ramsay said a few yards to his right. "I was coming for ya."

Jamie picked up a dead man's sword and gave it to Wishaway.

"I know you know how to use one of these," Jamie said.

"Lorca would not permit a princess of the—" she began.

"You're better than all of us, we need you," Jamie said, and grabbed a bloody scimitar for himself.

Just then an Alkhavan warrior burst through one of the lines and tried to push a large crooked knife into Ramsay's kidneys. Without hesitation, Wishaway stabbed the Alkhavan in the back. "Uhh," he groaned, and Jamie kicked the dying man to the ground.

"See?" Jamie said to Wishaway, and turning to Ramsay

he went on. "Listen, it's all over. We got to get out of here if we can. We need your brother. He's in that platoon over there, surrounded by our guys."

Ramsay nodded breathlessly. "Brian! Brian!" Jamie and Ramsay yelled together.

Arrows thocked around Brian and Anna in the center of a collapsing Oralands infantry square.

"I'm over here," the big Irishman yelled, picking up a huge battle club from a fallen Oralands marine and thumping it heavily into an Alkhavan sergeant's chest.

"Can you get over here?" Jamie yelled.

"Aye!" Brian yelled.

Brian turned to Anna. "Stay close," he said.

He eased his way out of the Oralands square and began swinging the two-headed club as if he'd been born to the task, battering his way through the throng of soldiers until he found Wishaway, Jamie, and his brother.

"Brian!" Ramsay exclaimed. "Good to see you're in one piece."

"Tell me something," Brian said as he stepped forward and smashed his club into an Alkhavan bowman who had just broken through the line.

"Tell you what?" Ramsay said.

"Is it always like this when you come here?" Brian asked.

Ramsay nodded. "Pretty much," he said.

"Wee idea—bring a machine gun next time," Brian

said, and thumped the club into the rump of a *draya*, sending the animal careening off into his fellows and knocking over half a dozen Alkhavan soldiers who were trying to cheat round the flank.

We need Lorca now, Jamie thought as he saw the Lord Protector's cavalry hack its way closer and closer to them.

"Lorca, are you still alive?" Jamie yelled.

Brian picked up a two-headed axe and threw it to his brother.

"Come on, bro. We're a foot taller than all these guys. We can do some damage if we work together," Brian said.

"I'm coming," Lorca said from somewhere.

He fought his way to his friends, wielding his sword beautifully in both hands, dispatching clumsy enemies with all the deftness of years of training in the royal armories.

"Lorca!" Wishaway cried when he got to the little group.

He hugged his bride happily and almost fell into her arms with exhaustion.

"We've all made it," Jamie said.

"Yes, we will make our stand here together," Lorca cried happily, brandishing his sword.

Jamie shook his head. "We're getting out," he said.

Lorca laughed. "We are totally surrounded," he said.

"No, not totally surrounded. They've left one way open if we can get there. North," Jamie said.

Lorca shook his head. "Up onto the glacier? That is certain death," he scoffed.

"*This* is certain death. Right here. Right now," Jamie said.

"We can fight them," Brian said, swinging his club.

Jamie knew that this foolishness had to end immediately. He punched the big Irishman on the shoulder. "Brian, you're smarter than that. We're not going to win this battle. We've lost, we've got to get out of here," Jamie said.

Around them men were screaming, fires burning, *drayas* howling.

"*Ga va sha kaaa!*" the Lord Protector yelled in wild Alkhavan as he hurled spear after steel-tipped spear at his sworn enemies. He could see the Lord Ui Neill just a hundred paces from him on the other side of a ragged line of Oralands marines.

"Ksar will be here in a matter of minutes," Jamie pleaded. "We've got to go."

Brian nodded slowly, as if a violent red mist was clearing from his eyes.

"You're right," he said. "Go. Not stay. Our only chance. OK. We'll go. Ramsay and I'll clear the path. Follow us. Come on."

Lorca shook his head. He looked haggard, broken.

"I cannot desert my men," he said, tears in his eyes now.

"You must save your wife," Jamie replied.

Lorca hesitated for a moment, but only for a moment. "Then south to the ports, we must go south," he said.

"No. Lorca. We're trapped, there's only one way, the one place they don't think we can go," Jamie said.

Lorca nodded. "Then lead on," he said, sounding broken.

"That way, Brian," Jamie cried.

The two huge Irishmen clubbed and axed their way through the soldiers to the north while Jamie, Wishaway, and Lorca protected their flanks with sword thrusts and parries. In the utter chaos of the melee it wasn't difficult for a determined group of six people to battle through the lines.

Ramsay and Brian worked like Trojans, butchering anyone who stood against them, and they fought utter exhaustion as they shoved, pushed, and killed their way through the hordes. They weren't stopping to get into individual combat, they were merely using their momentum to take them through the path of least resistance.

They were helped when it began to snow heavily, and in only ten brutal minutes they had slashed their way to the rear echelons of the Alkhavan northern flank. Behind them the elite Alkhavan guard were annihilating the last Oralands sailors and marines, but out here on the edge of the conflict they found mostly monks from Balanmanik who had been given staffs and spears and told to protect the pathways to the glacier. "Get rid of them, guys," Jamie said.

Brian yelled menacingly at the monks, brandished his club like a hammer, and swung it sickeningly down into the snow with an almighty crash. It did the job. Most of the monks dropped their staffs, and all of them ran for their lives.

With the messier parts of the battle behind them, Jamie checked to see that everyone was OK. "Anyone hurt?" he asked, grabbing an Alkhavan monk's shoulder bag from off the ground. It contained a little dried food and a small bottle of water. "No one's talking. OK, I'll take that as a yes. This is the plan: We're going up onto the glacier. I've got some dried meat and *juha* in my backpack. It's not much but it's all we've got," Jamie said.

Again nobody had anything to add.

Well, there was no point asking for opinions. Jamie knew that they didn't have much time. Even if the Alkhavans hadn't noticed their flight, the Lord Protector would soon learn of their escape, and he'd be after them with the entire army if necessary.

Jamie scanned the way ahead. There were dozens of paths up onto the glacier. They had to pick one. Brian and Ramsay turned to him. "Well?"

Jamie pointed to the way that seemed most traveled.

They began ascending a series of wide, slippery steps up the ice face.

The weather had deteriorated and snow was now falling slantwise and hard. Lorca hoped that the blizzard would allow some of his brave soldiers to escape.

A small hope. He sighed, fought back tears of shame, and went on.

It was only a vertical climb of a few hundred feet, but it was very difficult on the unfamiliar ice.

The sky began to darken.

The wind picked up.

And finally the sound of fighting diminished.

In an hour they reached the top and lay exhausted on the vast, featureless expanse of the Gag Macak glacier.

"Has anyone got any water?" Ramsay asked.

"Snow," Jamie said.

Ramsay scooped some into his mouth.

Jamie got to his knees and took out the map Lorca had given them.

"Let me help, I've got a compass on my watch," Brian said.

"You would," Anna said with a smile, her first words in an hour.

"Will it work on this planet?" Ramsay said skeptically.

"We're on a different planet, but the laws of electromagnetism are the same everywhere in the universe . . .

Unless we're not in the same universe. We could have jumped to a universe in a brane parallel but close to our own in the ten-dimensional multiverse, and in that case the laws of phys—"

"Look, Jamie," Wishaway said, pointing back the way they'd come.

He peered over the edge of the glacier. Down below a group of Alkhavan pickets on *draya*-back had seen them ascend the ice stair. Some were already on the ice steps, others were riding back to the Lord Protector to give him the information.

"Jeez, they'll be up here soon," Ramsay said, stating the obvious.

"What do we do now?" Brian asked.

Everyone was looking at Jamie. He had to make a snap decision.

He examined the map. "We'll make for one of the ruined cities north of here. This one called Near Balan. It doesn't seem that far away. We should have enough rations to get us there," Jamie said.

"And when we get there, then what?" Lorca demanded.

"We'll assess the situation," Jamie said.

"I think we should find somewhere to hide here," Lorca said, "and when the battle's over, we can try and make it back to the ships. Come, Brian, you can see the sense of that? No one can survive on the glacier."

Brian thought for a second but shook his head. Even though Jamie was a mere slip of a lad, for better or for worse, just like in the Ayatollahs of Funk, Jamie was the leader, and they had to do what he said.

"We can't discuss it. We've got to move, come on," Brian muttered.

Lorca looked at Wishaway. "Tell them it is suicide," he said.

But Brian was convinced, and as the biggest and the second-oldest person there it was easy for him to fall back into the role of bassist, the one who controlled the rhythm, the one who drove the beat. "Discussion over. Come on. Let's go," Brian said, and began walking north.

Lorca hesitated, shook his head, but then slowly set off behind him. Wishaway followed Lorca, and next came Anna and Ramsay. Jamie took up the rear.

Once, but only once, he stared back at the city and the terrible battle that raged beyond. The devastation and the horror were immeasurable, but they had made it out, and already night was coming to cloak them in its embrace. They had done it, they had survived an awful day. How many more such days they could live through in this icy wasteland only time and the Gag Macak would tell.

Chapter X
THE GLACIER

DAWN OVER THE VAST emptiness of Gag Macak. A mocking, faraway, heatless sun. Yesterday's cold joining today's cold.

An infinity of cold.

Perhaps death was like this: a white nothingness that stretched to oblivion.

Skin-burning air.

Tongue-freezing air.

Endless land.

Shipwrecked sky.

A day shuffling in furs caked with frozen sweat. Six hours with a break in the middle to drink snow and eat dried meat. Already it was too painful to talk, to walk, even to breathe. But there was no choice.

The army behind them still.

Up and on again.

There were two ways to experience the glacier: When the wind wasn't blowing, the temperature was bearable, perhaps ten or twenty degrees below freezing, the ground was flat, and the sun gave up a sliver of warmth. But when the gale raged everything changed. Snow, hail, and particles of ice came tearing at them from the north in a blinding, terrifying blizzard with a windchill that was a seething torture on any exposed skin. When the wind came, the easiest thing to do was huddle together en masse and move like a Roman army "tortoise" a step at a time, achingly slowly.

Jamie's conversation with himself was simple. Put one foot in front of another. Just keep going. If Wishaway and your mother can do it, so can you.

Six people, hunted across the frozen waste, stumbling together over the antiseptically dead terrain.

A long, short day.

Two more hours walking, and the sun sank behind the horizon.

Still they went on, fear driving them.

Jamie on point with Ramsay, Anna, and Brian in the rear, the two Altairians in the middle.

And yet despite the closeness of the others, Jamie felt alone, abandoned, lost. How could you not in such a desolate place?

If this were a pole on Earth at least there would be animals. Penguins, seals, albatrosses in the south, polar bears, foxes, wolves in the north.

Wolf mother. Bear mother. Help us.

But there was no help.

Only the howling wind, the racing moons. The stars asleep in the jet-black night.

Anna's voice. "We must rest."

"Yes."

A snowbank offering protection against the wind. Brian and Ramsay digging a hollow. Everyone climbing in. Tumbling on top of one another like sleeping pups.

Brian put an Oralands Army tarp over the snow cave hole.

Jamie's eyes were heavy. "Eat this," his mother said.

He slipped his hands out of the *moxy* sleeves.

He ate it.

Sweat unfreezing on the fur. The tarp blew down and ripped away across the plain. Side view of Orion and what might be Sirius.

Dog star. White night. Frozen earth.

But warmer in here. The icy hand releasing its clutch on his heart.

Wishaway buried in Lorca's arms, shivering still.

"Wishaway," Jamie said, and slept.

Morning.

Jamie's eyes opened at the sound of voices. The two big McDonald boys.

Brian and Ramsay, strong, awake, talking in murmurs: ". . . the Altairians will suffer the most with their thin frames and delicate features."

"What do you mean?"

"This planet was obviously much warmer in the recent past. These people are not adapted for the cold like us with our stocky bodies and body fat. Huge help too is our comparatively big noses, which warms the air before it enters our lungs. The good news is that the whole army behind us should be suffering too."

"Yeah, and they don't have these expensive furs like we do."

"And of course because you've been here twice you must have noticed that the planet's tilt is much less than on Earth," Brian said.

"Tilt? Uhm, not really," Ramsay admitted.

"It means less pronounced seasons. It means that this climate change is going to be a global phenomenon, everyone is going to be affected, not just on Alkhava, but sooner or later even down in the equator. You say you thought that maybe this was a binary star system?"

"Wishaway spoke about a legend of another star or something."

"Well, if we are in an elliptical orbit about a second unknown star, obviously we're moving away from it and it's getting colder, but maybe eventually we'll get back into the goldilocks zone—not too close, not too far away—and things will improve again."

"So all we have to do is wait a few thousand years," Ramsay said.

Brian chuckled. "Yeah, but we could also be in terminal decay. If that's the case Altair's orbit is going to slip until its sun gets farther and farther away, and then one day the sun will finally be gone forever. The atmosphere will freeze, the unprotected oceans will evaporate into space, the entire planet will become a dead hunk of rock and ice with no hope at all of life, never mind civilization, ever coming here again."

Ramsay smiled. Gloomy guts yes, but Brian was a thinker. Maybe he *was* the smarter one of the two of them, and for once this thought didn't fill Ramsay with resentment but actually made him a little bit proud. It was good to be related to such an observant and perspicacious older brother.

"So for their sake you gotta hope that the stable binary star theory is correct."

"Well yes, but either way these people and their culture are pretty much screwed," Brian said.

"It's certainly very cold," Ramsay muttered. "And this is their summer."

"What do you think, Anna?" Brian asked, noticing that Anna was awake and eavesdropping on their conversation.

"You're awake too?" Jamie whispered.

She grinned at him.

"What do I think? I think it's no worse than walking

over the George Washington Bridge in January," she said.

Jamie could think of no occasion when his mother had walked across the George Washington Bridge in either January or indeed any other month, but he let that slide.

"You think we can make it to the city on the map, Brian?" Anna asked.

Brian looked at the compass and the icy plain beyond the snow shelter.

"I think *we* can. Whether *they* can is another question," he whispered, and jerked his thumb at Wishaway and Lorca.

Jamie leaned over and said in a low voice: "Either we all make it or no one makes it."

"Yeah, of course, but—" Brian began and suddenly had a brainwave.

He rummaged in the backpack and found the Salmon.

"Maybe this will help," he said.

He located the fish eye and turned the device on. Sure enough the Salmon heated up a little. Not much, but it was better than nothing.

"Put that between the two of them for a bit," Brian whispered.

Jamie nodded and gently placed the Salmon on Wishaway's arms . . .

Two hours later.

Jamie walking in the rear.

Looking at his feet.

The glacier flat, featureless.

The pain in his body no longer localized but instead one huge, amorphous agony of sores, blisters, windburn, and most terrifying of all, the early stages of frostbite.

Hard, dry snow falling slantwise at the fulcrum of land and sky.

A blizzard.

A pause while Anna distributed a rock-hard piece of bread and a kind of milky Alkhavan cheese she'd gotten from somewhere,

"Eat the bread and cheese with the snow. Carbs, liquid, and protein," she said.

They ate, rested, and went on again for another three hours until mercifully Brian called a halt. Jamie saw that he and Ramsay were in a discussion, looking at the compass, wiping the snow off the map.

Lorca and Wishaway had collapsed onto the ice, exhausted.

Ramsay was pointing. Brian shaking his head. Hand gestures, voices raised.

Jamie walked over to them. "What's going on?" he asked.

Ramsay looked pained. "Uhm, we may be in trouble."

"Why?"

"We think we've reached the area on the map that supposedly is the site of Near Balan. On the map it said that the city was a ruin. I know we kind of assumed that there had to be what was left of an old building or two, perhaps a street, maybe some roofing material we could use as kindling . . ."

"Yeah? And?"

"Look around you," Ramsay said.

Of course there was nothing like that. Only the pitiless emptiness of the flat glacier.

"This is it? Are you sure we're in the right place?" Jamie asked.

Brian checked the compass and map. He nodded solemnly.

"You must have made a mistake. Where's the city?" Jamie insisted.

Brian pointed at the ground. "Two hundred feet beneath us," Ramsay said.

Anna shook her head. "No. It can't be," she said.

"The glacier destroyed it?" Jamie asked.

"It just rolled right over it, obliterated it," Brian muttered.

Lorca, who'd been listening absently, struggled to his feet.

"The map said the city was still there, as a ruin," Lorca protested. "You have made an error in your calculations."

"No mistake, mate. The map is wrong. There's no ruin. The city has been pulverized," Ramsay said bitterly.

"Oralands intelligence is the best on the planet. It is never wrong. You must have gotten us lost," Lorca said, trying to grab the map from Ramsay's hand.

Just then the wind began to blow again from the north. Everyone winced.

"What are we going to do now?" Anna asked.

"Not much choice. Find the army behind us. Surrender," Brian suggested.

Ramsay looked at him furiously.

"Surrender to those dogs. Never. Never. They'll get the Salmon," Ramsay said.

Brian shook his head. "So they'll get the Salmon. We'll live, they'll live, big deal," Brian shouted over the ever mounting wind.

"Are you nuts? Have you lost your mind? If they get the Salmon they can come to Earth," Ramsay snorted.

The two brothers got into it—yelling and hurling accusations at each other.

Jamie let the voices drown out for a moment.

He closed his eyes.

Tired. So tired. He stamped his feet to get the cold out of his limbs.

"Can I tell you what your problem is?" Brian yelled.

"Go ahead. No one ever stopped you from speaking, big brother."

"Your problem, my friend, is that you are on the wrong side in this war. Your lotus-eating pals in Aldan and

Lorca's mates in Byzantium are living large on the install-
ment plan. The planet is doomed, and you really can't
blame the Alkhavans for wanting to get off it."

"They're monsters," Ramsay insisted.

"The Queen seems pretty reasonable to me. She uses
the old scare tactics a bit, but for all their methods, at
least the Alkhavans are trying to do something to save
themselves," Brian said.

"Jeez, Brian. You've really gone, mate. I think its called
Stockholm Syndrome. You're identifying with your cap-
tors. Patty Hearst, remember her? Yeah, that's it, he's
gone native, Jamie," Ramsay said to his friend.

"Perhaps Brian has a point," Lorca said. "If we turn
back now, we can negotiate a truce with the Alkhavans.
An equitable exchange."

"Oh my goodness, don't tell me you're losing it too,"
Ramsay said bitterly.

"There's no sense going on. We might as well go
back," Brian insisted with all the authority of his big
frame and booming voice.

There was a long silence.

"There's no sense going on? You should tell them what
you really think, Brian," Anna said at last.

"What's that?" Brian said.

"What you said in the prison. Stay here, go back, surrender, go on. You don't see the point of any of this. Of
any life. You think we're just meaningless blips in the

eternity of the universe. What does it matter if we live or we die? Isn't that what you said?"

If Jamie's eyes were open he would have seen the look of irritation on Brian's face.

"What of it?"

"But really that's just an excuse. It's about you. Your life. Your life is stalled. Your life didn't work out the way you wanted. Your plans went down the tubes. Your illustrious physics career didn't pan out the way you wanted. It's not about the universe, it's about you. You're paralyzed by your own feeling of helplessness," Anna said loudly.

Brian laughed. "No, it's not actually. Unlike you, I've really thought about this. There really isn't any point to any of this. We are doomed. We might as well take the path of least resistance. Go back, give ourselves up."

"But don't you see that's what gives our life meaning in the first place? The fact that we're all doomed. Every breath we take is a cosmic act of defiance," Anna said.

Brian shook his head sadly. "I won't argue with you. We need to keep our energy," he said.

But Anna knew this wasn't some philosophical debate. They couldn't go back. The Queen would kill them all to have the Salmon.

"We have to keep going until the army gives up the chase. Only then can we turn south. We have to outlast them," Anna said.

Jamie saw the sense of that. He took a deep breath and opened his eyes. "She's right," he said, finally breaking his silence.

"Of course you'd say that," Lorca muttered. "She's your mother."

Jamie glared at him. That guy was really pushing his luck.

"I say we take a vote," Anna suggested between shivers.

"A vote to decide our lives? No, we must think on it and use reason, we cannot listen to what the dull majority would do," Lorca muttered.

Anna ignored him and ducked as a chunk of ice blowing across the glacier nearly knocked her over.

"OK, the first choice. A vote to go back. We surrender to the Witch Queen and throw ourselves at her mercy. Who votes for that? Raise your hands. Come on."

No one raised their hands.

"I refuse to participate in this foolishness," Lorca said. "We must go back. There is no choice now. We came here hoping for a ruined city. There is no city. Wishaway cannot go on. Voting is not the answer."

Wishaway, who had not uttered a word, looked up at the mention of her name.

"There's six of us. What do we do if there's a tie?" she asked.

"OK, Lorca, tell you what, if there's a tie we'll go back to the army and surrender. Eh? You've two chances to win. Either you get the majority or you get a tie. What do you say, have you got the numbers?" Ramsay asked, and threw back the hood on his fur coat so everyone could see his grinning face.

Lorca was wavering on the question. He knew that he and Wishaway would vote to go back and probably Brian too. That would mean three votes. That would be enough.

"I don't know," he said.

"Come on. If it's a tie we'll go back. OK? 'Course, it won't be a tie, I can see the way it's going to go already," Ramsay said.

"I will participate," Lorca muttered finally.

"OK," Anna said. "Who votes to go back?"

Lorca and Brian raised their hands.

Ramsay laughed. "That's it. Measly two votes for surrender. OK, who says we go on? Keep heading north. Try to wait them out?" Ramsay asked.

Jamie, Ramsay, and Anna, raised their hands.

"That's it, a majority," Ramsay crowed.

"Not quite. Wishaway will vote with us, making a tie," Lorca said.

All eyes turned on the Aldanese girl. "Wishaway, come on, you can see the way the wind is blowing. Literally. We have to go on," Ramsay said.

Wishaway stared at the tall Irishman.

She was so cold. Confused. Lorca put his arm about her.

"Let me speak to you," he whispered.

He took her to one side, away from the rest of them.

"We will throw ourselves on the Queen's mercy. She will not dare harm our royal personages. I am the king's grandson. A prince of Oralands. You are my princess. We will be safe," he said in a whisper.

Wishaway peered into his handsome face. Frost had covered his long eyelashes. His blue eyes were earnest and true.

"And the others?" she asked.

"I will insist upon their safety. Needs be that we must give up the Salmon, but we all shall live," Lorca said in a voice that was kind but insistent.

He took Wishaway's cold, fragile hand and squeezed it.

Over his shoulder he could see Jamie looking at him. Jamie caught the glance and turned away.

"Come, Wishaway, let us put an end to this foolishness," Lorca said.

"To the Queen you are the king's grandson, but Lord Ui Neill has no power over her. No country. The Witch Queen will do with him as she will," Wishaway said.

"No, you are wrong. Why dost thou think she follows us deep into this wind-blasted desert? She cares not about her soldiers or her people, she wants that thing from them, the Salmon, that is all. When she gets that, her wishes will be satisfied," Lorca said.

"I don't know."

"Come. We will go to her and present our terms. She will accept them. In a day or two we can be at the coast and on my ship. We will return to Oralands with Anna and Brian, the two hostages, safe and sound. It will appear as a victory to my brothers and the king."

Wishaway looked at him strangely. "Is that what you care about? How things will appear?"

Lorca forced a laugh. "Goodness no. I care about the well-being of you and your friends," he said.

He spoke quickly and sincerely, but Wishaway did note that he said "your friends" not "our friends" or "my friends." Yes, he cared about Jamie, Anna, and the others, but could she believe him when he said that the Witch Queen would let them go? She had seen the Lord Protector and his sister's handiwork before. The Alkhavans had invaded her city, they had destroyed the White Tower of Aldan, they had poisoned the minds of the Aldan Council. They were capable of anything. It was foolhardy to put one's trust, one's life, in their hands.

Wishaway nodded, released Lorca's grip from her hand, walked back to the others.

"Well?" Ramsay said.

Wishaway raised her hand.

"I vote to go on. We are not yet sunk so low that we would prostrate ourselves to the Alkhavans and beg their mercy," she said.

Jamie laughed. "Four to two. A clear majority. We go on," he said.

Lorca could not conceal his fury.

"This is madness. Wishaway, reconsider at once," he said in the harsh imperative speech of formal Aldanese.

"I have cast my vote," she replied in English.

Lorca angrily seized her by the arm and led her away.

"If you love me, you will do as I say, change your vote. We must go back. Think on it, Wishaway," Lorca hissed.

Wishaway burst into tears. She had never been treated so roughly by anyone who said they cared for her.

She broke free of his iron grip. "I do love you, Lorca. But—but—I have to make my own decision," she sobbed.

"You defy me?" he asked.

"I do," she said between tears.

"Then what you call love, I call sham," Lorca said.

"Hurry up, you two. Wishaway, is that your final answer?" Ramsay said.

Wishaway wiped away the tears freezing on her cheeks.

She turned and faced the others.

"Yes," she said.

"You're voting to go on?" Jamie asked, looking all the time at Lorca.

"Yes."

Jamie nodded, as if sensing the subtle power shift between the couple.

"OK, well, I'm changing my vote too," Brian interjected. "I've been thinking about what you said, Anna. You know, you might be right—maybe I've become a bit too infected with negativity, with nihilism . . . I mean . . . I mean, we're not dead yet."

Ramsay punched the air and gave his brother a high five. Lorca shook his head sulkily. Wishaway seemed horribly torn and upset.

"OK, folks, the decision's made. Let's go," Jamie said.

Lorca's face reddened with fury. "You march us to our deaths," he said, and stood there, hands on hips, fuming as they made their preparations.

"Coming?" Ramsay said.

He did not reply. Still seething with anger, he watched them get themselves together and head north.

He fiddled with the king's ring on his finger.

She had lived in that university city all her life. She was spoiled. Eventually she would learn about the real world.

A year or two in the seraglio would teach her.

He let them trudge away for another full minute, but then, with a heavy heart, he kicked the snow off his boots and followed them north, deeper and deeper into the wasteland.

In half a day they had made it to where, according to the map, the Tomb Road was supposed to be, which led to a place called the Tomb of the Ice Gods; but, of course, there was no road. Or, if there was, it existed hundreds of feet beneath them under the glacier ice.

Snow had fallen constantly throughout the afternoon and evening. Wet, moist snow from the west that was easier to melt and drink. It was as good a place as any to camp on the featureless glacial plain. Since it was almost dusk, Brian and Ramsay, still the two strongest, made a cave in the snow, and the motley group bundled themselves inside.

Lorca, still furious from earlier in the day, did not lie next to Wishaway, although in such a cramped space they couldn't help but be in physical contact.

Brian turned on the Salmon, and it gave off a little residual warmth, not as much as a good campfire would have done, but at least it was something.

Not long after dark, the snow and the wind ceased, and the two exhausted Altairians fell asleep.

Anna was next to doze off, and although Jamie tried to stay awake to have a conversation with Ramsay and Brian, he too succumbed to sleep later in the evening.

The wind dropped and the night became still and very cold.

Brian regretted the tarp he'd lost, but the gap allowed them to see into the expanse.

"Hey, Bri, look over there, that's them," Ramsay said in a low tone so as not to wake the others.

In the distance, beyond the horizon, Brian could make out the glow from what could only be the remnants of the Alkhavan Army still in pursuit.

"Yeah, I think you're right. Cooking fires. If we do decide to surrender at least it won't be hard to find them."

"Hey, listen to that," Ramsay said, ignoring him.

Brian took down the hood on his fur jacket. Very faintly, he could hear singing and the sound of drums. Whether the drums were a form of prayer or a marching song or an attempt to intimidate them wasn't clear, but they were certainly unnerving.

"How far away do you think they are?" Ramsay asked.

"Seven, eight hours behind us, not more," Brian said. "We should rest."

They tried closing their eyes, but neither Ramsay nor Brian could sleep.

"Are you still awake?" Ramsay asked after an hour or two. Even after a wearying trip across a glacier, Ramsay's brain wasn't letting him sleep that easily.

"Yeah. You?"

"Yeah . . . Let me ask you something," Ramsay said.

"Ask away, *mon frère*."

"Are you sorry you came here? I mean, all you've experienced is a prison cell and this polar landscape."

Brian smiled in the darkness. "Sorry? Are you kidding?

The chance to go to another world? To experience a wormhole? This is the stuff they dream of at MIT, and I've done it for real. No, I'm not sorry at all. I wish I'd seen more though. The mountains, the cities, the ocean, but I certainly don't regret what I *have* seen."

"We were on the ocean. It's green, you know—I couldn't figure out why."

"The sea is green? Hmmm. Must be a high iron concentration. Hey, have you noticed sometimes that there's a slight red tinge to the sky?"

"Uhhh, well, no, I hadn't."

"There is. The atmosphere's thicker here than on Earth. Hence more refraction of white light and a shift toward the red end of the spectrum. Sunsets over the ocean must be spectacular."

"They're not actually. The sun sets very fast."

"Really? Well, anyway, higher concentrations of all the inert gases too, I'll be bound, and iron dissolving in the sea. Very interesting."

Ramsay had a sudden thought. He took out his cell phone. He typed something in and pointed it at the stars. He pressed Send.

"What are you doing?" Brian asked.

"In case we don't make it. I'm sending a text message to oblivion."

"Good idea. Send one for me too."

Ramsay sent the message, and then after a while both

brothers, strangely comforted, fell into a deep, dreamless sleep . . .

❀ ❀ ❀

Another morning.

Jamie helped Wishaway get up and gave her some melted snow. The party assembled itself and got moving.

This time everyone heard the morning drums of the Alkhavan Army. Their pursuers seemed closer.

Lorca looked pointedly at Ramsay.

"No more discussion. We've made our decision. Come on," Ramsay said.

Jamie was the last to leave the ice cave. He didn't want anyone to know that the feeling was going in the finger-tips of his left hand. The one that the Salmon had made for him.

He buried his fist deep in the sleeve of the fur coat. But it was still agony. Going farther north would be serious trouble. But what choice was there?

They set out.

At least the wind was giving them a respite, and that made it easier today, or at least it did until it started snowing again.

Jamie began to lag back.

The pains in his left hand grew worse. Perhaps the Salmon had not quite fitted the nerve endings properly, made them more vulnerable to cold than they should be.

In an hour no one had noticed that they were a hundred feet ahead of him.

The snow was falling in huge slantwise flakes, almost obliterating them from his sight. It would be easy to let them get ahead, to lie down here in this powdery haze of crystals. An embrace of this big, white blanket of nothingness.

Snow in his eyes, ears, mouth.

An end to all this misery as his existence gently, ever so gently, guttered out like the last candle of Tenebrae.

A brief sleep.

And then what?

And then—

An arm about him.

He looked across.

"Hi," Anna said, startling him a little.

"Mom."

"Hey, you were falling behind there. We can't let that happen," she said with a tiny grin.

"No."

"You were muttering. What were you thinking about so intently?" she asked.

"What?" he managed, his tongue feeling like a piece of leather in his mouth.

"What were you thinking about?" Anna asked again.

"You don't want to know," Jamie replied.

"Tell me."

"What Brian was saying. You know. Death and what comes next."

"And what does come next?"

Jamie put his hand out. His left hand. He let the snow land on it flake by freezing flake. He licked his fingers and felt the moisture in his throat.

"Well," he began, "if you're Lorca you believe that the sun god takes care of your soul and shepherds it to a place of eternal repose. If you're Wishaway you're caught between the ideals of your father who believes that personality does not survive death, and her mother, who had a different, less logical, more comforting view that we're all part of some grander cycle in which we'll eventually be born again in a new body. If you're Ramsay you're doubtful about an afterlife but willing to believe in ghosts and the supernatural if there's evidence enough. Brian, apparently, says our life doesn't matter in the big scheme of things, we're just an insignificant bump in an infinite cosmos."

Anna could see that his arm was in pain. She took a handful of snow and put it in Jamie's mouth. "And what do you believe?" Anna asked.

"I used to think that when we die, that's it. I remember that during my surgery there was nothing—nothing, just blackness."

"You used to think that?"

"Yeah."

"And now?"

"Now I don't know," Jamie said. "I really don't know. The universe is really huge, but everywhere you go the people seem to believe in something bigger than themselves."

They walked together in silence for a moment.

Anna smiled to herself. Jamie had missed the obvious question: Mom, what do you believe?

Anna had thought more about death than any of them.

Death had been her constant companion during her son's surgery and all those months of chemotherapy.

Anna also didn't know what happened after you died.

But she did know one thing.

Death was cunning, and he could get you ten thousand ways.

Death was the enemy and you had to fight him tooth and claw.

Death wanted her firstborn and only son.

She knew that they were all fading, the strong and the weak. And she knew it was up to her. No one was going to slip to the rear on her watch. No one was going to do a Captain Oates and dart out of the cave at night to give the others more of a chance.

Death would not have them. They were all going to live. Either they'd break the will of their followers, or they'd give up, but not a single one of them was going to die.

"Come on," she said to Jamie. "Let's catch up with the guys."

She put her hand under his arm and helped him walk a little faster.

"Hey," she called to Brian. "We walk at the pace of the slowest. Remember?"

"Sorry," Brian yelled back. "Ramsay, take it down a notch."

Ramsay looked back. "Sorry," he said.

The group re-formed. They walked north for the rest of the day at a much reduced pace.

That night only Brian had the strength to dig a cave, shoveling a small hollow in the fluffy snow with his two hands. By the end of it he was utterly exhausted.

They ate the last of their meager supply of *juha* and dried meat and huddled next to the Salmon for warmth, all of them piled practically on top of one another.

For some reason, though, that night they all slept better.

The next morning was overcast and there was no sun, but Brian was convinced that it felt, perhaps, a little warmer.

As if to counter that good feeling, the sound of the Alkhavan drums was definitely closer. Miles away on the far horizon they watched smoke from the campfires of their pursuers.

"They're putting the fires out. Getting ready to move on again," Lorca said.

"So should we," Jamie muttered.

"How much farther?" Lorca asked in a quiet voice. "Wishaway is nearly at her breaking point."

"I'll look after her," Anna said.

"She is my wife," Lorca said with a flash of anger.

"I know, but she's weary, tired. You and me both, we'll both help her, we'll all help her," Anna said.

They woke Wishaway and got her to her feet and gave her some melted snow.

They began marching north.

They had only gone a couple of miles with Jamie on point, when the snow gave way in front of him, and he stumbled and almost fell into a half-kilometer-deep fissure. Brian grabbed the back of Jamie's fur jacket and pulled him backward.

"That was close," Jamie said.

"Yeah, it was," Brian agreed.

The others looked into the deep chasm. It was only a few feet wide but terrifyingly deep.

"A crevasse. Actually noticed several of them in the last few hours. The landscape is changing," Brian said with a conspiratorial grin.

"What's going on?" Jamie asked.

"Well, I thought it was my imagination at first, but now I know it's not. The glacier for some reason is beginning to slope downward. It's not as thick as it was a mile back, and it's getting thinner all the time. Hence the cracks. I think we should rope ourselves together now."

They improvised a rope from belts and the lining of Jamie's Alkhavan backpack, and they walked in single file, tied together, for another hour or two.

They avoided two more crevasses in the snow, but the journey was the easiest since they had climbed up onto Gag Macak in the first place.

Sure enough the glacier was sloping downward, and the air did appear to be getting warmer.

Brian was the first to notice the old Tomb Road appearing slowly beneath the ice.

"Down there everyone, look, do you see that?"

"What is it?" Anna asked.

"Up here the glacier has thinned to such an extent that the buried road to the Tomb of the Ice Gods has reappeared," Brian explained.

"Aye. It's the thing on the map. It's the road," Ramsay said, his eyes filled with renewed fire.

They edged down the slope, along the thinner and thinner glacier and finally onto an old granite road, made from massive boulders that would have lasted thousands of years had it not been for the ice.

They stopped to get their bearings and take another drink of snowmelt.

"Come on, folks, let's go all the way to the tomb, bound to be shelter there," Ramsay said excitedly.

The Altairians did not have the strength to speak, but Anna knew they were close to utter exhaustion. She looked at Brian significantly. They weren't going anywhere at the moment.

"Nah, my leg's gone, give me a minute or two," Brian said.

They rested for a good hour and then set off again.

Walking on the road was far easier than on the surface of the glacier.

Ramsay looked at his brother. "Feeling better?"

"Yeah."

"Good. Need to pick your brains. Didn't want to ask in front of the others. Spook them, you know. But what's going on? It should be getting colder as we go north, instead it's getting warmer."

"I don't know. I thought it was just the cloud cover from the snow, but it's not. We're getting closer to the tomb. Maybe something to do with it is altering the base air temperature," Brian mused.

"Aye, maybe the tomb is really a volcano or something, or a hot spring," Ramsay said excitedly.

"Yeah, could be, or maybe it is just a tomb, but the reason they put it here is because of the different weather, because it's a little oasis of warmth in the middle of this ice desert."

"We'll soon see at any rate."

The road continued for a half mile with the gently sloping glacier on either side of it, then it began to narrow again between massive canyons of ice.

But still they weren't worried.

Something was up.

Something *was* warming the air.

It wasn't so warm that they could take off their coats, but it was definitely getting close to the freezing point, perhaps even a little above.

The microclimate had improved considerably.

They began to see clumps of moss, and in direct sunlight, once, a pool of standing water.

The road twisted and turned through the glacier cliffs, and it was impossible to tell what was round the next bend.

It was Jamie, on point again, who saw it first.

Walking on the granite highway between the two sheer sides of the ice canyon, he turned the next bend and spotted it immediately.

He didn't say anything.

He just stood there.

Amazed.

Remembering after half a minute that he had to breathe.

Ramsay turned the corner next.

"Wow," was the best that he could manage.

Finally the others came one by one, with Brian in the rear.

Brian had traveled and seen something of the earth.

He had comparisons in his head.

Perhaps it was like that first glimpse of Petra between the rocks of the Jordanian desert, or dawn over Machu Picchu in the gap between the Andes mountains, or sunset at Angkor Wat through the canopy of the Cambodian jungle.

But no, it wasn't like any of those things.

Was it a hallucination? A fantasy? A mirage? A thing you see to comfort yourself in times of need?

The hell it was.

Summoning the energy from some artesian reserve Brian started to run.

The others started to run too.

They stopped when they were twenty meters away.

And then they all just *looked*.

Ramsay finally stated the obvious.

"It's not a tomb at all. It's a spaceship," he said. "An alien spaceship."

* * *

It was, undeniably, an alien spaceship. A massive, symmetrical, oval vessel. Fifteen feet high, perhaps a hundred feet long.

There was no obvious power system, bridge, or distinguishing external features. Its hull a smooth, matte black—clean and apparently unmolested by the most hostile of hostile environments.

It was sinister, and even the glacier seemed to surround it with caution, keeping its distance, as if knowing that it would do no good to attempt to absorb it into its geography.

Curved at the ends, it could have been a surfboard built for a giant; or if you were desperately hunting for analogies, you might think that it was like some ruined warship or nuclear submarine, beached on its side and abandoned here on a foreign shore.

But that would have been a stretch, for, unlike nearly everything else on Altair (political systems, cultures, even biology), which had parallels or antecedents on Earth and could be comprehended within a human frame of reference, this was a thing inescapably alien.

Actually, it wasn't quite a true oval, nor even an oblong.

In fact it was cut to an angle no man would have made, which perhaps explained why the Alkhavans had thought that this was a tomb carved by or for their "ice gods."

It didn't look like it could fly, and yet Brian saw that this was how it had gotten here, centuries ago, before the glacier had begun to migrate south, when this was woodland, or at least steppe.

Now the plants were all but gone and what remained was a dark brick of sinister warmth in a sea of whiteness.

It looked dead, inert, but if you got close and put your

ear next to its complex metal skin, it seemed to make a noise, like singing.

They walked up to it.

Touched it.

A hull like no other, seemingly manufactured from the same superconducting material as the Salmon itself.

It wasn't big, but it was big enough.

They all knew that if they could get inside, they could live comfortably for a long time and if they could get it working . . . Well, the possibilities were endless.

For some reason everyone found its oppressive form ugly, except for Brian, who argued that perhaps for a species uninterested in aesthetics, utility was beauty enough. No one could deny its engineering properties. For the whole afternoon they explored it. Walking on it, walking round it, looking for symbols, writing, anything. But either the aliens didn't believe in marking up their ships or the centuries of weathering had taken a toll. Considering the state of the hull, the former seemed the most likely scenario.

They hadn't heard the Alkhavans all day, but around dusk, far off in the distance, Anna thought she could make out the sound of drums. Perhaps the army setting up camp.

It was an alien spaceship, it warmed the local environment, but they needed more than that. They needed it to help them. They rested, drank some of the water lying in clear pools about the vessel, and set off to explore it once again.

Night was coming and their morale was starting to flag a little when Wishaway found the door.

A large circular porthole near one of the ends, it fit perfectly into the rest of the hull and was barely visible as an entrance.

"Here," she cried. "Come here."

They quickly gathered there and looked at it.

It hadn't been opened in millennia, but everyone saw that that was about to change.

A croissant-shaped slot next to the door was obviously fitted for a device such as the Salmon.

Without a word Jamie took the Salmon out of his backpack.

"Go on then," Ramsay said.

But Brian stopped Jamie's hand. He knew that this was a seminal moment. He could picture it all in his head. Before the environment had gotten too fraught for anyone to venture here, he could imagine the hundreds of attempts that various Altairian peoples had made to get inside this thing. Stone tools, fire, metal tools, acids, bases, perhaps even primitive explosives. None of it would have worked. This ship was built to withstand interstellar travel. It was built to last. The technology this vessel represented was centuries ahead of anything on Altair or Earth.

You didn't go inside a spaceship like this without at

least appreciating the awe of the moment.

"What?" Jamie asked impatiently.

"We're about to come into contact with an ancient culture, maybe the most ancient culture in the universe. Think of Hiram Bingham or Howard Carter or one of those guys. This is something you do with rever—"

Jamie removed Brian's hand from his wrist.

"Open the pod bay doors, Hal," Ramsay said.

"This isn't a time for levity, we don't know what's in there," Brian snapped.

"It's just like *Expedition to the Barrier Peaks*, from D and D," Ramsay explained.

"Expedition to the?" Brian asked.

"A Dungeons and Dragons module. I helped write the Wikipedia entry. I'm ready for an alien spaceship. Come on, let's get in," Ramsay said.

"Brian, if we don't get inside we're going to be in trouble," Anna said softly.

Ramsay looked at his older brother and sighed. "Brian, mate, the Alkhavans are coming. We're gonna be up the creek if we don't get in."

Brian sighed. Of course they were all right. "OK, Jamie, do it," Brian said.

Jamie nodded, inserted the Salmon in the slot, and opened the door.

Chapter XI
THE SHIP

PHANTASM. MIRAGE. GHOST SHIP. A thirty-meter oval coffin of black steel lying on the ground as if it had been there for all eternity.

It labored under no dust, no snow, no ice.

A wonder of old-universe technology. And, apparently, as good as new. After the Salmon was inserted, the door slid across, lights came on, and the ship powered itself up.

"Just like an old Toyota pickup," Ramsay said, and went immediately inside.

The rest followed, inside a "flying saucer" that had been hibernating for thousands of years. It was a thing so fantastic that the very idea took the breath away. Unknown aliens had built it, powered it, flown it, and although they were long, long, gone, tantalizingly silent it had sat there, a secret keeper holding within it the quiet of eons.

And yet . . .

And yet no one would quite admit that the interior of the spaceship was something of an anticlimax.

Unlike the entire afternoon they had taken to explore

the exterior of the ship, the inside they had pretty much sussed in about twenty minutes. The problem was that about 95 percent of the craft's volume was taken up with what appeared to be an engine—a huge black tubular device that resembled a particle accelerator that had been cut into thousands of sections and piled on top of one another. There seemed to be no moving parts, no flashing lights, and the engine made no sound whatsoever.

To Brian's immense frustration you couldn't actually get into it, and it was only visible through a couple of small access ports in a bulkhead. How it was maintained or supplied with energy was a complete mystery.

The remaining 5 percent of the ship was obviously where the crew lived and flew the thing.

A small bridge, a few side chambers, a tiny storage or possibly sleeping area, a couple of odd triangular rooms that might have been meditation zones or a sort of mini squash court or, well, anything really.

It wasn't big, and Jamie felt that you certainly couldn't spend a lot of time on this ship without wishing you had a good book to read. Ramsay and Brian speculated that the engine was so powerful that interstellar voyages were of short duration, but, regardless, either the aliens did not spend long periods on board awake, or, if they did, they had an incredible capacity for warding off boredom. To everyone's huge disappointment there was no food, no supplies, no water, no futuristic video games. There were a couple of portholes in the floor through which you could see compacted dirt.

"Let's hope that at least I Spy in space is going to be fun," Jamie said to no one in particular.

The bridge was by far the most interesting part of the ship. It looked like one of the many "white rooms" Brian had seen at MIT and when he'd interned at Motorola. There weren't any seats and no obvious controls save a series of tubular holes penetrating a long, featureless, metallic dashboard. No monitors, joysticks, buttons, nothing but the "control panel" and its tubes.

When their thorough exploration was done, Jamie sized up the situation and looked at Brian.

"Well, Einstein, what do you think?" Jamie asked.

"About what?" he asked.

"The army will be here in the morning. I don't know what they can do to harm the ship, if anything, but I don't want to find out. OK?"

Brian still wasn't getting it. "So?"

"We're going to get this thing to fly," Jamie said with a grin.

"How do you know that?" Brian snapped with condescension.

"I know it because if we don't get this thing to fly we're not getting back to Earth," Jamie said.

"Why are you looking at me?" Brian asked.

"Because you're the smartest," Jamie said. "I'll get Ramsay to help ya."

"I don't think that—" Brian began.

"Forget about it. With the army hot on our heels, there isn't time for the usual pointless arguments. Now we're going to get some sleep, and in the morning you and Ramsay can figure out how this thing works," Jamie said, slipping in a little New York attitude.

And after only a few more pointless arguments they all curled up together on the bridge, and one by one they drifted into a warm dream-filled sleep.

Morning.

Ramsay and Brian began playing with the control panel while the others went outside.

It was snowing again, but the ship's mysterious heat was stopping the snow from accumulating. The little flakes fizzled on the saucer's surface and evaporated. This effect carried on for hundreds of meters around the vessel.

Still the air was chilly, and they put the hoods up on their coats.

"We'll fan out and look for something to eat," Jamie said.

Lorca nodded sullenly and took Wishaway on a circuit around the ship.

Anna looked at her son. She was in a difficult position. She wanted to question Jamie, but she couldn't do it in front of the others. She was his mother, but he was the acknowledged leader of the group. She bent down to tie the laces on her brand-new Nikes, now horribly broken in because of the ice and cold.

Jamie stopped beside her. When Wishaway and Lorca were well out of earshot she stood again.

"Jamie, tell me the truth, what on earth are we doing out here? You know there's no food."

Jamie nodded. He sometimes forgot that his mom was pretty smart too.

"Look, if we'd been in the ship Brian would have been too embarrassed to try anything. Now that we're not in there, he and Ramsay can get in blazing arguments, hit things, jump on things, try stuff, and really maybe get that big beast working."

"So we're just killing time out here in the snow?" Anna asked.

"'Fraid so. Look around ya. There's no plants. No plants, no animals, nothing."

Jamie was right about a lot of things, but he wasn't right about everything. The ship had created a huge island of warmth in the middle of the glacier, and this had developed a microclimate in which, surprisingly, things could indeed grow.

Wishaway and Lorca saw that there wasn't anything interesting around the "tomb," but just on the other side of a huge finger of ice, at the bottom of a glacial valley, there *were* plants growing—brown, stubby things with what looked like red berries on them.

"Look," Wishaway said.

"I see them," Lorca concurred.

They ran down a fairly steep slope that led to the bottom of the glacial depression, slipped, fell, got up, ate a couple of sweet-tasting berries, and hugged each other for joy.

Excitedly they stuffed their pockets and, bursting with excitement, brought a full batch of berries back up the slope again.

"Everyone is going to be shocked," Lorca predicted.

They were holding hands and burbling with joy as they walked past the massive finger of blue glacial ice, but when they got back to the ship they found that their amazing discovery was being outrageously upstaged.

Inside the saucer Brian and Ramsay were experimenting with the ship's flight controls, the big holes in the dashboard, into which tentacles or trunklike appendages must have been thrust in the past. They had discovered that if they worked together, sticking their arms into the tubes, holographic screens appeared in front of them, showing them what they were doing.

And outside what they were doing was getting the ship to hover above the ground. The first time it had flown in probably thousands of years.

Jamie and Anna were watching the vessel with admiration and amazement.

"Berries," Wishaway said, coming up next to him.

"Oh great. Thanks," Jamie replied absently. He pointed at the ship. "Do you see that? How long did that take them? Twenty-five minutes? I'd give Brian a PhD, wouldn't you?"

When the ship landed the door opened, and they all ran inside.

"You did it!" Wishaway exclaimed, and kissed Ramsay on the cheek.

Anna hugged Brian and kissed him too. Rather longer than Wishaway's little peck. "You guys really did it," Jamie said.

Brian nodded and grinned with amazement at himself. "Yeah. It's uhm, I guess, it's all fly by wire. User-friendly apps. Did you see? We managed to get the ship to levitate off the ground, bank a little to the side, and land again."

Jamie nodded. "We all saw," he said.

"Perhaps if we spend the next few days and weeks learning in increments, little by little, in due time, we'll get this thing into space," Brian said with an odd humorous note in his voice.

Jamie frowned. This was not a time for joking around.

"The army's coming. We don't have a few weeks, Brian, as you well know," Jamie snapped.

Ramsay started to laugh and winked at his brother. Brian winked back.

"OK, what is it?" Jamie said.

"Fortunately I don't think we're going to need weeks," Ramsay said.

Jamie saw now that Brian had discovered something else. The brothers could not quite contain their delight, and their attempt at subterfuge was very annoying.

"Spill," Jamie said.

Brian grinned. "Spill the beans, he says. Well, OK everybody, take a look at this, it's good," he said.

"Better than getting the ship to fly?" Jamie asked.

Ramsay nodded. Brian nodded. "Much better," Brian said.

"What could be better than getting the ship to fly?" Anna asked.

"You'll see," Brian said.

"He ain't kidding," Ramsay added, making Jamie more annoyed than ever.

"Just show us!" Jamie yelled.

Brian reached onto the control table and put his fist into a shallow opening, a flat disk into which the aliens must have placed their tentacle/trunk/arm.

"OK, you want to see something really cool?" Brian said.

"Yeah, come on, let's do it," Jamie said, expecting disappointment after all this brotherly hype.

Brian did something inside the tube, and immediately a holographic image appeared in front of them.

An image of a world.

A blue-green planet rotating in space, orbited by a single moon.

Earth.

It was the Earth of perhaps fifteen thousand years ago, when ice covered most of Eurasia and North America. So much of the planet's moisture was locked up in the ice caps that there were land bridges between Ireland and Scotland, between Russia and Alaska, and across many of the narrow seas of modern times.

"It's the Earth of the last ice age," Brian said. "I guess that means the aliens haven't been around for ten thousand years. They were here and now they're gone. Virus, disease, war? Who can say what happened to them or where they went. Imagine a galaxy brimming with life with hundreds of planetary cultures suddenly vanishing into the—"

Jamie stopped him before he got carried away. "What does this mean?" Jamie asked. "This picture of Earth?"

"It's the computer asking us to engage the, uhm, warp

drive, the interdimensional gate, whatever you want to call it," Brian said.

"What?" Jamie said.

"The warp drive, Jamie, the ship does the same thing the Salmon does, but without the need for one of those fixed towers or the splitting up of our atoms. This ship is one big quantum tunneling device," Ramsay said, waving his arms about excitedly.

"Yeah but what does *that* mean?" Jamie insisted.

"It means that we can leave today. Right now in fact. We've been wasting our time messing around with the flight controls when, in fact, we don't even need them to take off. All we need to do is engage this: the warp drive. It'll take over the flight controls, zip us out of the atmosphere, and create a wormhole that'll take us to Earth," Brian said.

"Are you sure?" Jamie asked.

"Well, I mean, obviously the ship hasn't flown there for ten thousand years, but I don't think it's forgotten how," Brian said.

Anna gasped and hugged Brian.

"Is it safe?" she asked in disbelief.

Brian laughed. "As houses. If I engage the drive, the ship's computer will take us straight home. The computer will find our star, find Earth, and take us there."

"How do we do that?" Jamie asked.

"I engage it by pressing down and to the side of this tube. I'm not going to try it now. Once we get started there's no stopping us. It's home or bust," Brian said.

Lorca had been getting agitated during this conversation. It wasn't that he didn't follow what they were saying. He followed it all too well.

"But you're learning to fly the ship. We don't have to go to Earth. Once you get up into the skies, we can go back to Oralands or Aldan. We don't have to go to Earth," Lorca said.

It was not in Jamie's nature to be manipulative, but he saw that this was his last and only chance. He couldn't read Lorca's thoughts, but he could guess them. Earth would be a disaster for him. If he went to Earth his life would be over. The exiled prince, among strangers who knew nothing of their lands and customs? It would be Bonny Prince Charlie drunk in Paris, it would be Alex Rodriguez playing for the Yankees. It would be lame. Pathetic. Not only would he lose his power, his position, his whole raison d'être, but there was also that chance that on Earth he would lose her too. There was that spark between Jamie and Wishaway that could not be denied.

Jamie took Ramsay to one side. "Listen, buddy, what I'm going to need from you is clarity. Explain the situation. We're going to Earth. Earth, OK? You and I both know that it's going to take weeks, months, probably never for you guys to fly this thing, whereas the autopilot is going to take us straight to Earth. That should be our focus. Get me?" Jamie whispered.

Ramsay looked at him strangely. "Of course. Why the cloak-and-dagger?"

Jamie led Ramsay out into the corridor even farther from the others.

"Because, Ramsay, if I know Lorca, and I *know* Lorca, he doesn't want to go to Earth. His world is back there in Oralands," he whispered.

"Why do you say that?" Ramsay said.

"Don't you see? Here he's a prince of Oralands. On Earth he's a nobody. He's not going to come and he's going to make Wishaway choose. And she's seen Earth and seen that fool's paradise in Oralands, and if she chooses to stay with him here, well then I lost fair and square. See?"

Ramsay nodded. "Let the chips fall where they may," he said.

"Exactly," Jamie replied.

"What do you want me to do?" Ramsay asked.

"Nothing dishonest. Just tell it like it is."

"OK. I got your back, mate," Ramsay said.

Lorca looked at them suspiciously as they walked back onto the bridge.

"OK," Ramsay began, "Jamie and I have discussed it,

and this is my take. There's no time to waste. The army's coming, our supplies are gone, Brian can get this working, and once the process is started we're going to be going directly to Earth. Forget flying to Aldan or wherever. Has to be the warp drive to Earth. It's our only hope."

No one said anything.

"Earth. OK? Any objections? . . . Lorca?" Jamie asked. "No? OK. Good. All right then, we need to start working. First, we don't know how long the flight's going to be, so we're going to have to bring in a few bags of snow that we can melt for water. Mom, you and Ramsay go outside and get the snow, OK?"

They nodded.

"Good. Now, Brian, you'll stay here and try and master those flight controls. Lorca, you, me, and Wishaway will gather all the berries that we can find on the far side of the ridge. That should stave off the hunger pangs for a while."

Wishaway nodded.

"OK, everyone, that's it. We'll meet back here in, say, sixty minutes at the most, and then the next stop: home."

Anna was so proud of Jamie that she couldn't help but lean forward and give him a kiss on the cheek. "Well done," she mouthed.

And everyone else was excited, happy.

Well, nearly everyone.

Lorca had grown increasingly quiet. Jamie had noted it. He looked at Ramsay to get his spin. The big Irishman had seen it too. Lorca's eyes had become narrow slits. Sullenness had formed above him like a cloud.

"OK, Lorca, come on, let's go outside and we'll pick us some ice berries," Jamie said cheerfully.

Lorca nodded. "Go ahead, Lord Ui Neill, I will catch thee," he said carefully.

"Nah, too dangerous, we'll all go together," Jamie insisted.

Lorca looked at him. The boy was trying to provoke him.

There was nothing else for it.

He had to tell her.

He took Wishaway to the doorway of the saucer and led her outside.

He held her hand. "Wishaway, my love," he began.

Wishaway smiled. This was the first sign of real affection that he had showed her in days.

"Yes?" she said.

"Wishaway, I must tell you, I will not be going to Earth," he said simply.

Wishaway looked at him. "What are you talking about?"

Lorca knew better than to cast the debate in terms of

personalities, a battle of him versus Jamie. "My duty is to Oralands. My father will be king one day; I must help rule the country. I cannot desert my people. You yourself made the same decision when Jamie left us in the White Tower. You could not leave Aldan. Nor I my own people."

"We must help the Lord Ui Neill go to Earth," Wishaway said.

"No," Lorca said.

"There is no other way to get back," Wishaway protested.

"I will find another way."

Wishaway pointed back at the glacier. "There is only ice and death."

"No. We will march to the Alkhavan lines. The pickets will find us and take us to the Queen. No one of royal blood will harm another sovereign. Besides we are too valuable alive. She knows that if she ransoms us, my father will pay heavily."

"They'll kill us," Wishaway said.

"They will not kill us. I understand them now. I understand their desperation after being up here on the glacier. I will tell them that I wish to help them. Perhaps we *can* help them somehow."

"They'll kill us, Lorca. All they care about is the Salmon."

Then we must give it to them, he almost said. Rather

he knew that he had to assert his authority. Wishaway was weakening. She had to see the rightness of his position.

"Come. Say your farewells. We are leaving. As Jamie said, the army will only be a few hours behind us now," Lorca explained.

Wishaway let go of his hand.

She started to cry. "It's madness," she said. And she meant it. Why would they even dream of gambling their lives with the Witch Queen when they could all go to Earth? What was Lorca thinking?

"I am leaving," Lorca insisted.

She stared at him. "I cannot go with you," Wishaway said.

Lorca looked at her with fury. "I insist upon it," he yelled so loudly that the others couldn't help but hear and come to see what the disturbance was.

Jamie tried to approach them. "Guys, listen—"

"Keep back, Lord Ui Neill, this is not your concern," Lorca interrupted. "Come, Wishaway, we shall go."

But again, stubbornly, she shook her head.

"I command it," Lorca said.

"No."

"You dare defy me? Your husband?"

"We're not quite married yet," Wishaway said softly.

That was the final straw. Lorca raised his arm above

his head. Wishaway took a step backward. Lorca's face flushed and then, horrified, he let his arm fall to his side.

"I'm sorry, I didn't mean to frighten you, I . . ." he said, his cheeks burning with shame.

"Save your words for the women of Oralands," she said.

Jamie was finding it hard to conceal a smile. Lorca looked at him. Suddenly, he had the feeling that he had been tricked into this, that he had been set up. His fury overflowed. "Thou. Thou hast poisoned her. This was thy plan all along," Lorca said spitting out the words with hate.

"You're crazy," Jamie said.

Lorca went for him. He tried to hit him, but Jamie stepped to one side. Lorca slipped, grabbed Jamie's feet, and dragged him to the ground. Punches flew for a few moments until Brian and Ramsay pulled them apart.

The prince of Oralands got to his feet. He pushed his hair out of his face and tried to retain his dignity. "Come, Wishaway," he said, and tried to grab her arm.

"No," Wishaway yelled.

"Come, I will not tell you again."

"I have given you my answer," Wishaway said. She shut her eyes and shook her head firmly.

Brian removed Lorca's hand from Wishaway's sleeve.

"You heard the lady. Now go if you're going."

Without another word Lorca walked away from the spaceship.

"Come on!" Jamie yelled, full of guilt. "You'll die out there."

"Then die I must," Lorca said without looking back.

"We've got to go after him," Jamie said.

Ramsay shook his head. "Don't worry about it. He'll be back, you'll see."

The Queen was going to say something, he could tell because she had pulled the curtain across on her window. Ksar smiled and looked across to his sister's litter. They were both being carried along the old Tomb Road. Not terribly comfortable but it was the only option. *Drayas* could not survive on the glacier, and the dignity of their offices did not allow them to go on foot like a common soldier.

The litter was being carried by four strong Alkhavans who would have fought one another for the honor of bearing the Queen and Lord Protector, had such a thing been seemly.

"If only your *rantas* could withstand the cold, we would have spotted them by now," the Queen said.

Ksar nodded. Unfortunately the *rantas* could not bear ice on their leathery wings.

Still it was an intriguing idea. A *ranta* as their forward observer. Perhaps even as an attacker. That would have been delicious. The Ui Neills being shot at from the air by men with crossbows.

"Do not worry, with every hour that passes their position becomes more desperate," Ksar said.

"Yes," the Witch Queen said, but she had already noticed that the air temperature was warming up. She knew if the Ui Neills had made it to the tomb, they would not, at least, freeze to death.

Of course she kept this information from her brother. What he didn't know would not harm him.

And anyway even if the Ui Neills did make it to the tomb, what then?

They were trapped.

She looked behind her at the army. They had taken five hundred men with them up onto the glacier. Losses had not been particularly bad. Perhaps a few hundred had suffered frostbite and ice burns. No more than fifty had died. It was a small price to pay when the fate of the entire population of Alkhava was at stake.

Two hundred healthy soldiers could surely best half a dozen barbarians and minor royals.

She noticed one of the fast pickets, no longer on *draya*-back, run to the Lord Protector's litter. He clearly had something to say but would not speak until bid.

"Yes?" Ksar asked after a pause long enough to demonstrate his supreme authority.

"Sir. Protector Krama at the head of the column sent me straight to you, sir."

"Well, what is it?"

"A prisoner, sir."

Ksar tried to conceal his surprise. "A prisoner?"

"Yes, sir. We found him marching toward our lines. He said he was surrendering. We brought him to Protector Krama."

"Who is he?" Ksar asked.

"Protector Krama questioned him. He claims to be Prince Lorca, sir. Protector Krama believes this to be the case. He sends his compliments and asks if you wish to see the prisoner?"

Ksar nodded. "Tell Krama to send him here immediately."

The messenger ran back along the line of soldiers.

"Did you hear that?" Ksar asked his sister.

"What is it? Another setback?" the Witch Queen asked sarcastically.

"Prince Lorca has surrendered to us," Ksar said.

"Indeed? Indeed. Perhaps he may be of some use," she replied.

Two minutes later Krama and half a dozen guards brought the young Oralands prince to Ksar's litter.

"Krama, halt the column while we talk to our honored guest," Lord Protector Ksar said. He got out of his litter and bowed to Lorca with great dignity. The Witch Queen descended from her carriage, but she did not condescend to bow to the man who had attacked her city.

"Why have you come here?" Ksar asked.

"I throw myself at your goodwill, Lord Protector Ksar and my lady the Queen of the Alkhav. And as a sign of my goodwill, I present my person and I bring you information," Lorca said in a passable Alkhavan dialect.

"Speak it," Ksar replied in English.

"The Tomb of the Ice Gods is no tomb. It is an alien vessel that the Lords Ui Neill will use to journey across the stars. They are there ahead of you on this road. Their plan is to fly the ship and escape this world."

"A vessel, I knew it," the Witch Queen said.

The Lord Protector looked at his sister.

"I suspected it," the Witch Queen corrected herself. "Since the days of Master Sarpa and the Twenty-seventh Queen, we have believed something of the kind. We were never able to penetrate the vessel's hide, and of course in the last few decades conditions here have been abominable."

"You would never have been able to get inside. Only the Salmon of Knowledge unlocked the secrets of the 'spaceship,'" Lorca said.

"The Salmon. Always that. We were right to covet it so," the Witch Queen said bitterly.

"If thou wilt hurry thy army, ye will catch them before they leave. Ye shall have the ship and the Salmon and the Lords Ui Neill themselves," Lorca said excitedly in English.

Ksar looked at his sister. Was this a trap? What did she make of it? The Witch Queen saw her brother's questioning face and nodded. She would probe this further.

"Tell me. What ails thee, Prince?" the Witch Queen asked gently.

"Nothing, I—"

"Tell me," she said again.

Lorca looked into her stern, handsome face. She seemed to know already, so perhaps there was no harm in speaking plainly.

"My, my wife flees with the Earth boy. I do not wish her to go. I could not force her to come with me. The Ui Neills stopped me from taking her. I will not allow her to go."

The Witch Queen nodded. The oldest reason in the world. Why hadn't she thought of that before as a potential wedge between them?

"You have a bargain for us no doubt, Prince Lorca. What do you suggest?" she asked.

"I will lead you to them. If they are inside the ship thou wilt not be able to get in. If ye conceal thy force I will draw them out and ye may seize them," Lorca said.

"Hmm, there will be a struggle," the Lord Protector

said, sighing. "There may be casualties, your friends may be hurt."

Lorca nodded. "I understand, but this I must stress: On no account must my lady, the Princess Wishaway, be harmed. We will have no agreement unless you promise me that . . ."

The Lord Protector looked at the Witch Queen. She gave the slightest of bows.

"Princess Wishaway will not be harmed, Prince Lorca," the Lord Protector said. He nodded to Krama.

"You have heard?"

Krama nodded.

"The prince will guide us to the Ui Neills, he will draw them out, and we will spare his wife. Not a hair of her head must be touched. On pain of death, Krama," Ksar said.

"Understood, sir," Krama said.

Ksar turned to Lorca. "Anything else?"

"Wishaway and I will be allowed passage to Oralands. My father will pay any reasonable sum in ransom for our—"

The Witch Queen interrupted him. "If ye deliver to us the Salmon, the Ui Neills, and this alien vessel, no such ransom will be necessary. Thee and thy bride will be free to return to thine own country," she said. And almost meant it. For really what would any of this matter after she had the Salmon in her power?

Lorca nodded.

"Then ye art satisfied?" Ksar asked.

"I am," Lorca said.

"Well then, lead on, young prince, and if you are taking us to an ambush, I assure you that you and your bride will die," Lord Protector Ksar said in a fair approximation of the royal dialect of Oralands.

Lorca didn't even hear that threat.

His eyes were still blazing with fury.

How could she do this to him? How could she humiliate him like this? It was their influence. Their foreign words. Their talk of Earth and its foolish joys. Well, he would show them. He would lead the enemy into their camp.

That would teach them.

That would teach her.

He walked down the valley and turned the corner between the ice cliffs. It was still there in all its horrible foreignness, this monstrosity from another world.

They had not left yet.

"Jamie! Ramsay!" Lorca called out.

His voice echoed off the disgusting alien vessel's hull. There was no sign of any of them. He walked to the closed entrance. They had to be inside.

Lorca banged heavily on the odd metallic door.

"Who is it?" a muffled voice asked.

"It is I, Lorca, I have returned," he said with some embarrassment.

He heard Anna's voice. "Brian, it's Lorca, can you figure out how to open the—"

The door opened with a quiet hiss.

Anna grinned. "Lorca, you came back. I am so glad," she said and gave him a hug. She shouted inside: "It's him!"

Lorca looked at his boots. "I have come, I had to, uhm . . ."

Brian and Ramsay appeared. Brian shook his hand.

"I knew you'd be back. Well done, mate. Swallowed your pride. You're a bigger man than I thought," Brian said.

"Where are Jamie and Wishaway?" Lorca asked.

"They're finishing up the berries. Already got a whole bag of them. Jamie thinks they can get another," Ramsay said.

"On the other side of the ice ridge?" Lorca asked.

"Yeah."

Lorca nodded. "All of you please come over here, there is something I wish to show you," he said.

"What is it?" Ramsay asked.

Lorca's mind raced. "It is a surprise. It will help us on our journey," Lorca said, desperately trying to make his voice sound natural.

They followed Lorca to the beginnings of the Tomb Road without suspicion.

"What is this?" Anna asked.

"A little farther," Lorca said. He needed them well away from the ship, so that the troops around the corner could seize them without bloodshed.

A look passed between Brian and Anna; both had picked up on his nervousness.

"I think we should get back to the ship," Anna said.

They were fifty paces from the door. Lorca knew he would have no better chance.

"Now! Now!" he yelled in Alkhavan.

From around the corner of the ice cliff the Lord Protector, Krama, and a dozen of his finest men came charging toward them.

Lorca jumped on Ramsay and tried to pull him down.

"Back to the ship," Brian said, and pushed Anna behind him. He kicked Lorca in the back and threw him off his brother.

The two fastest Alkhavans were on top of them. Big men with knives. The first swung at Brian's head. He ducked and kicked him in the shins.

Ramsay barreled into the second of the Alkhavans and shouldered him to the ground. Brian punched the second man in the stomach, kicked him in the head, and grabbed his knife.

He growled and threatened the Alkhavans with the blade. Brian's fearsome expression and wild red hair were enough to stop the other Alkhavans in their tracks.

Lorca scrambled to the approaching soldiers.

"Traitor!" Ramsay yelled.

"Forget him!" Anna shouted. "Come on, boys."

Brian threw the knife at Ksar, grabbed Ramsay, and ran the short hop back to the ship.

They got inside, sprinted straight to the bridge, and shut the hatch. Lord Protector Ksar made it to the saucer just as the metal door closed with a resounding hiss.

Ksar smashed his fist into the ship's hull.

"Lorca, you fool. You did nothing to prevent them," the Lord Protector bellowed.

The Witch Queen walked sedately to her brother.

"He has let them get inside," Ksar said.

"They will fly now?" she asked, concealing her fury.

Lorca smiled. "We must act quickly. Come. They will not be going anywhere. Jamie and Wishaway are on the other side of that ice ridge gathering berries for the journey ahead. Ramsay and Anna will not leave without Jamie, this I assure you."

Ksar's burned face lit up. He took out a vial of his pain medication and swallowed the whole thing. "Show me," he said.

"This way," Lorca said. "Place some men here at the

ship's door and we will climb the glacier, walk down the ice slope, and trap them in the next valley . . ."

Ksar ignored the boy's insolence and ordered Krama and fifty men to guard the entrance to the spaceship while he took twenty others and followed Lorca to the top of the ice ridge.

And there beneath them in a narrow valley Jamie and Wishaway were throwing berries into a large bag they had made from someone's shirt. They hadn't heard the shouting and were oblivious to the fact that they were being watched.

"We have them," the Lord Protector whispered.

"Yes," Lorca agreed. For Jamie and Wishaway to get back to the spaceship, they would have to come up to the top of the glacier again, battle through Ksar and the Witch Queen's guards, climb down the other side of the ice ridge, and fight and kill the fifty men guarding the spaceship entrance. Impossible.

Ksar, the Witch Queen, and Lorca knew it was all over.

"There's a path down the glacier to the bottom, it's an irregularity in the ice, not steep, if you let me go—" Lorca began.

"You wait here. I will take them myself," Ksar interrupted.

"Remember, Wishaway is to be unharmed," Lorca said.

"I remember," Ksar replied.

The Lord Protector turned to the Queen. "I will go down with my men. I will attempt to take the Ui Neill alive so that we can offer to exchange him for the Salmon. The prince is right, his mother will not leave without him."

"You will let the Ui Neill go?" the Witch Queen asked, surprised and even pleased—perhaps her brother was learning to play the long game at last. What they needed was the Salmon so that their people could escape this dying world. Personal vendettas were, at best, a distraction from the grander goal.

"The Ui Neill will die one way or another. He will pay for what he has done to me!" Ksar snapped.

The Witch Queen sighed.

"If they try to escape up onto the glacier, perhaps your bowmen will discourage them from that idea," Ksar said.

The Queen nodded. "And the prince?" the Witch Queen asked.

"He is of no further use to us," Ksar said.

The Witch Queen nodded and signaled two members of her personal guard to seize him.

"You have broken your word," Lorca said.

The Witch Queen regarded him. "Be quiet, Oralands invader, no one has broken their word. Yet."

One of the Queen's guards placed a knife at Lorca's

throat to prevent further outbursts. Ksar and his men ran down the steep slope to the valley. There were more than thirty of them. Some skidded on the incline, and one even managed to slip over the side, crashing to the valley below with an awful scream.

Jamie and Wishaway turned and spotted them for the first time.

"I have you, Ui Neill," the Lord Protector shouted with glee.

Lorca saw Jamie and Wishaway drop their bag of berries and look desperately for an exit. But there was no way out. They were trapped in the valley.

The soldiers reached the bottom of the incline and began walking languidly toward the frightened pair.

"Remember, Wishaway is to be spared," Lorca said to the Witch Queen. She ignored him and cooly watched her brother advance on Jamie and the girl.

Jamie doesn't even have a dagger, Lorca thought.

He felt sick. Physically sick. He pushed aside the man guarding him, dropped to his knees, and began to retch. But even that was a failure. He'd eaten so little in the last few days that nothing came out.

"What have I done?" he muttered to himself.

Below him Ksar was triumphant. "Stand fast, Ui Neill!" the Lord Protector yelled, now only a dozen paces from Wishaway and Jamie.

Jamie muttered something but Lorca couldn't hear it.

"Load weapons," the Lord Protector cried, and his soldiers began to put bolts in their crossbows.

"Come to me, Princess Wishaway," Ksar said firmly.

Jamie yelled something and one of Ksar's men loosed a crossbow.

Two other jittery men fired their weapons.

Jamie narrowly missed being hit.

"Come, Wishaway," Ksar said while his men reloaded. Jamie put his arms round her protectively. The soldiers aimed their crossbows.

"They'll murder both of them," Lorca groaned.

"This is your final chance," Ksar said.

Before Jamie could reply, there was a sudden, high-pitched, whining noise from the west. For a moment everyone froze to see what it was.

It grew louder and louder.

Lorca stopped dry-heaving and looked up.

A terribly unearthly burr that was like the sound of a ship running aground, or metal grinding in a forge or—

Just then the glacier seemed to explode in all directions as the alien spaceship crashed sideways through the ice wall between the two valleys.

Screaming, yelling, and utter terror from the Alkhavan soldiers.

The saucer hovered clumsily for a moment, then

landed heavily, sliding across the valley floor and crushing most of Ksar's platoon, only narrowly missing the Lord Protector himself.

As it was, the Alkhavan leader was bombarded by a shower of razor-sharp pieces of ice that cut him in dozens of places.

There was a long, stunned, sickening silence before the spaceship door opened.

Lorca saw Anna standing there.

"Run, Jamie, run!" she yelled. "Brian's going to get us out of here."

Jamie was only fifty paces from the door, but there was a mountain of crushed ice and huge chunks of glacier between him and his mother.

The Lord Protector got to his feet. Jamie ran to him and thumped him in the face. "Do you never learn?" Jamie said.

Ksar weakly swung his dagger, but Jamie bent down, wrestled the injured Ksar and drove his arm backward, stabbing the Alkhavan leader in the stomach with his own knife. Blood poured from the wound. Jamie stepped back.

"Thou . . ." Ksar managed.

Jamie hadn't time for last words.

"Come on, Wishaway, let's go!" Jamie yelled.

"I think I am injured, Lord Ui Neill," she said.

Jamie turned. There was blood on her legs.

"What happened?" he asked, but no answer was necessary. He saw it clear enough—a huge piece of ice had slashed into her thigh. Fortunately, it looked to be only a small laceration, not a fracture, or worse.

"Is there anything broken? Can you stand?"

She nodded.

He put his arm under her shoulder and they began limping over the boulderlike pieces of glacier toward the open saucer door.

The Witch Queen surveyed the scene with pinch-lipped calm.

"Come," she ordered, and her personal guard followed her down the slope to the valley floor. Lorca did a quick calculation in his head. Even going single file, the soldiers would be at the bottom of the incline in a minute. Jamie and Wishaway would need at least two or three minutes to get over the ice field to the spaceship.

They weren't going to make it.

He loosened his limbs and flexed the fingers in his sword hand.

"Hurry," Lorca found himself saying. "Hurry, Jamie."

Jamie and Wishaway were scrambling over the ice, but the Witch Queen's guards were getting closer.

Even Ksar now was getting to his feet again.

Lorca shook his head.

He'd watched long enough.

If Jamie and Wishaway were to get to the ship, then he had to follow the Queen down the slope and fight his way through her guard. The soldiers would kill him, but maybe he would buy Jamie and Wishaway enough time to make it to their ship.

He nodded at the Alkhavan sergeant in possession of his sword. The sergeant nodded back. It was an arresting scene. Dead men lying all over the valley. The spaceship humming. Anna shouting, the Witch Queen yelling, snow tumbling from the sky.

Lorca smiled.

Yes, he would fight her and all of them. It would mean certain death. It would mean that he would die alone and without honor. He had turned his back on his friends, and now he would betray the Queen, to whom he had given his word as a person of royal blood. They would cut him down and kill him. He would lose Wishaway, and she would never know what he had done. None of them would. Forever they would think of him as the man who had deserted them and betrayed them and led their enemies to their door.

But . . .

If he could succeed in making it to the Queen, it would mean that Wishaway would live.

He didn't need to think anymore. He knew what he had to do. He got to his feet. He took off his fur coat.

"Where do you think you're going?" the sergeant of the guard asked him in base Alkhavan.

"I must go down there, I have something to communicate to the Queen," Lorca said simply.

"Tell me," the sergeant demanded.

Lorca knew that there was nothing else for it. He head butted the sergeant in the nose, ripped his own sword from the sergeant's hand, and smashed the man in the face with the hilt.

He set off down the slope, sliding and tumbling as he went.

He went head over heels and crashed into the last of the Witch Queen's troops, an older man who looked like a peasant from his own country.

"Afa gall?" the man asked angrily.

Lorca thrust his sword into the man's gut and stood up.

The other guards turned. "It is the prince!" they yelled in Alkhavan.

Lorca assessed the situation. There were, perhaps, a dozen of them. He looked back—more than that in pursuit, coming gingerly down the slope, led by the angry sergeant. Better get moving then. He slashed at the nearest of the guards, blocked an axe blow at his head, drove his blade into another guard's shoulder, and bundled him and the man next to him off the ice path.

The Queen turned to see what the commotion was.

"Kill him!" she screamed, and now they all came at once.

He slashed, parried, ducked, stabbed, punched, kicked, and drove his way through the guards. He had the advantage of the hill, a superior weapon, better training, and he was helped by the narrowness of the path. He slew one guard and another and another. He shoved the bodies off the ice cliff like a merciless killing machine.

"Run, Jamie, run," he found himself chanting like a mantra.

Cruel knives and axes nicked him on the shoulder or the ribs, but he parried away the killer blows.

Still they came.

A man with a spear he stabbed quickly in the ribs. Another with a short sword he pierced in the eye.

Exhaustion was almost crippling him, but he knew he had to stand here alone and fight for as long as possible to prevent them from reaching his beloved. It was like that tale in the *Book of Stories* of the Spartans at Thermopylae, save that they were three hundred and he was only one.

"Use the bows!" the Witch Queen yelled, and a hail of arrows came at him. One hit him in the stomach, another in the thigh.

He thrust at a small Alkhavan soldier attempting to throw a net at him. Another leaped at him with a knife. Lorca killed the first with a sword swipe to the neck and took the knifeman out with a blade in the lungs.

He fought his way through the remaining guards, slaughtering them in this confined space until he was down to three—the Witch Queen herself and her final two men, a big blond-haired bruiser who was almost as tall as Ramsay and a dark-haired man armed with two curved daggers.

Blood was in his teeth and hair. His eyes were wide with fury. He looked fearsome, terrifying. If only Wishaway could see him. If only she could know what he was doing.

But that was a dream. No one would see. No one would know.

The big blond came at him with a hammer. He ducked the blow, jumped, turned in the air, and drove his sword through the man's face, leaving it there.

"There he is! Fire!" someone said behind him.

The sergeant from the glacier top with a dozen bowmen.

Thock, thock, thock.

He felt three arrows hit him in the back.

The man with the curved daggers stabbed him in the shoulder.

"Is that the best you can do?" Lorca said in Oralands and shoulder-charged the final guard off the ice path.

She was alone now.

"Just you and me," Lorca said.

There were arrows in his back, his legs, his shoulders. There were slash wounds all over his body.

The rest of her men were scrambling to reach her along a path strewn with bloody corpses. She knew that they wouldn't get there in time. It would be she alone who would decide this day. She smiled. She liked that. Happy the person who has her own fate in her own hands at the very end. *She* would save herself and her people or *she* would not.

Lorca looked behind him. Jamie and Wishaway were close now. Ksar was getting to his feet but was too far away to do any harm. They'd make it as long as he could take out the Queen. Lorca removed his sword from the dead man's face.

The Queen appeared to cower from him, backing away, her eyes frightened, disbelieving.

Lorca picked up his fallen sword.

He raised it above his head.

He wasn't to know that her fear was merely a feint. Her knife penetrated his stomach in a blur of movement. He hadn't even seen it. Blood from a severed vein entered his mouth.

The world was closing down.

The light fading.

"Thou diest, *Princeling*," the Witch Queen said, insulting him with that mocking word. He stared into her ice blue vampiric eyes. She was laughing at him.

But it didn't matter. He was past that now. He could see that Jamie and Wishaway had made it inside the ship.

He stepped back and with a savage upthrust he drove his sword into the Queen's belly, driving it up through her organs and into her heart. She gasped and slumped forward almost on top of him. He spat the frothing blood out of his mouth. He wanted to be clearly understood. "Thou, also, Queen of the Alkhav," he said into her ear.

Her face contorted in fury at his superior manners. She tried to speak, but she was beyond words. She would not save her people, she would never see Earth. Her eyes lost their fire and her last breath exhaled.

He laid her body gently on the ground.

Ksar saw his sister fall but he had no time to mourn. He had reached the field of ice boulders. He saw the way through to the saucer.

"I can do it," he muttered to himself.

He too had lost a lot of blood.

He couldn't walk. He was crawling. But if he could make it to the ship . . .

"I must, I must," he said.

And somehow he got to his feet.

"Wait for me, wait for me," he said.

All around him death, slaughter, the smell of blood and ice.

The door was closing.

His last hope.

He leaped.

Dived.

Slipped through.

He was inside. He landed with a thud on a black, glassy surface.

"What was that noise?" he heard Lord Ui Neill's voice shout from the bridge.

Ksar had to think quickly. He was injured. He had no weapons. No place to hide.

He looked at the ground. No blood trail. Yet. But he couldn't stay here. The floor was solid, the walls, impenetrable. He had to get somewhere, a room, a corridor, a—

Up. Above his head there was a small panel that perhaps someone could climb into. "I'm sure I heard something," Jamie said.

"Check the door," Brian said.

With a superhuman effort Ksar pushed open the tiny hatchway. He was cut all over his body from the ice splinters, his stomach was in unbelievable pain, but he managed it. He pulled himself up. Slithered through the hole. Breathed hard.

He saw Jamie appear beneath him.

Carefully he replaced the panel.

"Nothing here," Jamie said.

Safe. For now. Ksar allowed himself a sigh of relief. He had a place to hide, he had air to breathe, and if he could just stop the blood loss he might have a fighting chance.

"Is the door shut?" Brian yelled.

"Yup."

"OK, our work here is done, let's go home."

The ship lifted above the ground.

It crashed sideways into the glacier, knocking off huge chunks of ice. It wobbled on its axis, but then it seemed to stabilize. It lifted higher into the air and flew above the army, frightening everyone from youngest recruit to oldest veteran.

"Steady there, men!" Krama yelled, trying to master his own terror. With the death of the Queen and Ksar, he was in charge now. "Steady, men. Like the fireworks of old, it is merely an Aldan trick."

Some trick, Lorca thought as he watched the ship lift into the sky and disappear into the gray clouds.

He sank to his knees and tumbled face-first to the ground.

The bloody-nosed sergeant turned him over, looked into his dying eyes, and pulled the royal ring off his finger.

"We showed you," the sergeant muttered, and moved down the slope to steal the Witch Queen's rings too.

Lorca didn't care.

The cold was gone.

The battle no longer raged.

He saw falling snow and a dead monarch and the vapor trail of a flying ship.

All of it became dim, and when the light was finally gone he smiled, knowing that he had bested the Witch Queen and the Lord Protector and that his friends were safe and that he had saved Wishaway, his wife, his one true love.

He closed his eyes and felt ice in his lungs.

And then he died.

Chapter XII
THE RETURN

T HE SUN WAS RISING and over the airwaves, Pirate Radio 252 was in a ten-song block of Glenn Miller, Jim Reeves, Patsy Cline, Buddy Holly, John Denver, Lynyrd Skynyrd, Ritchie Valens, Aaliyah, Ricky Nelson, and Otis Redding.

It was Plane Crash Tuesdays on Pirate Radio 252, one of their many tasteless gimmicks to grab listeners in their broadcasting area, which they claimed stretched as far north as Glasgow and as far south as Dublin. The Pirate Radio 252 ship was a converted trawler that cruised out beyond the three-mile limit somewhere between Ireland and Scotland. Because of this, it was not regulated by the British or the Irish authorities and was listened to mostly by youngsters who liked its cheeky defiance as well as its mix of old and new music.

Since it was a ten-song segment, Donal McCawley (the captain/chief engineer) and Phil O'Brian, one of the DJs, were on deck having a smoke. The station feed was playing through a loudspeaker so Phil could tell when he might be needed below. For Phil, any break from Dave Higgins, the other DJ, was extremely welcome. Dave was a professional misanthrope who complained about the boat, the weather, the boredom, and most of all his fellow DJ, Phil. The listeners couldn't get enough of it.

"Should have brought my fishing pole," Phil said to the chief engineer between puffs of his cigarette.

"Aye. Nice day isn't it?" Donal replied.

It was indeed a beautiful day. The pink lough water was as calm as could be, and Scotland to the east and Ireland to the west were green and lovely. Seals were barking, and a few lazy-looking gulls were caging for scraps at the stern of the boat. The dawn had banished the low clouds, and the sun was casting a golden light over the funny little boat with its squat hull, unused trawling nets, and seventy-foot radio antenna bolted onto the cabin roof.

Otis Redding's "Sitting on the Dock of the Bay" ended.

Phil threw his cigarette over the side and ran downstairs.

"The late, great Otis Redding. Now, at six-fifteen, it's time for the local news and weather. Over to you, Phil," Dave said in a ridiculous transatlantic voice that was as phony as his hair, résumé, and tax returns.

"Over to you, Phil," Dave said again as Phil dived into the booth. Phil grabbed his headphones and took a breath.

"The weather is going to be mild and sunny today, Dave. High around twenty degrees Celsius, which isn't bad at all for early spring. Light winds from the west, clear skies tonight . . . The local news is still dominated by the disappearance of four people from Muck Island, three of whom were in the Islandmagee band the Ayatollahs of Funk, an up-and-coming group that placed sixth in the Ireland's Most Talented Youth Belfast heat."

There was a brief moment of dead air.

"You judged that competition, didn't you, Phil?" Dave asked, going off the script.

Phil shot him a look. There was a smug expression creeping around the edge of Dave's mouth. He had obviously done a bit of research about this story.

Phil was immediately suspicious. "Yes, I did actually, Dave, you're right. I was there in Belfast judging that competition for the station," Phil said cautiously.

"And how were the Ayatollahs?" Dave asked with apparent innocence.

"Well, uhm, to be honest, Dave, we, uhm, me and Marty, that is, the overnight guy, we, uhm, left before their set . . . It was raining and we heard that their bassist was thirty years old, so they would have been disqualified anyway."

Dave raised his eyebrows. An unhelpful gesture on the radio.

"You didn't actually hear them play?" Dave asked, surprised.

"No . . . Well, uh, Marty heard the start of the first song, it was about Kurt Cobain, I think."

"Huh. And yet you judged the competition and gave them sixth place?"

"Er . . . yeah."

"Hmm, with that kind of treatment from their elders, really, Phil, is it any wonder that kids run away?"

This time the silence was even longer but eventually Phil cracked first and hit the Play button, sending "Sweet Home Alabama" blaring over the airwaves.

"You better think of something to say, mate. We've got another six hours to fill," Dave said off the air as he cued up the next CD.

"Six hours. With you in this mood it feels like sixty."

Dave laughed. "Huh, that's a different take than your usual happy optimism. I guess I'm rubbing off on ya."

Phil winced and thought about that. Really there was no point in stooping to Dave's level. "Yeah. You're right. If you looked outside you'd see that it's a lovely morning and the day's rich possibilities are ahead of both of us."

Phil guffawed. "There are no rich possibilities. You wanna know how it's going to be? I'll tell you how it's going to be. It's going to be another tedious, boring, dull day, spinning records and talking crap in the middle of the dreary Irish Sea where nothing exciting ever happens and time takes freakishly long to eventually pass you pay,"

Dave replied, in what, in about two hours, would prove to be one of the least accurate predictions he had ever made in his life.

※　※　※

Even his enemies would have had to admit that Irian Ksar, of the Ninth House of the Northern Alkhav, former general of the Combined Armies and current Lord Protector of all the Alkhavan peoples, was a tenacious and extremely talented survivor.

In a little over a year, he had been stabbed, beaten, given a deadly Earth virus, wrestled, horrifically burned in a wormhole accident, frozen, pelted with ice, and finally stabbed again.

And yet.

He lived.

As a boy he had studied many disciplines under the Black Monks of Balanmanik. From Master Ninar he had learned some of the science of the Old Ones. From Master Ada he had been taught English as well as the teachings and the knowledge of the Ui Neill. From Master Anak he had studied the play of sword and shield. When they had progressed to the third level of the fourth year, Master Harala had taught the boys the secrets of unarmed combat, the way of ice fighting, and finally, in the closed conclave, the discipline of the Fast.

The Fast was something that had come to the monks

from the people of the north country, hundreds or maybe even thousands of years before.

It was a form of hibernation that the northerners used if they were trapped in a blizzard. They would build a snow cave with an airhole, lie down, and Fast until the storm passed. The Fast would last at least a day, sometimes days, on occasion a week or more.

As a form of deep healing meditation it was very effective; but it could be dangerous—there were several recorded incidents of monks who could not be awoken and had perished from a slow starvation.

It was therefore to be used only in extremis.

Ksar had never had occasion to use it, even when he had been burned by the wormhole's fire. That time the monks and his sister's minions had cared for him.

But now all he had was himself.

He knew that he alone could climb from this yawning grave.

First things first. He had to get out of this cramped and dangerous place above the corridor.

Still bleeding from his stomach and arms, he crawled through a cylindrical conduit until he came at last to the area above a large central chamber or control room. The spaceship was old, perhaps ancient, and although it was extraordinarily well built, there were several small microfractures in the composite materials of the tunnel duct.

Through a long, narrow fissure in the floor he looked

beneath him and saw clearly the four humans and one Altairian who had thwarted his plan.

Jamie, Ramsay, Brian, Anna, and of course that interfering girl, Callaway's daughter, Wishaway.

Five people who, through their own selfishness, had condemned his world to suffer and die.

Why should they live while his people froze to death and perished over the coming centuries?

Perhaps with this vessel he could ferry some of them out of the dying world into the new world. It was too late for his sister, the Witch Queen, killed by Lorca's treachery, but it was not too late for the rest of those lost souls in Alkhava.

Yes, he would do something.

First he would have to get strong.

Recover.

Time for the Fast.

Smothering the pain, he rolled over and lay down on his back. He stretched his legs to full extension and folded his arms over his chest.

He repeated the mantra the monks had taught him all those years ago.

"Hury ma na sta, fa ccar la. Hury ma na sta, fa ccar la." Feel the presence of the ice gods, let them hush you into sleep. Feel the presence of the ice gods, let them hush you into sleep.

He reduced his breaths to five per minute.

His heart rate slowed.

His oxygen intake eased.

The muscles in his face relaxed.

The bleeding in his stomach ceased.

He slept . . .

Directly beneath the meditating, recovering Irian Ksar, Brian had been looking at the alien control panel for over an hour now.

"Well?" Ramsay said at last.

Brian wiped a bead of sweat from his forehead.

"I think," Brian said finally. "I think we *are* going to Earth."

Ramsay pursed his lips. "And you can tell that how exactly?" he asked.

After takeoff, a holographic control panel had emerged in the air in front of them—it was basically a luminous dial on which strange, incomprehensible orange symbols occasionally appeared. There were several portholes in the flying saucer, but the view out of these was disturbing in the extreme. No stars, no nebulae, nothing. Only a silvery blackness that seemed to stretch to infinity in all directions.

They had briefly experimented, putting their arms into the many tubes on the control panel again, but the ship had refused to respond to any of their commands. This worried Ramsay a great deal, but Brian not at all.

"I still believe that we're traveling through a wormhole or possibly a series of wormholes on our way back to Earth," Brian said.

But now that Ramsay didn't have to sell the idea to the others he could be a bit more combative and skeptical. "Pure guesswork. And wishful thinking too, I might add," he said.

Jamie, Anna, and Wishaway were looking at Brian hopefully, and he knew he had to contradict Ramsay for their sake, even if he didn't really believe it that strongly himself. How was the ship going to find Earth's sun after ten thousand years of hibernation?

"No. Not really, Ramsay. It's a logical deduction. The part of the wormhole network that we're familiar with goes from Earth to Altair. It would make sense that that's where the ship was going."

"We could be going to the Vancha home world, or the heart of a sun, or a black hole, or anywhere really," Ramsay said. "When we traveled through the wormhole by ourselves it was almost instantaneous."

Jamie could tell his mom and Wishaway were getting nervous. "There's an explanation for that, isn't there, Brian?" Jamie said with a knowing grin.

"Uhh, yeah . . . When we went by ourselves our

molecules were broken up and we zipped on through. Obviously it would take too much energy to do that with a spaceship; so once we're in the wormhole we have to fly through it. It's like going through the Channel Tunnel from Britain to France, except that this is a tunnel in space-time," Brian explained.

"If that's true, how long do you think a trip like that could take?" Anna asked. They had water, but very little food.

Brian had absolutely no idea, but he smiled reassuringly.

"Oh, couple of days at the most, I would have thought," he said confidently.

"So we'll soon be on Earth?" Wishaway asked with a big, hopeful smile.

"Absolutely. We will all soon be safely home on Earth," Brian said.

Ramsay opened his mouth to say something about tempting fate, but Jamie cut him off with the finger-across-the-throat gesture. Jamie felt that they'd had enough of this discussion. It was all moot. They were going where the ship was taking them, and that was the end of it. Any more of Ramsay's doubt bombs—although entertaining for him—would be bad for morale . . .

By the second day, for Jamie, the excitement of flying in a flying saucer, an actual spaceship, an *alien spaceship*, had begun to dim.

The place was cramped, smelly, unhygienic (there were no bathroom facilities), and actually quite boring.

During the cold war, American submariners discovered that the biggest enemy was not the Soviet Navy but rather the twin hydras of claustrophobia and tedium. Sure, you could at any moment get a call from Cent-Com to launch World War III, but the real crisis would come if someone lost the dice for the Monopoly set. Similarly Sergei Krikalev, the Russian astronaut who spent more than a year aboard the spacestation *Mir*, was only able to keep sane by learning English from Beatles albums and playing hundreds of games of chess with ground controllers.

Even for supernerds like Brian and Ramsay, the novelty of interstellar travel wore off fast.

Finding something to do was the only way to stave off boredom and incipient worry at the thought of the possibly unknown object of their destination.

They had tried games of I Spy, Charades, Hangman, Tag, Invisible Man, Kick the Tin, Find the Flag, Name That Tune, and Rock-Paper-Scissors.

They had exhausted all of their jokes.

By the evening of the second day they had ended up just chatting, telling each other elaborate stories, and whether they were entirely truthful or not didn't seem to matter as long as they were lengthy.

Jamie spun yarns about New York, and those went down well because the Big Apple was a place where anything seemed possible, good and evil, the tragic as well as the very funny. Anna talked about the city too. She'd been born in Brooklyn and like everyone with that blessing/curse, couldn't talk enough about that diverse borough.

Brian didn't have any good stories about Boston, but he did know several long Bob Dylan and Bruce Springsteen songs that had a strong narrative arc.

Wishaway, however, was the master.

She had learned oratory and formal recitation at the university in Aldan and could recite from memory entire passages from Morgan Ui Neill's *Book of Stories*.

She had already done four tales and six prose poems in a row and was clearly fading a little when Ramsay cajoled her into a final one before they tried to get some shut-eye.

Wishaway's throat was getting dry and she *was* tired, but she had to admit that she loved telling tales.

She took a cup of melted snow and wet her lips.

"Shall I do one more from the *Book of Stories*?" she asked Jamie.

"Anything you like. If you're up to it."

"It is one I just reread again recently. A dark one."

"The darker the better," Ramsay said.

"Good. I read it again on my wedding night to L—" she began and paled. No one had even mentioned that name once. They knew it would hurt her. He was probably on his way back to Oralands by now. In a few months he would be married again to some local girl or a princess from Kafrikilla. Wishaway winced at the thought of it.

"We'll just go to sleep, it's too late for stories," Jamie said, sensing her discomfort.

She shook her head. "I will tell it." And she began:

"Some call the lost kingdom that existed between Ireland and Scotland the Land of the Lost and still others, the Land of the Drowned. Many are the tales of this harsh place, which, like the Atlantis of Plato, has since sunk beneath the gray waters of the Irish Ocean. Here, in the Chronicle of the Fintoola, bard Nacallum tells his story. 'In the Land of the Lost there were two souls walking . . .'"

She recited from memory the whole saga of the two strangers meeting and their shadows quarreling. At the end the shadows died and the travelers died with them.

"'Such is the harsh way of the Land of the Lost. We can expect no happiness or reward in this life. All comes to us in the future time in the Kingdom of the Saved,'" Wishaway concluded, and put her hands in her lap.

There was a long period of quiet.

"Wow, that was pretty intense," Jamie said.

"Tell us a happy one," Ramsay whined.

Jamie shook his head. Even if Ramsay was an insomniac, the rest of them needed rest and recuperation.

"No, Ramsay, no more. She needs a break. It's time for sleep now anyway," Jamie said. "Isn't it, Brian?"

Brian looked at his watch. "Yeah, I think it is," he said.

"Hey, you wanna hear one of my stories?" Ramsay asked, brightening.

Jamie shook his head, but Anna, who couldn't quite get the primary school teacher out of her system, said: "We'd love to, Ramsay. One more story before bedtime."

"Well, there was a great MERP adventure I did once—it's kind of like Dungeons and Dragons set in Middle-Earth. Anyway, it took place twenty years after the *Lord of the Rings* ended. We burgled this house in Gondor and got sent up before Aragorn, the high king, you know. He was the judge. Anyway, he executed us. Tough guy. After the book was over he became a bit of a tyrant . . . That's it. OK, is it Wishaway's turn again?"

There was a confused silence, not least because no one knew what Ramsay was talking about.

"OK, now it's definitely time for slee—" Jamie began.

"Wait, I never told you what happened in my science-fiction novel. The one about the evil aliens coming to Earth, uh, no offense," Ramsay said, looking at Wishaway.

"You write novels, Ramsay?" Anna asked.

"Don't encourage him, Mom," Jamie groaned.

Ramsay grinned and filled in the others on his plot for *A Screaming Comes Across The Sky*. As he told it, he got very loud and very animated.

Above him, Lord Protector Ksar, who could hear all of this with one part of his mind, began finally to wake from his deep healing sleep.

"OK," Ramsay continued, "so the aliens come to Earth to investigate Earth's religions. They've been cooped up on their ships for thousands of years waiting for the secret of the universe and when they realize humans don't have the answer they go nuts."

"Then what happens?" Wishaway asked, trying to follow him.

"They pick one obscure religion and decide that all the false religions have to be exterminated. We're following the female UN chief as she tries to convince the aliens not to kill everyone, but the aliens say convert or die, and since most people don't convert, the aliens wipe out the whole planet, and that's the end of the book," Ramsay said with satisfaction, and banged his fist on the metal floor.

Ksar's heart rate increased and his breathing began reaching normalcy.

"The book ends with Earth getting more or less destroyed?" Jamie asked, surprised.

"Absolutely. Classic sci-fi ending."

"Isn't it a bit bleak?"

"No it's good. It's a metaphor for the meaninglessness of existence," Ramsay said with a nod to his big brother.

"I don't think an advanced species would exterminate all the humans," Brian protested.

"People said the Germans were the most enlightened country in Europe before the Nazis came. And my story's good because it shows that the aliens could be just as dumb as us," Ramsay said.

"And the UN lady dies?" Jamie asked.

Ksar's eyelids flickered.

"Everybody dies."

Jamie shook his head. "You'll never find a publisher."

"You think? OK, well let me tell you about another book I've got in mind—"

Mercifully, before Ramsay could continue, Brian noticed something.

"Wait a minute. Everyone be quiet. Listen," he said.

"What?" Wishaway asked.

"You hear that hum?" he said.

"Yeah," Ramsay said. "So?"

"It's a different hum than before," Brian explained.

"It is," Jamie agreed.

"Stars, look. Stars!" Wishaway cried, running to one of the portholes.

Everyone dashed to the windows, and sure enough gone was the disturbing streaky background, and there through the thick polymer glass was a familiar panoply of stars.

And not just stars.

"The sun," Ramsay said.

"Where?" Anna cried.

"There in the distance. Two o'clock. Getting closer."

"And there," Anna cried, grabbing Brian by the shoulders, "There, look, that's Earth, isn't it? Isn't it?"

Brian turned to her and nodded.

"I guess Brian was right," Ramsay said to Jamie sotto voce so his brother wouldn't hear.

"OK, OK, listen. We're out of the wormhole. We're heading for Earth," Brian said. "Everybody better grab a seat."

"I thought the plan was that we'd get a good night's sleep before trying to land," Anna said.

Brian shook his head. "I'm sorry, it's out of our hands. We're going for it. Everybody better sit. Now."

"Who died and made you Commander Adama?" Ramsay said.

"Just get down, Ramsay," Jamie said sternly, and Ramsay, like the others, found a place to sit on the floor.

"What do we do?" Jamie asked. "Should I try and operate the air brakes or something?"

Brian shook his head. "Don't do anything. My guess is

that it will pilot itself. It's programmed to take us right to the lighthouse on Muck Island. Just sit back, relax, and we'll soon be home."

And above him General Ksar opened his eyes.

❖ ❖ ❖

A melody drifting on a floating island in his mind. A tune disturbing the wind. A place of belonging. A place of loneliness.

Night on the ice cliff.

Yes.

I remember.

Stars moving backward across time. Across these long years. And that melody? A song of childhood.

White mirror sky. Weak summer sun. Clouds flitting across the last moon.

Morning.

He had passed the test. (One of many.) His father was looking at him with disdain. A blow. His father's hand pushing him down into the frozen snow. "Singing is for widows. The men of Alkhav do not sing."

Laughter then.

Tears.

Relief that at least Krama was not here to see this humiliation.

Krama. What happened to you? Are you also among the many dead?

A metallic taste in his mouth.

Pain in his back and legs.

Where?

A craft. A ship made by the Old Ones. Taking him to Earth. He didn't know how long he'd slept, but he knew it had been days, not hours. He was weak, hungry, above all thirsty. The craft was making a strange noise.

Slowly he felt the blood return to his extremities. He rolled over on his chest and peered through the crack in the ceiling.

There they were, sitting, waiting.

The Lords Ui Neill. The mother. The brother. That girl from Aldan.

The men of Alkhav do not sing.

What do they do?

Ksar sighed. They kill or be killed. What a sterile, lonely trajectory that was. Kill or be killed. In Balanmanik, in the olden days, before the ice had wiped clean the city, they had shown plays. Men would stand before an audience and pretend to be other men. They would speak words written for them by others, they would do deeds preordained and inescapable. They had no choice.

Kill or be killed. If not for his father, for Krama and the Queen and all the others they had slain.

Yes.

He took the long knife from his boot and, slowly, crawled back to the hatchway near the door where he had come in.

He flexed his arms and hands, put the knife between his teeth, opened the hatch, and lowered himself to the ground.

The spaceship was very loud, but in any case he walked along the corridor and came to the bridge with all the noise of a butterfly alighting on a flower.

He crept behind the four humans and one Altairian. All of them watching the orange holograms above the control panel. None of them armed. None of them expecting anything.

Lord Brian first. The biggest. The strongest. The only real threat. Then Lord Ramsay. Then Lord Jamie.

He grinned to himself.

Maybe his father was right.

Alkhavans do not sing. Alkhavans kill or be killed. Perhaps he would spare the women.

When he returned the ship to Altair, they could become part of his harem. Altair. He wouldn't stay there. No. He would load the vessel with followers and retainers. And if they pleased him he would permit them to escape that dying world too.

"Looks like we're entering the atmosphere. Nobody touch anything, this is going to be the most delicate part of the whole procedure," Brian said, completely absorbed by the alien symbols in front of him and the view out the window that was changing from black sky to blue heliosphere.

Now, Ksar told himself. Now.

He crouched low and approached the semicircle of sitting people. He moved the knife from his palm to his fist. A stab into Brian's throat. One blow. Then a thrust into his chest before he could even get out of his seat.

He crept closer.

Wishaway sniffed the air.

Ksar slipped behind Brian. He felt the cool blade in his fingers. He raised his arm.

The spaceship started to rock.

"Hold on, everyone," Brian said.

Wishaway sniffed again. She recognized that smell. She turned her head.

"Ksar!" she screamed. "*Haga* Ksar! Behind thee, Lord Brian."

Ksar stabbed down with his knife. Brian rolled to the side at the last second. The knife tore into the dead air. Ksar slashed at Brian's throat, but Brian dived away from him.

Two seconds had elapsed since Wishaway's warning.

Enough time for Jamie and Ramsay to get to their feet.

"You really don't know when you're beat, mate," Ramsay said.

The Lord Protector leaped at the big Irishman. Ramsay blocked the knife thrust with his forearm, the dagger nicking his wrist.

Ksar lunged again, but a slight bounce in the flying saucer's motion sent the knife an inch past Ramsay's ear.

Jamie jumped on the Lord Protector's back and threw him forward into the control console. Ksar turned and struggled free of Jamie's grip.

"Thou will not," Ksar said in furious English, and with two vicious blows kicked Jamie to the floor.

In an attempt to blindside him, Ramsay hurled his fur jacket at Ksar's head, but the Lord Protector brushed it to one side.

He slithered off the console, brought his knife hand to full extension from his body, and surveyed the five people standing in a semicircle about him.

"The game's up. You're outnumbered," Anna said. "You might as well drop that thing."

"Ye underestimate me, Lady Ui Neill," Ksar replied, and with surprising agility he leaped at her and would have landed on top of her had not Brian jumped and crashed into him like a Patriot missile taking out a Scud.

Ksar landed heavily on one of the spaceship's control tubes.

It must have done something to the autopilot because suddenly the ship lurched sickeningly to one side and almost went upside down before righting itself again. Jamie and Ramsay were thrown into Wishaway. Ksar was splayed heavily across the console, then he was lifted into the air and the back of his head thumped very hard into one of the angled spaceship walls.

Jamie and Ramsay got to their feet and ran to him.

"Hunnnh," Ksar was saying.

"Hit him," Ramsay said.

"No," Jamie replied, for he saw that it was nearly all over.

The Alkhavan general was lying in a pool of blood, his head smashed in, the wound in his stomach open again.

Blood bubbled on the Lord Protector's lips.

His hands were shaking.

"Thouuuu," he said.

"He's trying to speak," Jamie said.

Summoning a last gasp of strength from somewhere, Ksar raised himself up and looked Ramsay in the face. "I heard thee. Thou art a s-storyteller then, Lord Ramsay?" Ksar managed.

Ramsay nodded. The Lord Protector blinked the blood out of his eyes. He felt the cold of the ice cliffs. That wind again. That perfume from the past. That melody drifting in and out of his brain.

"When ye shall sing of me, bard, t-tell them, I have done my b-best for my people," Ksar said.

Ramsay looked at Jamie. Jamie nodded.

"I will," Ramsay said.

"Good," Ksar said, and coughed and closed his eyes.

His body wilted to the floor.

"That's it then," Ramsay said.

"That's it then," Jamie agreed.

Suddenly the spaceship began vibrating and bucking in Earth's atmosphere.

"Get over here," Brian said. "Everyone sit. Now. Fast."

Jamie and Ramsay left the dead man and returned to their space on the floor.

"Now that the autopilot has been disengaged, broken in fact, the angle of reentry is all wrong," Brian said.

"What are you talking about?" Ramsay asked.

"Autopilot's smashed. Can't you see?"

Ramsay nodded. If that smashed thing on the control panel really was the autopilot, then they were in big trouble.

"How will we get down, Brian?" Anna asked.

"Oh gravity will take care of that," Brian said confidently.

"But what are we going to do about the entry?" Ramsay asked.

"Hmmmm?"

"What are we going to do about reentry if the autopilot's gone?"

"We'll fly it manually," Brian replied.

"How?"

"By listening to me. Ramsay, get control of that yaw device. Jamie, you work the thrusters—those tubes over there. Anna, you and Wishaway are going to have to be in charge of braking, the tubes at the far end. Yeah, stick your arm all the way in," Brian said, barking the orders like he'd done this all his life.

Each of them went to their positions at the very alien controls. They certainly weren't designed for human hands, in fact they weren't designed for hands at all. It seemed that the creatures who had built this ship, and presumably the Salmon as well, had had many trunklike appendages. You had to put your entire fist into the sockets on the control panel, and even then you had to push incredibly hard to get any response from the ship.

"Ease off on the thrusters, Jamie . . . no, the other way, that's it. This is going to be tricky . . ."

"What are you doing, Brian?" Jamie asked.

"Well, here's the thing. We got to get the angle exactly right for entering the atmosphere. Too slight an angle and we'll bounce off the troposhere and continue on into deep space."

"Not good," Jamie said.

"No. Too steep an angle and we'll burn up and disintegrate."

"Also not good."

"No. Not good at all . . . OK, Anna, Wishaway, start the braking procedure, here we come."

Jamie stole a look at the porthole in the floor. The black sky was completely gone. Now it was shades of blue with streaks of red fire ripping across the ship's outer hull.

The craft was shaking horribly.

"Brian, tell us the truth, are we burning up?" Anna asked.

Brian grinned. "No, we're doing fine," he said looking out of the porthole. He did a quick operation on the calculator on his digital watch and adjusted the ship's entry position by several points. But even so, he was still just guessing the angle, hoping that the tolerances of the advanced hull material could accommodate a few degrees either way.

Red glowing fire out the window

"Where are you going to put us if we get down, Brian?" Jamie asked.

Sweat was pouring off Brian's face as he wrestled with the controls. He turned to Jamie and grinned unnervingly.

"The autopilot's initial trajectory is still going to try to take us across the Atlantic to Ireland. OK?"

"OK."

"We're going too fast, more air brakes please, Anna."

"And if we make it down to Ireland in one piece?" Jamie wondered.

"We'll be fine. If I can get control of the ship and get across the Atlantic, we'll plonk her down in the middle of Trafalgar Square. We'll be heroes. Ramsay, that's still too fast. You hear what I said? Yaw down, Ramsay. Jamie, get over there and help with the brakes, stick your fist into that socket if you have to . . . We're still going far too fast."

Jamie got up and stood next to Wishaway. He put his arms into the braking sockets, made a fist, and pushed hard.

But the vibrations only increased, and bits of the ceiling began to fall down.

A crack appeared in the floor.

Brian breathed deep and assessed the situation.

He had no way of telling what the altitude was or where exactly they were. Not a good thing in a spaceship heading toward the ground at Mach 5.

"Wishaway, get over to one of those portholes and tell me what you can see," he said.

Wishaway took her hand from the braking socket and ran to the glass.

"Clouds, sky . . . oh wait, the ocean, the ocean," she said excitedly.

So they were through the upper atmosphere.

Jamie and Anna still had their hands into the braking sockets, but they were still traveling at over five thousand miles an hour across the Atlantic Ocean. Brian knew he would have to bring them down to close to sea level, where the air was thicker and friction would help slow the ship.

But he didn't want to get too close.

"Wishaway, I'm going to lower us. Tell me when we get to within a couple of hundred feet," Brian said, and lowered the spaceship still farther.

The vibrations began to ease, the thick air caressed the flying saucer, sucking the velocity from its sides. After five minutes of gradual reductions in altitude, Wishaway said something in Aldanese.

"What?" Brian asked.

"Stop!" Wishaway cried. "We are above the waves."

"How far?"

"Two *stasa*, perhaps three."

"English. How far in yards and feet?"

"Ten Earth yards?" she said.

Brian immediately leveled off. "Ten yards! Good grief. Thanks for the information," Brian muttered, but the sarcasm was lost on the Aldanese girl.

"We're still breaking the sound barrier," Ramsay said.

"I know. Ramsay, over to the brakes. We have to retard

the speed—Jamie, see if those thrusters are working," Brian said.

"Thrusters are off-line," Jamie said looking at the smashed control panel.

Ramsay shoved his arms into the braking lines.

"Think we're slowing," Ramsay said.

"OK, let me see," Brian muttered.

He ran to the window, and with relief he saw that they were definitely slowing, but they weren't out of the woods yet. The vessel was partially out of control, skimming above the surface of the Atlantic by only a few meters and still going far too fast. He couldn't gain altitude because that would only increase their velocity.

"Jamie, what are you doing with those thrusters?" Brian asked.

"See for yourself, they're kaput," Jamie said.

"There's land," Wishaway said, and pointed at a green shape out the window.

Brian ran to the porthole. "Yeah, we're still on the old course for Muck Island and the lighthouse. That must be the north coast of Ireland," Brian said.

That was good, but their speed was five or six times what it should be.

"Anna, Ramsay, can you get anything more out of those brakes?" Brian asked.

The brake tubes were still operational, but only just.

"We're slowing her, but the power couplings are fraying at the edges. You're going to have to get us down now," Ramsay said.

Brian shook his head. "She's still going several hundred knots, come on, Ramsay, get this baby to ease up, use the antigravity shielding if you can—"

"I can't slow her any more."

"Try," Brian demanded.

"I am trying."

Anna yelped as a circuit sparked and a flame jumped from the console.

"The power coupling's just gone!" Ramsay yelled. "Get us down, Brian, or we're going to drop out of the sky like a falling brick."

Brian ran back to his position and wrestled for control as the ship began to rock from side to side.

"I told you, looks like you're losing your gyroscopes," Ramsay said with increasing urgency.

"So I see," Brian said, trying to keep the irritation out of his voice.

"The yaw compensation is retarding our speed," Ramsay noted.

Brian grimaced. "Is it? I wish I could see . . . Are we slowing by much, Wishaway?" he asked.

"Not by much," she said, peering through the glass.

"OK. Fine. Are we over land or over water?"

"We have passed over one large island and in the distance I see another," she said, straining her eyes to peer through the thick glass.

"Scotland," Jamie said. "We missed the rendezvous with Muck Island."

"Yeah," Brian agreed, and checked the instruments. He ran to the window again. The ship was still traveling at least a hundred miles an hour and heading closer and closer to the mountainous coast of Galloway. He sprinted back to his seat.

Now he did try to gain a little altitude. He shoved his arms into the control tubes up to his elbows, but with the vectors damaged the system would not let him raise the ship.

He pulled so hard he almost broke an arm, but he couldn't get her up.

"Damn," he said to himself.

"What's going on, Brian?" Anna asked gently.

"The gyroscopes won't let us gain altitude. Down yes. Up no."

"And what does that mean?" Anna asked.

It meant that if they kept on this course, at this speed, at this height, they were going to pancake into a mountain.

There was no longer any choice.

"Wishaway, Jamie, Ramsay. Everyone get back on the ground, get into a brace position," Brian said.

"Why?" Ramsay asked.

"Just sit!" Brian barked.

When they had all sat down, he began gently lowering the ship.

No choice, he told himself. If he didn't ditch her now, he was robbing them of any chance of survival.

"Everybody grab something to hold on to," Brian said with forced calm.

"What are you doing, Brian?" Anna asked.

"I'm going to have to put her down in the sea," Brian replied calmly.

"What about landing in Trafalgar Square?" Jamie asked.

"That's not going to happen. I can do a semicontrolled descent into the ocean or a crash somewhere in the middle of Scotland. Everybody strap yourself in. Grab something. This ain't going to be pretty," Brian said.

"We can't ditch in the sea, Wishaway can't swim," Jamie said.

"I'm sorry, this is all we've got," Brian said.

Brian looked across the ship to Anna, who was wrapping herself into ball. She gave him a little smile.

Jamie and Wishaway were together near the galley. Ramsay was sitting next to his brother at the main console.

"Those side panels will make pretty good flotation devices," Ramsay added.

Brian tried one more time to reduce their speed by

veering the craft slightly off the vertical. He got it down to what he guessed was about seventy or eighty miles an hour. Still far too fast, but with western Galloway getting closer and closer and the power couplings all but burned out, that was the best he was going to get.

He began slowly lowering the ship to sea level.

Steady, he told himself.

"We're going to make it," Ramsay whispered to his brother. "You can do it, Brian, I know you can."

"Yeah," Brian replied, and winced as he felt the waves touch the bottom of the flying saucer.

Two more meters.

He nudged the controls still lower.

"OK, everyone brace for impact!" he yelled, putting the spaceship down into the Atlantic.

G forces ripping the ship apart.

A huge, dreadful crash.

They were upside down. Noise. Sparks. An explosion. Screaming. Yelling. And then the ship broke apart like a wine jug smashing on a marble floor.

Wishaway was spinning through the air. She hit something hard. Blood in her mouth. In her eyes.

Blackness.

The cabin burst and began to fill with water. Huge torrents of foaming sea, bubbling and breaking around her.

"Jamie."

"I'm here."

Terrible ice-cold water reached her face. She gasped. She saw sunlight. She was out of the ship. Outside. There was fire around her. She was sinking.

"Jamie?"

"I'm here."

"Where are we?"

"Safe. Between Ireland and Scotland," Jamie replied and tried to grab her.

Between Ireland and Scotland.

Like in the story. The land of the lost. The land of the drowned.

"Jamie," she said, and swallowed a mouthful of the frigid, briny ocean.

Her head disappeared beneath the water.

She clawed her way to the surface.

"Wishaway," Jamie said from somewhere behind her.

She turned. There he was. Unhurt. Coming for her. She touched his hand.

The last of the spaceship sank beneath the sea in a frothing, fiery mess.

Jamie's hand slipped from hers and Wishaway found herself going under.

"No!" Jamie screamed. "No!"

Over a year ago he had fought this sea for his mother's life. He had beaten it, cheated it, and now it seemed that in recompense it wanted to take Wishaway.

The Atlantic would not be denied. The scales would be balanced. A life for a life.

"Wishaway!" he yelled.

He would not let it happen.

"Wishaway," he screamed, but he couldn't see her anymore.

She was gone.

Down.

Down.

Down.

A current carrying her. The sea wrapping itself around her. She fought and scrambled to the surface.

Gasped air.

Saw no one.

Struggled against the gray waves.

Sank again.

Truly this place was cursed. To get so close but to be denied.

She cried inwardly and thought of her mother and her father. Lorca. Jamie. All of them. Even Ksar and the Witch Queen, who had been driven to desperation by desperate times.

The cold was a knife in her chest. The ocean sucking her to the bottom. Her lungs bursting. Her heart slowing.

If she opened her mouth and breathed, it would at least be over quickly.

Yes.

So welcoming, so simple.

If she opened her mouth . . .

No. I will struggle to the end, she thought. She fought back, scrambling toward the light, but it was too hard, she was too deep.

And then she felt something on her legs.

Something touching her feet.

The bottom of the sea?

Surely she had not sunk that far?

Perhaps death himself had placed his loop about her ankles. Perhaps he—

Something hard, a piece of cloth, a rope a—

A net.

A net pulling her.

Pulling her up.

Sunlight.

The surface.

Men.

Men dragging her onto a boat with a huge metal tower. A sign in English that said PIRATE RADIO 252, whatever that meant.

Words. Faces. Anna. Brian. Ramsay. And yes, wet, bedraggled, smiling, happy: Jamie. She fell into his arms and gulped air.

Someone wrapped her in a blanket.

She was exhausted. "Oh, Jamie," she managed.

He held her.

She closed her eyes.

Dozed.

Woke.

A lighthouse.

A lighthouse house.

A small islet.

They were getting close to land. A man gave her a hot, sweet drink.

The sun setting behind the lighthouse and the rock. A green sea. A tin leaf sky. A sliver of crystal light from the impossibly big moon rising among the stars.

She shivered and Jamie kissed her and held her and said something about having two hands again on Earth! And his joy was wide and abundant, spreading from horizon to horizon and shore to shore. And in an undertone he added, "Don't tell them we came by spaceship, they think we ditched a light aircraft."

And she didn't understand but nodded anyway.

She wrapped the blanket about herself and breathed the heady oxygen-rich air of Earth. Night was coming, and she knew it would be beautiful and filled with stars.

Jamie was speaking once more. Asking her something.

"Are you OK?"

And she looked about her and realized that the *Book of Stories* was wrong.

"I am OK," she replied, for although she was still in that perilous place between Ireland and Scotland, now she saw that this was not the Land of the Lost at all. She was alive, safe and happy, at peace with her beloved, in what could only be the Kingdom of the Saved.

ABOUT THE AUTHOR

ADRIAN McKINTY has been called "one of his generation's leading talents" by *Publishers Weekly*, and his books have been described as "unputdownable" by the *Washington Post* and "exceptional" by the *San Francisco Chronicle*. Adrian was born and grew up in Carrickfergus, Northern Ireland. Educated at Oxford University, he then emigrated to New York City, where he lived in Harlem for five years, working in bars and on construction crews and enjoying a stint as a bookseller. He currently lives with his wife and daughters in Denver, where he teaches high school. *The Lighthouse War* is the second book in his *Lighthouse Trilogy*.

This book was designed
and art directed by
Chad W. Beckerman.
The text is set in 11$\frac{1}{2}$-point
Adobe Caslon, a font designed
by Carol Twombly and
based on William Caslon's
eighteenth-century typefaces.
The display type is set in Eremaeus.

Enjoy this sneak peek at

THE LIGHTHOUSE KEEPERS

BOOK THREE OF
THE LIGHTHOUSE TRILOGY

C ow excrement was the least colorful of the many pejorative epithets that Dan Connolly, the acting deputy director of the CIA's Special Projects Division, could have used upon reading the latest memo from Victor Astatin in Section 22.

Dan was new on the job, not only in Special Projects, but actually in the CIA itself. He was an outsider who had previously worked for the FBI in its Witness Protection Program. He had no loyalties to anyone in the CIA and no preconceived notions. The president had appointed him with the mandate to be a new broom who would clear away some of the dead wood.

The first thing on his agenda was Section 22.

Dan was a chubby, skeptical, streetwise man, the son of a New York City beat cop and a schoolteacher. He'd done well in the FBI and got the reputation as a hard-headed reformer who would slay sacred cows if necessary.

On the first day in his new job he'd been briefed about Section 22.

He had tried hard to contain his amazement behind a coughing fit and then a supposed need to go to the bathroom.

This all had been necessary because Section 22 was a revival of a discontinued Cold War CIA plan to hire psychics.

Psychics.

Dear, oh dear, thought Dan in a stall in a bathroom of an anonymous-looking gray building in Langley, Virginia.

Still, he'd taken the job.

Two weeks in now, and he had thoroughly digested the entire compendium of Victor Astatin's monthly reports.

They were not pretty reading.

Apparently in the entire five-year history of Section 22, Victor's team hadn't turned up one single piece of worthwhile intelligence. But then how could they? They were obviously charlatans and con men, the lot of them. They couldn't know the future. No one could know the future. Section 22 was a sad chapter in many recent sad chapters of a once-great agency.

Now only a few days away from his confirmation hearings in front of the Senate Intelligence Committee, Dan had called this meeting with Victor Astatin to tell him that he and everyone who worked for him in Section 22 was going to be fired.

"Mr. Astatin to see you," his secretary, Mandy, said through the intercom.

"Let him wait," Dan replied.

Perhaps Section 22 had seemed like a good idea at

the time. His predecessor's attempt to think outside the box in preventing another terrorist attack on the United States. But with the psychics an obvious failure, he had to get rid of the lot of them before it became known to the press. If this came to light the *Times*, Leno, and Letterman would all have a field day. Back in the 1980s, when it had been discovered that First Lady Nancy Reagan employed an astrologer to arrange her husband's schedule, the late-night talk show hosts had been in clover for months.

Dan leaned back in the chair of his ground-floor office and watched planes making the final turn for Dulles.

He reached in a drawer of his polished mahogany desk and removed a pipe. His father's pipe. It helped him think. Of course, smoking was banned not only in every CIA building in Langley but up to fifty feet from the entrance too. You had to walk halfway into the parking lot if you wanted to light up.

"Mr. Astatin is still waiting," Mandy said with an insistent tone.

Dan put the pipe back in the drawer and closed it.

"Send him in," he said.

Victor came in.

"Take a seat," Dan said.

Victor sat.

He was a wiry, trim man in his fifties with dyed hair and a Botoxy, fading-movie-star face. Dan resisted the urge to feel sorry for him. Victor's vanity and delusions of grandeur were things to scorn, not to pity. Victor was a native New Yorker who had become famous briefly in the 1970s, bending spoons and fixing people's watches using "telepathy." Victor claimed to have psychic and telekinetic abilities, but they obviously didn't extend that far into the future since, after defrauding the IRS for years, he had finally been arrested, bankrupted, and sentenced to eighteen months in prison. The calamities mounted after that. His model wife divorced him and he was exposed (in a best-selling book) as a cheap fraud by his ex-manager. The book revealed in detail how he had pre-bent the spoons and switched keys from real ones to bent ones by sleight of hand. His ex-manager even revealed how he did his famous picture trick that had so impressed Johnny Carson. Before the show Carson had drawn a picture, sealed it in an envelope, and then Victor had read Johnny's brain waves and replicated the picture for the TV cameras. There was nothing psychic about it. In fact Victor's ex-manager had simply distracted *The Tonight Show*'s producers and looked in the envelope and then told Victor what Carson had drawn—nothing could have been simpler.

For Victor there had then been a long wilderness period when he'd worked for prospecting oil companies, a Vegas casino, and finally as a fortune-teller in Atlantic City.

There he'd been found by CIA scouts and brought to Langley, where he was recruited by Dan's immediate predecessor and given orders to assemble a team of empaths and psychics—people who supposedly had the ability to see into the future.

It was obvious to Dan that it hadn't worked. They had produced five years of absolute garbage. This meeting would be the very last time Dan would ever have to look at Victor's perma-tanned, unctuous face.

Or it *probably* would be, Dan thought uneasily.

Probably, because only this morning he had just had an incredible briefing from one of the CIA's moles in British intelligence. Most of it was uninteresting stuff. But one thing had made him take notice.

The Brits were holding a most unusual patient at a minimum-security hospital in Belfast, Northern Ireland. The man was in a coma, and why he was unusual no one seemed to quite know. But apparently he looked very strange, and the Brits had been pretty excited about their mystery patient for some time.

Victor coughed.

Dan looked up from his own reflection in the mahogany desk.

"Did you get my memo?" Victor asked anxiously.

Dan nodded. "Yes, I got it. I read it," Dan said with only a trace of contempt.

"We have the first name of the boy, the Evil One," Victor said excitedly.

"The, um, the boy that causes the end of the world," Dan said, deadpan.

"That's right. The Chosen One. Death Bringer. *An Fadras.* Evil incarnate . . . He's called Jamie. We know his name!" Victor said, pounding his hand into his fist.

Dan nodded. On any other day he wouldn't have

been able to take much more of this. He looked past Victor's head to the window outside. The sun was sinking over Virginia, silhouetting the cigarette smokers in the car park and the players on the CIA soccer pitch.

He pushed the chair back from the table, opened the drawer, looked wistfully at his pipe for a moment, and then removed a can of Fresca from the mini fridge he kept on the floor.

"Fresca?" he asked Victor.

"No," Victor said impatiently.

Dan popped the can and took a sip.

"You have to take this to the president," Victor said.

Dan looked at Victor square in the face. Of course, he remembered watching Victor when he was a kid. He'd been a wonderful performer. What a pity it was all a lie.

Dan shook his head. "Look, Victor, I like you personally, but I'll be honest with you. I'm afraid I just don't buy it. I don't see how it's possible to look into the future. And furthermore, I don't believe that some innocent little kid called Jamie does some crazy thing that leads to the end of the world."

Victor frowned. "Well, in the memo I suggest—" he began, but Dan interrupted.

"I mean, how do you suppose he does that, exactly?" Dan asked.

"I haven't a clue, I—"

"He builds a neutron bomb with his chemistry set? Invents a new killer virus? Come on. You're an intelligent man. Surely you can see that the whole thing is quite preposterous."

Victor spread his hands on the table.

He had encountered skeptics before. And the skeptics were only encouraged by all the fakers. Newspaper astrologers. Water diviners. Crystal-ball gazers. Palm readers. He had gone down that road himself for a while. Indeed, of the many, many people he had met in his life claiming supernatural abilities, perhaps four or five had had the genuine gift. And all of those he had corralled into his own team.

Their presence and dedication had given him his own gift back too.

"Mr. Connolly, I know what you must think. Yes, it's preposterous, but the thing is we've all seen it. Before last month I hadn't had a vision for twenty years and now even I've seen it."

"Seen what?"

"Terrible things. Fire from the ocean to the sky. Something very, very bad is going to happen, and this boy Jamie starts it somehow. Look, there's an Arab historian called Cide Hamete Benengeli who talks about the Chosen One who brings the end of the world, and Nostradamus himself—"

Dan raised his hand. "This isn't the Carson show, Victor, this isn't Coney Island. Explain to me in a simple sentence how you are supposed to be able to see into the future."

Victor was ready for this one. He had thought long

and hard about how anyone could see things that had not yet come to pass, and after much reading he'd come up with an answer.

"Have you heard of quantum physics?"

Dan nodded.

"OK, quantum physicists have been troubled for years by what Einstein called *spukhafte Fernwirkung*—spooky action at a distance. How two distant quantum events can happen simultaneously on opposite sides of the universe. This violates the theory of relativity. Nothing can travel faster than light so nothing can happen simultaneously, see?"

"No, not rea—"

"Ah, but the equations work if the light cone from those events taking place at the quantum level extends backward as well as forward along time's arrow. If a quantum event happens in the future and the signal gets sent back in time, then relativity isn't violated."

"Say that again more slow—"

"So, according to this theory, hints of the future, very small hints, sometimes leak into the present. And sometimes, if you're attuned and very, very sensitive, you get a hint. Especially if that event is going to be a catastrophe."

Dan looked intrigued.

"Really?" he said.

Victor nodded. He had him on the hook—now he had to reel him in.

"Pick a number between one and ten," Victor said.

"Oh, I don't think—"

"Go on, pick one, go on . . ."

"Four."

Victor reached into his inside jacket pocket, removed a sealed envelope, and placed it on the desk in front of Dan.

Dan opened it.

Inside the envelope was a note that read: "The number you are going to pick is four."

Dan got up from his desk, walked around it, reached in the side pockets of Victor's jacket and took out several more envelopes. He ripped them open, revealing the messages: "The number you are going to pick is five," "The number you are going to pick is three," et cetera.

"You're an old fraud, Victor," Dan said.

He returned to his chair and sat down. He took another sip of Fresca.

"Then why aren't you kicking me out of your office?" Victor asked.

Dan looked at him.

"Now, that is the smartest thing you've said all day. Why am I not kicking you of my office? There's a reason. Tell me about the man in the coma."

"The man in the coma?"

"According to your reports, you've been seeing a man in a coma, yes?"

"Yes. We have. I don't know who he is or what his connection is to the boy, but we've been seeing him for weeks now. Somehow the two are linked. We believe that the man in the coma will lead us to the boy."

"Have you seen his face in your . . . in your whatever you call them."

"Visions. Yes, we've seen his face. Hints of his face, yes."

Dan nodded. "And the man in the coma does what? Helps the boy destroy the world?"

"The man in the coma leads us to the boy," Victor said. "Or so we believe."

"What do you think we should do when we find this boy?" Dan wondered out loud.

"The consensus of the group is that we should kill him."

"And you?"

"I think we should kill him too. The signs are very clear."

Dan was glad that he wasn't taping this conversation or keeping notes. Plotting the murder of a teenage boy called Jamie probably wouldn't get him much praise in the *New York Times*.

He examined Victor. The tan, the fake smile. A pathetic con man or someone who really could see things that others couldn't?

"I'll be honest with you, Victor. I usually pay no attention to your memos, and I was on the verge of recommending the suspension or termination of your section, but, you see, something's come up."

Victor's eyebrows raised. "Yes?"

"How would you like to go into the field?" Dan asked.

"The field?"

"The field. We have a mole in British intelligence—well, several actually, but this one is particularly reliable . . . Anyway, I was reading a briefing from him this morning that, to be frank, gave me the willies."

"Go on."

"There's a hospital in Belfast, Northern Ireland, where, for the last year or so they've had a most unusual patient."

"Yes?"

"I can't tell you any more than that except that he's in a coma and he seems to resemble the man that you've all been talking about for the last month."

"Aha!" Victor said triumphantly.

Dan smiled.

"You're going to have to go take a look at him."

"Me?"

"You."

"Go to Ireland?"

"Yes."

"When?"

"Tonight."

"Are you kidding? I don't think I even have a passport, I—"

"Your group believes that the man in the coma will lead you to this boy that you all want to kill, to save the world, right?"

"Yes."

"OK, then, this is your big chance. You're going to have to go to Ireland and get a look at this patient that British intelligence seems so excited about."

"But I've never done field work before," Victor protested, the color draining from his face.

"Oh, there's nothing to worry about. The patient is in a private sanatorium just outside Belfast. Not a prison. No armed guards. It won't be dangerous. I'll have someone brief you further on all our procedures."

"But, I-I—" Victor stammered.

"No 'buts,' Victor. You want to save your job? You want to save the world? Well, let's see if your story holds any water or not. Can I count on you?"

Victor gulped and said nothing.

"Well?"

"Yes."

"Good. Take a look at this mysterious man, see if it's your guy, and if it is, question him about anyone called Jamie."

"How can I question a man in a coma?"

Dan grinned, crumpled his empty Fresca can into a ball, and threw it into the wastepaper basket.

"You wake him up, Victor. You wake him up."

Keep reading! If you liked this book, check out these other titles.

Fell
By David Clement-Davies
978-0-8109-1185-7
$19.95 hardcover

Tiger Moon
By Antonia Michaelis
978-0-8109-9481-2
$18.95 hardcover

Elf Realm: The Low Road
By Daniel Kirk
978-0-8109-7069-4
$18.95 hardcover

Visit **www.amuletbooks.com** to download screen savers and ring tones, to find out where authors will be appearing, and to send e-cards.